Additional Praise for

THE LOBSTER KINGS

"A powerhouse of a novel. Alexi Zentner proves himself to be a writer of the first rank with this story of one woman's determination to carry on her family's legacy in the face of the encroaching pressures of modernity and the strictures of a patriarchal culture. The bold and endearingly stubborn Cordelia Kings is a protagonist we can root for, flaws and all, as she struggles to reconcile the past with the present." —Ben Fountain,
National Book Critics Circle Award–winning
author of *Billy Lynn's Long Halftime Walk*

"This masterfully written book is many things: a heartbreaking family saga, a myth-enshrouded ghost story, a thickly calloused ode to work and to art—not to mention a pulse-pounding mystery. Alexi Zentner commands both the malevolence and the magnificence of the natural world like no writer I know."
—Michael Christie, author of *If I Fall, If I Die*

"Zentner displays more talent and controlled craftsmanship in *The Lobster Kings* than many other writers will manage in a career's worth of novels." —*Toronto Star*

"Zentner's second novel . . . is brutal and beautiful. . . . His fusion of myth and mission, fury and beauty, as well as the palpable sense of place in this unique corner of the world add up to a memorable tale." —*Publishers Weekly*

"Just as compelling as the dragons, mermaids, and selkies that may inhabit the waters of Loosewood Island are its year-round residents, besieged by tourists, art historians, and drug smugglers. With a knowing nod to *King Lear, The Lobster Kings* follows a patriarch's fading powers and a dynasty's uncertain future in the face of a changing world. As in his wonderful debut, *Touch*, Alexi Zentner gives us a family saga that contains the origin story of a magical, once-timeless place where the past and present must inevitably collide."

—Stewart O'Nan, author of *Last Night at the Lobster* and *Emily, Alone*

"So big on legend, rich in style, and crowded with the kind of people who simultaneously seduce you and tear at the foundations of your understanding, it makes you want to drop your life, call the movers, and buy a one-way ticket to Zentner's universe. *The Lobster Kings* confirms what *Touch* already prophesied: Alexi Zentner is one of the greatest literary architects and mythmakers working today."

—Téa Obreht, author of *The Tiger's Wife*

THE LOBSTER KINGS

A Novel

ALEXI ZENTNER

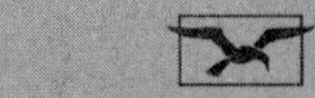

W. W. NORTON & COMPANY
NEW YORK · LONDON

Printed in the United States of America
First published as a Norton paperback 2015

For information about special discounts for bulk purchases, please contact
W. W. Norton Special Sales at specialsales@wwnorton.com or 800-233-4830

Manufacturing by RR Donnelley, Harrisonburg, VA
Book design by Mary Austin Speaker
Production manager: Anna Oler

Library of Congress Cataloging-in-Publication Data

Zentner, Alexi.
The lobster kings : a novel / Alexi Zentner. — First edition.
pages ; cm
ISBN 978-0-393-08957-8 (hardcover)
1. Lobster fishers—Fiction. 2. Family-owned business
enterprises—Fiction. 3. Love stories. I. Title.
PS3626.E445L63 2014
813'.6—dc23
2014002205

ISBN 978-0-393-35107-1 pbk.

W. W. Norton & Company, Inc.
500 Fifth Avenue, New York, N.Y. 10110
www.wwnorton.com

W. W. Norton & Company Ltd.
Castle House, 75/76 Wells Street, London W1T 3QT

1 2 3 4 5 6 7 8 9 0

This book is dedicated to all the men and women who work the water.

And to Laurie, Zoey, and Sabine.

THE LOBSTER KINGS

WE'RE NAMED THE KINGS, and we're the closest thing to royalty on Loosewood Island. The story goes that when the first of the Kings, Brumfitt Kings, the painter, came to Loosewood Island near on three hundred years ago, the waters were so thick with lobster that Brumfitt only had to sail half of the way from Ireland: he walked the rest of the way, the lobsters making a road with their backs. He was like Jesus walking on the water, except there was no bread to be found anywhere. Lobster there was plenty of. In 1720, the waters were crawling with them in sizes that no man today has seen. To catch his first lobster, Brumfitt didn't bother with boats or traps or anything more complicated than simply wading into the water at low tide and gaffing a lobster ten or twenty pounds or more. He caught lobsters five feet long. When I was young I heard old men down at the harbor and in the diner talking about how when *their* grandfathers were boys they saw lobster claws nailed to the sides of boathouses, claws big enough to crush a man's head. The lobsters are smaller now, but they've done well for the Kings. Back when I was a girl in school, we were told about how lobsters used to be cheap trash fish for filling bellies, but it's hard to believe. Daddy and I both drop pots and haul lines and he's raised all three of us girls on the money the lobsters bring in. Raised us well enough, too. Carly, the youngest, teaching in Portland for the last few years after Daddy put her through Colby College, hard cash that could have gone to buy a third boat. Rena, the middle daughter, like so many of us living on an island that is claimed by both the U.S. and Canada, taking some schooling on both sides of the border—she started nursing school at Dalhousie University, in Halifax, and finished up as an accountant at the University at Albany, SUNY—and now is married and back to the island, running the fish shop and managing our books, with her husband, Tucker, trained as an architect but working as Daddy's sternman. And me. The oldest daughter. I went to college, too, and I studied art, but as much as I love to paint, I never wanted to paint anything other than Loosewood Island, never wanted to do anything other than live here and walk the same beaches and paths, painting the same famous landscape that Brumfitt Kings painted, and, girl or not, to head to sea to work like Daddy and his daddy before him, and so on and so forth all the way back to Brumfitt Kings, Kings of the ocean, lobster Kings. I have two sisters, but I'm the one who works the ocean with Daddy, Cordelia Kings, heir to the throne.

Daddy likes to say that you can find both the history and the future of the Kings family in Brumfitt's paintings. You just have to know where to look. Sometimes I wonder if Brumfitt could have imagined a future with me working the water, if Brumfitt really predicted that a woman would be the next to wear the Kings crown. I said this to Daddy and he laughed and said that Brumfitt painted all of the memories of Loosewood Island, even the ones that hadn't happened yet, and what I had to do was look at the right paintings. But that's the problem. At night, when I'm up late worried about the legacy—and the burden—of being a Kings, working my way through Brumfitt's paintings feels too close to trying to divine my fortune through tea leaves or fortune cookies: I can read things any way that I want. Any future and every future for the Kings family is laid before me in *The Collected Works of Brumfitt Kings* if I just pick the right paintings in the right order.

Some of my skepticism tonight is the heat that has settled in over the island and chased me out of the house. It's late, late enough that it's close to being early, and I've given up on the tangled sweat of my sheets. Instead, I'm sitting at the edge of the dock. Trudy, my dog, is pacing behind me. I wish I could explain to her that I'm just restless, sleepless, turned out by the heat, that we're not heading to the *Kings' Ransom* to go fishing. I can hear her panting behind me, but I'm forcing myself to look out over the water and watch the heat lightning paint the sky instead of turning around and doing what I really want to do, which is to stare at the crooked elbow of houses that embrace the harbor. There, by the shoulder, is Daddy's house, the light in his downstairs den left on through the night, and there, near the wrist, is Rena's house, dark for hours, my sister and her husband and the twins all asleep. There, too, is Kenny's house. Kenny Treat. My sternman for the last five years, lying in bed with his wife.

Out over the water, the lightning spills in ripples and lines, like a circulatory system drawn in the night, but there isn't even a lick of thunder, a hint of rain. If I wanted to pick a Brumfitt painting to match the weather, it would be *God's Wrath*, but *God's Wrath* wouldn't do anything to explain the dizzy spells that Daddy's been having, and *God's Wrath* wouldn't tell me what to do about the talk of James Harbor's drug trade pushing into our waters. And there isn't a Brumfitt painting in any of the books on my shelves that tells me what I want to hear about Kenny Treat or shows me how to deal with either of my sisters. There's no Brumfitt Kings painting to chase the heat of this night away from me, no hidden messages in the weather. There's just me and Trudy, sitting on the dock, just the play of lightning in the sky and the way it's reflected in the water. But with the lightning—and there, the first push of thunder—I don't need Brumfitt to know that a storm is coming.

My own memories start on a boat. I was small enough that Daddy had cut me down a rod, I think, though it might even just have been a stick with some twine tied to it. Whichever it was, it did the trick: I went to cast my line and I hooked Daddy's lower lip with my lure. The metal was speared completely through the flesh. Blood spilled out of Daddy's mouth, the silver dangle of the lure flashing in the sun. I remember that I cried when he yelled at me, but he says that I've got the story wrong, that it was the other way around, that he yelled at me *because* I cried, and that sounds about right for my father. He can't remember why it was just me with him out on the boat, what my sisters were doing—"probably at home with your momma, just waiting for your brother to be born"—but he can remember the weather and the low tide time for every day stretching past more than forty years. He says that was why he married Momma, so he'd have somebody to remember things for him, like birthdays. That's the only way he talks about my mother anymore, as if she were some sort of prank he pulled.

We weren't out in Daddy's lobster boat, the *Queen Jane*. I remember that, too. The boat was small, a skiff or something borrowed, and my feet got wet from water in the bottom of the boat. I remember being cold, but there again my father says I'm remembering wrong. It was the beginning of June, he said, the week before Scotty was born, and hot in a way that comes as a surprise any day on Loosewood Island, but particularly that early in the summer. It makes sense that it was June, when the lobsters are busy tucking themselves into rocks and growing new shells. Loosewood Island has its own particularities with the lobstering season, and there's a moratorium on catching lobsters from June through the middle of August. It's different in different places, but that's the calendar we work by. So my father would have just been maintaining traps, fixing up the *Queen Jane*. Plenty of downtime ahead of him, enough time to take me out fishing.

He cut my line with the knife he always kept clipped to his belt—or to his slickers when he was working—and he told me to quit crying, his voice now soft and calm, the lure hanging bloody from his lip. I put my fishing pole down on the bottom of the boat, snuffled, and wiped at my nose with my sleeve. He worked at the hook for a little, trying to see if he could thread it back out the way it had come, but he had been hooked cleanly, the barb pushing up and all the way through. The fishing line flossed in the soft breeze like a streamer. "You've caught yourself a whopper, darling," he said to me. The hook in his lip turned his words into a bloody mumble, and he gave me a smile that made the lure jiggle in the sun. The spoon of the lure flashed at me. I had a magpie moment, wanting just to grab at the shininess of the metal, but I kept my hands down. He pulled out the tackle box and rooted around in it, calmly and slowly, as if he didn't have my hook stuck full through him. The blood flowed, drip, drip, dripping down his chin and onto the floor of the boat. It mixed in with the seawater that had been wetting my feet, clouding out, diluted and strange. He took out a pair of pliers and said, "This will serve."

He pulled his lip gently and nestled the pliers against the hook. For a second I thought he meant to just yank it, ripping out the flesh, and if I hadn't been so afraid, I would have started crying again. Instead, he used the wire cutters on the pliers to snap through the hook. He moved the lure away and then worked out the small piece of hook that still hung in his lip, holding on to the barbed end with his fingers and drawing the sheared end out of the flesh. As soon as he pulled the metal out, the blood welled up stronger and started to pour down his chin. Still, he was careful to put the lure and the sharp spear of the cut hook into the tackle box so that nobody would accidently step on it—the same sort of careful consideration of future actions and calamities that served him well as a lobster boat captain—before he pulled off his shirt and wadded it up as a bandage, pressing it against his lip.

"We'd best head in, darling," he said to me. "I wouldn't mind getting this cleaned up, see if I need a stitch or two. Besides, it's getting late enough that your momma will be looking for us. Looking for me, really, to give her a hand with your sisters. And who knows," he said, giving me a wink, "maybe the baby is on its way."

That memory, of hooking Daddy, blurs with my memory of meeting my baby brother, but I know they were two separate events. It would have been a week or so after the fishing trip that Scotty came home from the hospital. The thin, ugly stitches knotted on Daddy's lip were only partly disguised by the growth of his beard. I remember standing on the deck of the *Queen Jane* and getting my first look at my baby brother. It doesn't make sense to me now—why wouldn't Momma have been there with the baby?—but at the time it felt normal to be out on the *Queen Jane* without Momma, without my sisters. I'm sure there was nobody else on the boat, I'm sure it was just Daddy, my brother, and me.

Daddy sat in the captain's chair, cradling the baby. Scotty was crying, the sort of mewl that comes from newborns, and I thought, *He doesn't like it here, doesn't like it on the boat, doesn't like it on the water.* I understood right at that moment that he was just like my sisters: Scotty didn't belong on the *Queen Jane* any more than they did. As I had that realization, Daddy scooped me up and into his lap, and I thought, *Daddy sees it too.* I remember what it felt like to burrow against him, to be looking down at Scotty, the surge of pleasure at the understanding that I thought I shared with Daddy, the belief that I was the one who was meant to be out on the water with him. Daddy was a loving father, but he was certainly not a cuddly one, and to be on his lap was a privilege rarely afforded. I felt like a commoner sitting on the throne.

But as Scotty kept crying, Daddy looked at me and then nodded at Scotty and said, "Here, look at him, Cordelia. This is your brother. Look at him, because he carries with him the weight of our history, the lineage of the Kings family."

Even though I know that I can't actually remember the words with such exactitude, that I was only three and a half when Scotty was born, that those words wouldn't have made any real sense to me at the time, I can still hear every word that Daddy said. "Look at him," he said. "Look at this little boy, Cordelia, because he is both our past and our future, and there is going to be a day when he takes over the family business, when he is out on the water, when Scotty Kings is going to be the king of Loosewood Island." He leaned over and kissed me on the head then and asked me if I wanted to hold Scotty. I nodded, but I didn't really want to hold him. He was just a baby, I thought, small and loud and deserving of nothing, and Daddy had already decided to give him what I knew to be my birthright as the firstborn, girl or not: as much as I could feel Daddy's arms around me, holding me on his lap and holding Scotty steady, I could also feel something else, could feel with a certainty as loud as Scotty's increased cries, that this was not a boy who was born to rule the sea.

And I remember this, too, though I know it can't have been real: Daddy standing up, stepping over the edge of the boat, and walking across the water to the shore, with me and Scotty in his arms, walking across the top of the ocean, taking me home to Momma, Rena, and Carly. I remember the way he cradled me, like I was still a baby, even with Scotty in my arms, and I remember that there was part of me that wanted to close my eyes and let it be a dream. Instead of closing my eyes, however, I looked down at Daddy's feet leaving ripples on the surface of the ocean, and then out to the rocks and the shore of Loosewood Island, as he carried me across the water.

The wife of Brumfitt Kings, first of the Kings, was a miracle. Brumfitt was Scots-Irish, and when he crossed the ocean and ended up on Loosewood Island, he saw birds he knew: gulls and terns, eider ducks and cormorants. Gannets, with their vast expanse of wings diving from a hundred feet above the waves, striking into the water and emerging with fish that no other bird could scoop. And there were other birds as well. He described these birds in his journals, sketched out some of them with the loose attention to detail that art historians have lauded him for, but these birds are such that I've never seen around Loosewood Island and that I have never been able to find in books. I go back and forth between thinking Brumfitt was fanciful and believing that there is some truth to his sketches.

He left a dozen of his journals, leather-bound books filled with his crimped and spidered writing, his delicately shaded drawings of fish and bird and lobster, and they are the first records we have of the Kings. Most of the Brumfitt things that we own—two paintings, sketches, an unfinished canvas, knickknacks from his personal life—are on loan to museums, but Daddy has kept the journals at home. Every year or two an academic writes Daddy a letter asking for permission to come to the island to spend time looking over the journals. Mostly, art historians and academics are interested in the later books, eight through twelve, which read to me more like ledgers. Those are the journals that Brumfitt kept after he married and had his two sons. Occasionally there is a study for a painting that I recognize, but they are mostly lists and records of catches, purchases, the weather, and the few odd drawings of plants and fish. They have notes on mixing paints, studies of birds and fish and the coastline, the day-to-day drudgery of surviving on Loosewood Island, his household finances, lists of repairs or building projects to be undertaken. I've always been more interested in the first seven journals, however, since they show Loosewood Island as Brumfitt first found it, first imagined it, and as a girl I spent a lot of time curled up in a chair by the window reading through the journals, deciphering Brumfitt's tortured spellings, trying to piece together sentences that didn't connect or never finished.

At the end of the seventh journal—his last entry before moving on to the eighth journal a half year later, when his focus shifted to the detritus of life—Brumfitt writes about how he met his wife. Scholars have claimed that she was a native woman from one of the local tribes, though there is debate over which tribe: Micmac, Abenaki, Malecite, Passamaquoddy, Penobscot, or Beothuk. I find it hard to believe that Brumfitt married any native woman, however. The idea seems almost as far-fetched as Brumfitt's own story, because about that time the indigenous population was—with reasonable cause—hell-bent on wiping out the white men who'd come to their shores. No, according to the journal, his wife was neither a white woman nor an Indian, but rather a gift from the sea.

Brumfitt had been on Loosewood Island for eight years by the time he married. When the boats had started coming, they'd fished out the season and then crossed back over the ocean, the men returning home with the salted and dried cod, but after a while the companies realized they could do better if they left someone behind to keep the drying racks together, to keep a permanent encampment for the benefit of all the other men who fished. Brumfitt volunteered, and that first year he was the only man left behind. He seemed to thrive on the isolation of Loosewood Island. He spent a few hours a day seeing to company business, cooking, cutting firewood, or doing other chores of survival, and the rest of his time drawing. This went on for three years. During the season he worked the waters and he worked the shore, and as the boats left when the season was done, he waved them off. After the third year, a handful of other men stayed behind, and the year after that, those men fetched wives from England or Ireland and began to start families among the hardness of the new country.

After eight years on Loosewood Island, Brumfitt found himself surrounded by husbands and wives and children but still living alone. According to the journal, he went out one night to the edge of the island to draw by the glow of the emptiness of the sky, and he found himself, unexpectedly, crying. He realized that the island itself was not enough for him: he had want of a wife.

The night was clear and calm, with the stars and the moon making the soft lapping of the waves into pulses of light, but as he cried, a thin mist started drifting down from the sky. Then, with a crackle like ice breaking, the water suddenly flattened and then seemed to pull away from the island, leaving rocks that were normally just skimming above the ocean bare and dry, crabs and starfish recoiling at the sudden air. Brumfitt peered through the mist and walked toward where the memory of the ocean marked the land, and he looked out toward where the water stopped. And the water did stop, according to Brumfitt's journals. It was not simply that the tide had receded, but rather like something great and mighty had erected a wall of glass that held back the sea. The water lay absolutely still and flat on its surface, no sense of wind or waves. Then, from the flush of the moon, from the pinpricks of the stars, Brumfitt saw something roiling and bubbling out near the Sea Clift Rocks. The mist dropped out of the sky the same way that a silk scarf drops from a lover's balcony, leaving the night clear until, Brumfitt wrote, the roiling water suddenly sprayed into the air like a whale was clearing its blowhole.

And then he saw her, he saw his wife.

A miracle.

She rose inside the spray of water. Her eyes were open and fixed upon him, like she knew he was waiting.

The invisible hand holding back the ocean opened its fingers, letting go, and the water rolled back toward him, the first waves pushing over his ankles and soaking his feet, but he barely noticed, so intent was he on the woman gliding toward him. It was not that the woman herself moved, Brumfitt wrote in his journal, but rather that she was carried. He wrote it both ways, that she stood and that she sat—she sat upon a throne, she stood upon a chariot—but either way, she was carried on the waves, the seawater still dripping off of her. She was wearing a dress made of oyster shells and coral, a necklace of pearls, and she was delivered into his arms with a dowry.

The dowry was this: if Brumfitt married her, his children, and his children's children to each and every generation, would carry a blessing: the bounty of the sea.

I remember reading the story in the journal—Brumfitt's handwriting so rushed compared to the lushness of his drawings and paintings—and being thrilled. It seemed romantic to me. Sometimes I imagined myself as Brumfitt's bride, this queen of the waters, delivering the dowry, the bounty of the sea. Other times I pretended that one day I'd have my own prince wash ashore, that he'd step from the waves to take me in his arms. It was like having my own personal fairy tale.

But what I never thought about as a child was that, like in all fairy tales, the gift came at a cost.

With every blessing there is a curse.

When Brumfitt married, his wife's dowry was the bounty of the sea, but the price for each and every generation of Kings was this: a son.

Momma came into her marriage already knowing what it meant to be a lobsterman's wife. Momma was an only child, her father the last of the Grummans on the island—all the rest had moved to the mainland and were fishing cod and haddock—and she knew Daddy from the time she was old enough to know anybody. She was five years younger, too young to get anything but passing notice until after he came back from Vietnam and realized that little Mary Grumman had grown up into the kind of woman who could have been washed to shore upon a wave nearly three hundred years ago.

But even if she wasn't directly out of a fairy tale like Brumfitt's wife, Momma made for a pretty picture as a bride. The photograph of the two of them on their wedding day, which still hangs above the sideboard in the dining room, looks like it could have been painted by Brumfitt: Momma and Daddy standing on the rock beach by the docks, mid-July with the sun washing over Loosewood Island, Momma in an ivory dress handed down from her mother's wedding, Daddy, a late bloomer, in the dark suit he'd worn to his high school graduation, the sleeves so short that the white of his shirt showed from the forearms down. Daddy's facing the camera, his back to the water, but Momma, who is leaning into him, has her body quarter-turned, her gaze on the ocean behind him, like she was already practicing for him to be out working the waters, already waiting for him to come home.

People always say that it's Rena and Carly who remind them of Momma, and that I take after Daddy, a Kings through and through. But at least in that wedding photo, I'm a ringer for her. She looks beautiful in the same way that I've turned out sort of beautiful: she's lean and strong, a rope in the shape of a woman, freckles in the summer and skin that doesn't fade in the gray months of sleet and ice. Her hair, turned toward red from the sun, is braided and pulled into a crown twist, giving her an elegance that I've never mastered. She's barefoot, which I can tell because she has the hem of her wedding dress snatched up in her hand, keeping it dry from the threat of the waves. She's smiling so easily that I sometimes wonder if she even knew that she was having her picture taken.

She's not wearing it in the picture, but for their wedding, Daddy gave her a matched pearl necklace. The same pearl necklace, Daddy claimed, that had been worn by Brumfitt's bride when she was delivered by the sea. Before I was born, Momma said she used to walk out on the beach in the afternoons, waiting for the first sight of Daddy returning in the *Queen Jane*, and she'd touch the necklace every few minutes to remind herself that he'd be coming home soon.

"I knew," she said to me, "that as long as I had those pearls on my neck, Daddy would come home. It was a covenant between me and the ocean, between me and Brumfitt. I'd wear the necklace, and Brumfitt would deliver your daddy home to me. But still, some days, when the sky turned ugly, when I could feel the weather hunting the island, I couldn't breathe until I saw the *Queen Jane* come through the mouth of the harbor. I'd just worry those pearls and pace up and down that beach."

"How come you stopped?"

Momma laughed at the question. I remember that she laughed,

because it wasn't something that happened often. Like finding two pearls in one oyster. On some days, getting her to laugh was like finding an entire necklace, matched and strung, in the same shell. "I've got kids. I've got you three girls. I've got Scotty. I don't have time to walk on the beach and worry about Daddy. Things change."

They were married three years before Momma got pregnant, and once things changed, they changed fast: four kids in four years, all of us coming out straight and quick, bowling pins lined up just to be knocked down. Me first, and then Rena, Carly, and last of all, Scotty, the boy my father had been waiting for. Daddy worked the boat and Momma worked the house, and that's the way it worked between them. Not that Daddy wouldn't pitch in here and there—he was never the kind of man to be squeamish about folding sheets or washing dishes or even changing a diaper—but there'd be months of the year when he'd be gone before dawn and come home after dark, times when it seemed like he'd be gone on his boat for days. He was around more in the summer, when lobsters peeled themselves from their shells and scuttled deeper into the rocks to protect their newly soft flesh, when the industry on the island was tourists, and in the late winter and early spring, when the season was closed or when storms and ice made it so he'd only head to sea a few times a month. But when there was fishing to be had, Daddy was gone.

On the nights when Daddy was working the water late, Momma used to pile the four of us into her bed and sing to us before bedtime. Their marriage bed was small, particularly by today's standards, but it was sized to fit their headboard, which had been passed down for long enough that it might have belonged to Brumfitt himself. I'm sure that back when it was just a woodstove heating the house, the cold salt winds murdering their way through the slits in the siding, it was good to be snuggled close to your husband or wife in such a small bed. The full-sized mattress was separate from the headboard itself, which was attached to the wall and carved like a shell, the base wide and then cut in before flaring out and scalloping over the top. Around the edges, scrollwork ivied up and around, meeting at the top in a royal, gold-leafed clamshell. In places, the gold leaf had been worn down almost to wood by the touch of generations of Kings hands. Once Momma had us ready for bed, our teeth brushed, pajamas on, hair still wet from the bath, she'd turn the lights down low and place Scotty, Rena, Carly, and me underneath the quilts; with the gilded headboard above us, we looked like nothing more than the Kings upon their throne. I remember the way that my sisters and Scotty would snuggle in and wait for her to sing, but I could never seem to get comfortable there; I always wished that I was out on the water with Daddy instead of stuck inside the house.

I know that other mothers read stories to their children, but Momma sang her stories to us: she sang "Mermaids of Dover," "Tall Ships and Tall Sails," and "Mulroony Goes Courting," and we sang along with her; she sang "The Fishgutters," "The High Wave," and "MacAuley's Lament," and we listened quietly to the high, gentle tides washing over us; she sang "The Boatman," "Nine Ships for Nine Daughters," and "The Rocks of Wailing," and she'd sing those to us in Gaelic, halting here and there to search for a word or a phrase that she couldn't remember, telling us how her grandmother used to sing to her like that when Momma was no older than we were. She always ended with "Thief of the Ocean":

The thief of the ocean,
A king with his head held high.
Steal a fish from the ocean,
Repent not when you die.

I used to think that the king with his head held high meant Brumfitt Kings, and I remember one of the nights when I was eight or nine, all of my siblings had fallen asleep in the dark room, Momma's voice lulling them under, and I asked her about the song.

"No, honey," Momma said, as she led me down the hall to my bedroom, "it's not the Kings, just a king. Any king." She left Scotty, Rena, and Carly in her bed, for Daddy to carry to their own rooms when he got home from pulling traps. "The Thief of the Ocean isn't Brumfitt, it isn't Daddy, it isn't even Scotty. It's any man or boy who works the sea."

"Or girl," I snapped. I was ferocious at times with Momma. I had to be, to stay out of her grip. Even with Daddy pushing for it, saying that if I wanted to be out on the boat then I belonged out on the boat, she resisted. Oh, but Scotty belonged out there, she said. Momma sent him out on the *Queen Jane* when he was four, five, six, even though he would have been just as happy at home with Rena and Carly, up in aprons and mixing flour and eggs. When it came to me, I had to claw my way out of the house, had to fight for my birthright as a Kings.

Momma didn't answer me, but she didn't kiss me on the forehead when she tucked me in, either. As she stood up, however, I realized that I had another question. "What happens if the ocean catches you?" I said.

She took a breath to stay even, a sign I recognized to mean that she was ready for me to go to bed. On the nights when my father was not in the house, she did not have much left that she was willing to suffer by the time Carly, Rena, and Scotty were asleep. "If the ocean catches you . . . what?"

"If the ocean catches you stealing," I said. "Does it steal you back?"

She stood straight and looked down at me. Her carriage was erect, like she practiced walking with a cup of water balanced on her head, but she let her fingers drift to the pearls around her neck during the moment of time it took her to answer me. "Hush, dear. Time for sleep," she said. "That's enough from you." As she lingered by the light switch, it felt like there was something she was waiting to say, but then she turned. Before I heard her feet on the stairs I was sitting up in bed and calling to her. I could hear how frantic my own voice sounded, but when she came back in,

I couldn't think of why it was I needed her back, so I asked for a glass of water.

She touched my arm and then reached onto my nightstand and picked up the glass of water that was already waiting there. "Cordelia, do you know what my grandmother used to say to me?" I shook my head and took a sip of the water. It didn't feel like enough somehow, to simply sip at it, so I took few great gulps and then had to cough. Momma took the glass out of my hand and put it back on the nightstand. "*Is i mhàthair bhrisg a nì 'n nighean leisg*, which means, An active mother makes for a lazy daughter," she said, but in a voice that made me know that she didn't mind. She gently pushed me onto my back and brought the blanket up to my shoulders before leaning low and letting her lips linger on my forehead. I remember how safe, how warm, how dry I was, how there are moments of childhood that feel brief but last forever.

I slipped my hand out and wrapped it around the back of her neck, feeling the pearls rolling under my fingertips. "I'm sorry, Momma," I whispered.

"Well," she said, "maybe you can just look next time, to see if there's already a glass of water waiting for you."

I could feel her lips moving against my forehead as she spoke, but I didn't bother to correct her. I wasn't apologizing for calling her back to me, and I wasn't even apologizing for the way that I'd gotten sharp with her when I'd said that a girl could be the thief of the ocean. I was apologizing because I knew that I had no choice: girl or not, I had the blood of the Kings ebbing and flowing through my body. Nothing could stop me from getting on a boat. I was born to it.

Brumfitt Kings wrote in his journal about seeing a mermaid, but his mermaid wasn't something gentle out of a cartoon. She was pale and the fish part didn't end neatly at the waist; scales climbed the mermaid's body up to her shoulders, her eyes bulged, and her face flattened like a fish's. When he reached for her, she showed teeth that made her look more shark than woman, snapping at his hand and drawing blood from one of Brumfitt's fingertips. Brumfitt wrote that he stayed away from the water for nearly a week after seeing her. Daddy said that Brumfitt shouldn't have been scared. His wife came from the sea, after all—which meant, I guess, that all his descendants have fish blood running through our veins—and that should have afforded him some protection from what he saw.

There are other stories about mermaids, though none like Brumfitt's. The rest of the stories described beautiful mermaids who sang to sailors and seduced them. The boys liked to joke that if you jumped in the water after them you'd at least get a chance to see whether or not mermaids actually wore those little clamshell bikini tops before you drowned.

When Daddy told *his* mermaid story, however, he never joked.

It happened when he was six. He'd been playing on the shore, collecting shells or rocks or some such, and he'd turned his back to the ocean in the way that you're taught never to do. A wave had curled over him and brought him out under the water.

He said that it hadn't been at all like he'd expected. First there had been lung-searing blackness, and then he realized he could breathe underwater. The fish hung around him like birds strung from wires, seemingly oblivious to his presence. He walked across the rocky floor, heading down the slope and toward the dark of the deep water, and then he saw brilliant pinpricks coalescing into a great light before him. The light came from windows, and the windows were set into a castle that was unlike what he had imagined when he played war with his leaden soldiers. The castle was something more alive, as if it had been coaxed from the bottom of the ocean, the parapets pulsing with the movement of the waves. Daddy entered the castle, and even though light seemed to come from the walls themselves, there were dark and sad whispers swimming past him in the hallways.

He said he walked through corridor after corridor, but each door he came to was locked. And yet, he said that he never felt as if he were lost, and when he finally saw the entrance to the great hall, the wide doors thrown open, the light pouring out toward him, heard the tinkling of glass on glass, he was already half expecting what was in there: a lone mermaid waiting for him.

She was not like Brumfitt Kings' mermaid, Daddy said. She had long dark hair that seemed nothing like seaweed, and her tail could have been any color or no color at all, but the light made it shine. The mermaid welcomed him, and said this was his castle now, that he was to be the king, and told him to lean down so that she could put a crown upon his head, so that she could welcome him to his kingdom. But as he bent over and the mermaid reached for him, he said he heard a dog barking, and then saw his mother burst into the room. His mother pulled him into her arms, away from the mermaid. Daddy said that my grandmother carried him across the rocky ocean bed, and up the rise, the water seeming insubstantial to her. "Hush, hush, hush," she kept saying to him, her words the rhythm of the waves breaking over them. Daddy felt the waves trying to pull him back into the ocean, but each one of his mother's hushes beat back the water, breaking its pull on him, until the two of them broke through the dark tunnel of the salt water and onto the surface, the water flattening into a sheet of glass, the sun's light exploding off the surface of the ocean bright and gleaming: everything disappeared and all he could see was light, light, light.

My grandmother, who died when I was eleven, liked to point out that my father didn't include certain bits from the story. Like how when he'd finally opened his eyes again it was to the inside of a hospital room. Like how *she* didn't see any mermaid. Like how what *she* saw was a fisherman's Newfoundland dog going after Daddy and dragging his limp body from the surf. Like how Daddy was dead for at least a few minutes. But Daddy insisted. He went around the island telling anybody who asked how he was doing, and plenty of people who didn't, that he'd been under the ocean, that he'd met a mermaid.

Carly thinks he likes to tell that story as a lesson: we all have a place where we belong, and Daddy's place was above the water, on Loosewood Island.

I think it tells a different lesson, the same lesson that is in all of Daddy's stories: there's magic in the sea, magic on Loosewood Island. The problem is that some of the magic is like Brumfitt's mermaid: sharp with teeth.

Brumfitt Kings probably isn't a name you'd hear in your daily conversation, but he's famous enough that a good portion of the tourists who come to Loosewood Island come only for that reason. Others, of course, come for all the same reasons that tourists go anywhere: to see something beautiful and new, to play at being rich somewhere else, and simply to step outside themselves, to imagine that their lives could be something different. Every year we get a few tourist couples—they are always couples, but since I've grown up, some of the couples have been men—who fall in love with the island and decide that what we need is an upscale coffeehouse or a jazz bar or a shop that sells only olive oil, and they start their new business up. It doesn't usually take more than one winter for those people to realize that the reason they fell in love with Loosewood Island wasn't because of what the island was, but rather because of what Loosewood Island wasn't. It wasn't the life they wanted to leave behind. Still, some of them make a go of it year-round and become permanent islanders, and some of them are just tourists with a business interest, keeping shop during the summer months and closing up the rest of the year. There are plenty of islanders who make a good living looking after cottages and houses and businesses that are shut up for the winters.

Even the tourists who don't come for Brumfitt Kings have mostly heard of the island in the first place because of Brumfitt Kings. The bulk of tourists, Brumfitt Kings fans or not, come here during the summers, but the Brumfitt Kings pilgrims are less predictable. We'll get a few every month of the year, even into January and February, and you can pick them out because they are the ones who walk the island with coffee-table-sized books in their hands, trying to match Brumfitt's paintings to the views in front of them. We've encouraged it on Loosewood Island, keeping the Brumfitt Kings Museum open year-round. Islanders have grown used to seeing tourists stumbling across our lawns and getting lost in their search for the exact point where Brumfitt painted *Morning Breaks*, or *Broken Mast with No Hope for Shore*. The only people who get upset at the Brumfitt Kings tourists are the other tourists themselves, the summer people who built up their six-thousand-square-foot "cottages" and who think that buying into the island means that they've bought the island. Those are the ones who try to tell lobstermen whose families have been fishing the same spot for fifty or a hundred years or longer that they don't want their view spoiled by lobster boats. Those things work themselves out.

Those other kind of summer tourists, the wealthy ones, can be a bit much sometimes, thinking that Loosewood Island's a sort of fishing theme park, but they are mostly bearable. The ones who come to the island for Brumfitt Kings are almost always easy to deal with, however. For some of them, the trip to the island has been a lifelong dream, and for others it's something they do every summer.

I think that Daddy and I both look kindly on the Brumfitt tourists because we understand the pull. For Rena and Carly, the idea of the family legacy, of being the descendants of a famous painter, is appealing, but there isn't any urgency to it. A few years ago, when the Met installed Brumfitt's most well-known painting,

The Catch, neither of my sisters were interested in making the trip to New York with Daddy and me.

"I'm happy to go to the city if Tucker wants to watch the babies," Rena said, "but I'm not making the trip just to see a painting that I've already seen."

Daddy raised his eyebrows and then put down his beer with an exaggerated slowness and theatricality that made Rena start smiling even before he began his lecture.

"And where, exactly, have you seen *The Catch*?"

"It's in every Brumfitt book ever. Plus, all I have to do is head to the west side of the island to get the same view. Seems a lot quicker to take a walk over there than to drive to New York City," she said.

She was teasing, and she indulged Daddy and me in going to museums when we used to take vacations as a family, but she just didn't understand. Brumfitt painted the island, but in some of his paintings he saw a different island than the one my sisters did. *The Catch* was one of those paintings. The paintings that got Brumfitt "discovered" in the 1950s are menacing portraits of Loosewood Island: men drown, a body floating in the water is one that is ravaged by the seas, and a man in a boat is a man who despairs of ever getting home. Brumfitt also has his share of what I like to call "restaurant and hotel lobby paintings," even though that pisses Daddy off almost as much as when I say that Brumfitt is what you'd get if you combined Andrew Wyeth and Winslow Homer: paintings of birds caught on the wing, fish brushing against the surface of the waves, the ruggedness of the coast with all menace removed. My favorite works, however, like *The Catch*, are the ones that remind me of the stories Daddy likes to tell about Brumfitt: paintings where hands snatch at you from the ocean, where birds I've never seen before cover the air, where sailors beat back monsters from the waves.

The Catch shows the purpling skies of dawn, a lush light coming over the horizon, but enough shadows to make the ocean seem sinister, and a small, single-masted boat overmatched by the waters and the waves breaking on the rocks. There's a pair in the boat: a seasoned man and a boy who could be ten or eleven. The man is struggling to pull a single fish from the water. It's not clear what kind of fish it is—where the rope meets the water there is simply the froth of water—but the man's back is bent and his muscles and sinews seem to jump from the canvas, and the thing that *is* clear is that this is a large fish, and that this man with his son, and presumably a wife and more children at home, will use this fish to feed his family.

Despite the strain of the man, the movement of the catch in the water, the menace of the ocean, it's the son, however, who caught my eye as I stood in the museum with Daddy, and who always catches my eye when I look at prints of *The Catch.* The boy is smooth and delicate, more like a bird than a boy. He's looking over the side of the boat and into the water. His hand is extended, almost touching the water.

And this is why I love the painting, why it reminds me of the stories of Loosewood Island that Daddy raised me with: if you gave *The Catch* only a cursory glance you might wonder at the reflection of the boy's fingertips in the foam of the ocean.

Except it's not a reflection.

It's not the boy's fingertips at all, but some other person's fingertips—some other creature—reaching from the water to grasp at his hand, to pull him under.

Every time we boarded the *Queen Jane*, Daddy gave us the same lecture: watch our feet with the ropes, watch our fingers in the hydraulics, watch that we sit where we're out of the way, watch that we help when it is needed, and always, he'd add at the end, giving us a wink, watch to see if there's anything that Brumfitt might have painted out in the water.

By the time I was twelve I'd started showing breasts, though it was Rena, early at only eleven, a full year younger than me, who'd gotten her period already, and Momma had been making noises about how the *Queen Jane* wasn't a place for me or my sisters to be spending our weekends, that squatting on the deck to pee and hosing it off wasn't the best training for the kind of girls she was trying to raise. She'd never been warm to the idea of me, Rena, and Carly fishing, but she was always ready with an extra lunch for Scotty to take along. He belonged out there with his daddy, she'd say, because otherwise how would he learn to be a lobsterman? It might be in the Kings blood, but that didn't mean Daddy didn't also need to teach him how to be a man.

Despite Momma's urgings and Daddy's steady attention, Scotty was always the last one out the door. On a Saturday morning, when I'd already be in my boots and slicker down at the docks, checking the bait, re-coiling any lines that I didn't like the look of, he'd still be sitting at the table, as if his sugared cereal could stand to soak up more milk. Rena and Carly were somewhere in between. Sometimes they'd come fishing because I wanted to be there—and Scotty *had* to be there—and because they didn't want to be left behind. Sometimes they'd stay home to walk the island and bake with Momma or play with friends.

That Saturday, a fall day when the wind was hinting at what was in store for us with the coming of winter, was the last time that the four of us all went with Daddy at the same time, and it was also the first Saturday that Momma said it explicitly: "You girls are staying home."

Scotty was still upstairs, even though Daddy had woken him first and Momma had gone into his room twice to get him moving, but I was at the table eating oatmeal with syrup. Daddy was pouring coffee into his thermos. Momma packed him his lunch every day, but he liked to doctor up his coffee with enough sugar to offset the salt of the sea, and he always heated the cream before he poured it in, so that the coffee wouldn't go cold for him if he was still out on the *Queen Jane* in the evening. He rested the lid on top of the thermos, like he did every morning, to keep the steam in while he pulled the sugar from the pantry. He glanced at Momma when she said it, when she said, "You girls are staying home," but he didn't say anything.

Rena stuck her head out of the bathroom, where she was braiding her hair, but Momma glared at me and me alone. I hadn't said anything, hadn't responded, but she acted like I had. "That's right, Cordelia. You're staying home. It might be a weekend, but it's cold outside and I don't want you girls coming back home tonight with runny noses and skin that's chafed from the wind." She folded her arms under her small breasts and leaned back against the counter. She was wearing a blue dress that matched the sky more than the water, and I wondered how early she must have woken to have already done her hair and her makeup before starting to make breakfast and pack lunches. She uncrossed her arms, crossed them again, and then brought one hand up to her necklace. I could tell that she was nervous. She hadn't talked to Daddy, and she wasn't sure what he'd say. She seemed to consider it, and then let her fingers fall away from the pearls, standing up straight and crossing her arms. "The *Queen Jane* is no place for a young lady."

And this time I did speak. "Scotty can go fishing, but I can't?"

There was a long silence. Rena stood still on the threshold of the bathroom. Carly put down her doll. Upstairs, I heard the first movements from Scotty's room, the creak of his bed and then the floor. We were waiting for Daddy to respond.

He put the glass jar of sugar down on the counter and unscrewed the lid. He didn't seem to be in any sort of a hurry as he opened the drawer, pulled out a soupspoon, and started scooping sugar into the thermos. I counted the spoonfuls, five, six, the squeak of the spoon in the sugar, the occasional tinkle of the handle hitting the glass of the jar or the rim of the thermos. Fourteen and fifteen, and then Daddy dunked the spoon in the thermos and gave it a twirl. He didn't say anything, and the lack of voice was too much for me.

"Scotty's a baby, and he's still going fishing?" I said.

I was looking at Momma, and she was ready to respond, but it was Daddy who spoke. "Scotty's a Kings, and he'll be out fishing with me today, Cordelia."

"You and your sisters can stay home with me," Momma said. She was trying to make her voice sound bright, but all I could think of was glass breaking. "You'll help me with painting the back room, and after lunch we can bake some cookies if you'd like."

"I'm a Kings, too," I said. I pushed myself away from the table, hard enough that some of the milk in my glass sloshed out. I'd like to be able to say that I hadn't meant to push that hard, but I had, and more importantly, I meant what I said next. "I can't go fishing because I'm a girl?" I paused, so that the next words would really hit. "That's bullshit."

I think that I was hoping the word would drop like a bomb. The men on the docks swore without any real thought, and I'd heard Daddy talking like he meant to take the paint off the hull of the *Queen Jane*, but that wasn't the language we used in our house. I'd never heard anything stronger than a "darn it" come out of Momma's mouth. I pressed hard on the word, "bullshit," looking at Momma and waiting for her to respond. She opened her mouth, but it was Daddy who spoke.

His voice was calm and even, as if he were simply suggesting I wear rain boots instead of sneakers. "I don't think you're going to talk like that in front of your mother," he said, "but the point is taken." He picked up the thermos and screwed on the cap. "It *is* bullshit, Cordelia. You're right. You're a Kings, too, and if you want to be out on the water, you'll be out on the water. All the kids will go today, and if any of the girls decide that they don't want to be out on the *Queen Jane* in the future, well, they don't have to be. But if they want to fish, if *you* want to fish, Cordelia, I'll have you along." He didn't look at Momma as he said it, but he didn't need to. We all knew that what he said, as far as it came to fishing and the Kings name, was how it would go.

To her credit, Momma didn't storm out of the room, didn't do anything more than nod and pack up lunches for me, Carly, and Rena, to go with the lunches she'd already packed for Scotty and Daddy.

Out on the *Queen Jane*, things moved like they normally did. Carly had brought along her doll, Mr. Pickles, and she and Rena pretended that he was their captain, giving them orders for what lines to move, what traps to bait. They were too old to be playing with dolls, but Carly never went anywhere without the raggedy thing. I didn't care that they were acting like little kids. What I cared about was that they were out of the way, that it was just me and Scotty doing the real work. I wanted to show Daddy that I belonged on the *Queen Jane*.

By midmorning, my sisters had set themselves up with a snack on the deck under the cabin. We were across from Seal Coat Cove, and Daddy was working over a jammed trap with a pair of pliers. Scotty and I were working together to lift a baited trap and get it over the rail, but mostly it was me. I could see Scotty looking over at where Rena and Carly were sitting. I'd like to believe that I told him he should go over with them, that he should just take a break, because I was trying to be thoughtful. But even at the time I knew that wasn't the truth; I knew that I wanted him to go sit down with my sisters so that Daddy would see that he was weak, that he wasn't meant for the water. Scotty didn't think about my reasons. He immediately let go of the trap and walked forward to get himself one of the blueberry muffins that my sisters were eating.

I hadn't expected him to just let go, to leave me holding the trap on my own, and it banged down off the edge of the boat and smashed into my shin. "Fuck," I shouted. I didn't mean to swear that time. It just jumped out of my mouth. The second time I'd sworn in front of Daddy that morning.

He looked up from the trap he had resting on the platform in the middle of the deck and raised an eyebrow. He loved raising his eyebrow. "You all right?"

"Just slipped. I'm okay." I bit my lip. "Sorry about saying... that word."

"Not the best habit to get into, particularly for a twelve-year-old," he said, and then he glanced over at my sisters and at Scotty. "You three, come on. How about you help Cordelia out?"

Scotty blushed and shoved the muffin into his mouth before scampering back to me. I felt almost bad about it, but there was a part of me that was also happy that I was the one Daddy had seen working. Both Rena and Carly were slower to respond. I knew that they would have been just as happy to stay home with Momma. They'd worked the first hour we were aboard, but they were content to stay in the shelter of the cabin, out of the wind.

I wrestled the trap up myself and dumped it over the side of the boat. "We're good," I said, and Daddy nodded and moved up to the captain's chair, easing the throttle forward to move us to the next set of traps. I turned and started prepping bait. Scotty was already there, wiping the crumbs of the blueberry muffin on his slickers before putting his work gloves back on.

"Thanks a lot," Rena said as she joined us. "Yay. Bait."

Carly held up her doll to her ear as if Mr. Pickles were talking to her and then she said, "Mr. Pickles wants to know why we can't use something that smells better."

I didn't bother looking at them. "Don't be such girls," I said, with as much scorn as a girl that age could muster.

"You just wish you could be a boy," Carly said, "like Scotty."

I don't know if I did it because I was angry that what she said was true or because I was still angry that being a girl mattered so much to Momma, but I snatched Mr. Pickles away from her and stepped over to the rail. "Take it back," I said, and I held the doll out over the water.

The doll was dingy and faded, something that had been well used even before Carly latched onto it as something that was special to her. The fabric around one of his ears was puckered where Momma had to mend it, and the markings where his eyes had been were so faded that he looked more like something cooked up to scare a child than a favorite toy. But still, Mr. Pickles was Carly's. Where Rena and I had special blankets and Scotty had a teddy bear, Carly had Mr. Pickles, and she'd already started to cry.

"I'm sorry," she blurted. "I take it back. You're not a boy."

It wasn't just me trying out cursing that day, because it was Rena who spoke next. "Don't be such a bitch, Cordelia."

The doll fell into the water.

My hands were slippery from the bait, and we'd hit a wave so that the *Queen Jane* bucked. I'm almost certain it was an accident.

I blubbered that night while Momma paddled me. I had snot streaming down my face, and I told her it wasn't my fault, that I hadn't meant to, but it didn't matter much. The result was the same.

That was in the early fall, and by December, Rena and Carly had stopped coming fishing altogether. I was two months shy of thirteen, Scotty was nine, and our first dog, Sailor, had been dead long enough that Sailor II, who we all called Second, was past being a puppy. He was a big dog, even for a Newfoundland dog, at 150 pounds, black and gliding and never willing to leave Daddy's sight. Newfoundland dogs are gentle things, great slobbering balls of fur. Loyal and sweet. They shed like the ocean makes seaweed, but they're good dogs for a fisherman to have: Newfoundland dogs' coats keep the water away from their skin, so they're warm in the water even when the sea spray rims the boats with ice, and they've got webbing between the toes on their paws so that they can power through the swells. There are lots of stories of them saving men from the waves.

Me and my sisters had all been sick for weeks: the cooped-up, crouped-up, coughing crud you can get when you live hard against the ocean's edge and winter has come to settle itself in for good. School had just taken to vacation for the winter break, and we already had our Christmas tree cut and standing in the living room, trimmed with tinsel and ornaments that Momma unpacked from the same tissue-paper-filled boxes every year. Carly and Rena were still hacking, but I'd been clear of sickness for a few days, driving Momma crazy with energy, and Scotty had never taken to coughing, so when the weather broke clean and warm—or what passed for warm in December on Loosewood Island, just above freezing—Daddy bundled the two of us up in our woolens and rain gear, whistled up for Second, and took us out on the the *Queen Jane*. He'd pulled all his deepwater traps already, saying he expected some storms in the next week, but he still had twenty or thirty traps in the shallow water, on the shelf off the island, and he told Momma that he wanted to pull them as well. After that, he said he'd stay out for a while, either to catch something fresh for dinner, or maybe even to make a run across to James Harbor to pick up a few more small things to put under the Christmas tree. The sky was clear and we were squinting with the bounce of the sun off the water. I was sitting in the cabin, trying to keep out of the wind and the cold, huddled against Scotty, who was already whining about not being allowed to stay home.

We were barely out of sight of the docks—Momma could have seen us from the window if she'd been watching with a pair of binoculars instead of being busy cleaning up the mess from tending to Rena and Carly—when Daddy came to his first set of traps and started hauling them up.

Nowadays, about half of the men on the island have fiberglass boats made local in Maine, and a few have Novi boats, but the fleet is still choked with wooden boats like the *Queen Jane*. Daddy's made a few concessions to the times: the hydraulic hauler that his father did without, a citizens band, and even a tape deck—if a tape deck can be considered a concession to the times—that he uses to listen to Johnny Cash and books he takes out from the Loosewood library. He hasn't bothered with a depth finder or LORAN or GPS or most of the other things that the younger men and I are kitting out our boats with. For the most part, the *Queen Jane* looks like what it is, which is a lobster boat that was bought new in 1952 and handed down from my grandfather to my father, a boat that has seen a lot of weather but that has been taken care of like my daddy's life depends on it. Which it does.

I guess if you aren't familiar with lobster boats, one looks about the same as the other: a high bow forward of the cabin, and back of the cabin, low sides and stern to make it easier for hauling traps. The *Queen Jane* was no different. Daddy had off-loaded most of the gear so that he could make repairs, prepare for the resumption of day-in-day-out lobstering in April, but the bait barrel was still lashed against the starboard railing, and there was plenty of space for the traps. Daddy had been fishing these traps as pairs, which meant that pulling one trap actually meant pulling two.

Daddy gaffed the buoy, slapped the warp into the hauler, and let her rip. The traps broke the surface glistening with mud and a decent catch of bugs despite being an off time of year.

Daddy put the brass gauge against each carapace, checking to make sure we were legal, though I bet he could have done it by eye. He threw four overboard and kept two, and from the second trap he kept one and threw back five. "We're not looking to sell any, but maybe we'll get enough for dinner tonight," he said, which was what he said almost every time we were on the boat with him, as if this might be the one time he didn't get enough for our dinner. He pulled the second trap off the rail and put it on deck with the other and then said, "Here, Scotty, come on over. I'll rebait, but you separate the traps out. I want to put them back in as singles."

I got to my feet, but Daddy looked at me and shook his head. "I want Scotty to do it, Cordelia. He's nine. Old enough to start taking over more. He's a Kings, and he can earn his keep."

That was all he said, but it felt more like a kick in the gut. It wasn't just that Daddy wanted Scotty to do it, but that he *didn't* want *me* to do it. I spent as much time on the *Queen Jane* as I could. Daddy liked to joke that I was the youngest sternman on the island, but the price was right. I could haul a trap, empty it, and rebait it fast enough that I was more of a help than a nuisance, and Daddy never said anything about me being just a girl. I was a

Kings through and through, and Daddy knew it. I belonged out on the water. But Daddy never seemed able to see what I could see so clearly about Scotty, which was that my brother wasn't made for the ocean. Scotty tried, he really did, but only when Daddy was looking. When Daddy asked if Scotty wanted to learn a new knot, to see how to adjust the diesel engine, Scotty always said yes. When we were on board and Daddy called him over, Scotty scrambled like a puppy because he didn't want to disappoint Daddy, but the truth was that Scotty didn't want any of it for himself. Left to his own devices, Scotty would have been just as happy to be playing football with his friends or to be back at the house with Momma.

It killed me. No matter how often it happened, no matter how many times Daddy called Scotty over to do something on the boat that I could have done blindfolded in half the time, it still felt like a betrayal. Why could Daddy never see that only one of us was suited to the sea?

I stayed in the relative warmth of the cabin and watched Scotty untie the knots from the paired traps while Daddy rebaited and banded the keepers. And I didn't say anything when I saw that Scotty had only tied a line to one of the two traps. He struggled with that first trap, getting it up and over the rail, letting it splash into the water. The line played out of the boat as the trap sank. I waited for him to notice that the second trap was naked, that there was no line attached, no buoy, nothing to keep it from disappearing in the depths, but Scotty didn't notice. Scotty didn't notice, and I didn't say anything, and it was only when the trap was already up on the rail and starting to teeter over that Daddy saw the mistake my brother had made.

Daddy lunged for the trap, but it was too late. It fell from the boat, hit the waves, and sank. "Scotty," Daddy barked. Scotty had already started to realize what had happened, and I saw the way his face went blank, as if by not acknowledging that he'd thrown away a trap it would mean that it hadn't happened. "You didn't tie a line . . . how could you . . ." Daddy shook his head and pursed his lips. He didn't say anything more than that, but he didn't need to. Even from the cabin I could feel the way Scotty was trying to shrink into himself. It wasn't the cost of the trap—we lost gear all the time to weather and accidents—but the way that he'd lost it. Such a stupid thing to do. But then Daddy shook his arms, forced a smile back onto his face, and put his hand on Scotty's shoulder. "Don't worry about it, son. Mistakes happen. It's a good lesson. Always double-check to make sure you've got your gear ready to go. It could happen to anybody," Daddy said.

Except, I wanted to say, it couldn't. That wasn't the sort of thing that I would have done, I wanted to say. I didn't say any of that. I kept quiet even as Daddy moved the *Queen Jane* to the next spot on his line, even as he pulled the next pair of traps, measured the lobsters, kept one, and threw the rest back. He looked at the two traps and then shook his head. "We'll throw these ones back in the water and pull the rest of the line. The first two are rebaited, and I've got a couple on the backside of the island that will do for the family." He roughed Scotty's hair. "Everything else we pull we'll bring back to land. You kids stack them up and lash them."

I didn't bother moving from the cabin. If Daddy didn't want me to help when we were rebaiting and dropping traps, I didn't want to help now. Besides, Daddy was watching, so Scotty was acting the good son, was already dragging the traps across the deck. He was being quick and eager, trying to do the right thing, trying to make Daddy forget his mistake. Daddy came back to the wheel and pushed the throttle. He didn't say anything to me about not helping Scotty, but he gave Second a tap with his boot. The big Newf uncurled himself from under the wheel and walked over to where Scotty wrestled with the traps and the bounce of the boat over the waves. Second nosed at Scotty and let out a few barks.

It was the sort of thing that happens all of the time. A mistake. There's the weather, there's the waves, there's the lobsters themselves with their crusher claws. There's all sorts of hooked and sharp things aboard a fishing boat, and there's the hydraulic haulers to take a finger off. But most of all, there are the ropes. Warp scatters everywhere; good lobstermen will keep their warps organized, lines coiled and out of the way, where they need to be, and so will the bad lobsterman. Highliners and dubs alike, they keep the ropes neat. The only lobstermen who don't keep their ropes neat are the dead ones.

Scotty hadn't bothered taking the floating rope off the bridles on the traps, and he left the pair of traps still lashed together; the warp was tangled up in a bundle around his feet. Scotty was struggling to get one trap stacked up on the other, and the top trap was half on its twin, half on the railing, and that big, stupid fucking Newf, Second, was barking and nosing at Scotty. I can't remember if I was watching the whole time, if I saw Scotty straining with the traps, a nine-year-old trying to be a man, trying to live up to Daddy, to live up to the name that he carried with him everywhere he went on and off of Loosewood Island. I can't remember if I didn't offer to help because I was a twelve-year-old girl and busy with simply not being near him, or if I didn't offer to help him because I knew that he would never live up to the name that he carried with him, that he wasn't deserving of it in the same way that I was. What I do remember is the sound of Second's barking.

Daddy heard the barking, too, because he looked over his shoulder and yelled out, "Second. Get off him," but as he yelled at Second, the *Queen Jane* caught a wave. The boat gave an unexpected bounce, and it wasn't clear if Second stumbled into Scotty or if Second jumped onto Scotty, but the results were the same: the trap that Scotty was balancing on the rail went over, and Scotty fell in the tangle of ropes on the deck of the boat.

I wish I could say that something spectacular happened, that it was a scene from one of Brumfitt's paintings. I wish I could say that the ocean flattened into glass, sea turtles rose to encircle the *Queen Jane*, the weather crackled black, and the winds cursed at us, ripping a hole in the clear blue sky as water spouted into the air like hissing serpents. And I'd like to believe that we all had a chance to realize what was going to happen, that Scotty and I locked eyes, and that Daddy, in that moment, understood that the promise Brumfitt Kings had been given when he married—that the Kings would receive the bounty of the ocean, but that our sons would be at the mercy of the sea—was being fulfilled. But I know better than that. There was nothing to set this moment aside from all of the other moments that came before and all of the other moments that came afterward. There was no magical marker to delineate then and later, no animal from the deeps reaching out and drawing Scotty away from us. It was just an accident. It was just the ropes.

Scotty fell to the deck, slipping in and under the ropes, the first trap hitting the water and yanking tight the lines to its twin. The warp snapped against Scotty, and I could see a piece snug across his throat, his body slamming into the trap, and then the whole mess—line, trap, Scotty—crashed into the rail and flipped over and out into the water. The buoy line that hadn't tangled up with my brother smoked over the rail and left a scar that still marks the *Queen Jane* seventeen years later. The buoy smacked against the rail, the last thing out of the boat, bouncing into the air and then settling in the water. The traps, and Scotty with them, were already under the water.

Second, barking, went over the stern and into the water to save Scotty, unable to leave him alone even after he'd knocked my brother overboard. There wasn't time for Daddy to try to throw the boat hard in reverse—from Second knocking Scotty down to the time he was in the water wasn't even enough for a blink, like a car crash or a bullet wound—and instead Daddy did the only thing he could do, which was to slam the throttle full forward and crank the wheel, turning the *Queen Jane* nearly on her edge. He reached out to me and grabbed my shoulder, and it was suddenly like I had woken from a daze. "Turn her around," he said. "Line me up."

He moved back to the rail, and for a minute I thought he was planning to go in after Second, after Scotty, but he had already recognized that with the cold of the winter water and the weight of the traps and Scotty's body, he was best off in the boat.

Even though I was still short enough that I could barely see through the glass—I didn't really grow until I was in eleventh grade, and then I shot up five inches in a year, heading to my full height of five-seven, just like Momma—I kept the wheel hard to starboard. The boat turned against the waves and, though the sea was calm for that time of year, I glanced back to see Daddy stumble as he went for the gaff.

I stood on my tiptoes and could see Second moving swiftly across the water toward the buoy. The sky was clear and the sun hung up so that it bounced off the water, Second's black fur glistening in the light and the wet. A series of shadows cast through the water and under Second, a school of fish or just a play of darkness.

"Off the throttle, honey," Daddy called, and his voice sounded so calm, so reassuring, that I half wondered if I was in some sort of a dream, if Scotty was in a mermaid's castle, if my grandmother would come flying through the water, if Second would simply pluck my brother from the sea.

Second barked, and then barked again, and started swimming in a tight circle around the buoy. He kept ducking his head under the surface. I lined up the boat, one cold hand on the throttle, one cold hand on the wheel—I wasn't wearing mittens, for some reason—and I heard Daddy yell, "Stop her!" He meant for me just to throw the throttle into neutral, but I panicked and killed the motor, killed all the power on the boat, killed everything.

Daddy gaffed the rope neatly and slapped it into the hydraulic, but nothing happened. When I killed the motor I'd cut the power to the hydraulic; the rope hung tight, not moving, doing nothing to take Scotty from the depths.

How long did it take before Daddy pulled the rope back and started hauling it by hand? Half a second? One second? Two?

Second kept barking. With the motor cut, the sound of the dog and Daddy's breath competed with the waves and the few gulls overhead.

Maybe a minute had passed since the dog had knocked Scotty into the traps. I left the wheel and hurried to start stacking the wet warp—the rope—on the deck behind Daddy, though I had no hope of keeping up and no real sense of why such a thing would be useful. We were over the shelf, and the water wasn't that deep, three, four fathoms, which was the only reason why the buoy, with all that fouled line, still shone on the surface. By the time I got behind Daddy, he'd already pulled twenty feet of warp from the water, the first lobster pot breaking the surface. I gasped at the sight of my brother's body: he was pressed tight against the trap, a loop of warp around his neck, the rest of the line tangled against his nine-year-old body and the trap, his arms splayed out. When he broke the surface, he wasn't breathing and his skin had turned pale and headed to blue, though I didn't know if it was from the cold or the lack of air.

I couldn't look at my brother, and I couldn't look away, but there was something to the side of him that caught my attention: a small movement among all of the other movements of the waves and the water. I leaned over the rail and extended my hand toward the water, the sun and the reflection of my fingertips in the foam bouncing back to me, and for an instant I thought it was not a reflection, but some other creature reaching from the water to grasp at my hand, to pull me under, like in Brumfitt's painting. And then that instant was broken by Daddy's voice.

"Call it in, Cordelia," Daddy said.

I looked again at the water, but it was just my hand and my own reflection. I straightened up and watched as Daddy reached over and grabbed the trap and hauled it—and my brother's body—up from the ocean. At the time I could have lifted neither my brother nor a wet wooden trap. The trap could have easily hit eighty or ninety pounds, more with the second trap trailing behind, and Scotty must have weighed another eighty or ninety. But my father made it look effortless.

I ran to the radio and I remember that there was the sound of someone laughing and then a moment of static, a transmission cut off, before I grabbed the mic and started asking for help. It was George Sweeney who answered, and the few times he's talked about it with me he said that it still gives him the creeps how calm I sounded when my voice came across the radio and said, "We need help, George. We need help. Scotty's dead. Scotty's dead."

Except he wasn't. By the time I clipped the radio back to its mount, Daddy had gotten Scotty untangled from the trap, had pounded his back, had blown air into his lungs, and Scotty was puking water and coughing and shuddering, his lips blue and chattering, a red, raw line marking where the rope had pulled tight against his throat.

It only took George Sweeney five minutes to pull alongside, John O'Connor with him for the ride. Daddy had already stripped Scotty out of his wet clothes and wrapped him in blankets, pulled Second back on board, and reassured me that my brother wasn't going to die. The water was calm enough that George drew his boat almost touching ours, and John hopped over onto our deck. While Daddy cradled Scotty on his lap, John fired up the engine and ran the *Queen Jane* full-throttle back to the docks, where Momma and what seemed like half of the winter population of Loosewood Island were already waiting.

It wasn't exactly a party at our house that night, but neither was it anything but a party. The Christmas tree in the corner winked at the room, the tinsel breezing like seaweed. The fridge was overstuffed with beer, and ladies brought casseroles, more than we could possibly eat, as if they had started filling up their glass baking dishes the moment they heard me on the radio, and then couldn't stop themselves from finishing their cooking once the news went out that Scotty had survived. The women hovered over Scotty, rubbing his hair and kissing him on the forehead, and the men put a full drunk on, toasting Second both for knocking Scotty overboard and then for trying to rescue him, toasting to me for keeping my head, even toasting to the shelf that the trap had landed on, knowing that with the short rope on the traps, if the water had been twenty fathoms or even ten—anything deep enough so that the traps would have pulled tight the fifty feet of warp and sunk the buoy beneath the waves—there would have been no pulling Scotty back from the water.

Scotty was tired and pale, complaining that his neck was sore and that his chest hurt from the water he'd swallowed, and he was put to bed early, worn out from the cold and from the experience of both dying and being reborn. Carly and Rena and I were allowed to stay up late—despite my sisters hacking and coughing to seize the day—but there were still at least a dozen men sitting around the woodstove and drinking beer when I went to bed, Second curled up near my father's feet, celebrating a Christmas miracle.

Only the celebration had come too early. Sometime in the middle of the night Scotty started coughing, a pink, frothy ooze from his lips, and then his breath started coming in short gasps, and then nothing. He was dead before Carly, Rena, or I had woken. When the doctor finally got to the house, late in the morning and a thousand hours too late to help, he said it was delayed drowning, that Scotty had swallowed so much water when he had gone under that he continued to drown even after he was pulled from the water. Maybe if he'd been pulled out quicker, but the way it was, not much could have been done. Perhaps if Daddy had taken him to the hospital in Saint John, or even the clinic in James Harbor, but even then, whichever side of the border, a hospital probably wouldn't have helped.

Years later, before Rena dropped out of nursing school, she called me and said she'd studied it, studied what killed Scotty.

"It was hypoxemia. That's what they call it."

"I'm not following you, Rena."

"It was the salt. If he would have drowned in a river or a pool or somewhere other than the goddamned ocean, he might have lived, but it was the salt water. It pulled the water into his lungs."

A few years after that phone call, she told me that she might have had her facts wrong, that maybe freshwater was worse, that there was some disagreement, but that she was so excited to have something that made sense to her that she just had to call. She wanted to make sure I knew that there was something that could explain how we had a breathing brother at night and a corpse in the morning. But knowing it didn't change the fact: Scotty was dead.

Of course, there was more to it than that. The day of the funeral, December 24, Daddy slipped out early in the morning. I don't think anybody else was up—which in a fishing village meant it must have been god-awful early—or that he knew I was awake. I had been sleeping poorly since Scotty went overboard, bad dreams keeping me fitful. Even the night it happened, before I woke up to find out my brother had died, I had nightmares. Sharp-toothed mermaids, hands reaching from the deeps, dragons circling in the shadows: a Brumfitt Kings slideshow.

I was awake when Daddy left the house on the morning of the funeral. I heard footsteps on the stairs and then the less cautious movement of Second, behind him. A few bumps from the kitchen and then the opening and closing of the front door. I pushed myself out of bed and pulled on my jeans and sweatshirt from the day before, putting them over the panties and T-shirt I slept in. At the front door I stepped into my boots, the mix of felt and rubber inside odd and cool against my bare feet, and grabbed my mother's slicker.

I was maybe a minute behind my father, and I hurried down the path toward the harbor, moving through occasional pools of yellow light. It was wet, and the weather was cold enough that it came down in equal parts snow and rain. The snow stuck to the grass and the bushes, but it was liquid running down the arms of Momma's slicker and turned to puddles on the pavement. I was shivering by the time I caught up to Daddy and Second at the head of the dock.

I called out to him and he turned to look at me. If he was surprised by my presence he didn't show it. "Head on home, Cordelia," he said. "It's too early for you to be up yet. The funeral isn't for another five or six hours. Go back home and go back to sleep."

"What are you doing?"

"I'm going out in the boat for a while," he said. "Go on, now, go home."

"Come home, Daddy. It's raining. Or snowing. Both."

"Let it," he said. He let out a small, strangled laugh and looked past me toward the water. "Blow, winds. Rage, blow. Spit, fire. Spout, rain."

"Daddy," I said, and I was worried because he was right here in front of me, but he sounded like he was drifting away. "Daddy, please?"

He looked away from the water and at me, and his voice was his own again when he said, "Go home, Cordelia. Just go on home." He said it gently and started walking again, but I didn't turn around. I stayed next to him, following him as he climbed into the skiff. Second dropped himself over the gunwale, stepping onto the bench and then giving a quick circle before settling himself on the floor of the boat. I got in and went to the bow of the skiff, reaching out to untie the painter. Daddy sat down with his back to me and picked up the handle of the oars. There was a pool of water and slush on the bottom of the boat, but it didn't seem to bother Second none, and he looked like he might have already fallen asleep. I brushed the first takings of snow off the bench and tucked my jacket in under the ass of my jeans so I could sit down. A bead of water dropped off the hood of my jacket and landed on my knee, immediately soaking through. I wished I'd thought to throw on a pair of bib-pants under Momma's slicker. I wished I'd worn a warmer coat. I wished Scotty wasn't dead. I wished a lot of things.

Daddy didn't move the oars at all and he didn't turn around, but his voice came through clear, despite the guzzling of the waves and the constant patter of rainy snow on my hood and all around us. "You sure you want to come out with me, Cordelia?"

"Seems like fine weather for it," I said.

"You're not to question me or to get in my way," he said. He sounded stern in the way in which I rarely heard unless it was something that was well deserved. "The weather is the way the weather is, and I'm telling you that if you come with me, then you are telling me that you'll give me your obedience." He let his head hang down, and with his back to me, his voice became muffled. "I'm losing my wits here, Cordelia."

I didn't say anything, and that seemed to be enough for Daddy, because he bent his back into the oars and started moving us across the bay. It only took us a few minutes to get to the *Queen Jane*'s mooring buoy. I tied us off while Daddy held the rail of the *Queen Jane* so Second could navigate his way on board.

The diesel fired up without any complaint, and Daddy kept the motor low as he threaded his way out of the harbor. He kept quiet, but he saw me shivering and pulled a spare jacket and a pair of bib-pants from a hook in the cabin and handed them to me. I stripped off Momma's slicker, pulled on the pants, and then threw the jacket on before putting Momma's slicker back on. I was still cold, and my hands had begun to ache, but with standing in the cabin and out of the sleet I felt some relief from the weather.

Once we were away from the boats, he reached over to the controls and turned off all of the lights, leaving us running dark except for the thin glow from the dials behind the wheel. With sleet coming down on us, it felt like we were moving through ink. The lights of the village had already dimmed into nothingness, and when Second lumbered into my legs and then settled at my feet, I could only tell by touching him, his wet, black fur making him invisible. We motored like that for ten or fifteen minutes, Daddy steering by feel and memory and three hundred years of the Kings living and fishing off Loosewood Island, and then Daddy pushed the throttle into neutral and hit the lights again.

The lights came up bright and burning, and as soon as I could open my eyes again I realized that the sleet had turned completely to snow, the running lights bouncing back at us. The snow fell heavy and deep, and there was already a thin coating on the deck of the boat. It was mesmerizing in the way it fell, and I spent a few seconds trying to see if I could figure out a pattern to how it lined down in the lights. I could have kept staring out into the dark morning forever if Daddy hadn't reached down and grabbed Second's collar, hauling the dog to his feet.

Second came up eager enough. He followed as Daddy made his way aft, out of the cabin. Daddy motioned to the stern and said, "Up," twice, but Second didn't move until Daddy grabbed his collar again and half wrestled the dog up and off the deck. Second stood on the stern, looked out over the water, and then at Daddy. The dog turned to get back in the boat. "Go on, then," Daddy said, pushing back at Second, maneuvering him toward the edge. "Go on," he said again, and then he gave Second enough of a shove that the dog half stumbled and half leapt into the water. The splash was quiet, and Second didn't even let out a bark. I moved to the port quarter and saw Second treading water, staring up at me with the same eager almost-smile that he always had on his face. Daddy brushed past me and went back to the cabin. He opened a compartment and pulled out a plastic box and rested it on the captain's chair.

"What are you doing?" I asked, even as I recognized the box. He kept his old service revolver in there, a Smith & Wesson Model 10, smuggled home from Vietnam. He let Rena, Carly, Scotty, and I fire it off sometimes, when we were out on the boat with him and tired of lobstering or bored with waiting to get wherever it was we were going. We'd shoot at lobster buoys and empty glass bottles that Daddy threw into the water for us. If he wasn't looking, we'd occasionally take a shot at a seagull, missing every time we tried. The gun probably only weighed two pounds, but it felt heavier. We were all small enough that the square butt felt enormous in our hands, and even if we'd been on land instead of on the decks of the *Queen Jane*, it would have been hard for a girl my size to keep the sight steady. The Model 10 fired .38 Special rounds, so it was easier for us kids to handle than his new pistol, a Model 65 stainless steel chambered to fire .357s. He'd gotten the Model 65 the winter before, and he'd let me fire it once. The kickback was like a whale yanking at my shoulder, and I was so surprised that I didn't even notice the gun had bounced up and the barrel had smacked me above the eye until Daddy handed me a cloth to press against the open flap of skin in my eyebrow.

He didn't answer me, didn't look at me. He simply unwrapped the gun from the oilcloth he kept it wrapped up in to protect it from the salt air, flipped open the fluted cylinder, glanced at it, and then flipped the chamber shut again. Second gave out a sharp bark, and I looked into the water again. The snow was still falling, disappearing as it hit the surface of the ocean, and it seemed like a magic trick in the lights of the boat: it was hard to understand how something that looked so substantial could float from the heavens and then disappear as soon as it met the ocean.

Daddy walked over to the side of the boat, but I stood in front of him. "What are you doing?" I asked again. "The funeral is in just a couple of hours." I was twelve and my brother was dead and I wasn't letting him by until he told me what he was doing. I wanted to hear him say it.

"Uneasy lies the head that wears a crown," he said.

"Fuck you."

The words came out of my mouth as a surprise, but they didn't seem to surprise Daddy. He didn't react at all other than to say, "Step aside, Cordelia." His voice was low and soft. He had a deep voice and he talked with deliberateness, but he sounded tired. He was missing the sea foam in his voice.

"Did you hear me? I said, fuck you. I'm not stepping aside, not until you tell me what you're doing. Why did you push Second in the water? You're not going to shoot him," I said, but I wasn't sure if that last sentence came out as a question or a statement.

He tried to step around me, but I blocked his path. Looking back, I can't believe he didn't just push me aside. It wouldn't have taken much for him to move past me, but he let me stop him. "At the docks," he said, "I told you to go back to bed." He leaned his head back, looking up into the darkness and the snow, as if he were going to open his mouth and stick his tongue out like a little boy trying to catch a snowflake. His arms hung down at his sides and he would have looked innocent and hopeless if he hadn't still been holding the gun. The blued steel of the revolver wanted to sink into the shadows. "Yes, Cordelia," he said, letting his head sink back down and staring at me. "I'm going to shoot him."

I don't know what it says about him—or about me—that I wasn't surprised, that I had already known the answer. I think I knew the answer before I even left my bedroom. "Why?"

"I have to do it," he said. He looked at me, no break in his gaze, and I could see that he'd had no question about it, and if I hadn't been there he would have already shot Second and been motoring back to the harbor.

"He didn't mean to knock into Scotty," I said. I could hear my voice breaking, and I was cold again, despite the bib-pants and the extra jacket.

"But he did knock into Scotty, Cordelia." He said it patiently, as if it were something he was explaining to a small child.

"He's just a dog." I looked down at my feet and tried to swallow. I wanted to hit Daddy, but I couldn't. "I hate you," I said, and the words surprised me. I hadn't expected to say that, hadn't known those words were going to come out of my mouth, but Daddy didn't seem surprised at all. I looked up to see him nodding. "I hate you," I said again, like I was trying the words on. "It wasn't Second's fault."

"No, Cordelia, it wasn't Second's fault," he said. He sounded tired. Not like he was giving in or giving up, not like he thought for even a second of wrapping the gun back in its oilcloth and putting it away in the plastic case, but like he hadn't slept in a thousand nights, like maybe all those years since he'd been tugged under the water as a boy he'd actually stayed under the sea in the mermaid's castle, staying awake and waiting, waiting, waiting to resurface. "It wasn't anybody's fault except for mine, Cordelia," he said. He reached out and lifted my chin, his voice going hard.

Second barked again, and we both looked into the water where the dog kept swimming in circles. I began to think I saw something akin to panic on Second's black face. "So why—"

"Second went in after him, didn't he? That's what Newfs do," Daddy said. "They go in the water and they pull fishermen away from certain doom. I didn't even do that. I didn't go into the water. I stayed on deck where it was safe and dry and did my rescuing with a gaff and my hands, but Second went right to the water." He put his free hand on my shoulder and then glanced out at Second again. "Let me tell you a story, Cordelia, and it's not one I want to talk about again or want to hear you telling your sisters or your mother, okay? You don't get to repeat this."

He stared at me until I nodded dumbly. "You know George had a brother, right? Billy? That the three of us went overseas together, but only George and I came back." Second barked again, but Daddy didn't look away from my face. I could have been afraid to breathe—whatever Daddy was going to say, I was sure that I didn't want to hear it—but I was all reflex and stillness. "It's more complicated than this, of course. Everything is more complicated. I could string out the story, pretend there was something more to it, but in the end, it's as simple as this: Billy was killed. That's what happens in war, I guess. Billy was killed, and we did what we felt like we had to do, which was to bring a punishment down upon the earth."

He took a deep breath after he said this, and in the moment of quiet I remember thinking how that sounded both like and unlike Daddy: "to bring a punishment down upon the earth."

That sounded like the man I'd seen doing Shakespeare in summer stock plays, taking the part of Henry IV, Caesar, Coriolanus, and Iago, it sounded like the man that I knew from home, his voice roaring through the house when he read aloud a section from a novel that seemed to sing to him. But it didn't sound like the salt-grooved man who squinted over the water, who fished and hauled and never left anything undone.

"Billy died and we, in turn, killed. George and me and all of the boys who were with Billy when he went down, we killed until there was nobody around to kill and all that was left to us was Billy and the pieces of his body and the understanding that there are times when it isn't about what you want or don't want, about right or wrong, but only about what needs to be done."

He looked down at the pistol in his hand and his voice dropped into something quiet and falling, like the snow that kept coming down over the water and the *Queen Jane*. "Do you understand, Cordelia?" Second barked again, and whatever spell Daddy had fallen into seemed to break. "Of course you don't. You're just a kid," he said. There wasn't any scorn in his voice. Just fact. "I did what I had to do. And if I could do it again, if I could go back then, to when I was a kid myself, maybe I would have been able to tell myself, tell George, tell all of the other boys, that this *wasn't* what we needed to do, that Billy's dying was senseless and bad luck and bad decisions, that spilling more blood wouldn't do anything for what happened to Billy, but that's not the way it was. Not the way it is. And maybe in some later year I'll look back on now and think this isn't what had to happen." He took another heavy breath. I wanted to believe, in that momentary pause, that he was going to change his mind, but even then, even as a girl, I knew better. "Right now," he said, "right here, it's all I know to do. When everything is over, when everything that can be said is said, when everything that won't be said is swallowed down, I can't just do nothing. I wish I could just howl, that I could scream loud enough to make it right."

He looked down at his hand and seemed almost surprised to see the pistol, and then he cocked it. The sound was softer than I would have expected, nothing like the breaking click that I would have expected at that moment, and it was perhaps that quietness that made the sound pass through me with the impact of a bullet that hadn't yet been fired.

He swallowed hard and then his voice turned hard as well. "But all I know is that I'm not heading back to shore with that fucking dog."

I thought about Brumfitt Kings and his wife rising from the ocean, about what it meant to be a Kings, about the price we had to pay for being able to haul fish out of the ocean like they were called by our voice, and maybe Daddy was thinking the same thing, because when I said, "It's not his fault, it's not Second's fault," the broken glass in his voice smoothed over.

"You're right, Cordelia." He reached out like he was going to put his free hand on my shoulder but then let it drop. "It's not Second's fault. I should have taken care of the traps myself or helped Scotty out. I should have kept Second away from Scotty. I should have kept an eye on him, kept the throttle down until he was clear of the ropes. It was my fault, Cordelia, and it was Scotty's fault. He knew better than to leave the warp such a mess, connected to the bridles, to leave the traps tied together." He paused, coughed, glanced down to the gun in his hand, and then stared at me again.

"And you. It's your fault, too, Cordelia. You knew better than to kill the engines, kill the hauler, so I was pulling line by hand. Could have gotten him up faster, out of the water. Might have made the difference. And you should have been helping him. You should have been there to make sure your brother was safe. I thought he was going to be the heir to these waters, the next generation of the Kings men to work as a fisherman, but no. No. He's gone forever, and instead, I'm left here with three daughters and Scotty to be buried once the light comes up on the morning. It's my fault, it's Scotty's fault, and maybe you don't deserve as much blames as I do, but it's your fault, too, Cordelia. You should have helped him, but you didn't. And what am I left with now? What am I left with?"

Me, I wanted to scream, *You're left with me.*

But I was choking down a sob, and he answered his own question.

"I'm left without a son, Cordelia. That's what I'm left with."

He turned away from me and I couldn't keep it swallowed anymore, the tears and shaking coming out of me, but then he was turned back to me and taking me in his arms, and his voice had the air gone out of it. "I'm sorry, honey. I didn't mean that. You couldn't have done anything. It wasn't your fault. You did right. You did right by all of this, baby. Oh, honey, oh, sweetie. I'm sorry. You brought us around and lined us up, and we got him out of the water as quick as we could."

I cuffed at my eyes. "But why—"

He cut me off. "I stayed on the deck and pulled Scotty out, and Second went into the water. And it didn't matter, did it? I didn't save Scotty, and Second didn't save Scotty. But that's what I had to do, that's what Second had to do. And this is what I have to do now."

He moved to step past me again, and this time I didn't stop him. Maybe it was because I was still paralyzed by what he had said, by the way he had said it was my fault, with no doubt. Never mind the apology. I had already pointed at myself, already wondered if my mistake had been what pushed Scotty past the point of reclamation, but it was different when my father said it. To have a father like that, and then to have him say it was my fault, my fault that Scotty died? No matter that Daddy said he was sorry, that he was wrong, because I knew the truth: my father didn't make mistakes.

I walked to the cabin and sank into a chair, trying to dry my face with my sleeve as I turned to watch him. He stood alone and solid on the deck of the *Queen Jane.* The lights of the boat washed around him and made him seem like an absence against the snow that fell over the boat and the waters. He raised his arm and pointed it down and out over the water, like an accusatory finger.

And then, a lick of fire.

The shot came sharp and stark against the night. The only sounds were the lapping of the water and the hum of the motor in idle. The crack of the gunshot snapped against me like I'd been shot myself. There was barely a pause between the first and second shots, and then again between the second and third shots, one, two, three, and then there was silence, but in the space of that silence, it felt like the sound of the bullets echoed from every wave around, bouncing in and around the cabin and filling the boat. I tried to keep my crying to myself, but I couldn't stop myself from letting out a gasp and then a few sobs.

I saw Daddy's head drop, his whole body seeming to sag against the effort, like the snow that had started collecting on his shoulders was weighing him down. And then he began to howl and rage against the night, screaming like it would stop the snow and the waves. The snow streaked down and over him, breaking out of the darkness and framing him in the white. He lifted his arm and fired the gun out into the distance of the ocean and the dark that lay behind the curtain of reflected snow from the ship's lights, the last three bullets in the gun flaming into nothingness. His voice died in the night, leaving us again with only the hum of the motor and the constancy of the ocean, his screaming and the sound of the gunshots already fading to memory. He grasped the rail of the boat with one hand, and then, with the other, almost casually, he spun the gun out into the air and over the water. The metal soaked up the lights of the boat and the darkness of the sky, turning around and around, lost to my sight before it hit the water. By the time I heard the heavy splash, Daddy had already turned back toward the cabin, his hands empty, the gun sinking into the deeps.

We didn't speak on the way home, and I looked through the windshield out into the night. I was crying hard enough that things kept coming in and out of focus. Daddy tied us up to the mooring buoy and then we reversed our trip across the bay, a thin coating of snow sticking to all of the surfaces of Loosewood Island. When we got to the dock, I stepped out of the skiff and tied us up, but Daddy didn't move. He sat hunched over in his seat, his hands still on the handles of the oars. I let him stay there shaking for a few minutes, and then he wiped at his face and got out of the skiff, the two of us making our way through the snow and up to the house.

In the vestibule, he cupped his hand around the back of my neck. I didn't know what to do and wasn't sure what to expect. I think that I thought Daddy was going to say something, either to justify his killing Second, or something to comfort me about Scotty, or Second, or even just about his love for me. I wanted him—needed him—to say that he understood that he wasn't left with nothing, that despite the death of my brother, he knew that he had me, had my sisters, but he didn't say anything. He leaned over and kissed me on the top of my head, his breath warm through my hair, and he held me like that for an uncomfortable amount of time.

When he released me, he turned and walked into the living room, and it wasn't until the click of the lamp sent the shadows leaning away from the doorway and I heard the compression of the sofa, the thin crisp of paper in his book, that I snuck back upstairs to my room. I stayed in my bed, in and out of sleep until I heard the stirrings of Momma and my sisters. I didn't say anything when Daddy told them all that there had been an accident, that he had gone out on the *Queen Jane* just to clear his head, that Second had gone into the water and gotten tangled up in the propeller. Rena and Carly wailed for a while, but Momma just bowed her head, like she was all cried out. Daddy didn't look at me. Afterward, we cleaned up, ate our breakfast, and put ourselves into our black dresses for Scotty's funeral.

And past that, it wasn't something we talked about. Sailor II was gone. Scotty was gone. The ocean gave us our life and it also took life away.

The funeral was behind us when school started up again after New Year's. I turned thirteen in February, Rena turned twelve a few days later, and Carly made eleven in April. In the spring, sometime in May, Daddy took a day off of lobstering to make a run to the mainland and when we came home from school there was a Newf puppy running around the house, Sailor III. Third. We taught Third to carry a beer from the kitchen to Daddy's recliner in the living room.

And then, in June, around what would have been Scotty's birthday, and about the time Daddy pulled his traps for molting season, Momma put bricks in her pockets and walked off the edge of the dock, leaving Rena, Carly, and me alone with our father.

I don't know what Brumfitt Kings would have painted if he'd been looking out over the water and watching Scotty, Daddy, Second, and me on the boat that day, but the only thing he would have had to paint was the ocean. No monsters from the deeps were necessary. The water takes enough away on its own.

What Brumfitt did paint was a series of three paintings commonly referred to as *The Drowned Boy* paintings.

If you head from the village toward the schoolhouse, and then turn at the end of Coral Avenue, there's a path that leads up the hill toward the west side of the island. The Brumfitt Kings Museum has a donation box specifically for the upkeep of "Brumfitt Trails" on the island, and this is one of the most well used trails. There's even a small brass marker on the trailhead post that labels it THE DROWNED BOY PATH. During the tourist months, when the population of the island more than triples, there's a steady stream of people making their way along the path. It's about a ten-minute walk up a soft grade, and it doesn't feel like you are going anywhere because the trees grow heavy, and even on a sunny day there's not much you can see outside of the woods and the path in front of you. It's best in the winter months, because when you finally come to the top of the trail, the leaves are gone and the trees are bare; the trail suddenly bursts open in front of you, and you realize that you are standing on a sheer cliff a couple hundred feet above the sea, and you can see the same thing that Brumfitt Kings must have seen. In the winter, the waves hit the rocks sitting a hundred yards off shore differently. What in the summer is a rolling, smooth whiteness has become something ferocious and energetic. The waves smash against the rocks and send spumes of water into the air, a mist that carries across to shore if you take the shore path. The light falls differently, too.

There's a bench at the top of the path near the guardrail, and if you sit on it, you are sitting more or less in the same spot from where it seems like Brumfitt painted the first two paintings in the series. The paintings are large for Brumfitt—each one is seven feet wide and five feet high—and they are clearly a series; he dated the back of his canvases, and these were completed respectively in January, February, and March of 1740.

In the first painting, Brumfitt captures the waves and the spray of the water off the rocks, but nothing of the actual coast; it's as if you're only fifty or sixty feet from the boat. The boat itself is small against the waves, and the boy, maybe nine or ten, is at the oars and clearly struggling with the wind and the wash. The mast is broken, but that seems something that had happened before, since there is no evidence of sails or rigging, nothing other than the oars. There's fishing line and some sort of oilcloth tarp, indication that the boy wasn't out on a pleasure cruise, but had been getting food. Behind the boat, the sky is split between darkness and, if not exactly light, then not exactly dark, either; it's clear that the storm has come in fast and hard, and the boy has been taken unawares. There's a look of panic on his face. He's glancing back over his shoulder, but you can see that no matter how hard he's struggling to row, he's not going to clear the rocks where the water is breaking.

The second painting in the series is more expansive. It shows the coast and the spit of pebbled beach, the water between the beach and the offshore break of rocks. Between the break and the beach, the water isn't truly calm, but it doesn't have the manic energy and whitewash of the waves on the ocean side of the break. Out there, on the other side of the break, the ocean side, the wind has whipped up the water into nothing other than spray and foam, and the waves make the boy's boat look like some sort of a beach toy. And like a toy, the boat is caught up in a wave, turned at a three-quarter angle in the wave's gutter, the stern smashing into the break of the rocks; it's clear that if the painting were a filmstrip, the next frames would show the boat hung up on the rocks, tumbled end over end. The boy himself is already sliding from his seat. One hand is raised as if to ward off the rocks, the other still firmly fastened to the handle of an oar. That's what the eye is drawn to, but it's the figure on the beach that breaks my heart: at the edge of the picture, small enough that we know he's too far away to do anything, a man runs across the polished rocks of the beach. He's wearing a heavy jacket and boots. You can't make out any other details, but you can see the urgency and you know it's too late.

The third painting is from a different location on the island, and it's a spot that seems to draw all kinds of tourists, not just the Brumfitt tourists: the cemetery. There is a man digging out a grave. You can't tell for sure if it is the same man from the second painting in the series, but it's hard for me to believe anything else. The sky has cleared, the storm from the first two paintings blown past, and the sunlight is achingly bright, so that the body lying next to the grave has no shadows to hide it. It's the boy's body, wrapped in oilcloth. A flap is turned over by his head so that we can see his face. If you stand too close to the painting, the picture is smeared and blurry. It's only when you move back from the painting that it comes into focus and it's clear that Brumfitt wants you to see the face of a boy who was smashed against the rocks.

The series probably wouldn't have been considered so important if the dates and the events hadn't lined up so neatly with Brumfitt's own life: his oldest son died at the age of ten, in December of 1739, his boat overturned in a storm, his body broken against the rocks. The first Kings boy taken by the sea.

We floated together as a family for more than three years after Momma drowned herself. Her body spent three days in the water, and when they finally fished her out, she went right into a closed casket. I'd like to think that she looked calm and peaceful resting on the silk liner, a clean dress and styled hair, closed eyes, but I knew too much about what the water could do after three days: bloated and bitten skin, soft features smeared by the fish that fed on the bottom of the ocean.

By the time I was sixteen, Carly and Rena were completely done with pulling lobster pots. I fished with Daddy on the weekends and after school, hauling lobsters on the *Queen Jane*, while Carly and Rena went off with friends, fucking boys in the back of cars and in dank basements. With Scotty gone, Daddy took me on for a full share of what he pulled out of the ocean, and in response, my sisters separated themselves from him with a violent absence that turned me into the bridge between them and Daddy; it was as if the only way they knew how to figure out who they were was to obliterate the ground around them, a teenage policy of scorched earth. Or maybe it was the other way around, maybe it was Daddy responding to Rena and Carly pushing away by pulling me tighter.

Either way, it never occurred to me to worry about Daddy. He was always a self-contained man in most ways. That's not to say that he was always quiet. I can't think of a day that went by when he didn't tell me that he loved me, but he was a hard man, and I also couldn't think of a day when I felt like he *needed* me, *needed* anybody. Still, in retrospect, I should have been able to see that there were times when whatever it was that he was holding inside of him was beginning to leak out, that he was in danger of coming undone, but I couldn't see beyond myself.

It was that fall, nearly four years after Scotty drowned, that James Harbor made a play for our waters, dropping traps in Loosewood Island fishing grounds. I remember tense men crowded into our kitchen, talk of guns and fists and cutting traps. I was old enough to be around the fringes while still being too young to be in the thick of things, but I remember the way that every time I heard somebody talk about the kingpin of James Harbor, Al Burns, his name was prefaced with the phrase, "that cunt." The only person who didn't seem worked up over the poaching was Daddy. He'd let the men grumble and flame, and then he'd tell them that these things had a way of working themselves out, that "Brumfitt Kings claimed these waters for Loosewood Island, and that cunt Al Burns can't change that."

Out on the *Queen Jane*, with James Harbor buoys floating thick in our waters, it seemed like Brumfitt Kings was just a piece of ancient history. When I said that to Daddy, however, he snapped at me.

"You spend too much time looking forward, Cordelia. It would do you some good to look back more often."

I lifted a trap onto the rail and dropped it into the water. "I just think that we need to do something."

"What do you want to do, Cordelia? You think we should be cutting traps? You think we should sink a couple of their boats?"

"There are worse ideas," I said. I swallowed the words into

a mumble, and Daddy either didn't hear me or decided that he didn't hear.

"You're thinking about this wrong. This isn't about us against James Harbor. This is like Brumfitt and *The Sea Dragon*."

I knew enough not to groan. Daddy's only response to me complaining about getting yet another lecture on our family history was to tell me more of that history, as if by weight alone he could get me to understand its importance. And he always told me the stories about Brumfitt as if I had never heard them before, as if I hadn't read the same journals he had. I'd never actually seen *The Sea Dragon* in real life—it hung in a national museum in Denmark—but I'd seen reproductions and heard the story dozens of times. None of which stopped Daddy.

"There be dragons," Daddy said. "That's what they used to write on the edges of maps, in the undiscovered waters, and they weren't just words. We've got mermaids and selkies and the merrow, and those are still in the waters off the island, but there was a time when there were dragons, too. Sea serpents, some men called them, but doesn't matter what you called them, Brumfitt knew they were real. And you've got to understand that Brumfitt was alone when he painted *The Sea Dragon*. This was before he had a wife. It was just him, in a cold cabin, drawing and painting and trying to keep warm despite the winds coming off the ocean.

"And you've heard the winds yourself, but they were different then. They carried traces of Ireland, reminding him of the home he'd left behind, but they also carried crystals of ice and salt that worked their way through the cracks in the walls of his shack. Sometimes, at night, when Brumfit was trying to sleep, he heard the sound of a harp: it was a merrow trying to sing him to the deeps. He stuffed his ears with greased rags and sketched with charcoal to keep his body from wandering to the water."

It was a Saturday. We'd left the house early, keeping normal fishing hours. I wasn't sure if Rena and Carly were still sleeping, or if they hadn't bothered sneaking back into the house yet. It was a gray, cold piss of a day, and Daddy had spent all morning working at his thermos of coffee. Despite the weather, he seemed lazy, almost dreamy, as if we had all the time in the world to take the lobsters from the ocean. And after three hours of lackadaisically pulling traps, here we were in a stretch of water that was polluted with James Harbor buoys, a stretch of water that was supposed to be ours and ours alone, and Daddy had decided it was story hour.

"You can picture it, can't you?"

Of course I could picture it. *The Sea Dragon*, despite its title, mostly shows the interior of the shack that Brumfitt lived in during his first few years on the island, and it shows what a mean existence he lived. Even at sixteen, I understood how a man who lived like that could wake one day and suddenly realize he was in want of a wife. The painting shows the raised board with blankets that Brumfitt used for a bed, the stool and table where he worked, the poorly vented hearth that served both for heat and cooking, smoke glazing the room. The room is dark and crackling with shadows from the fireplace, and you have to look closely to see that buried in the blackness is something twisting and scaly.

"Brumfitt knew it was there," Daddy said. "He'd seen it circling in the waters, found the bones of deer and the feathered carcasses of fowl. At night, when the merrow wasn't singing for him, he could hear the slither and the scrape of the beast's scales and claws on the rocks. The night that it came into his shack, he heard the door groan open, could feel the whisper of the dragon creeping across the dirt floor, but Brumfitt didn't turn to look. Can you imagine that, Cordelia?" Daddy said. "Can you imagine how hard it must have been to know that there was a monster in the room with you, a monster come to eat you whole? And yet, Brumfitt didn't look. He didn't look, Cordelia, because he knew that the sea dragon could feast upon his bones if it wanted to. That's the thing about dragons. They can kill a man. They've got scales that coat their bodies like armor, teeth and claws, and a man who faces one will be left a bag of bones. And Brumfitt knew that he'd been marked, that this dragon had decided that he looked like easy prey."

"So, what?" I said. "Loosewood Island is Brumfitt, and James Harbor is the dragon?"

"Smart girl," Daddy said. He lifted his coffee mug to me, an acknowledgment.

James Harbor was bigger than we were, and they were already pushed hard against the limits of their waters. Even back then, when I was sixteen, before meth had taken a firm hold in James Harbor, they were nastier than we were. A place for drunks and men who left their women with bruises and plaster casts on their arms. Small compared to the world, but big compared to Loosewood Island. James Harbor was a place where just living felt like having your back against the wall. "We have to do something."

"If we fight James Harbor, if we go in mindless and stupid, they'll turn us back beaten and bloody." He leaned back against the console. "I thought you knew this story. You know this story, right?"

I shrugged. I knew it didn't matter what I said, he was going to tell me the story the way he wanted to.

"So he knows it's there, but Brumfitt waited," Daddy said, "keeping bent over the canvas he was working on, sketching the inside of that shack with charcoal. But when the dragon sprang, what it didn't realize was that in Brumfitt's other hand he held a blacksmith's hammer. Even a dragon has an underbelly," Daddy said, "a place where you can hurt it. And Brumfitt showed no quarter. He beat at that dragon until it fled, never to return."

He pushed himself back to a full standing, letting out a small grunt and then sauntering over to the rail. He leaned on his elbows, contemplating the water as he told me the story. I was cold and put out. I liked spending time with him on the *Queen Jane*, but Daddy's dreamlike spell that day meant that there was never a rhythm to our work; it was like dancing with a boy who can't keep a beat. I waited for him to say something when he finished the story, but after he said, "He beat at that dragon until it fled, never to return," he just stared at the water. After what felt like several minutes, I cleared my throat.

"Why didn't he kill the dragon?"

It seemed like a good question to me, and I realized that it had never occurred to me to ask it before. It must have seemed like a good question to Daddy, too, because he stood up and looked at me. "Well, I've never thought of that. I suppose that a dead dragon is just that: a dead dragon. But a live dragon, one you've beaten and caused to flee, is so much more than that. It's a message to all of the other dragons to stay the hell away from Loosewood Island."

"And I guess Brumfitt was never bothered again?"

"No," he said. "Not by dragons." Daddy took a sip of his coffee and then looked out over the water again. "I think we'll call it a day, Cordelia. I'll drop you off at home."

"So you want to wait until James Harbor really comes after us? We just wait around until then?"

"No." He shook his head, and then, almost bewildered, he said, "No," again. "Every man is a dragon when he's threatened in his own home." He turned to the wheel and kicked the throttle forward.

"That's it?" I said. "What about the rest of the traps? You want to at least cut their traps?"

"No. I think I'm done with that. I'm going to go have a talk with that cunt, Al Burns. This water was given to the Kings. You know the story of Brumfitt Kings as well as I do, and I don't think this needs to be going on anymore. Burns is going to have to get his men out of our waters." He glanced at me and then smiled. "There be dragons. Well, there are dragons in these waters. Remember that. 'Come not between the dragon and his wrath.' Shakespeare. All of the good lines are from Shakespeare." He paused and was about to say something, but then shut his mouth as if he were reconsidering, before opening it back up. "'Come not between the dragon and his wrath,'" he said again. He shook his head, clearly pleased with himself. "You want me to drop you off at home, or you want to come along to James Harbor?"

"I'll come along," I said, thinking that maybe I could do some shopping while Daddy took care of his business, or that maybe there'd be some boys around that I knew. Daddy sounded a little weird, but I didn't think much of it at the time. He always sounded a little weird, particularly when he was talking about Brumfitt.

"Brumfitt would have liked you," he said. "You're not afraid of anything in the ocean, are you?" I didn't answer, even though Daddy stood straight and looked at me. Whatever I didn't say was good enough for him, because he nodded and dumped the rest of his coffee overboard. He went to the wheel and drove the throttle hard until we were near the docks in James Harbor. Once the motor was quiet, he tied off and stood on the deck of the *Queen Jane* for a minute, his hands on his hips, staring at the building where Al Burns, who both fished and served as the buyer for James Harbor, which was a lot of how he got his power, kept his offices. "Cordelia," he said, without turning around, "get me a hammer. There are two of them in the toolbox, but I don't want the claw hammer. The regular one for whacking nails. Get me the ball-peen hammer instead. It's got a flat head on one side and a rounded head on the other."

"I know what a ball-peen hammer is," I said.

"Of course you do, honey."

"You going to smite the dragon?"

"Something like that," he said.

I went belowdecks and got him the ball-peen hammer and then held it out to him. He took it, and he looked like he was thinking of taking a sleep. "I'll be right back," he said. "Stay here."

I watched him walk up the dock and across the parking lot. I was thinking that I had close to forty dollars with me, and that maybe I'd try to find a new pair of jeans. Even then, James Harbor was run-down, nothing like Halifax or Saint John or Boston, but there was more shopping in James Harbor than I could find on Loosewood Island. I thought I could convince Daddy to stay an hour or two, maybe even take me to the mall. I watched Daddy saunter toward the building. A pair of slickered men smoking cigarettes standing outside of the office building watched him as well. It was only when Daddy opened the door and disappeared inside that it fully hit me that I had handed him a hammer. An actual hammer. There was no reason he needed an actual hammer.

I ran.

By the time I got inside the office I could already hear Al Burns screaming. The two men who had been outside were hard on my heels.

Al was on his knees, his free hand scrabbling at Daddy's arm, his other arm pinned at the wrist on his desk. Daddy was facing me, and he was concentrating fiercely on the task at hand, which was smashing Al's hand into nothingness. Daddy had all of his weight leaning onto Al's wrist, and he didn't seem to notice the other man's struggle. He kept swinging the hammer in the sort of rhythm that had been missing from our fishing, as if he were keeping the beat to a song. I watched him swing it once, twice, a third time, crushing Al's fingers, before the two men tackled him, pinning him to the floor. Al Burns collapsed on the floor, cradling his destroyed hand against his body. I couldn't look at the desk. It was a mess of blood and flesh and bone, but it wasn't better to look at Daddy, either: beneath the two men pinning him down, he was staring at me, and even with a small grin on his face, the splash of blood flooding across one of his cheeks, there was a blankness that was terrifying.

He repeated it to me before the cops took him away: "Come not between the dragon and his wrath."

He was gone for four months, to a psych unit in the Halifax hospital. Maybe it was something catching up to him, Scotty's death and Momma killing herself, his time in Vietnam, or maybe it was something else entirely, but Daddy didn't talk to me about it, and the James Harbor lobstermen cleared off well before he got back. When I picked him up in the *Queen Jane* we sailed through waters that were clear of James Harbor buoys.

Daddy wasn't like most of the other lobstermen on Loosewood Island. Obviously, there was the trip to the loony bin, but it was more than that. For one, he'd been off to war, choosing the U.S. side of the border and enlisting with George and Billy Sweeney, but from there he made a four-year pit stop at college besides, and still he'd come back to the island: a barely noticeable limp a souvenir from Vietnam, and an undergraduate degree in theater a souvenir from university. He joked about the little limp—patting the star-shaped scar on his calf—and was willing to make fun of himself for his degree: majoring in theater didn't help much out on the boats. Still, acting was a passion that stayed with him. He was usually given a leading role in the two summer stock plays Loosewood Island put on at the band shell on the commons, one a Shakespeare and one something more contemporary and light, often a comedy, and he once had a brief speaking role—"Watch out for those deeps, Captain Spindle!"—in a movie that was shot locally but stayed in the theaters only long enough to be a disappointment.

And I might as well get this out of the way, too, if it's not obvious enough already: my name. Cordelia. Straight out of

Shakespeare, and god thank my mother for exerting at least a small amount of restraint on Daddy for the rest of the children. Cordelia. The name was my father's idea of a joke. We were the Kings, and so he'd give me the name of the king's favorite daughter, the one banished but true. When I finally read the play, my junior year in high school, I went up to my father in a huff, pointing out that the play ended with me dead.

It was February. More than a year since Daddy had flattened Al Burns's hand and taken his tour of the loony bin. There was enough weather outside that Daddy had spent the day tending to equipment and was now at his desk, a small shoved-into-the-corner-of-the-kitchen table that he used for paperwork. He had a pair of reading glasses perched up on his forehead, and he was fingering a bottle of beer and staring out the window at the sea instead of actually paying bills or writing letters or whatever he was supposed to be doing. Third was curled up under the table and my father had tucked his feet under the dog's furry mess. I pulled a chair out of the dining room, moved it next to Daddy, and spun it around so I could sit on it backward and look at him.

"I see we're working on appearing ladylike today, Cordelia."

"Ah, go suck an egg."

He didn't even bother trying to suppress his grin, and I both saw and didn't see the way the scar on his lip from where I'd hooked him thinned and lightened as his mouth spread into a smile. "Go suck an egg? Are kids still saying that? Or maybe I should ask, are they saying that again, because I think that even before I was a kid, 'Go suck an egg' was no longer in fashion." He spun his pencil around in his fingers twice and then placed it on the table. "Are you saying that you don't like your name? That there is something unworthy about being named after King Lear's daughter? Are you saying that you are not a fan of the Bard?"

"I'm saying that I end up dead."

"Never!" He shouted the word and I jumped back in my chair. He'd come home from the loony bin seeming like the same man that he'd been before things went wrong with Scotty, and that left me nervous: If I didn't see it coming before, why would I see it coming again? His outburst left me all tilted, but the next words came out more softly. "Never. Never. Never. Never." He shrugged. "The professor who taught me *King Lear* was a Shakespeare nut. He was losing his sight. Huh. Going blind. I guess I never thought about it in the context of the play before, but that's kind of funny. He was going blind, and he'd decided to try to memorize each and every one of Shakespeare's plays before he lost his sight entirely. He'd almost done it, too. He had all the ones we did that semester, and when he was up there in front of the class, he acted it out for us." Daddy shook his head, a real smile on his face. "It's unbelievable to me how clear that is, probably the thing I remember most from four years at university. This was in the first few weeks of my first term at school, and I still didn't know what to expect from my professors, and here we go with him up in front of the class." Daddy stood, and his voice dropped lower. "And my poor fool," and back to his own voice, "meaning you, meaning Cordelia. Even if there is a fool in the play, he means Cordelia. Lear is overcome with grief, his kingdom ravaged, his one true daughter dead, madness descending, and you could hear it with my professor, too, that he had that same kind of grief." He looked at the kitchen cabinets as if they were an audience, and let his voice change again. "And my poor fool is hanged. No, no, no, no, life? Why should a dog, a horse, a rat have life, and thou no breath at all? Oh, thou'lt come no more," Daddy said, and then let out a breath. "And here he goes, and the entire class was still. I had goose bumps on my arm, and I can tell you, every single student in that class was paying attention." Daddy tapped the table with his finger each time he said the word: "Never, never, never, never." He shook his head, and I could see how much Daddy was enjoying acting this out for me. "And then his voice got soft and you could see that he was almost ready to cry—this old, bearded, almost-blind man, about to cry because of some words from a play written four hundred years ago—and he lets out one more 'never.' The fifth and final 'never.' And it came out, that last 'never,' in an almost-moan. And that was the moment I said to myself, 'I'm going to be an actor.' Right at that moment. It was all that passion."

"And here you are, an actor," I said.

"Don't be a smart-ass, Cordelia. I was twenty and all I'd known was Loosewood Island and Vietnam, and those two worlds sure as shit didn't come together with what I was learning at Williams."

He rarely just mentioned Vietnam casually, as a place where he had once been, and I wanted to take the opportunity to ask him about it. He talked around Vietnam all of the time, what it was like at basic training, what it was like to go to Hong Kong on leave, what the hospital was like after he was shot in the leg, the flight home, but he almost never actually talked about what it was like when he was there: what it meant to be gone from everything he knew, what it felt like to be scared and only a year or two older than I was at that moment. Walking through the jungle with a bunch of other boys who were eighteen, nineteen, carrying machine guns and all the other paraphernalia of war, each one hoping that he'd make it back to wherever it was he came from. And other than that one day on the boat, when he shot Second, he never talked about Bill Sweeney, George's older brother, who went over with Daddy but never made it home.

I didn't think about any of that at the time. What I said was, "So why did you come back to the island?"

He studied me, like he didn't even understand the question, and after a second I realized that he *didn't* understand the question. "Don't you know? I thought of all my daughters, you were the one who'd understand. I mean, have you even been listening? Didn't you just ask me about your name? Cordelia? You're the one, true daughter, the rightful heir."

"Because you couldn't do anything else. Because of the sea."

He nodded and sat back down, picking up his beer. "Because of the sea. I loved acting, and it was fun, still is fun during the summers, but I could never fully imagine myself as being anywhere other than Loosewood Island and working on a boat. Maybe that's why I've never been a better actor. A failure of the imagination. I like to think of it as something else, something mythical and primal, like the sea just pulls at me and will never let me go. We're connected to the earth and the earth is connected to the sea, and once you've had a taste of the ocean—if you're a true child of the ocean—nothing can keep you away."

I raised my eyes at him and he leaned back in his chair. "Wow, Daddy. Very moving. I guess you're trying to be an actor *and* a poet? Or maybe you've been drinking?"

"You know, just because you and your sisters are all teenagers doesn't mean you have to mouth off."

Even though I was only seventeen, I wanted to call bullshit. I wanted to say that I knew his talking, his joking, his willingness to say things that other lobstermen wouldn't—his frequent professions of love for me and my sisters, the way he admitted he was afraid of drowning, afraid that the catch would dry up and we'd go broke—covered all of the other things he didn't say. That his talking was meant to be an ocean in and of itself, so that we'd be washed away by the words and never wonder about the things he didn't talk about: Scotty, my mother, Vietnam, his own father. And most of all I wanted to call bullshit because he'd only been back from the loony bin for a year since then, and we never talked about the way he'd gone blank in the face and taken a hammer to that cunt Al Burns's hand. We never talked about the way that he had left my sisters and me to fend for ourselves while he swallowed pills and wore a bathrobe in the psych unit. We never talked about what it was that had bent him enough to grab the hammer in the first place, whether it was Scotty or Momma, whether it was something to do with Vietnam, or whether it was something more disturbing to me: that he believed his own stories about Brumfitt Kings, that he actually thought that Al Burns was a dragon circling the dark and waiting to strike. I wanted to call bullshit on all of that.

But I was only seventeen. Maybe that's the sort of thing that I can only think about now that I'm older and past the age of thirty, but either way, I let him steer the boat back to where he had always wanted it pointed.

"It's a tragedy, Cordelia. There are Shakespearian comedies and there are Shakespearian tragedies, and *Lear* is a tragedy."

And then he did something that surprised me, because he'd never done more than say, "Sorry I was gone," never said anything about his recent trip to the loony bin. He said, "You don't have to worry, Cordelia. I'm not going to end up crazy like Lear did, wandering around on the heath. I'll never, ever, ever leave you and your sisters again. I'll never leave you, okay?" I looked down at my hands and was suddenly unsure what I should do with them. I could feel my shoulders slumping, knew that I looked like a sullen teenager, but it was all I could do not to start crying, not to jump up and wrap my arms around him, to curl up in his lap like I had when I was a little kid. I could feel him staring at me, and finally, I nodded.

"Did you know I wanted to name all of you girls after the daughters in *Lear*?" he said.

"Reggie and Goneril?"

"Regan. And yes, I thought it was romantic, but your mother decided otherwise. She pointed out that Goneril might be too close to gonorrhea. Well, that and she also reminded me that the other sisters were evil bitches." I started to open my mouth to make the obvious joke, but he shook his finger at me. "Don't," he said, but he was smiling. He reached up and slid his glasses down onto his nose and then picked up one of the bills on the table before him. "Jesus. We should turn down the thermostat."

"I'm already wearing wool socks and a heavy sweater, Daddy, I'm not sure how much lower we can turn it."

"You'll just have to wear wool underwear as well," he said.

"How'd you end up with Carly and Rena's names, then?" I wanted to steer the conversation back to what he'd just said about never leaving me again, but I knew that we'd passed that point.

Sometimes you can't turn a boat in time. It was all I could do to ask him about Carly and Rena. I couldn't even make myself ask him about Scotty's name; it wasn't that we never talked about Scotty, but it was just that I hated that hitch I always heard in his breath if someone other than Daddy was the one to say Scotty's name. He sometimes brought Scotty up himself, said "Scotty would have liked that," or "Scotty would have done this," and we had pictures up in the house, but it was different when somebody else said Scotty's name, when my father wasn't expecting it.

"I've never told you?" He looked genuinely surprised. "Carly's Carly because your mom liked that singer, and Rena was the name of one of my great-aunts. Or maybe one of your mom's great-aunts." He looked down at his feet and gave Third a nudge. "Damn it, Third. Quit your farting." He looked back up at me and gave a shy half-smile, the kind I associated with little boys hiding behind the legs of their mothers. "Doesn't that beat all to hell? I can't remember if it was my great-aunt or your mom's great-aunt. Well, it was somebody's great-aunt, that's for sure." He reached down, grabbed Third's collar, and then hauled the dog out from under the table. "I'm going to take her down to the boat with me for a bit, at least let her stink up the ocean instead of the house. In the meantime, why don't you make yourself useful and start putting dinner together? What are we having?"

I stood up and left the chair sitting next to him. I didn't want to bring it back into the dining room, to tuck it under the round table. We only ever kept four chairs there, neat and ready for their four occupants, a defining limit on the number of people living in our house now. I knew Daddy would put it back. "Lobster," I threw back at him over my shoulder as I left the kitchen. It's what I always said, what all of us always said to his question of what we were having for dinner, and it never failed to elicit our intended response: a quick, deep chuckle that sounded more like a coughing dog than a man's laughter.

I remember that, from my room, I looked out on Daddy and Third climbing down the steps to the wharf. Third was a girl, and small for a Newf, which meant that she topped out at about 110. I remember her as a puppy, though I know that she would have been four or five the year I was seventeen. Walking next to Daddy, she could have been a version of his shadow.

I knew I'd missed my chance. When we were sitting at the table and Daddy said that I was named Cordelia after the king's one true daughter, that I was named Cordelia because I was the rightful heir, what I should have done was asked him if he was sure of that, if he'd known that for sure when Scotty was alive. I should have asked him if he'd always known that I was going to be the one to follow him onto the water, to take up the mantle of the Kings.

I should have asked him this: If he could go back and make a bargain with the ocean, would he have traded my life for his son's?

Our waters stayed clear of James Harbor buoys for nearly fifteen years after Daddy destroyed Al Burns's hand, but nothing lasts forever.

There'd been trouble the year I got back from university, and Daddy had taken me and George and a couple of other men to James Harbor, and we'd marched right into Al Burns's office. I'd made sure Daddy wasn't carrying a hammer, but all it took was for Daddy to say, "Your boys are fishing our ocean again," for Al to clamp things down. Still, that had been more than a decade ago. More than fifteen years had passed since Daddy smashed Al's hand and headed to the loony bin, and things had changed. There was a new generation of boys who were working the boats, and the story of Daddy flattening Al Burns's hand with a hammer was just that to them: a story. There were rumors that James Harbor lobstermen were planning to make a push for our waters again. The fact was, generations of overfishing in their waters had taken their toll. There were rumors, too, that something uglier was going on than simple lobster poaching, that James Harbor had gotten run-down with drugs—meth in particular.

With Daddy's history, a resumption of our fishing wars with

James Harbor should have left me nervous—his trip to the loony bin had left its mark on my sisters and me—but the truth was that I was preoccupied with something that felt more pressing than my worries about James Harbor: in the fifteen years since Daddy smashed up Al Burns's hand, he'd started to get old.

He'd been aging well. He was trim from decades of hauling lobster traps, and at fifty-seven he could probably still have fit into the same suit that he was wearing in his wedding portrait, though that suit didn't have a particularly fine fit even at the time. When he did wear a suit, which was rarely, only to weddings and funerals, he looked good, the silver in his hair like the cut of a fast boat through the water, his skin worked over by the sun and the wind, leaving him looking rugged. Put him in a tuxedo and it would be leading man looks from Hollywood before Technicolor came along.

But the rest of him wasn't holding up. His dizzy spells had turned to fainting spells: I'd gone over to Daddy's house for our weekly dinner and found him out cold on his kitchen floor. His dog—Sailor V, Fifth—was curled up beside him, like the two of them were just taking a nap. He claimed it was nothing. Low blood sugar or just standing up too quickly, Daddy said, the sort of thing that could happen to anybody, nothing to worry about, but of course I worried. He'd been in the middle of prepping food. There was a loaf of bread, a pot of stew simmering on the stove.

I set him down on the couch while I finished getting our meal together, and after I badgered him for a while he admitted that his energy had been down the past few weeks.

"Nothing to mind, Cordelia. A flu bug or something like that. Another ten days until pots go back in the water. I'll maybe just take an early bedtime tonight."

I put the tray with our dinners down and slid the coffee table closer to the couch. The broth in the stew trembled. "You'll do more than that," I said. "You'll be going to the doctor's tomorrow."

He took a bite of his stew and grimaced. "Eh. You'd think I'd learn to let it cool down. Burned my tongue again." He broke off a piece of bread and put it under the table for Fifth. "You planning on going to the mainland before the season starts? I've got a few odds and ends I need picked up. Nothing big, and I can ask George or one of the other boys, but I—"

"Don't you change the subject, Daddy. You're going to the doctor tomorrow."

He grumbled and tried to weasel out of it, and after dinner he insisted on heading over to the Grumman Fish House for a beer. I'm not sure if he really wanted to get out or if he was just trying to convince me that he was hale and hearty, hoping I'd forget about him going to the doctor, but once we were actually at the Grumman Fish House Daddy had complained that I was treating him like he'd gone old and senile overnight. "Next thing I know, she'll be taking the *Queen Jane* from me, telling me there's only room for one of the Kings to be on the sea," he said, but even if he told the boys about it with a smile on his face, there was something about it that didn't ring funny to me, because I knew that there would probably come a day when I *would* have to drag him off of the *Queen Jane*, and I worried that he'd be out on the water past the point where it was safe. I'd be staring a long, long time if I looked to my sisters to say anything. Rena would kiss a squid to stay in Daddy's good graces, and the only person Carly was interested in pissing off was me. But maybe this was an opportunity. Maybe this fainting spell of Daddy's was a chance to broach the subject with him, to see what his plans for the future were, see when he was ready to step down.

I sleep better when I'm sharing the bed, but it had been a couple of years since I'd had a serious boyfriend, and that meant that there wasn't anything keeping me tethered to the bedroom if I woke in the middle of the night. My dog, Trudy—a Newf, of course, and on the smaller side for the breed—was used to my restlessness and kept me company through the brutal hours. Mostly I read histories or biographies or the specialized fishing stuff that is only interesting to somebody in the business. I'd also gotten hooked on watching the cricket matches that my satellite dish picks up. I don't understand the rules, but there is something in the pristine white uniforms, the ritual of the matches, that appeals to me. Sometimes, when a strange heat and lightning rolled over the island, I liked to head down to the water to wait for the night to pass.

But the night that Daddy passed out I slept straight through. I wouldn't have thought it would be the night for it, not with worrying about Daddy, but the storm that had come in a few nights before had turned from a biblical torrent into a solid, cool, windless rain that tangled with the metal roof and kept me soothed until dawn.

With the rain, I hadn't been much out walking or running—the graveled tourist walks were the only paths that hadn't gotten slopped out in the weather—and I'd been feeling cooped up in the house. I could only read or watch television for so long. I'd tried working on some of my paintings, but couldn't concentrate with the grayness. Besides which, it felt like I was touching up things that didn't need to be touched anymore, working on them for the sake of work. I was itching to take my pochade box out and start something new. Some of the other painters on the island could bring what they saw inside with them, used the winter and the gray and rainy days as a chance to paint from what they remembered, but I'd always been somebody who needed to stand out there and work with what was in front of me. Once I got properly started I could finish indoors, in foul weather, but I'd used that up a couple of days ago, and to start something new I needed to be in front of it. It meant I looked like one of the tourists during the summers: with my pochade box flipped open and attached to a tripod, if I was working somewhere that was of particular importance in the Brumfitt canon, I might be one of a line of a half dozen painters scraping away at the water and the cliffs. I couldn't help it. I needed to be outside to capture that sense of being outside.

I didn't have any illusions about my paintings: I was serious in my intent, but I knew I'd never be better than competent. It didn't matter, because I enjoyed it, and on Loosewood Island, being an artist was almost as common as being a fisherman. Most of us did at least some of both. We had the history of Brumfitt, of course, and another half dozen or so minor artists who had either lived here or painted works on the island, the sort whose work might seem familiar even if their name didn't. We had the seasons, too, and with the weather and the way that lobstering tacked back and forth between brutal days and stretches of inactivity, you had to have some sort of a hobby. There were enough people who took up drinking or smoking pot, but arts and crafts came in a pretty popular second to self-destruction.

I'd started painting more seriously since Kenny Treat had

moved to Loosewood Island nearly a decade before. Kenny hadn't been born here, and even if his wife, Sally, who teaches kindergarten through third grade, had been raised close by on the mainland, in Lubec, most of the islanders still thought of them as outsiders: coming from off the island is something that longevity can't change, but it was more than that. Kenny worked for Daddy for five years, and then moved to my boat, the *Kings' Ransom*, once Rena's husband, Tucker, took to the water and started working on the *Queen Jane*. Kenny went to college at Yale and everybody says he comes from money, but he never talked about buying his own boat, like he had no aspirations to do anything more than be a sternman and paint his pictures. That lack of ambition is the sort of thing that can only come with a safety net, and left some of the boys suspicious, despite my attesting to Kenny's work ethic. I couldn't imagine having a different sternman than Kenny. He was funny and kind and he saw lobstering the way I did: as a chance to prove that the sea can never beat us. Though, of course, it does sometimes.

I'd gone to college, too, and raced through four years in three so that I could come home and start working my own boat. I was on the island when Kenny moved here. The first time I saw him was down at the docks. I was working on the engine of the *Kings' Ransom* and tied up two boats closer in than the *Queen Jane* when he came walking toward me, Daddy at his side. I was struck by the way Kenny moved. This was before Kenny had worked a day on the *Queen Jane*, before he'd done anything but take a pleasure cruise, but he came toward me with his knees tilted out, the sway that you get from spending years on the ocean. He was taller than Daddy, broad across the chest and shoulders—something that I learned later came from time on the crew team when he was in college. Each step Kenny took was solid, his hips open, his boots ticking against the wood of the dock. He had his head tilted down, listening to something that Daddy was saying, and I remember that as he came over to me, he gave a small smile. I don't remember what we talked about that day—it was probably nothing more than an exchange of names and a few pleasantries—but I remember the way he looked at me.

The island being as small as it is, it took maybe twenty minutes after I met Kenny before I figured out he was married, and that he and his wife had bought a small two-bedroom Colonial one road up from Gull Street. I decided to go over there and welcome her. I hadn't been up there in a few months, hadn't even realized the house was up for sale, and as I walked up the street I could see that Kenny and Sally had painted it blue. There was a wheelbarrow on the lawn and the freshly turned dirt in front of the porch where they'd planted bright flowers: black-eyed Susans, asters, and blue flags. It looked like a hopeful little house.

I'd gone with a cheap bottle of white wine. Sally was sitting on the front steps, a bottle of beer in her hand. She had a pair of gardening gloves next to her and a small smear of dirt on her legs. She had makeup on and her hair done up. She looked like she expected Kenny to take her away from gardening and out for a fancy dinner. Even though she was sitting, I could see that she filled out her clothes nicely. Not to say that I don't have a good body, but I take after Momma. I look taller than my five-seven, and I've got breasts, but they're not like Rena's or even Carly's; I eat like a horse, but with all of the time I spend out fishing, I don't have any extra meat on me. Or maybe it's just a good metabolism. Either way, while nobody would mistake me for a boy, I'm definitely built for speed.

As I came up the walk to her I held the bottle of wine out in front of me, but she didn't make a move to get up or do anything other than simply watch me come to her. I handed her the bottle of wine and said, "Welcome to Loosewood Island."

"Thanks." She reached out and took the bottle. "It's cold."

"Straight from the fridge."

She put it on the step next to her. "I'm not going to open it now," she said. I suppose that I must have flinched at that, because I saw her try to recover. "I can offer a beer." She sighed and shook her head. "Sorry. I'm just still trying to wrap my head around the idea that I moved back. I always swore that once I left Lubec I'd be gone for good, but Kenny wanted it."

"Well, Loosewood Island isn't exactly Lubec."

She laughed and then finished her beer. "No kidding. At least in Lubec I could drive somewhere if I wanted."

"I'm Cordelia. Cordelia Kings."

"I know," she said. "It's a small island."

"Well, looks like your husband's going to be working as a sternman for my father."

"You fish, too, right?" I nodded. "Early mornings, I guess." She pushed herself to her feet and then bent down and picked up the bottle of wine. She tipped it in my direction. "Thanks for the wine. I'm Sally. And now I'll go put this bottle back in the fridge. I've got some unpacking to do."

She didn't slam the door behind her as she went inside, but she might as well have, for the impression it made on me. I don't think it took that long for her to put other people off, even the boys who were taken by her looks at first. It's not that she was deliberately nasty or cold. There was just something tight about her. I don't think she was aware of the way she was acting, but she never stopped complaining about being on Loosewood Island. She didn't get along well with any of the women I knew, and she was never more than indifferent toward me. Despite that, I felt bad for her at times, particularly after she started having miscarriages.

Over the years she had three. Kenny told me about them, but it wasn't the sort of thing you could keep hidden on a place as small as the island anyway. And for a couple of years she had a drinking problem, too, which made me feel bad about giving her a bottle of wine for a housewarming present. Ten years on and we all thought we knew everything there was to know about Sally Treat. Gossip got around the island quicker than a divorcée spending a week's vacation on the rock.

Maybe if Sally had been a different woman we'd have become friends and I'd have looked at Kenny differently, or maybe if I'd known from the first moment that Kenny was married I wouldn't have gotten the thought of him as somebody to be attracted to, but those twenty minutes of meeting him were just enough to turn him into a splinter lodged under my skin. Of course, once I actually got to know Kenny, it got even worse. As Daddy's sternman, he was somebody who was in my constant orbit, and then, five years ago, when Tucker and Rena moved to the island, Daddy took on Tucker, and Kenny moved on to the *Kings' Ransom* with me.

It didn't take long before I was trying to impress him. It's not like I didn't read much before Kenny, didn't watch movies unless shit was being blown up, didn't go to museums when I went to Montreal or Boston, but it was different after Kenny started working as my sternman. He'd mention a book he'd read and then when I said I hadn't heard of it, a few days later he'd show up to work with the book stuffed inside a plastic bag. I'd read the book, and then later, back on the boat, as we were pulling traps, stuffing bait bags, slapping the brass measure against the backs of bugs, we'd talk about it. Same thing with a play he'd see in the city or a piece of art at a gallery. Next time I was in a big city—and I went every couple of months—I'd go where he told me. If there was a new band he heard, he burned me a CD; a magazine article he liked, he'd clip it out for me. We argued about some of the things. He made me read a novel that had won the Pulitzer, and even though I passed it on to Daddy and he thought it was brilliant, I had to tell Kenny the truth, which was that I didn't get what all the fuss was about. He was enamored with an indie rock group out of Columbus, Ohio, that sounded like two dogs fucking a cat in a garbage can, and after about the thirtieth time he put it in the boat's CD player I threw the disc out into the ocean.

But what happened was that after a while I realized I wasn't reading this stuff or going to check out paintings at galleries or online—living on the island, that was sometimes my only option—because Kenny had told me I should, but rather because I wanted to. Before long, I was bringing him my own book suggestions or telling him about some movie I'd read about that I thought sounded good. We couldn't agree much on music, though he finally grew to appreciate Johnny Cash.

We probably spent the most time talking about Brumfitt Kings. Kenny had been an art history major at Yale, and he wrote his senior honor's thesis on Brumfitt's lighter works, arguing that they deserved an equal place to his darker works. There was no reason, he wrote, that a painting showing a mother and young son picnicking on a stone beach in clear weather was inherently less important than one that showed a mother and son in peril from a bank of black clouds. Since then, he's come around to my point of view, which is that the Brumfitt's paintings that show the Loosewood Island from Daddy's stories are better than either his lighter pieces or his more menacing, realistic paintings.

I didn't fool myself that it was romantic when we were on the *Kings' Ransom*. We flirted at times, the sort of aimless brushing against the line of two people who are attracted to each other but know that nothing can happen, because while Kenny may have been unhappily married, he *was* married. I missed the flirting in the off-season, but more than anything, what I missed was the regularity of having him with me out on the *Kings' Ransom*, the intimacy of the two of us out on the water, the rhythm of working together. Sometimes, when things were going well on the boat, it was an odd sort of dancing. I saw him in the off-season or touched base with him on the phone, but it was different.

Still, he was the person I wanted to call to talk with about Daddy's fainting spell, but it was too early. Waking up before dawn was a habit that was hard for me to break in the off-season, but it wasn't something Kenny took too long to adjust to. Instead of calling, I decided to hop in the shower and see if Daddy wanted some company on the way to the doctor's. By the time I made it down to the docks, however, the *Queen Jane* and Daddy were gone to Saint John. I was already slickered up and not interested in watching the rain through the glass doors of my living room, so I rowed out to the *Kings' Ransom* instead. I didn't have anything that needed to be done on board, but I decided that I could find something. We were barely more than a week out from the spring season and I was itchy to get started. Part of it was that I just loved being on the water, and that fishing meant spending time with Kenny, but part of it was the rumors that the James Harbor boys were going to make a play at our waters again.

But even without worrying about James Harbor lobstermen horning in on my grounds, I still would have been antsy. The way we ran the lobster fishing season worked well for us—we pulled the traps out of the water during the summer tourist season, for chunks of the spring, fall, and winter—but between our schedule and the weather, there were often days on end when the seas kept me at home. I should probably have been going over paperwork, but that had never been my strong suit. It drove Rena crazy. She ran the fish shop, but the fish shop was only ever busy in the tourist season, and with her accounting degree she handled the books for Daddy's rentals and business concerns, for the *Queen Jane* and the *Kings' Ransom*, and did all of our personal taxes, too. All that Rena asked from me was to handle my own day-to-day records, expenses, gas, daily catches, and she figured out the rest.

I poked around for a while on the *Kings' Ransom*, trying to keep my mind off Daddy's doctor's appointment and going back and forth on whether or not I should call Carly down in Portland to tell her about Daddy fainting. Every time I heard a boat's motor I'd pop my head up, like some fucker from James Harbor was going to just sail up to the *Kings' Ransom* and tell me that he was going to try to poach my fishing grounds. I was both keyed up and bored at the same time. I tried mucking about in the engine, and then I pulled out my fishing rod and threw a few halfhearted casts. I sat on the bow in my slickers and let the rain wash over me, slowly working the lure through the water. Trudy stuck her paws up on the bow to see what was going on, and then curled up again on the deck. I didn't have much of a thought to catch anything, which was just as well, because after ten minutes or so I hadn't gotten a nibble yet and was done with it. Still, even with being anxious about the season being a week off and James Harbor getting pushy, there was something nice about being down in the harbor when nobody else was there. During the season, mornings are the busiest time of the day: lobstermen up before dawn, heading out with the throttle full-on, men readying themselves for a day at sea, a few wives walking down to see their husbands off.

By ten, about the time I turned to head back in, the rain had stopped. I stowed my rod, stripped off my slicker and hung it in the cabin, and then climbed into my rowboat. Trudy set up shop on the stern bench. She looked pitiful and soaked and smelled like what she was: a wet dog. I checked the knot on my mooring buoy, making sure the *Kings' Ransom* was set in case something blew in, and started pulling on the paddles. Most of the men had five-horsepowers or nine-point-nines on their skiffs, but I'd bought this rowboat from Daddy when I was fifteen for two hundred and fifty bucks. I'd used it for the rest of high school, dropping my first set of double traps in the shallow water I could reach with oars, and eventually expanding to ten traps, which was a lot to work from a crappy old rowboat. More than fifteen years later, I was still using that rowboat for lobstering, even if just to get me back and forth to the *Kings' Ransom*. It wouldn't have hurt me much to drop three grand on a new nine-point-nine, but I liked the way rowing out and back from the *Kings' Ransom* framed my day.

I backed in to the dock and heard Kenny's voice.

"Where's the *Queen Jane*?" he asked. "Woody told me he wasn't going to be out on the water, for pleasure or otherwise, until the season started. Though your daddy's been known to lie about what he is or isn't doing with the *Queen Jane*." He grabbed the rail of the boat and held it steady while I tied off the stern, and then reached down and grabbed the bow painter and cleated it off. Trudy jumped out and rubbed herself against his leg while she wagged her tail. Kenny stumbled a little and then scratched at her chest. "You're a big, smelly darling," he said. He looked up and winked at me. "Just like your mommy."

"Working on that raise, Kenny?"

He grinned at me and stuck his hand out to pull me up and onto the dock. I would have bristled if any other of the boys had done it, but from Kenny it was somehow charming, just more proof that despite how hard he worked and the decade he'd lived on Loosewood Island, he still didn't have what it meant to be an islander quite figured out. He was wearing a pair of paint-spattered jeans and a button-down that had seen better days, and he was carrying his portable easel and paint kit. Kenny was a good painter. There was some sort of emotional openness in what he painted; a way in which what was on his canvases took hold of you. Carly's girlfriend, Stephanie, an artist herself, said that Kenny had a nice command of light. That's what she said: a command of light. I didn't have anything more intelligent to say. Kenny's paintings were good enough to sell, and they did, not just on the island but in galleries in Halifax, Bar Harbor, and even New York.

"Well," I said, "Daddy wouldn't start setting traps without telling me. Besides, if he started setting traps today, he'd be out of his mind. Even if the season was open it isn't worth any bother for at least another week. What do you think he's doing, putting out the traps unbaited just so they can soak up some water? No, we'll start fishing next week when the season opens, but it will be a few days past that when we are actually pulling anything up." I'd wanted to call Kenny earlier in the morning, but right then I could feel my mouth staying closed. I don't know why I didn't want to tell Kenny that Daddy had gone to the doctor's.

"All I can tell you, Cordelia," Kenny said, "is that if Woody started setting traps on Christmas Eve, nobody on the island would be unwrapping presents the next day."

"We've got the seasons all set. You've been on-island long enough to know that, Kenny. Nobody, not even Daddy, is going to fish outside the dates."

"James Harbor would," Kenny said. He stared at me and then nodded. "Yeah, me, too. The rumor's going around. Everybody seems to think it's a done deal, that the James Harbor boys are coming for us."

"Well, it won't change when we start our fishing. If the James Harbor boys are making a play for our waters, we'll deal with it when the season starts."

"You know, the season starts when your father says it starts. Woody *is* the island, Cordelia. He wanted to change the dates, they'd be changed. Maybe it takes somebody who wasn't born here to point that out to you."

He was right, and it annoyed me to hear him say it, so I tacked back to him. "Where you off to? Painting?"

"You feel like modeling?"

"I'll get naked if you do, Kenny."

He grinned and then shook his head. "Promises, promises. Maybe someday."

That was what he always liked to say. Maybe someday. It let the flirting stay casual, but I don't think Kenny understood that I wasn't sure I was joking. If he wasn't married, I might have wanted someday to be today.

"I'm going to set up at the end of the dock for a spell. Take advantage of the lull in the rain." He glanced up at the village and then said, "You going up to the fish shop?" I could tell that he was itching to get on with things. "Be sure to say hey to Rena and the twins for me," Kenny said.

"Paint me something beautiful," I said, hoping he might make another joke about me modeling for him, but he just nodded back and headed out to the end of the dock to set up his easel.

I thought about heading up to the fish shop, like Kenny had asked, but Trudy had a mind of her own and had turned toward the house. Instead of calling her back, I followed behind her and then fixed myself a cup of tea and set myself in front of the phone. There was a brief message on it from Daddy: the doctor wanted him to spend the night in the hospital for some tests, and I wasn't to worry. Not for the first time, I wished that he carried a cell phone with him when he was off-island.

I deleted the message and put the phone back down in front of me, trying to gather my energy. I knew I should have called Carly the night before, but I hadn't been up for it. Calling her now, while she was at work, meant that she couldn't be mad at me for not calling her. It also meant that I could just leave her a message. I hoped that by the time she was done teaching and called me back this afternoon I'd have some sort of better news for her.

It only rang once before Stephanie answered the phone.

Stephanie and Carly had been together for a few years now, ever since Carly had set up shop teaching second grade in Portland after college. Daddy seemed to keep himself surprisingly oblivious to the idea that Carly and Stephanie might be lovers. Carly had always been after boys in high school, and despite her dating a few different women in college, it had seemed to me just to be another way of acting out her women's studies classes and showing that she wasn't "under the yoke of patriarchy." It took me a while to realize that she and Stephanie were serious.

"How's the lobster business?" Stephanie asked.

"Keeping me in cashmere," I said, our usual exchange.

"So you excited about the news?" Stephanie said. I didn't say anything, and then Stephanie stumbled nervously. "Carly hasn't told you yet? I figured that was why you were calling." And then, muffled, the phone pulled from her face, "you haven't told your sister yet? I thought you were going to call."

Carly came on the line. "So much for keeping surprises, I guess."

"What are you doing home on a weekday? Did you get fired?"

"Jesus. That's your first thought? That I got fired? And, what, you called on a weekday hoping I'd be at work so that you could leave a message?"

I loved Carly, but sometimes it seemed like she'd never gotten over the day I accidently dropped Mr. Pickles over the side of the *Queen Jane.* She wasn't always angry with me, but where Rena had settled into her role as a mother—as the middle sister and the peacemaker—Carly and I had taken more antagonistic roles in our relationship to each other. She accused me of overreaching, and I accused her, more or less, of being a spoiled brat.

"You getting married?" I said.

"What?"

"I heard lots of you folks have been heading down to Mass now to get married since that ruling last year."

"No, we're not getting married." To Stephanie, I heard her say, "She said lots of you folks have been heading to Mass now to get married." There was something indistinct from Stephanie, Carly laughing, and then back on the line to me. "Honey, it's 2005. You can't call gay people 'you folks.' You sound like one of those people from Alabama who say 'the gays.'"

"Give me a break, Carly. Rena's the one who thought you shouldn't tell Daddy, not me. And I'll say what I've always said, whatever makes you happy."

"And I'll say what *I've* always said, it's not about whatever makes me happy. It's just the way it is."

"I didn't call you to pick a fight," I said, though at that moment it felt exactly like I had called her to pick a fight. "I was calling about Daddy."

Even through the phone lines, I felt like I could see Carly stand up straighter. She and Stephanie had a small apartment near the Maine College of Art, where Stephanie worked part-time teaching pottery. It was a light, small place with a galley kitchen that they'd kitted out with junk sale furnishings, and despite the fact that it was a one-bedroom, even after Daddy visited in the winter of 2002, he still referred to Stephanie as Carly's roommate. They had an old Bakelite rotary phone in the kitchen, though I'd been teasing my sister about buying a cordless, and I heard her moving something around on the counter, the beep of a microwave. "What about Daddy?"

I knew she was holding the phone tighter than she needed to, because I would have been doing the same thing. When you go through what we did as teenagers, losing Scotty and Momma, and having Daddy beat another man's hand flat with a hammer and then disappear for a couple of months of psychiatric treatment, you never get over your wariness.

"What about Daddy?" she said again.

"What about your surprise?"

"I'm moving back to the island."

"Bullshit."

"Nope. Happened real quick. Sally Treat told Principal Philips yesterday that she's finished. She's off the island once the school year ends. I'd mentioned to Principal Philips a year or two ago to give me a call if anything came open, and he gave me a call. I'll be teaching kindergarten through third grade come September. You just can't keep the Kings away from Loosewood Island, I guess. I've been itching to get back."

It felt like I'd been hit in the head by a rock. Sally and Kenny were leaving Loosewood Island? Sally had told Prinicipal Philips this *yesterday*, but barely twenty minutes ago, when I'd seen Kenny at the docks, he hadn't bothered to tell me? Jesus. Kenny was leaving.

"Cordelia?"

I tried to swallow, but my mouth felt dry, like I was coming off a four-day drunk.

"Cordelia?"

I tried to sound breezy and natural, but the idea of Kenny leaving made the words hard to get out. "How'd you pull that off without Sally or Principal Philips telling Daddy?"

"I told him I wanted it to be a surprise for Daddy's sixtieth birthday," she said. "He won't say anything to anybody just so that he can have the satisfaction afterwards of telling people that he was the only one who knew, that he knew something Woody Kings didn't."

I didn't say anything about Kenny keeping it secret from *me*. Instead I said, "Daddy's only fifty-seven."

"Yeah, but that's almost sixty, right? He's getting older, you know, and it will be good to be home again."

I didn't like that she said it out loud, that Daddy was getting older. I looked through the window; rain had started falling steady again, over the harbor and the rest of the island. Everywhere else it was spring, but on Loosewood Island it was shit season, mud everywhere, no good for lobstering, not good for much of anything but catching up on chores and resting up for the hard work to come. One boat moved slowly through the harbor, but I couldn't tell whose it was through the rain. Maybe Timmy's boat or Chip and Tony Warner's boat. "What's Stephanie going to do?"

"She's coming with me. She's going to set up a small studio, do pottery, sell pots and cups and stuff to tourists in the summer, wants to try lobstering once the tourists head home, figures she can be a sternman during the season," she said. "Thought I'd ask Daddy if he could take her on. No pay to start."

"Not sure that's a good idea," I said, except that even as the words came out of my mouth I realized that Daddy would be so happy to have Carly back home again that he'd take Stephanie on no matter what.

"You don't think we should come home because we're gay?" Her voice had turned hard.

"No, Carly, I'm not talking about you coming home. I'm saying that I don't think it's a good idea for Stephanie to try to work as a sternman: she's five-foot. It's hard to imagine her carrying a wire trap on dry land, let alone hauling one out of the water when it's oozing mud and full of bugs," I said. "I don't think the lobsters care much one way or the other if she's gay." I waited for a laugh, but none came. The truth was that despite my protests, I wasn't sure that having Stephanie on the *Queen Jane* would be so bad. Maybe it would slow Daddy down a bit. With Stephanie on board he'd be more likely to take few breaks throughout the day. "Might be tough, living on the island. You know how it is. The boys here aren't exactly the progressive type. You move here with Stephanie, the two of you living together, it's not going to be much in the way of a secret."

"Wasn't thinking of keeping it a secret," Carly said. "We'll lay it out like it is."

"Well, that's probably for the best, but it's up to you and Stephanie."

"Jesus, Cordelia. Just come out with it. You don't want me moving back."

"Carly—"

"You're afraid that I'll come back and rock the boat and maybe with both me and Rena on the island you won't have as much of Daddy to your precious self. You're still such a child, Cordelia."

"That's not true, and that's not fair," I said. I paused and waited for her to say something, but she was quiet, and I hoped she realized that she'd stepped over the line. "I'd love to have you back." I thought I meant it, but I wasn't entirely sure if it was true or not.

It's true that some part of me wanted to keep Carly in Portland. I already had one sister on the island, and Carly was the baby, the one whom we circled the wagons around after Scotty died and Momma drowned herself, and she still acted like a baby plenty of the time, throwing tantrums when she didn't get her way. And maybe that was some of what made me worried about the idea of Carly coming back. I wanted to please Daddy as much as Carly and Rena did, but I went about it differently.

If I'd been a different person, maybe it wouldn't have even occurred to me to worry about it, but I showed my love to Daddy in the only way I knew how. I told him I loved him, but more than anything, I tried to be the kind of person I thought he was: I pushed back at him as hard as he pushed me, I worked the water like he worked the water, and I tried to be the kind of daughter who could replace the hole left behind by the death of his son, and maybe help him through Momma's death, too.

A few Christmases ago, Daddy had told me that I looked like Momma but I was nothing like her. "You're a Kings through and through. And Rena, she might act like your momma, trying to take care of us and step in with the mothering, but it's an act. Now, Carly," he said, "well, that's different. She only looks like your momma a little, but she fills up a space like your momma used to. Turns her hands out, pauses on the same words. Sometimes having her back on the island is like having a ghost in the house."

And I was jealous. I hated him for saying that, and I hated Carly for being more like Momma than I ever could be. But that wasn't the sort of thing I could tell my sister. "I don't get to see enough of you up in Portland, and you know I don't love talking on the phone," I said. "I only call you because if I don't call, I won't get to talk to you at all. You want to move back to the island, move back to the island. It would make Daddy happy," I said, and those were words that I knew were true.

"Yeah, it would make Daddy happy. He keeps dropping hints, you know? And speaking of which, you called because of Daddy. What's wrong?"

"He fainted," I said. "I found him passed out on the kitchen floor yesterday."

"Jesus."

"He was annoyed at me for fussing over him. Claimed it was just a dizzy spell. I browbeat him into going to the doctor. He's up in Saint John. He just called to say that they're keeping him in the hospital overnight for some tests."

"Well, he's taking care of it," Carly said. "That's something, at least."

"The fact that he's going to see a doctor is what's gotten me the most worried. I've been working on him for years just to start getting his annual physicals, and he agreed, but you know what he said? He told me that if any doctor shoved a finger up his ass he'd shove his fist into that doctor's face."

"That's Daddy. Always a charmer." She paused. "You're seriously worried about it?"

"I don't know. He's only fifty-seven, but that's old for a lobsterman, and with his dad's heart kicking out at fifty, it makes me nervous. He isn't going to live forever, is he?" I said. The boat that had been moving slowly in the harbor completed its circuit—what it was moving around for in this weather, at this time of year, I didn't know—and headed back toward the wharf. It was George Sweeney's boat, I realized. Just the sort of foolish errand he liked to engage in, wasting gas and exposing himself to the weather when there was no need. "Are you serious?" I asked. "About coming home to stay? Because if you come home and don't stay, you'll break his heart. You can't get here and realize that Loosewood Island isn't as welcoming of two lesbians as you think and then take off again for Portland. I'm serious. You know how Daddy gets when he's excited about something. Remember what he was like after the twins were born and Rena told him she was moving home? She was all he could talk about."

"Things have changed, Cordelia," Carly said. "Trust me. I'm sure that most of the island already knows that Stephanie and I aren't just roommates. That's not going to be a problem."

"Yeah," I said. "I know. I guess I just wanted to give you an out before you told Daddy."

"Don't you think Momma would have wanted me to come home?"

We were both quiet for a few seconds. I stepped over to the doors and put my forehead against the cool glass. I didn't want to talk about Momma. "Sure," I said. "Probably."

"You remember that story Daddy told us when we were kids?"

"Which one?"

"The one about how he was taken under the water by a wave and then Grandma rescued him from a mermaid?"

"Yeah."

"It's like that," she said. "The point of the story is that we've all got a place we belong, and I've had fun in Portland, but I'm ready to come home. I've got a job, and I've got Stephanie, and I'm ready to come home. I've been scrubbing and scrubbing, but I guess I can't get Loosewood Island out of my skin."

"What about Stephanie? She doesn't have Loosewood Island in her skin. She's never even been here."

"She knows what she's getting into," Carly said.

I liked Stephanie, but I didn't think she knew what it meant to be a sternman and to work the water, and I didn't know how she'd handle the winter, when the island mostly emptied out, stores and restaurants shut down, and the ocean beat at us. If Stephanie thought that living in Portland had prepared her for living on the island, she was in for a rude awakening. She'd been born and raised in Iowa, for god's sake, her father an insurance agent and her mom staying at home with Stephanie, her sister, and her two brothers. She'd never even seen the ocean before she'd gone to Brown, never eaten a lobster until she moved to Portland and started dating Carly. She looked like she belonged ensconced in a suburban McMansion somewhere; she was blond and petite and had a cute little turned-up nose that made how good she looked seem less threatening, made her seem like somebody you'd like before she ever opened her mouth. Most of the time when I saw her she was wearing khakis and a T-shirt covered with clay and glaze from her studio, but once or twice we'd gone out somewhere nice for dinner and she'd put herself into a dress, and I'd wonder how anybody could help but fall in love with her.

No, I didn't think Stephanie knew what she was getting into by agreeing to move to Loosewood Island—and I didn't know how things would turn out for me, with another sister at home and with Kenny gone—but instead of saying that, I promised to call Carly when Daddy came home the next day, and promised not to tell him that she was coming home until she told him herself. Then I hung the phone up, opened the glass doors, and looked out over the water.

My house wasn't something I'd have been able to afford on my own. Daddy let me live in this house free and clear, and he hadn't been subtle about the fact that there was room in the house for a husband and children both; he reminded me all the time that early thirties wasn't too old to get started. He'd set up the same sort of deal for Rena and Tucker, too. Other side of the harbor, but waterfront, same as mine. He'd even bought bunk beds to put in each of the twins' rooms, thinking ahead to when the kids would want to have sleepovers. Rena and I both offered to pay rent, but he said not to mind it. He had two other houses that he rented out to summer folk as well as the fish shop, the warehouse where the lobster pounds sat, two buildings on Main Street that held six different businesses that operated year-round—which was more impressive when you figured that Loosewood Island only had about three dozen businesses open during the off-season—and his own house, the house I'd grown up in. He didn't have loans on any of them, and that's the way he liked it. He was old-fashioned about being in debt and always said if you dealt in cash you didn't have to keep buying whatever it was that you bought. He was no dub—a fisherman who couldn't cut it—and that was part of things, but part of it, too, was that he seemed to understand that things were changing on Loosewood Island before anybody else did, and he bought before the tourists hijacked the island. There were lots of things about Loosewood Island that he seemed to understand better than anybody else, and sometimes I wondered if there was more to those stories he told me about Brumfitt than he let on. Either way, it worked out well for the Kings.

Maybe somewhere else, men would have been jealous of him. Even without him flaunting his money—his house had beautiful views, but was as old and beaten down as any other lobsterman's—every one of the boys in the harbor knew he had the money to buy something bigger and newer than the *Queen Jane*, that he had enough put away to weather the downs of the markets, the crash in lobster sales after the terrorist attacks in New York, that he could even weather the weather itself. But this was Loosewood Island, and more often than not I thought of our name as a description. Kenny was right about Daddy. He was the king of the harbor just as his father had been the king of the harbor, and his grandfather before, and there would come a day, probably, when I'd take over. We made decisions as a group—to shorten the season, to fish less traps, to stop letting cruise ships dock in the harbor—but anytime we made a decision, big or small, there was always the moment when every man would look to Daddy to see if he agreed.

Daddy was the reason we had the lobster co-op. Loosewood Island only has one wharf, though a few of the more ritzy cottages that are in sheltered coves have put in deepwater docks for their yachts so that they don't have to bother with the harbor. The lobstermen own the wharf. And I don't mean that like some silly gang slogan. I mean it in a purely literal sense. When Daddy said we should start a co-op, the lobstermen went together to buy out the old, crooked mainlander dealer who was nickeling and diming us to death. We could have forced him out—it's amazing how quickly somebody recognizes a deal when their truck burns up and their boat mysteriously sinks—but we offered him a fair price. When he took the money and left for Florida, we started the Loosewood Island Lobster Co-op. This would have been twenty years ago or so, before I started lobstering, before Scotty died.

The first few years of the co-op were kind of rough. They'd hired Mr. Taber to run the shop. He was an islander and when he fished he'd been a highliner—the kind of lobsterman who constantly outfished other men—and that seemed like qualification enough. Unfortunately, Mr. Taber was an old-school fisherman, born and raised to it, without a day of school past tenth grade, and he was taking on water from the beginning. He didn't know shit about marketing or buying or selling or paperwork or accounting or any of the hundred things you need to know to actually be successful buying and selling lobsters. He was over his head. He immediately upped the offer price, buying for fifty cents a pound more than that shit-ass dealer we'd run out. But, of course, after buying the lobsters for fifty cents a pound more than the going rate, Mr. Taber ran smack into the problem of not being able to demand a higher rate from the wholesalers in Boston and New York who used to buy from our dealer. We lost some money there. And then he forgot to do some simple things that we'd all taken for granted, like order fuel, so the pumps ran dry and several boys had to stay tied up for a week until more fuel arrived. And then he forgot to order bait, and everybody had to take their boats to the mainland, wasting fuel and time that nobody had. That sort of thing went on for about two years, but nobody, not even Daddy, wanted to be the first to tell Mr. Taber it was time for him to go. He'd been well respected when he worked the water, and his family name meant a lot on Loosewood Island: the Tabers had been on the island almost as long as Momma's side. They had fought on both sides of the War of 1812, which made for some mixed-up loyalties and even better dinner conversation back in the day. Fortunately, before anything had to be done about it, Mr. Taber had a heart attack and died. Then the men, at Daddy's urging, did something that was almost unthinkable: they brought in an outsider.

Paul Paragopolis had a name we couldn't pronounce, but he also had a business degree and some experience in the lobster trade. His family ran a wholesale business in Boston, and despite being young—he was barely twenty-four—he knew what he was doing, and he turned the co-op around in less than a year. He even got a bunch of the boys to run "lobster tours" in the summer off-season, letting tourists pay fifty bucks to pretend to be lobstermen for a couple of hours. He got the co-op in the black real quick, and soon enough the lobstermen counted on wholesale prices on gear and a year-end bonus once the co-op had covered costs and Paul's salary. By the time he married Lucy Swift, a fifth-generation islander, a couple of years later, the boys had stopped referring to him as "the new kid." It's funny how some men can come to the island every summer their entire lives, move here after college, work, live, raise children here, and still, forty years out, be considered "new," and yet Paul managed to become part of the island in only a few years simply because he helped the boys make more money. About five years ago they had a big party to celebrate the last repayments for the loan used to buy the wharf and the dealership in the first place, and when Paul got up to give a speech the boys hoisted him up, carried him down the dock, and threw him in the water. Paul came out complaining that the water was cold as shit—even in the height of summer, the water never gets much past fifty degrees, and a man can freeze to death on a sunny day—but he had a grin on his face all the same.

The thing is, even though Paul runs the co-op, nobody would mistake him for the man in charge: everybody understood that the Kings' word is the final word. Daddy usually let us talk things out among ourselves, but the few times he settled a matter, it was settled.

I thought about calling Carly back to insist that I *was* happy—or at least that I *wanted* to be happy—that she and Stephanie were coming home, that I thought it would all work out, but I didn't have it in me. I needed to get out of the house, to shake loose my worries about her coming home, Kenny leaving, and Daddy having to spend the night in the hospital being poked and prodded. Maybe if I'd lived on the mainland, someplace where I could have called Carly back from my mobile, I could have walked and talked, but being inside felt too close to being stuck. I headed outside instead, never mind the rain, and then stopped short at the coat hooks when I realized I'd left my slickers aboard the *Kings' Ransom* earlier in the morning. It wasn't cold enough for my winter parka, and I'd be damned if I was going to walk around the island carrying an umbrella. I dug in the closet for a minute and came up with an old oilcloth coat that I thought had belonged to my momma's daddy. I had to roll up the sleeves a couple turns, but it fit me well enough, the voluminous hood keeping my head out of water.

I looked into the diner through the front window and saw about whom you'd expect: the old boys, most of whom were down to lobstering part-time now, just something to keep their hands in the game, nursing the same cups of coffee they'd had in front of them since they finished up their lunches. I skipped past the Bronson Gallery, Island Ice Cream, and the Sandwich Shoppe, all closed for the season, past the Brumfitt Kings Museum, which was open only Wednesday and Saturday or by appointment until summer, past an empty storefront, and popped into the Coffee Catch, thinking I'd get something before heading over to see Rena. In the back, Timmy Green, Chip and Tony Warner, and Petey Dogger, all lobstermen closer to my age, were sitting and drinking from oversized mugs, looking as if they'd been there for a while. Timmy Green—who was actually not green, but black, and a third-generation islander—raised his hand at me and got up from the table.

"You hear about the shoot-out at the docks in James Harbor, Cordelia?" He handed me a copy of the *James Harbor Tide* so I could see the picture of a lobster boat and read the caption: "Meth Death Bloodbath." He waited for me to look back up at him again and then said, "Petey told me his brother says that there's some sort of a turf war going on." Petey Dogger was like most of us who'd been on the island for any length of time: part of a family of international mongrels. His sister was a dental hygienist in Lubec, Maine, his brother a cop in Yarmouth, on the tip of Nova Scotia, and Petey had stayed on Loosewood Island, which some years was part of the USA and some years Canada, and most years was just tangled up in the bureaucracy of two countries who disagreed about where exactly the border ran. The border dispute's been going on as long as Loosewood Island's had people on it: before the U.S. and Canada *were* the U.S. and Canada, it was France and Britain fighting over possession of the island. Today, despite the USA's official position that they don't recognize dual citizenship, both countries claim us as citizens. We're supposed to file taxes in both the USA and Canada. Of course, in the confusion, there are more than a handful of islanders who haven't bothered to pay either country. Loosewood Island is a kind of borderland, a no-man's-land.

"Sure it wasn't one of Brumfitt's monsters come to life, going after the James Harbor boys for being such pricks?"

Timmy smiled at me and it made me blush hot for a minute, thinking about the way he used to smile at me. We'd had a thing for a year or two, when I'd first come back to the island after college, but despite being good together in bed and even on the water, we couldn't hack it in the same house. When the season wasn't going on we'd get to picking on each other so fierce. One time I hit him in the head with a coffee mug. He hadn't been hurt, but we took it as a sign that we'd be better off if we weren't an item any longer. He moved on quick enough, marrying a Japanese tourist who'd rented a house on the island for a summer and never left—Etsuko does translation work—and Timmy and I had become close friends again since the wedding. Still, every once and a while he looked at me with that sharp smile and I'd think of the last time we had sex: he'd grinned at me and said, "For old times' sake, huh?"

For a while, I'd been in love with him. Or, if not in love with him, in lust with him. His boat, the *Green Machine*, wasn't anything special as far as lobster boats go, but Timmy knew how to keep his boat tight and clean, and that was as good a description of Timmy himself as anything. He wasn't tall, but he was solid in the way that you can't get from lifting weights, that you can only get from spending your life working; when he'd reach out and hook me around the waist and kiss me on the neck, just under my ear, it made my legs feel like they weren't used to the buck and bounce of a boat. Maybe Timmy and I weren't cut out to be boyfriend and girlfriend, but we loved each other in that weird sort of way that broken couples can be great together when the music stops, and I was genuinely happy for him. Plus, Etsuko and I, in some roundabout manner that I wouldn't have expected, had become friends. They'd already asked me to be the godmother for the baby they were expecting in the fall.

Timmy lowered his voice, though the coffee shop was empty other than him and the other boys, all of whom seemed caught up in their own discussion arguing the merits of engine power versus gas efficiency and noise. My motor on the *Kings' Ransom* was old as dirt, but I'd had it overhauled two years ago. I'd ended up having to have half of the motor rebuilt, and I wasn't interested in something new, so I tuned them out. "Nah," Timmy said, "none of Brumfitt's monsters. Just meth. But I don't know. From what Petey's brother"—the cop—"says, meth is going to be a bigger problem for the island than anything that Brumfitt ever came up with. There's a whole mess of men and women there who are cooking it up, running it over the border, trying to turn it into a real business. It was bad enough when it was just those morons taking it recreationally." He shrugged. "I guess it gives you energy. No big deal to pull traps all day and all night if you're tweaking, and I guess I didn't think about it that much when it was just James Harbor. I mean, how much worse can that shithole be, even with a meth problem? But Petey's brother says that it's spreading. Says it's a real cancer, and wanted to be sure to give us the heads-up, particularly if James Harbor boys are trying to move into our waters."

Loosewood Island couldn't pass for a puritanical paradise by any measure. We didn't have more than a couple of real bars in the off-season, but that was a function of the island's size, not any comment on temperance. During the U.S. Prohibition, the island firmly declared itself to be under Canadian control. We all drank, some of us to excess. Pot smoking wasn't much of a problem, either, and by that I mean nobody seemed to have any problem if you smoked pot. There were a dozen or so older residents—die-hard hippies who moved here in the late seventies and made their living as potters, and a few third- and fourth-generation fishermen—who liked lighting up a joint on a regular basis, and there was some of it with the teens and with the other people in their thirties and their forties. But weed was about where it ended on the island.

I'm not trying to make it sound like islanders were somehow above temptation. We sure as hell had enough drunks, and when people moved off-island or fished on ocean crews with mainland outfits, we had our fair share of people who turned into cokeheads, meth addicts, heroin, opium, crack addicts, whatever else was out there. But *on* the island, things were different. The simple explanation was that we more or less kept the island clean of any sort of serious drugs. Sure, there were tourists who'd bring in their own stashes, but we tried to keep it on the mainland. When there was somebody who didn't understand that there were unspoken rules about what we were willing to tolerate, we made things very clear. Every year or two there'd be somebody, sometimes a prodigal son but usually an outsider—always a man—who'd move to the island and come trailing bad ideas in his wake. Coke or heroin or pot or whatever it was, it didn't take too long before the word got around, and then Daddy and few of the lobstermen would visit and persuade that man that he wasn't welcome on Loosewood Island. Usually words were enough, sometimes a beating, and every once in a while a boat would be sunk, a truck smashed. Sooner or later, whomever it was would get on the ferry and not come back.

Was it hypocritical? Yeah. No question. Chip and Tony had worked as mules to get the money to buy their own boat, running pot south from Canada. They could make eight, nine, ten thousand dollars running two hundred pounds of weed over the border, and a few quick nights of risk put them in business as lobstermen, which was all they wanted. Petey had never done it—his brother was a cop and had him scared shitless about what jail would be like—nor had Timmy, but they both had friends on the mainland who supplemented their fishing incomes with a run now and then. I'd never done it, but then again, I'd never needed to with the money that Daddy had. But even if I had, or Petey or Timmy had, we would have said the same thing that Chip and Tony said: it's just pot, and it wasn't something we brought home. As long as we kept the island clean—and that was a line that was etched in the rock—what was the big fucking deal?

Maybe meth was going to be a different matter. According

to Petey's brother there was a wave coming, a wave that wouldn't pass Loosewood Island by. "Is Petey's brother worried that the James Harbor boys are going to start dealing here?"

"Seriously?"

"What?"

He looked over his shoulder to the table where Chip, Tony, and Petey were still sitting. "You don't know?"

"Know what?"

"Give me a second," he said. He touched my arm and then walked back to the table with the other boys. He leaned low to speak, and after a minute, he nodded me over.

"Something that needs telling?" I said. I sat down at the table and put the *James Harbor Tide* in front of the Warner boys, tapping on the picture. "We got more of a problem with James Harbor than just fishing?"

Tony was the one who did almost all of the talking, so I was looking at him, and when it was Chip who answered instead, I knew there was going to be trouble.

"Depends," Chip said, "on whether you think of Eddie Glouster as a James Harbor problem or a Loosewood Island problem."

I leaned back in my chair. "Eddie's not working for Daddy anymore. You know that. Hasn't been on the *Queen Jane* in more than a year."

"But he's still on the island, Cordelia," Chip said.

"So?"

"So," Tony said, reaching out to take the newspaper, "how do you think he's making money if he's not fishing?"

I could feel my shoulders slump. "He's dealing."

Chip reached in front of Tony, to stop his brother from speaking. "We're not blaming Woody for giving Eddie a chance. Woody likes those sort of reclamation projects. Hell, he let me and Tony work for him when you were at college and our dad kicked us off the boat. I'm just not sure that Eddie really wanted to be saved," Chip said. "So, yeah. He's dealing. It's Jenny."

Jenny. Chip and Tony's little sister. I guess she wasn't that young—fifteen and supposedly she'd been sleeping her way through the half dozen boys who were her age—and Chip said she'd been scoring meth from Eddie Glouster.

"Okay," I said. "What's the play?"

"Our dad's going to talk to Woody," Tony said. "I'm assuming they'll run him out."

I thought of Daddy spending the night at the hospital. The way those cotton gowns can make anybody look old and sick. Fluorescent lights and pulse monitors and blood draws, the doctors trying to figure out why he'd fainted. I thought of Daddy and Mr. Warner and probably George, three men who were older than they wanted to believe, facing up against Eddie Glouster. And I thought of the way Daddy looked passed out on his kitchen floor.

I didn't like it.

"No," I said. "We'll take care of it."

Petey Dogger leaned forward, his voice eager. "We will?"

I looked around the table at Chip, Tony, Timmy, and Petey. I realized they were all eager, not just Petey. Timmy was my age, and Petey and Chip and Tony were younger than me, but none of us were kids anymore, and they felt like I did, that we could handle things just as well as the old guard. "Can't let Daddy and all of those old farts have all of the fun, can we? It's our island, too, and it's something we can take care of, so we will," I said. They all nodded, and I wondered if any of them knew that Daddy was in Saint John getting tested, that my desire to take care of the Eddie Glouster problem was as much about keeping Daddy out of it as it was about it being time for us to start taking care of the island on our own.

"When?" Tony asked.

"Tonight," I said, thinking we needed to take care of it before Daddy got back from Saint John. I reached out and took the newspaper back. "At least it's just Eddie we're dealing with, not all of James Harbor."

Petey shook his head. "Not sure that's going to last. My

brother said it's a real shitshow in James Harbor. It's not like the old days, when we were just fighting over lobsters. Half those boys are users and need the money to keep tweaking. Things are going to get messy, and it might not be enough just to carry a hammer."

I knew he wanted me to say something about Daddy smashing Al Burns's hand, but instead I said, "You trying to say I should have a gun on board?"

"You don't already?" Timmy looked at me with his half-bit smile. "This isn't exactly the pirate coast, but with James Harbor pushing into our waters, I figured Woody's the kind of daddy who wouldn't give you much choice about being armed."

In fact, Daddy would have been pissed if he'd known I stopped carrying my shotgun on board the *Kings' Ransom*. He'd given me his father's Remington Wingmaster when I'd started running my own boat. He stuck with the company that had worked out just fine for him and his own father, and bought himself a new, nickel-plated Remington Marine Magnum shotgun for the *Queen Jane*. He had at least two pistols on board as well, and I'd occasionally find one of my buoys with a bullet hole in it, Daddy having gotten it into his mind to take target practice on the high seas. I kept my Wingmaster loaded with double-aught, but I hadn't bothered carrying it on the *Kings' Ransom* for a few years. It was a pain in the ass to keep it registered in both Canada and the U.S., though I bet Daddy didn't bother with registration in either country. More importantly, I'd never needed a gun. "Way I hear it, you're telling me I should make sure I got it handy," I said.

Timmy looked over my shoulder and nodded. "One for him wouldn't be such a bad idea, either."

I glanced back and saw Kenny ordering at the counter.

I stood up and grabbed the newspaper. "I'll see you boys tonight, but in the meantime, I've got to go. Kenny and I have something to talk about."

I stepped up to Kenny as he stood at the counter, but before I could say anything, he asked, "You hear about James Harbor?"

"The shoot-out at the docks?" I said.

"Yeah. No, what?" I handed him the copy of the *James Harbor Tide* that I was holding and showed him the "Meth Death Bloodbath" headline. He took the paper out of my hand, gave it a scan, and then put it down on the counter. "No, but I mean, Jesus. Nah, I'm talking about James Harbor dropping pots in our waters."

"Well, yeah, that's what you said this morning, that the rumor is that they're coming."

He shook his head. "Nope. Not a rumor. They're here. I ran into George on my way here. He found a couple James Harbor traps in our waters when he was pissing around on his boat this morning. Fucking peckerwoods."

"Shit. I knew it was coming, but the season hasn't even started yet and there are already real live traps in our waters? Can't Al Burns keep his boys in check?"

"I think things have changed. He's just an old man now. It's not the same as when you were a teenager, not the same as—" He stopped and looked at my hands and then back to my eyes.

"It's different. Been long enough that there's a new, young group of fishermen, and they're looking to extend their range, and they aren't listening to Al Burns," Kenny said. "That's my understanding." He pulled out his wallet. "Buy you a coffee?"

I shook my head, unsure of how to bring up what Carly had told me, that he and Sally were leaving the island. Out the window, the rain had broken momentarily, but a new wave of dark clouds seemed to be swimming over the island. It would start raining again soon, but I didn't want to ask Kenny about his moving away in front of the boys. When Kenny picked up his drink and came over I took his arm and steered him outside.

As soon as the door closed, I hit him with it: "When the fuck were you going to tell me?"

He was staring over the water and up at the incoming clouds, and instead of turning to face me he gave me the corner of his eyes. "What are you talking about, Cordelia?"

"You and Sally leaving the island."

That made him turn toward me. "We aren't leaving the island."

"I just talked to Carly. She said Sally gave notice at the school yesterday. Principal Philips called up Carly, hired her to take over K through third, and there we have it. Said Sally told Principal Philips you were headed off the island."

I could see it in Kenny's face as I was talking, but I somehow couldn't stop myself from going forward: he didn't know. He turned pale. He opened his mouth, but nothing came out for a moment. "You sure about that, Cordelia?"

"You mean you didn't know? Oh, Jesus, Kenny. I'm sorry. I thought—" I shook my head and then grabbed his elbow. "Come on; let's get out of the doorway. Walk down to the docks." He came along. "I just assumed . . ." I shook my head again, not sure what to say, but Kenny left it at silence, and as we headed down the slope I tried again. "I was mad at you, you know? I couldn't figure out why you hadn't told me. But, well, fuck."

"She's leaving me," he said.

"Maybe." I wanted to say something better, but all I could add was, "I'm sorry."

"I mean, we've talked about it, splitting up. Sleeping apart for most of the last year. Jesus. She's leaving me. We've been having problems, you know?"

I did know. We talked about it sometimes on the boat. Not much—Kenny didn't bring up Sally that often with me—but it was something that came up occasionally. I would have known anyway. Sally had been heading mainland every Saturday for therapy, and on Sundays it was both of them going over for couples counseling, and there was no way to hide that kind of thing from the island.

"But I thought things were getting better. Sally's been acting happier lately." Kenny stopped walking and turned to look at me and I could see that he was trembling, that despite all of the things he and Sally had gone through, he hadn't believed that it would come to this. "You really think she's leaving me?" he said, and I thought if I didn't answer him quick—any answer would do—he might just start walking again and not stop when he came to the end of the dock.

"I'm not sure, but you need to talk to her," I said. "I'm sorry, Kenny. I really am."

"You're right. I know you're right. I need to go talk to her," he said, and then he looked at his watch. I realized that he was thinking that Sally was still at school, that he was going to have to go home and brood until the children left Loosewood Elementary and Sally could make her way back to the house; that glance at his watch was such a tender, domestic action that it was all I could do to stop from taking him in my arms and pulling him into me. "Jesus. I've got to go, Cordelia," he said.

He turned, but I grabbed his elbow again. "Kenny, you call me if you need. You know I'm here for you, okay?" He just nodded, and then he started walking up the slope and away from the dock, breaking into a half jog after a few feet.

I watched him disappear and then looked out over the harbor

again. Was I actually sorry? It was complicated, and it wasn't my business what happened with him and Sally, but there was also a part of me that reacted to the thought that he might end up single.

I could see George Sweeney's boat on its mooring buoy. I couldn't make out his features from where I stood, but I knew it was George up on deck hosing it clean. He raised a hand to me—though I doubt he could tell who was watching him—and I waved back. The swell of the water soothed me, and I stared off into nothingness for a while, letting my eyes lose focus on that middle distance past the harbor and before the horizon. Daddy wasn't set to be back from the doctor's until the next day, and I knew he wasn't going to call just to set me at ease. I could feel my anxiety creeping back again. This wasn't right, this having to worry about him instead of the other way around. He'd looked so goddamned pale lying on the floor of his kitchen that for a moment I could picture what he'd look like lying in a coffin. He was fifty-seven. If he'd been an accountant or a lawyer or something that didn't involve the demands of lobstering, he wouldn't be that old, and as much as I wanted to be able to show Daddy that I was ready to take over, I wasn't ready to be without him. I might not be willing to admit it to him anymore, but I still needed him. This wasn't the natural order of things. I was used to Daddy looking after me.

At least there was getting rid of Eddie Glouster to distract me from waiting for Daddy to come back from the hospital. I couldn't do anything about Daddy's tests, but I could do something about Eddie Glouster. Daddy would be pissed if he knew that we were planning to deal with Eddie while he was in Saint John, but I didn't have to ask for permission. If Daddy was going to be pissed, he'd be pissed, but he'd also have to see that I could take care of the island just as well as he could. And things were complicated with Eddie Glouster and Daddy.

There was a piece of dried seaweed half off the dock and I gave it a shove with my foot, watching it flutter into the ocean.

"Fuck it," I said, and then turned to head back to my house to wait for the night to come.

Eddie Glouster's dad moved to Loosewood Island from James Harbor when Eddie was already sixteen or seventeen. Ostensibly, it was to get Eddie away from a rough crowd he'd been hewing to in James Harbor, but with his dad commuting to a job at a processing plant on the mainland, Eddie seemed cut adrift from the first. He was the sort of boy who was probably in his prime during his mid-teens, before he came to Loosewood Island, in the few years where his early growth spurt let him be a bully without worrying about the consequences. By the time he made it here, the other boys had filled out as well, and they were solid in a way that he wasn't, turned hard from the grind of pulling traps and working on the water.

He was a few years younger than me, and I was at college when he lived on the island, so I didn't see him much. The year after he graduated from high school, which was the year I came home from college, Eddie lit out to Portland, getting a job as a security guard at some mall and then signing up with the army before washing out. After that, he drifted south to Boston, where he seemed to bounce from job to job. Mr. Glouster wasn't a bad guy, even if he was a bit of a drinker, and the boys liked him well enough, but when Eddie came to visit every few months, while Mr. Glouster would quietly hunch over a dozen beers at the Grumman Fish House, Eddie would get drunk in a loud sort of way that didn't sit too well.

About two years ago, Mr. Glouster got sick enough that he went in for some tests, and by the time they figured out whatever kind of cancer had been eating him, he was already dead. I don't think Mr. Glouster was in the ground more than a week before Eddie showed up on the island with a wife and a baby in tow and moved into his dad's house. I didn't stop by, but a few of the ladies who brought pies and cookies said that Eddie didn't waste any time in bundling his dad's stuff into garbage bags, including the decoys that his dad had carved with such excruciating care and proudly loaned out to the library for display every year.

I'd see Eddie's wife occasionally, out pushing a baby stroller around the paths on the island. Nelly was a small thing, and the jacket she wore was so big on her that she looked like she was playing dress-up. It must have been Mr. Glouster's old winter jacket. Nelly kept the hood up, and kept wearing the coat through the winter and spring and well into that summer. It was that fall when Tucker got tangled up in the ropes and fucked up his knee, and Daddy took Eddie Glouster on as a temporary sternman.

It raised a few eyebrows around the docks and there was some talk at the Grumman Fish House over beers. Mr. Glouster might have moved to Loosewood Island as a way of getting the high-school-aged Eddie away from James Harbor, but as an adult, with Mr. Glouster dead, there was nothing to stop Eddie from bringing James Harbor to Loosewood Island. Eddie and Nelly regularly had visitors at their place, off-islanders showing up on the ferry and disappearing into the Glousters' house. Late nights the lights would still be on, music loud enough that their neighbors—despite their distance—said it was a nuisance, and in the mornings, a deathly stillness, empty bottles spread over the lawn. And aside from that and from generally being disliked, Eddie just didn't seem like a lobsterman. He was big, but despite his penchant for drinking and talking loud, he seemed soft.

Still, he was Daddy's hire, and we were used to Daddy taking on young men who needed some taming. Daddy kept quiet about it the first few days, but by the end of the week he had that familiar little smirk of his that he got when he knew that he'd been right. Eddie might have been soft and not used to the work of lobstering, but he was willing to try and, according to Daddy, despite not being born and raised on Loosewood Island, Eddie was a quick learner. After two weeks, Daddy was even talking about keeping Eddie on once Tucker was done rehabbing his knee.

I'd never spent much time with Eddie, or at least as little time as you could spend with somebody close to your own age on an island as small as ours, but maybe a month into Daddy's experiment Kenny got food poisoning and Daddy broke a crown and had to go to the dentist, so I ended up with Eddie on the *Kings' Ransom* for the day. He showed up fifteen minutes late, and while he didn't seem drunk or high, or at least he wasn't fucked up enough that it was obvious to me, he looked like he hadn't slept, and he reeked of beer and cigarettes. When we were motoring out to the first set of traps, instead of getting his gear together, he leaned over the rail smoking and staring at the water.

I eased up the throttle and brought us alongside my buoys, but Eddie kept dragging on his cigarette. "Eddie." My voice had a snap to it, but he took his time pushing himself off the rail.

"Late night last night," he said. "Had some friends over from the mainland." He gave me a half-assed salute and a smile that I'm pretty sure was supposed to be flirty. He was a big man, probably six-foot-two, but gone to seed and pushing two-fifty, two-sixty pounds, the sort of guy who loved playing high school football because he could toss around kids who weighed a hundred pounds less than him. Rounding his late twenties and headed to a burnt-out thirty, he had the start of a gut. His hair, already thinning, hung in a sharp part and fell to his cheekbones, but out on the *Kings' Ransom*, with the early morning sun skipping off the water and burnishing his skin, I could see how some women would find him attractive. I wasn't one of those women, though.

Even though I didn't like him, I hadn't expected any problems: Daddy had vouched for him. I still can't figure out if he was one of those guys who couldn't deal with taking orders from a woman, or if he was just generally an asshole but had managed to keep it hidden from Daddy, but the day didn't start well and it went downhill quickly. The first few sets of traps were fine, but once we started moving, I didn't have the same rhythm with him as I did with Kenny: I had to step back quickly to avoid getting a trap swung into me. I didn't like the way he stuffed the bait bags—there was too much spillage—and three or four times I noticed that he'd put a lobster in with the keepers without banding its claws. Plus, Eddie was just slower than Kenny. By nine in the morning I'd already barked at him a half dozen times. Each time I corrected something he did, he'd look at me with his eyes half lidded and then take his time before getting back to work.

And then I saw him sort through a trap and drop a lobster into the keeper bin without measuring its carapace. Even from where I was standing I could tell it was too small. A cardinal sin. I stomped over, pulled the bug, and slapped my brass measure against the shell.

"What the fuck, Eddie?" He dropped the rebaited trap into the water and then turned to look at me. I held up the lobster. "You didn't measure this one." I pinned it down and put the measure on it. "It's not big enough. If it's not a keeper, it's not a keeper." I picked the lobster back up, walked to the rail, and dropped it over the side.

He pulled his pack of smokes out from the pocket of his overalls, flipped the lid, and then tapped it against his hand until one stood at attention. He touched the pack to his mouth and pulled it away, the cigarette dangling from his lips. "Jesus. What's your problem? You've been on my ass all day. Can you hear yourself?" He made his voice higher, mimicking me: "If it's not a keeper, it's not a keeper." He tucked the pack of cigarettes away again, cupped his hand against the wind, and sparked his lighter. "It's just a lobster. You need to relax."

"And you need to do your fucking job, Eddie."

He leaned back against the rail. "Don't get your panties in a knot."

"You want to swim back to shore?"

He took a drag on his cigarette, staring at me, and I saw the way his eyes flicked down my body and back up. He pushed himself off the rail, stood at his full height, and stepped toward me until he was closer than I was comfortable with. I didn't step back, but I wanted to. For the first time, I was scared on my own boat.

"You threatening me?"

Behind me, I heard Trudy getting to her feet, and then felt her pressing up against my leg. There was the low rumble of her growling, and I remembered what Daddy had always said about dogs: Stare them in the eye until they look away. Be the boss or be the bitch.

I looked straight at Eddie. "I'm telling you that I'm the captain, and you'll listen to me on my boat, and you better think real carefully about what you do and say next."

He put the cigarette back in his mouth and sucked at it, still staring at me. I thought he was going to blow smoke into my face, but at the last second he turned his head to the side and then stepped past me.

"Fuck you," he said.

I couldn't stop myself. I grabbed his arm. "What did you say?"

He knocked my hand off his arm, and then, before I realized it, he'd shoved me.

Maybe he didn't mean to push me that hard, but we were on a boat and there was gear everywhere. I stumbled backward, caught my heel on something, and fell. As I went down, I felt my arm scrape against the bolt of an exposed hose clamp. I could tell it wasn't a deep cut, but it was long, running from my elbow almost to my wrist, and it started to bleed right away.

Eddie hadn't moved. The scowl that he'd had on his face was gone. Instead, he looked surprised. Almost scared. Maybe if he'd still been looming over me, maybe if he still looked like he wanted to punch me, I would have stayed down, but instead I got to my feet and pulled out my work knife.

Eddie took a step back. He held up his hands. "I'm sorry. I shouldn't have done that."

I kept the knife up for another second, but even though I was angry, I wasn't stupid, and while I wasn't sure that Eddie was actually sorry, he did look like he regretted what he'd done. I put the knife away and went to move past him.

"Your arm," he said. He reached out to where I was bleeding, but I pulled back.

"Go take a seat at the stern."

He stared at me, but then he looked down at the deck, headed aft, and turned his back to me, staring out over the water.

I didn't bother telling him he was fired. I didn't say a word to him. I just ran the motor until we were in the harbor, and then I watched him climb out onto the dock and walk away.

Of course, that afternoon, when Daddy got back from the dentist, I had to tell him that I'd fired his sternman. And then I had to tell him why.

Daddy didn't say much about it. He sat there and rubbed at the temporary crown on his canine. But the next day, I saw Eddie and Nelly out walking with their baby, and Eddie had a black eye and a cut under it that looked like it had taken a half dozen stitches.

That was the last of Eddie Glouster working for the Kings. At the time, it didn't seem like much of a big deal. Fishing isn't a gentleman's game, and sometimes tempers got hot. I'd notice at the Grumman Fish House that Eddie would get a little quieter if Daddy was around, and sometimes he'd rub at the little worm of a scar that lingered under his eye from where Daddy had hit him, but nothing seemed to come of it.

I tried calling over to Kenny's a few times, but the phone rang through to voice mail. Finally I gave up and just watched television until it was time to head out and meet the boys. By then it was late enough—close to eleven—that the island had mostly gone dark. Fishermen are early risers, in season or not. There was an occasional breeze, enough that the stray hairs I didn't have tucked in my ponytail wafted over my face, across my forehead, and the wind carried the cool of the water over me.

There aren't enough roads on Loosewood Island for there to be back roads—every road is a back road—but Eddie Glouster lived on Coral Avenue, which led inland and away from the docks. The closest thing we had to the wrong side of the tracks. The house itself was set back down a rain-washed gravel drive, in a small hollow of trees and rocks. The moon came in three-quarters full, and the stars seemed to swell and sway the way they always did when the nights were clear, as if they were breathing in and out.

I met Chip, Tony, Timmy, and Petey near the Grumman Fish House. Chip was carrying a rifle. I looked at him and he shrugged, and neither of us said anything about it. In fact, for the five minutes it took us to walk to the corner and down Coral Avenue we all stayed quiet, other than Petey's occasional cough, a dry, short force of air that made it sound like he had the husk of a piece of popcorn caught in his throat. Our steps on the asphalt seemed heavy in the quiet of the island at night, and the only other sounds were the ocean—which you could hear from almost anywhere on the island—and the occasional float of voices and laughter coming from the direction we were walking.

The silence of the island was overbearing for some of the tourists who came from bigger cities, or even from smaller college towns, where there was always some sort of background noise. Inside a rental cottage it didn't bother people: there was the hum of electricity, the refrigerator motor working to keep lobsters and chardonnay cold, the tick of the baseboard heaters kicking on, the echoes of breathing and movement coming off the walls and ceilings, breaking the silence. But at night, sitting on decks or walking on the beach, the absence of man-made sound seemed to collapse the darkness in a way that made some of the tourists jumpy, afraid that Loosewood Island was going to turn out to be the setting of a horror movie. Of course, the same silence, the same absences—no trains, no highway, no taxi drivers leaning on the horn, no broad-cover floodlights from parking lots erasing the stars, no neon signs leaking through the curtains—was one of the reasons tourists came here in the first place.

For islanders, however, the reverse is also true. We go to the cities for the things that we don't have here—shopping, restaurants, theaters—and just for a chance to be somewhere else, to be *someone* else, for a few days, but also because of the closeness, the bustling hustle of people brushing your shoulder on the sidewalk, the crushed-together rides on the subway, the chance to be part of a crowd for once. It's something I love a few times a year, despite which, the prospect of living full-time in a big city makes me shudder. There are some of the islanders who, like tourists who can't handle the absence of man-made sounds at night, are overwhelmed by the cities, the simple weight of so many people in one place. They shut down, withdraw to their hotel rooms, and come back to the island swearing they'll never go to the city again.

That night, walking toward Eddie Glouster's place, the quiet was reassuring, like a cocoon. With the sound of the ocean faded by distance, and with our footsteps on the asphalt, the stray voices coming from the direction of the Glousters', it was easy to stay inside the moment, to stay with the idea that I was doing what I had to, that I was there because I was part of the island, and I had to excise a cancer.

We were all there for a reason: Chip and Tony because it was their sister; Timmy because his being black was enough to make him seem scary to Eddie and his crew; Petey because he *was* scary, a former wrestler and boxer, a hulk of muscle and meat that moved like he was always ready to pounce; and me because I'd do what needed being done to protect Loosewood Island. I suppose there were other people that Chip and Tony could have confided in, boys more their own age, but we were ones they knew they could count on.

When we came up to the driveway, the house itself was dark, but there was a bonfire going in the yard. I could see a half dozen people circled around the flames. One of the logs popped, and a few sparks drifted high into the air, going dark as they reached the canopy of the trees. We were maybe twenty paces back—close enough that I could see the people around the flames, four men and two women, but hidden in the darkness from Eddie and his fire-blinded friends—when Chip called out. One of the women startled a little, and the group quieted down, but Eddie stood up from the stump he'd been sitting on and came over to us. He moved with no particular hurry. Eddie had one of those closed-toe walks that I always associated with men who'd never been to sea; instead of staggering a little from side to side as he walked, he almost floated over the dirt. He had a beer in his hand, and when he came up to the five of us, he seemed like he'd been expecting a visit.

"Closed party tonight, boys," he said. Then he lifted up his beer and tipped the neck toward me. "She's welcome to stay if she wants. Can never have too much pussy at a party."

I could feel all four of the boys start to gather the beginning of the kind of energy that inevitably leads to punches, but I couldn't help it. I laughed.

Chip looked at me, and it was as if, simply by laughing, I made some of the charge dissipate.

Eddie shifted back a step and then raised his beer but didn't drink from it. "You think that's funny?" Even with the light from the fire shifting and the shadows moving across him, I could see how he'd already started seeing the damage of too much beer and drugs etching lines on his face, and how in a few years he'd look hollowed out and only a woman as empty as him would be drawn in.

"Well, yeah, I guess I do think it's funny," I said. "When I heard you were dealing, I figured, well, let's have a talk with Eddie, let's see what's going on, let's see if he's as much of a douche as he seems. What do you think, Eddie? Are you the kind of guy we can just have a conversation with?"

Eddie leaned over me. His breath was beery but also sort of sweet. "Fuck you."

I put my hand up and lightly touched the scar high up on his cheek. "Yeah, I can see why Daddy busted you one in the eye." I glanced at Chip. "Anybody who thinks that saying 'You can never have too much pussy' is a good way to actually get pussy doesn't seem like somebody bright enough to get the point unless we spell it out for him."

Eddie swatted my hand away. "And what's your point?"

I could feel Chip, Tony, Timmy, and Petey edging closer to me.

"My point is that this is our island, and we don't want you selling drugs to our kids."

Eddie shook his head. "Jesus. You and your dad." He pulled a can of beer out of the pocket of his sweatshirt. "Tell you what, why don't you and your friends get the fuck off my property?"

The other men around the fire had come up behind Eddie, and while they didn't seem much of anything—Eddie was by far the biggest of them, and none of them spent their days hauling lobster traps or working or doing much other than drinking beer and smoking meth—I suddenly regretted my bravado from a minute ago. I recognized one of the men, knew him as a James Harbor boy. Oswald Cornwall. I knew his brother more than I knew Oswald. His brother fished out of James Harbor, and was as decent a guy as came from that shithole of a town, but Oswald was already on his way to being a burnout. He'd done at least two stints in prison for cooking meth. He wasn't exactly imposing, but I could hear Daddy's voice in my head, telling me, like he'd told me before, that you should always try to avoid a fight if you can, and here I'd come in and basically stuck my hand in the wasps' nest. The two women drifted over as well, lingering behind the group of four men, and I realized that, whatever I thought about the physical fitness of Eddie and his friends compared to Chip, Tony, Petey, Timmy, and me, pushing Eddie into a corner wasn't the best strategy. Everybody always says that you need to stand up to a bully, that they can never take a punch, and whether or not that was true, the one thing that I knew was absolutely true was that if you take a bully and embarrass him in front of his cronies, sooner or later he'll figure out how to hurt you. I wouldn't have minded cutting him up a bit, and I'd already had my hand tucked back behind my hip, resting on my belt knife, but I forced myself to let my hands fall more naturally to my sides.

One of the women—she had her arms wrapped around herself like she was cold, despite the heavy sweatshirt she was wearing, the hood up and over her head—took another step forward, and then I recognized her as Eddie's wife, Nelly. She was someone who you could tell had once been pretty, but it was as if she'd sunk into herself, faded out, and she looked both older and younger than the twenty-four or twenty-five she must have been. She touched Eddie on the shoulder, and as she did, I realized that the other arm cradled a sleeping baby against her chest. Their daughter. "What's going on, honey?" Nelly said.

"Take Cindy over to Marissa's house," he said, not even bothering to look at her.

"But I—"

"I said, take the fucking baby, and go to Marissa's." This time, Eddie glanced over his shoulder at Nelly, and she leaned away from him, like she half expected him to hit her. "Go on," he said. The second woman tried to keep her face down, but it was too late. Even if Eddie wouldn't have said her name, I recognized Marissa.

Nelly slouched over the baby and brushed past me, heading toward the lane. I grabbed Marissa's arm, but didn't say anything. Marissa was the kind of trash that washes up on the island every few years, and I knew that if she didn't decide to move back to the mainland on her own, I was going to have a talk with her soon, to let her know it was time to wash away. Marissa didn't struggle, but she didn't look up at me, either, and I let go of her arm. We were all silent for a few seconds, listening to the sound of Nelly and Marissa's footsteps on the gravel as the two women walked away.

Part of me felt bad for Nelly that Marissa was the best she could do for a friend on Loosewood Island, but there was a bigger part of me that wanted to laugh at Eddie again. I had to imagine that there was something good about Eddie, that maybe he was a doting father, in love with baby Cindy, or that alone with Nelly he was tender and compassionate. Maybe he was funny and warm with his friends, the sort of guy who was always available with his pickup truck when you needed to move a couch or a fridge, but standing there in his yard, the flames of the bonfire sucking in and then raising higher as the logs shifted, he seemed like an unredeemable, unrepentant dick. I wanted to see what he'd do, what sort of stupid thing he'd say next, and then I wanted us to just laugh and walk away, wanted to go get a beer with the boys and spend a couple of hours joking about how pathetic Eddie was.

I could feel Timmy sliding up beside me, and I don't know if it was because we used to date or because I was already on edge, but without looking at him I could feel how twitchy he was, how small a provocation it was going to require for him to be the one to take the first swing. Which was the moment that Eddie chose to say, "What you staring at, nigger?"

Like I said, Eddie was a dick.

The amazing thing is that even after the quick scuffle and the few thrown punches, it didn't escalate. I told Eddie that if he was on the island at sundown tomorrow, if he sold drugs to another kid on Loosewood, I'd have the boys pin him down while I personally cut his nuts out. Not surprisingly, Eddie's reaction was to tell us to go fuck ourselves, but he and his buddies disappeared into his house.

Standing out by the fire, we could hear the music cranking up from inside of Eddie's house, and I couldn't help but think of their little girl, how she was screwed having Eddie for a father, and how maybe this was one kid who'd do better without both her parents in the picture. Petey spread his hands out in front of the fire and said, "You know, we ought to do this some nights." There was a crest of blood on the knuckles of one of his hands, and it caught the glimmer of the fire.

"What?" Chip said. He planted the butt of his rifle at his feet and then leaned over the cooler that was next to the fire and flipped up the lid. "Get in fights? Threaten to cut somebody's nuts off?" He pulled out a piece of ice and pressed it against his cheek.

As near as I could tell, he was the only one of our gang who'd actually gotten punched—Petey had definitely nailed one of Eddie's friends, and I thought Timmy had clipped somebody—and Chip was going to have a bruise to show for it. Served him right, I thought, for bringing his rifle along in the first place. He was lucky that things hadn't gotten to the point where he was tempted to use it. But then again, I could see how he thought that might send a certain message to Eddie, who seemed like the kind of guy who might take a hint better if it came at the end of a rifle's barrel.

"No, dickwad," Petey said, "build a fire like this. But do it on the beach. Bring down a cooler of beers, a few chairs, maybe get Kenny to bring down his guitar, and have a get-together." He laughed. "Any left in there?"

Chip reached down in the cooler again and pulled out a can of beer. "What do you think? Were they all high?" Chip asked. He tossed the beer softly to Petey, who fumbled it before pulling it in to his chest with both hands.

"Thanks, man," Petey said, and then pulled open the tab. "Beats the fuck out of me, but yeah, I sort of assume they were all high."

"That guy is such a shitbag," I said.

Petey raised his beer. "Here's to dealing with problems the old-fashioned way."

And that's when we heard the shot.

I wish I could say that we sprang into action, or even that we were smart enough to drop to the ground or run away, but all five of us stood there dumbly, looking around. It couldn't have been more than a second or two before Tony said, "Was that a gunshot?"

I looked over at Petey, and he was holding the can of beer out in front of him, staring at it like he wasn't sure what exactly was in his can, and I noticed that a stream of beer was leaking out the bottom. He looked at me and then said, in a voice that seemed more amused than frightened, "They shot my beer."

I heard the click of the safety and saw Chip pulling the bolt of his rifle back, but Timmy had already grabbed the barrel of the rifle and tilted it up before I turned. "You don't want to kill anybody," Timmy said.

"I sort of do." Chip shook his head. "I can't believe they shot a can of beer."

"I'd bet that they were trying to shoot over our heads and just aren't so good with a rifle," Tony said. "Actually, that's not so reassuring. Let's get out of here."

"You know," I said, as we turned to start moving down the

driveway, "I'm kind of impressed at how calm we're being about this." I reached down to grab a couple of beers for the road, and that's when I heard Eddie's voice calling, "Get out of here, you cunt."

I didn't think about it. I just said, "Fuck it," and then I pulled a log that was half eaten with flames from the fire. With one motion, I spun and swung it hard toward Eddie's house.

The burning log landed on the porch and sent up a shower of sparks.

"Yeah," Tony said with the sort of wryness that sounded like he'd been expecting me to do it, "that's calmness at its best."

"Guess we're burning them out tonight," Chip said, clearly gleeful, and he was already reaching into the fire himself, swearing when he caught an ember, before grabbing the unburnt end of another log and chucking it onto the roof of Eddie's house.

There's not a lot more to it than that. By the time the other guys had thrown a few more burning logs I was laughing, and then we took off, running away from there as the house went up in flames. I'm not proud that I laughed at it—I think I was laughing more from the stress of it than anything else—and I'd like to think that if Nelly and the baby had been in the house instead of just Eddie and his buddies, I wouldn't have done it, but at the time, it was exhilarating.

I'd showered before bed, and I showered again in the morning, but I could still smell the smoke on me. I took a book and went to the diner for breakfast, but other than a few sideways looks from some of the older fishermen, nobody said a word about Eddie Glouster or the fire. I was finishing up my hash browns when Tony slid into the booth across from me. He leaned forward, his voice quiet.

"Gone," he said.

"Gone?"

"The early ferry. All of them."

I squeezed some more ketchup onto my plate and dipped a forkful of potatoes. "Eddie?"

"All of them," Tony said. He looked around furtively, but nobody was paying attention. "Ain't nothing left but a pile of smoke and char."

"Stupid," I said. I took a sip of my coffee. I saw Helen coming toward me with the coffeepot, but I waved her off. "We were stupid. That could have gone south."

"What we were was right," Tony said. "You should have seen yourself. Woody would have been proud."

A bit of the hash browns got caught in my throat and I gave a cough. Would he? Would Daddy be proud? I wasn't looking forward to telling him what had happened.

Tony reached across and tapped the back of my hand. "Chip and I," he said, "we owe you. You did good, Cordelia. You took care of things like Woody would have. Trash like that doesn't belong on Loosewood Island."

He pulled his hand back and then picked at the skin around his thumb. He looked away from me and sank lower into his seat.

"Something else?"

He put his hands down on the bench and straightened up, but he still wouldn't look at me. "Kenny."

I knew what he was going to say, but I asked anyway. "Kenny, what?"

"Kenny was on the ferry, too. Had two big bags with him."

I was staring at Tony, but I was glad that he was looking at anything but me. I don't think he would have believed my words if he had seen my face. "I know. He's taking a little time."

Tony nodded. "Okay," he said. "Just so you know." He lifted himself out of the booth, reached over to bounce his fingers off the top of my hand again, and then walked out.

I took a sip from my coffee even though it had gone cold. I had to do something to give myself a second. Kenny.

I checked my watch. It was late enough for school to have started, for Rena to be at the fish shop. I needed to talk to her. I dug some cash out of my jacket pocket and dumped it on the table.

The fish shop wasn't officially open in the off-season, but I knew Rena would be in there, either doing the books or playing on her computer: she'd gotten involved in an online knitting community and spent a couple of hours each day chatting with ladies on the forums.

As I wiped my feet and pulled off my jacket, I was surprised to be greeted by my nephew, Fatty. Fatty had just turned six, and his name isn't Fatty; if anything, he looks skin and bones, though

I'd seen him knock away plenty of chicken nuggets and fries when he put his mind to it.

Back when Rena had Fatty, he'd come as a surprise. It wasn't exactly a surprise that she was having a baby so much as a surprise that she was having *two* babies. Even the doctor was surprised at the twins, which led Daddy to comment that maybe Rena and Tucker needed a better doctor. When they were born—a boy and a girl, a perfect pair—all Tucker had said was, "Well, I'll be painted with herring. We're going to need another crib." I don't know what the hell "painted with herring" means, but I can guess what Tucker thought it meant. It was just Tucker's way of trying to impress Daddy, saying something that sounded vaguely like a lobsterman might say it. I suppose being surprised like that—and make no mistake, getting an extra baby *is* a surprise—can make you say some strange things. Tucker's become a decent lobsterman in his own right these past five years.

He and Daddy have a complicated relationship. Daddy isn't exactly easy to please, and he's been happy with Tucker on the boat. Things can be different on land, however. There was a spell when Daddy was talking like it would be Tucker taking over the business instead of me, but then Rena and Tucker hit a bit of a rough patch in their marriage. Daddy didn't pry too much, but it was enough to end the talk of Tucker being slipped in as the heir to the Kings. It left some bruises, though, both with me and with Tucker, and I wondered how Daddy and Tucker would fare on a boat with Carly's girlfriend thrown in the mix. It was going to be a sight to see Stephanie, Tucker, and Daddy together on the *Queen Jane*.

Tucker and Rena had named the twins Johnny and Mary. Johnny after Tucker's dad, who lived in California, where Tucker had grown up, and Mary after Momma. You could see Daddy wasn't sure how to take the name of his granddaughter, and he did what he usually did, which was to pretend there wasn't anything to it. Still, he never called Mary by her name. He called her Guppy from minute one, and once he started, it took off with everybody on the Island. Even Tucker and Rena were calling her Guppy before the first month was out. Johnny, however, got his nickname later.

Daddy had opened the fish shop even before the twins were born, and he'd given over the running of it to Rena when she returned to the island. When the kids were still too young for school they spent most of their time up there with her, and had their run of the place. During the summer Fatty was three, we had a real heater—ninety degrees for three weeks on end—and there wasn't a building on Loosewood Island set out with air-conditioning. Guppy was her usual sweet self, but Fatty had been a high holy terror, screaming anytime his mommy or daddy, or even when I, who was always his favorite, tried to get him into a set of clothes, even just underwear. So after a few days of this, Rena gave up.

"Let him walk around with his dick flapping away," she said. "What's the difference? The kid's three, it's hot enough to melt an iceberg, and if some tourist gets his pants in a bunch because Johnny's not wearing clothes, well, they can buy their fish somewhere else."

There wasn't anywhere else, of course, and nobody complained. But each and every time somebody came into the shop, Johnny came running out yelling, "Look at my belly! I'm a fatty!" It was both horrifying and hilarious, and of course, lobstermen being lobstermen—which is to say, maybe not as aware of the niceties of things—the name Fatty had stuck. At six, he'd turned into a sweet kid, finally matching Guppy's temperament, and when I looked up as he called my name I saw that he was sitting on the stool behind the counter, holding the *James Harbor Tide*. "You reading the newspaper?" I asked.

"Nah. Just looking at pictures."

"Aren't you supposed to be in school, Fatty?"

"I had a fever last night, so Mom kept me home today. I puked, too," he said.

I hung my jacket up on the hooks behind the counter and

pulled him into a hug. I kissed his forehead, letting my lips linger on his skin like I was a mother myself. "Not too hot."

"No," he said. "Haven't had a fever at all today."

Rena stuck her head out of the back room and scowled. "Is it true?"

"You heard?" I meant about Kenny, because that's why I'd come. I had to choke the words out, but that wasn't what Rena meant.

"Of course. The fire's all anybody's talking about today. That and James Harbor making a play."

Fatty looked up. "What fire?"

Rena stepped over to her son and stood behind him, resting her arms around his neck. She leaned down to him and said, in the same voice I sometimes recognized her using with Daddy when he started to get belligerent, "You want to run over to the coffee shop and pick up something sweet for you and Guppy to split when she gets home from school?" He jumped from the stool and was almost out the door when Rena called him to a halt and made him get a raincoat on.

"You involved in that fire, Cordelia?"

I wiggled my hand. "Something like that."

"Daddy's going to have a fit."

"Daddy needs to understand that I can handle my own business," I said. I went over to the cooler and pulled out a can of soda water.

"You going to pay for that?"

I popped the tab of the soda water. The hit of the bitter bubbles felt good. "Add it to my tab."

Rena gave me the finger, but then she held out her hand. "Grab me one, will you?"

I handed her a can and then I leaned back against the glass door of the fridge. I looked down at my hands. My nails were chipped. I never bothered painting them during fishing season, but when the traps were out of the water I usually kept them neat. When I looked back up, Rena wasn't drinking from her soda water. She squinted at me and then said, "It's something else, isn't it? You didn't come to talk about Eddie Glouster."

"No," I said, but I started with Eddie Glouster anyway. I told her everything that had happened the night before, and then I told her about Carly coming back to Loosewood Island, and then I told her about talking with Kenny and about Sally's leaving.

"Shit," Rena said. "I don't feel strongly about Sally one way or the other—" I rolled my eyes and she said, "Come off it, Cordelia, she's not *that* bad, and they had something once, and maybe they would have made a go of it somewhere other than the island. But that's sure a crappy way for a husband to find out a marriage is over."

"It's hard, sure," I said, "but don't you think that maybe it's for the best? I mean, I feel bad for Kenny. He looked like he'd taken a punch in the face, but they've been having problems from the jump."

Rena pushed Fatty's stool back to the counter, folded the newspaper, and closed the door to the back office. "Sometimes it's worth working through things."

She wasn't talking about Kenny and Sally. I knew that. There'd been a rough stretch for her and Tucker, but they'd righted the ship.

Rena peered over my shoulder and out the window looking over the ocean and then glanced up at the clock on the wall. "Daddy's back."

I felt sick all of a sudden, like I did when I was a kid and Momma told me I was going to have to wait for Daddy to get home to give me a punishment. Whether or not it was the right thing to do, I wasn't looking forward to explaining what had happened with Eddie Glouster. "He shouldn't have been back until this afternoon," I said.

"Well, that doesn't change the fact that he's walking up from the harbor."

"Not a word about Carly," I said, and Rena nodded.

We stopped him before he got to the diner.

"What are you doing back so early?" Rena said. She folded her arms over her chest. I realized I was already standing in the same position. A few of the old boys in the diner noticed us confronting, Daddy, and through the window I could see them laughing.

"There's nothing pernicious about it," Daddy said. Pernicious. Him and his five-dollar words. "They told me I could come home. Boat ran smooth and I made good time."

"And?" Rena said.

"And nothing," he said. "She ran some tests—"

"She?" I said.

"Yes, Cordelia. It's 2005. We've got lady doctors," he said, pointedly not looking at me as he added, "and even lady lobstermen now." I gave him a scowl for that. I could see Rena was trying not to laugh, no doubt thinking the same thing I was, which was that the idea of Daddy dressed in just a flimsy gown in front of a female doctor seemed ludicrous. Even getting him to go to Dr. Jamison, whom he'd known for thirty years, was always a struggle. "She did one of those heart things with the lines, drew some blood, made me piss in a cup, and had me sleep with a bunch of tubes and wires attached to me. Anyway, she said she'd give me a call in a couple of days."

Fatty came running out of the coffee shop carrying a bag with some sort of pastry in it, and ran over to us. He wrapped himself around Daddy's leg. "Grandpa! Want some cookie?"

Daddy chuckled and shook his head. "No, thanks, Fatty. It's all yours."

Fatty nodded and then looked at Rena and said, "I'm going to head over to school and wait for Guppy."

"You come right back with her," Rena said, "and don't you touch any of your sister's cookie." Fatty nodded and then ran off.

Daddy turned and looked at me. "I heard the news, Cordelia. You okay?"

The certainty I'd had the night before that we'd done the right thing at Eddie Glouster's evaporated. "You heard about the fire already?"

Daddy glanced at Rena and then back at me. "No. But I'm about to."

"What—"

"I was asking about Kenny. I saw him getting off the ferry with his bags. Had a little chat." He rubbed my shoulder. "You okay with this?" I nodded, but it was purely a mechanical action. I felt a little dizzy. "So what's this about a fire?"

I glanced at the door of the coffee shop and then took a few steps away. Daddy and Rena followed. "Eddie Glouster," I said, and I could see Daddy tighten up.

I told him the whole story, from my conversation with Tony and Chip through to me throwing the log.

When I finished, Daddy nodded. "Saw him and his wife getting off the ferry, too. He didn't look too pleased to see me. Chalked it up to the usual."

"I think she did the right thing," Rena said. I felt a swell of love for her. Rena and I were close, but she didn't always take my side of things with Daddy, and it meant something that she spoke up before Daddy weighed in. I started to give her a sideways smile, but then Daddy spoke.

"And I think it was foolish. You know better than that, girl." I looked down at the ground. "Look at me," he said. His voice wasn't loud, but there was a snap to it, and I looked up. "That was dangerous. Next time you come talk to me and I'll take care of it."

"No," I said.

I hadn't expected the word to come out of my mouth, and when it did, I felt my hand start to rise, like the word was a physical thing that I could snatch back.

"Excuse me?" he said.

But the word was already out there. I kept my gaze up this time. "No. I can't have you always taking care of things for me, Daddy."

Even though I was looking at Daddy, I could see Rena swiveling back and forth, staring at us. Daddy was quiet for a few seconds. And then he nodded.

"Okay," he said. "I suppose it's going to happen sometime or other. We done, then? Because I could use a coffee."

Daddy turned and put his hand on the door of the diner, but Rena stopped him. "Daddy," she said, "what else did the doctor say?"

He looked at Rena and then he looked at me, and neither one of us gave any ground. He sighed and then pulled a bottle of pills out of his pocket. Rena snatched them out of his hand.

"Fiber?" Rena looked up at Daddy and then back at the bottle of pills again. I took them from her, read the label, and then echoed her.

"Fiber? The doctor gave you fiber supplements? Why?" I turned the bottle over to look at the back of the label, as if that would explain it to me.

Rena closed her eyes firmly and then opened them. "So, you're saying that you passed out in your kitchen, went to the doctor, had a round of tests, and you're coming home with...

fiber supplements? Cordelia finds you out cold in the kitchen and the doctor is worried about your bowel movements?"

Daddy took the pill container back and stuffed it into his pocket. "Well, at least that time you spent in nursing school is good for something," he said. "Yes, the doctor is worried about my bowel movements. Not that it's any of your business, but yesterday, when I stood up from the toilet, I got dizzy. When Cordelia found me, I suppose I didn't want to have to tell my daughter that I'd passed out because I was trying too hard to take a shit. Okay? There."

I tried to keep my face straight, but I couldn't. I started to giggle and so did Rena.

Daddy scowled. "Oh, grow up, you two. I like to keep my own things as my own things, but what the doctor said, more or less, is that I'm getting old. She said all of the usual things: eat better, watch my weight, multivitamins, baby aspirin, less salt. She'll call me with test results in a couple of days, but in the meantime, she wants me to take fiber supplements and to try not to get myself too worked up." He let a little scowl soften and he poked me in the shoulder. "Which means that if you can avoid burning any other houses down, that would be terrific. And if there is anything else that the two of you need to know, I'll tell you, okay? Now," he said, with a smile that I wasn't sure was entirely real, "is there anything else, or can I finally go get a coffee?"

"Decaf," Rena said. "If the doctor is saying she doesn't want you to get too worked up, make it a decaf, okay?"

I realized that he hadn't looked at me. There was something he wasn't telling us. That was nothing new. There was always something he wasn't telling us. Maybe he figured it was something we didn't need to know. Which reminded me: "Daddy," I said, "did you talk to George?" He shook his head. "Word is that George found some James Harbor buoys out in our waters while he was motoring around today."

Rena glanced at me and then at Daddy. "Lobster season doesn't start until next week. Shit. I think Tucker has a color-coordinated chart of television shows he means to watch before heading back out on the *Queen Jane*."

"They aren't trying to catch lobsters," Daddy said. "They're just trying to horn in on our territory. Figure if they get the traps out it will be a fait accompli. By the time our season starts and we're out and fishing it will be too late."

"What are we going to do about it?" I said.

"You know I just came back from spending the night in the hospital, right? That the doctor's telling me not to get too worked up? And I'm gone for twenty-four hours to find that Kenny's off the island, you decided to burn out Eddie Glouster, and James Harbor is already in on our waters." He rubbed his hand on the stubble on his cheek. "What are we going to do about James Harbor? What do you think, Cordelia?" he said as he hauled open the door of the diner. He paused, glancing in the diner to make sure everybody was paying attention, and then looked back at Rena and me, his voice loud enough to carry both inside and out. "We'll encourage the James Harbor boys to get out of our waters, and if that doesn't work, we'll go to war."

That, to me, didn't seem like the best way of keeping himself from getting too worked up.

Daddy looked around at Carly, Stephanie, Rena, Tucker, and me, and then he placed his hands flat on the table. "I feel like King Lear trying to divide up his kingdom," Daddy said. "But it's better to do it now than to have problems later." I made a face, and he laughed.

"What?" Rena asked.

"I've read *Lear*," I said to her. "It ends poorly."

"You know what else ends poorly?" Daddy said. "Dinner without dessert. And while we're at it, a little salt won't kill me. The doctor said to watch what I eat. Cut down on red meats, less fat, olive oil instead of butter when possible, and less salt. Not no salt. Just less salt. A little salt." He pulled himself straight up in his chair and looked down at his hands. The five of us waited. "I'm not fixing to retire, but the truth of it is that all men age, and Carly," he said, "if you're seriously intent on moving home and shacking up with Stephanie"—he nodded toward Stephanie, who blushed—"we've got some logistics to work out." He stood up, like he'd forgotten something, and walked over to the window. There were some high, gray clouds kiting across the sky with speed, and out in the harbor there was enough wind to bounce the waves white. I thought it was going to be a rough ride across to the mainland for Stephanie and Carly after lunch; they'd come down for the weekend to tell Daddy about their plans to move to the island, and they'd looked like they were feeling it on the way in on Friday night. Stephanie, I knew, didn't have much experience on a boat, despite her intentions of becoming Daddy's new sternman, and Carly had gotten used to life with her feet on the mainland.

"This is what I've got," Daddy said, waving off toward the water. "You know I love you, and I've been straight and fair with all of you, haven't I?"

"Yes, Daddy," Rena said. Carly echoed with a quick yes of her own, and for a moment it looked like she wanted to add something else, to put in more than Rena had, but she changed her mind. I didn't say anything, but in the swiftness of my sisters' answers, I suddenly realized how generous Daddy had been.

I guess it says something about me that I hadn't thought much of it. Or maybe it says something about Daddy? Either way, Daddy had been fair with us, not splitting things down the middle—or three ways—but divvying up as things needed to be divvied. Rena and Tucker had gotten the biggest house, because they'd come to Loosewood Island with the twins, and Daddy had given over the fish shop to Rena's care and taken Tucker on as a sternman. He'd written checks for Carly, helping her pay rent those first couple years when she was teaching, and he'd set me up with my boat, paying for the bulk of the *Kings' Ransom*. He paid for college for all of us and bought Carly her last car.

"Carly," Daddy said, "you've already been sneaking around my back with Principal Philips, so you're taken care of with a job, which means that Stephanie, you're up first. Carly's been asking if you can be my sternman. What my baby asks for, my baby gets. If you want the job, I'll take you on. So you know, I won't pay you a penny until you've earned it. That seem fair to you?" Stephanie nodded, but Daddy kept looking at her. "You sure that's what you want, Stephanie? It's hard work."

"I can do it," she said. She actually believed she could. She looked almost like a child sitting on the other side of Tucker. She was small, even next to Carly, but she had no doubt that she could handle the waves, no doubt that she could handle stuffing bait bags and sorting and gauging lobsters and the constant lift and pull and carry of working on a boat. And I don't know why, but suddenly, even if it was just for a minute, I believed she could do it, too.

"Excellent. And now that you're my sternman, my first order is for you to go into the kitchen and get some dessert." We all laughed, but Daddy frowned. "I'm not joking. Go get some dessert, Stephanie."

"Don't do it, honey," Carly said, putting her hand on Stephanie's wrist. "You aren't on the *Queen Jane* yet." She had a big grin on her face, and I could tell that she felt that having Daddy take Stephanie on as his sternman was like passing a test. Maybe she didn't get to work the water with him, but her girlfriend would. Now all Stephanie had to do was to be damn good at the job.

Daddy sighed and looked to me. "What I have to deal with from you girls."

"I would have gotten you dessert," I said.

"I'm sure you would have," Daddy said. "That's why you're my favorite."

The words curdled the smile on Carly's face. It wasn't a joke to her. I don't think anybody else but me noticed, because Daddy had already turned to look at Tucker.

"Well, then, Tucker," Daddy said, "I guess you're probably wondering just what the hell we'll be doing with a second sternman, but the short answer is, you're fired."

He winked when he said it, and his voice sounded warm enough that there wasn't any real cause for concern, but that didn't stop Rena from clicking her tongue and saying, "That's not funny, Daddy."

"Oh, simmer down, little hen," Daddy said. "Tucker isn't fired, but he's done working on the *Queen Jane*. It's been a long time coming, Tucker, but we'll have to move you to your own boat. Rena's been badgering me and badgering me, and I suppose I've been putting it off because you've been such a good sternman. But you'll make a fine captain, and with Stephanie coming on as a sternman, your job's taken anyway. Besides, this way I can get Rena to stop harassing me."

"I haven't been—"

"Come on, Rena," Daddy said. "You know how you do it. Stopping by the house with your, 'Oh, I just happened to be baking brownies and I thought I'd bring some over and don't you think Tucker would run a boat just fine?' sort of questions." Rena blushed, but she laughed with the rest of us, because it really was the way she got all of us to do things. "Anyway," Daddy continued, "I've gotten tired of Rena asking, so I called around this morning, and I found a promising-looking boat for us to see in Saint John. She's got some miles on the body, but she's in good shape with a new engine and it's coming from a fellow I trust at a fair price. If she checks out okay with you, I'll buy it and you'll run it the way you want to. She's called the *McMolly*, so obviously you'll have to give her a new name." He offered up a smile. "I'm not letting my son-in-law fish a boat called the *McMolly*. As for everything else, well, I've already made a call about you getting your own license, and that's set, and I talked to John O'Connor, and Colin will be your sternman. Now that Colin's past being a teenager, it's getting too much for John to be working with his own son. Colin's learned well and he seems to have gotten over needing to get drunk every night and sleeping with every tourist wearing a skirt. He'll do well by you, and it will be a couple of years before he'll be looking for his own boat. Who knows? Maybe by that point Stephanie will be ready for her own boat, too, and we'll need to find a whole gaggle of new sternmen."

Tucker sucked in his stomach and looked like he wanted to burst from his chair to give Daddy a hug, but all he said was, "Thanks, Woody."

"You earned it," Daddy said. "Otherwise I wouldn't be doing it."

"Thanks, Daddy," Rena said, and I saw her move her arm so that she could take Tucker's hand under the table. I knew she'd give Daddy a hug later on.

"So, Cordelia, that leaves you," Daddy said.

"Yeah?"

"Carly asks for a job on the water for her girlfriend, Rena asks for a boat for her husband, and you? You don't ask me for anything? You're playing a little too closely to your name, girl." He grinned and then said, "Well, I guess if you ask for nothing, you get nothing. How about I buy you a beer the next time we're at the Fish House?"

"Big spender," I said, and I got up to clear the dishes from the table. It was the sort of thing that Rena normally took care of, but I needed to get out of the room. It had only been two weeks since Daddy had fainted, since Carly had told me she was moving back to Loosewood Island, but that was two weeks of Kenny being gone as well. I hadn't seen him since the morning of the day I'd burned out Eddie Glouster: Kenny was gone, off the island, a ghost.

I hadn't asked Daddy for anything, because I didn't have anyone to ask for.

Brumfitt Kings wrote near the end of his first journal that he saw a lobster the size of a horse. Not a big horse, but still. He compared the lobster to a horse. That's a big fucking lobster.

This would have been when he was still the only man living year-round on Loosewood Island. When the fishing boats were there, he worked catching codfish and he worked on the shore as well, putting the fish out on flats for drying and making sure that the boats would return home with the cash crop of the sea. He fished whatever his captain told him to fish, and whatever boat he was on had the kind of hauls that the men could barely keep up with. Once the boats left, however, he went after lobster.

I've read that back in the old days prisoners were fed it so often that they petitioned to have lobster taken off the menu, but Brumfitt seemed to recognize early that lobsters meant something special to the Kings. He has dozens and dozens of drawings of lobsters in his journals. Minute, detailed sketches of mouths and antennae, of the lobster's gills and swimmerets, of female lobsters with their undersides coated with eggs. When the boats were gone and he was left to his own devices, he ate a lobster almost every day, walking down to the ocean and snagging one with his hands, that's how thick they were around the island nearly three hundred years ago.

Lobsters figure in to some of his paintings, but mostly in the paintings that are light and airy, free of menace, and I sometimes used to wonder if it was the presence of lobsters themselves that made those paintings easier. Sort of like, for Brumfitt, a lobster meant everything was going to be okay, and in those other paintings, where there are no lobsters, that's when things go all to hell. But there are a couple of exceptions to my little theory.

Lobster Pot and Fisherman's Wife, which is about what you'd expect, and *Tucking In*, which shows a couple of boys, about the age Scotty was when he died, eating a bunch of lobsters with gusto, are the prints you are mostly likely to see in a seafood restaurant. In those, the lobsters are obvious, but in the rest of the lighter paintings, even if it isn't somewhere obvious, there's a lobster hidden somewhere. The more menacing paintings, the paintings that cemented his reputation when he was "discovered," rarely feature lobsters. I'm most interested in that weird group of paintings, however, that falls outside either of those other two groups, and with those fifty or so paintings, there's no making sense of the presence of lobsters. Sometimes they serve as a sort of talisman, breaking the winds and the storms, and at other times they seem the destroyers of the deep, crusher claws grasping at fishermen's arms, or swarms of them threatening to overtake the land.

If Brumfitt wrote his journals now, I'd read them as some sort of fiction, or maybe as the product of mental illness, but I think that when Brumfitt wrote that he saw a lobster as big as a horse—"one fit for a large child to ride, or to pull a small cart"—it was as real as anything else he painted or saw. I believe in Brumfitt's stories and paintings the way that I believe in Daddy's stories of Loosewood Island; Brumfitt was just trying to capture the sea and its power and how little control we have over it. He was just trying to capture the darkness.

If Brumfitt's lobster was real, I'd be curious how big it would be now, if it could possibly have survived. Scientists have said that the older a lobster gets the less often it sheds its shell, but each time a lobster sheds its shell, it pumps itself up with seawater and grows a new shell that lets it get about fifteen percent longer and increase its body weight by fifteen percent. How big would that lobster be nearly three hundred years later?

The next week, on an off day, Daddy and Tucker went to Saint John to look at the *McMolly*. Evidently the boat was to Tucker's liking, because he came home with it, and we had a small ceremony to rechristen it the *Twin Torpedo*.

Rena stood with me on the dock sipping from our tiny plastic glasses full of champagne. We watched Tucker—who was drinking fizzy apple juice with Guppy and Fatty—giving the twins a tour of the new boat. We couldn't hear what he said, but Guppy gave him a big hug, and then Tucker lifted her up and put her on the captain's chair.

"Huh," I said. "If that was Daddy, Fatty would have been the first one of the kids sitting there." I tried to drop my voice into an imitation of Daddy. "Here you go, son, you're the future."

"You'll never let it go, will you?"

Rena put her hand on my back and gave it a gentle rub. I knew she was trying to be nice, but mostly it pissed me off, which was why I shot back, "I should let it go like you just let everything go? That it? The way you let things go with Tucker?"

She looked away from her kids and stared at me. She wasn't trying to hide the fact that she was angry. "It's been three years,

Cordelia, and things were different. Sometimes marriages go through a rough patch. I've forgiven Tucker. Even Daddy's let it go. You can't?"

I looked back at her and tried to keep my gaze steady. I felt shitty about it. I told myself to let it drop, but I couldn't. "Daddy hasn't let it go, Rena. He still doesn't even know the whole deal with what happened with you and Tucker. Do you think Daddy would still be okay with Tucker if he knew that Tucker had cheated on you? What Daddy thinks is that Tucker was drinking too much and then quit and that you've patched things up. Daddy's given Tucker a second chance, too. That's not the same thing as letting it go."

Rena and I just stared at each other, and I honestly didn't know what to do. She'd always backed down before, always let me have my way. That was the way she worked. But there was some defiance there, and it made me wonder if maybe there were some things about my sister I didn't quite understand. Thankfully, after what felt like hours but was just a few seconds, Fatty called to Rena from the deck of the boat. She looked away to wave at her son, and then she shrugged. "He hasn't had a drink since we got back together. He was different when he was drunk. You know that."

What I knew was that, at least at first, Tucker's drinking hadn't seemed like much of anything. When he and Rena had moved to the island, Kenny passed over to me as sternman and Tucker had taken on with Daddy. It worked out well. Kenny and me hit it off—both work and personal—and things seemed good with Daddy and Tucker on the *Queen Jane*. The first week or two, Tucker had busted ass for Daddy. Rena said that even with the work gloves he was coming home with his hands raw and blistered, but he kept at it, and by the end of that first season Daddy had gotten to telling anyone who would listen that Tucker was a first-rate sternman. It was funny to watch how Tucker had puffed out at that. I suppose I did the same thing when Daddy talked about how I'd turned into the kind of lobsterman he thought was worthy of the name Kings. So Tucker took to having a few beers with us on Friday nights when we got together, had a few more when we celebrated at the end of the season, and it didn't seem anything to think of.

Then, in the middle of Tucker's second season, it seemed like Tucker was doing a little too well as Daddy's sternman for my taste. Daddy didn't go so far as to say he'd be handing things over to Tucker, but he started making comments about how it seemed like Tucker had been born to it, how even though I'd been out on a boat since I was a kid, Tucker more than held his own. There were even a couple of times when Daddy said that Tucker worked the water like he was a Kings. It brought back some of the bullshit from when I was a kid and Daddy couldn't understand that I was suited for the water in a way that Scotty wasn't. It was like Daddy saw Tucker and saw what he could have had if Scotty were still alive, but in seeing Tucker that way, it made me invisible. I probably should have talked with Daddy about it, but I didn't. I sulked instead. I pulled into myself and my boat, spending my free time on the *Kings' Ransom* or out with Kenny and with Timmy and Chip and Tony and the boys. I did my best to stay away from Daddy and Rena and Tucker. For a while I couldn't look any of them in the eye. And maybe that's why I didn't realize at first that things had gone totally to shit in Rena and Tucker's house.

I guess it goes to show you that even on an island this small, it *is* still possible to keep some secrets if you try hard enough. It took two years for things to come to a head, and by then Rena said Tucker had gotten up to a six-pack every night, more on nights when he knew he didn't have to work the next morning.

Tucker is mostly an okay guy. He tries too hard with Daddy and the other boys sometimes, trying to make up for what he can never make up for, which is a bad childhood in California. Rena tells me that he's the one who always comes up with the idea for my birthday presents. He's a pushover with the twins, and he adores the shit out of Rena, always kissing her and touching her and calling her made-up names that should sound funny coming from a grown man's lips but end up being endearing. But he found it harder than he expected on the island, and he turned out to be an easy drunk.

And all the while, Daddy didn't notice anything. He kept talking about how good a job Tucker did on the boat, and how he could see Tucker keeping things up when Daddy retired. But that kind of talk ended when Rena moved out of the house with the twins. She told Daddy part of the truth, that Tucker's drinking had gotten out of hand, but didn't tell him the rest, which was that Tucker had been carrying on with another woman. There was a month or two of things being touch-and-go, and then Tucker came crawling up to the door, telling her that he'd changed, begging her to give him another go. She had, and things had been good for them ever since, but Daddy seemed like he'd forgotten any talk of Tucker being the kind of man who could have been born a Kings.

"I guess everybody deserves a second chance?" I said.

"You've heard Daddy say it often enough. A second chance, but never a third. Tucker knows it, too. He hasn't had a drink since the troubles."

I tilted back my cup and took down the last of the champagne. "At least Daddy doesn't think he's the second coming of Scotty anymore."

Rena stood up and stared at me again, like she had a few minutes earlier, and it scared me. She looked angry.

"I'm not a fucking pushover, Cordelia. Just because you're out on the water working with Daddy doesn't mean that you know everything." She glanced down at the plastic glass I was holding and then took it from me, slipping it under hers. With her hand free again, she poked me in the arm. "You haven't been *chosen* by anybody or anything. And no matter how hard you work, you'll never make up for the fact that Scotty's gone and Momma's gone. You'll never make him forget that."

She closed her mouth and then took what seemed like an

involuntary step. "Oh, my god," she said. "Oh. I'm sorry. That just slipped out."

I took a deep breath and then gave myself a moment to let it out. "Well, then. I guess, don't hold back?"

She stepped to me and then wrapped her arms around me. I didn't move away, but I didn't hug her, either. "Oh, I didn't mean that. I just..."

"No," I said. "I'm sorry. I was attacking your husband, and you took a swing of your own."

She squeezed and then let go and wiped her eyes. She was crying, which wasn't a surprise to me. She was always an easy cry. "Marriage is complicated, Cordelia. You just don't know. That was a hard time. It wasn't as simple as Tucker being the bad guy. He wasn't the only one who was having a hard time with our marriage."

On the boat, Fatty was sitting in the captain's chair, and Tucker had opened the engine compartment and was looking in it with Guppy by his side. Guppy pointed to something, and Tucker shook his head and then guided her hand to the side. "He's something else with those kids, isn't he?" I said.

Rena leaned onto the rail. She smiled. I wasn't sure if it was at Tucker or at me. "He never seems to run out of patience with them, even when they're both ganging up on him."

Tucker looked up at us, and when he caught Rena's eye he smiled so fully and easily that it stung me to watch. I don't know that I'd ever be able to get past what had happened, but in almost every way he'd turned out to be a good guy.

I couldn't deny that he loved my sister or that she loved him back.

Near the end of July, I slept with a tourist named Otto. It was exactly what I needed: an excuse to stop thinking about Kenny.

That sort of getting together between tourists and islanders happens more than you'd think, though not usually with me. Usually it's one of the boys who puts on his slickers for a lonely housewife from Indiana or South Dakota who thought taking a month-long rental on the island would be just the thing to spark her inner artist. Sometimes the women were single or married but traveling alone and just wanted "a taste of the local seafood," as Rena liked to put it, and sometimes those things ended up working out, like with Timmy and Etsuko. Usually it didn't mean anything beyond a few nights of fun. The boys like to joke that you got to break out the fishing pole more during the tourist season than you did when you were actually fishing. Of course, there was also the long-running joke that when the single boys on Loosewood Island weren't catching lobsters, they were catching crabs.

I'd been having a hard go of it. It had been nearly three months, and I missed Kenny. Sally waited until school finished before she had her boyfriend move her out—turned out the therapist she'd been seeing on her own had been putting her on the couch in a serious way—but there just wasn't a trace of Kenny from the day he found out. I suppose if we would have lived somewhere other than Loosewood Island, somewhere with cell phone reception, I might have been able to call his mobile, but there wasn't any way to get in touch with him that I knew of. Some nights when I took Trudy out for a walk I detoured by his house, but with Sally gone, the lights stayed off and the house was just a blot against the darkness of the sky.

I fished without a sternman for the spring, but once the season ended, I was left with trying to keep myself busy, trying to pretend that I wasn't just spending my time waiting for Kenny to come back. June and July were broken-up days of doing a bit of everything: I fixed stuff at the rental houses, painting and doing general maintenance, ran "lobstering" tours for tourists, took visitors on Brumfitt Kings walks, gave Rena a hand at the fish shop, and took the twins two nights a week so Rena and Tucker could have "date nights." It was make-work, but still, I had plenty of downtime. I even took a week with Daddy to fix up the garage behind my house—we'd decided I'd move into the smaller of the rental houses so that Stephanie and Carly could take my house—into a studio for Stephanie to do art when she wasn't on the *Queen Jane*.

And that still left too much time for me to think about Kenny.

I'd started jogging in the mornings, heading out early, trying to work off my fretfulness. With Kenny gone, I was up to six miles a day. I still wasn't sleeping much, so it was only about five-thirty by the time I'd gotten halfway into my run and I stumbled across Otto.

I'd taken one of the oceanfront paths that the island maintained out of its general funds, which only meant that we paid some of the teenage boys to keep it in shape, threw down crushed shells every few years. I was maybe three miles in when I saw Otto sitting on a rock and staring across the water.

I can't say what it was that made me stop and talk to him. Perhaps it was his stillness. He was just sitting and looking at the water, and that seemed like it was enough for him. For the week we were together, he seemed content the whole time, whether it was sitting there on the rock, having a beer with me and some of the boys at the Grumman Fish House, lying in bed after we'd had sex, or even out in the *Kings' Ransom* with me. Well, not as much in the *Kings' Ransom*, since being out on the water didn't seem to agree with him.

We talked for an hour or so, mostly me telling him what it was like to be a lobsterman—"But you are a woman," he said, which, despite the fact that he spoke English fluently, seemed particularly charming with his accent—and him telling me about his job as a curator at the German Maritime Museum in Bremerhaven, which I later realized was kind of funny given his inability to keep his food down on a boat. He told me that despite the presence of the ocean, Loosewood Island wasn't anything like his home in Germany.

There was nothing more to it than that. Neither one of us pretended we were falling in love. I suppose if we had more time together it might have been possible. He was good in bed—as graceful as he was, he was also forceful enough that I didn't have to worry about myself. I liked his fingers skittering across my back, snapping open my bra, threading down and across my hips. His lips whispering against my neck, the length of his body pressed against me, the way he shuddered in my arms when he came. Each moment with Otto was a moment with Otto and nobody else.

Actually, when Otto and I weren't having sex, mostly what we talked about was Brumfitt and painting. He was fascinated with the idea that I could trace a direct line to Brumfitt. Maybe the third or fourth night, I was lying on my stomach and Otto was propped up on one elbow, lightly rubbing my back with his free hand. The moon was strong enough that it felt like we were covered in light. He'd asked me what it had been like to grow up thinking of Brumfitt as something personal, as part of my own history rather than as an artist.

I rolled over onto my side so that I could see him. "I don't know," I said. "That's kind of like asking a fish what it's like to breathe underwater." Otto looked down at me, but he didn't seem to understand. "It's always been this way. It's not the same for my sisters, but for me, for Daddy, Brumfitt isn't just some guy who we're related to. Wherever I go on the island I see Brumfitt's paintings. I don't think, oh, there's a rock, there's a wave. I think, that's where Brumfitt painted *The Whale's Tail*, there's where he painted *Wife on a Winter's Day*. That's what I see when I'm on the island."

"But so do I," Otto said. "That is why I have the guidebook."

"No," I said. "It's not the same. You see the paintings, but I see the way that the paintings tell the story of the Kings. There's no Loosewood Island for me without Brumfitt." Otto lowered himself so that we were both lying down and facing each other. "Daddy likes to say that Brumfitt painted both the history and the future of the Kings family in his paintings, and all you have to do is look at them in the right order."

"Is this true?"

I leaned forward and kissed him lightly. "I don't know. But there's no question that Brumfitt hid something in his paintings. You know about the Harel find, right?" He shook his head. "Really?"

"I like Brumfitt, yes? I come here because of Brumfitt, but I am not living here."

"This would have been maybe fifteen years ago," I said, though I know exactly when it happened, because it was the summer after Scotty died, after Momma killed herself. "There was an academic, C. C. Harel, who had this theory that Brumfitt left a coded message in the landscape of *Sea Bounty*. A sort of map. She spent three months on the island with a team of graduate students, and they eventually found a chest buried inside a cavern on the lee side of the island. There were more than twenty Brumfitt paintings in the chest."

"Where are the paintings?"

"Tied up in court. Things get complicated pretty quickly

when both Canada and America start fighting. But we get a steady stream of tourists who come to the island with a shovel and the idea that they're going to find themselves a treasure trove."

"Has anybody else found any?"

"No," I said. "The tourists all leave disappointed."

He smiled and moved a little closer. "I'm not going to leave disappointed."

He was quiet for a few seconds, and just when I was beginning to think that he was planning to kiss me, he said, "Do you think there are more paintings to be found?"

I pushed his shoulder down so that he was flat on his back and then swung my leg up and over so that I was straddling him and looking down at him. "Yes," I said. "No. Maybe. Daddy claims there are others, that he knows of a stash of hidden Brumfitt paintings and he's just waiting for the right time to bring them out. Sometimes I think Daddy's a little bit crazy"—I winced when I said it, but I don't think Otto noticed, and he certainly didn't know of Daddy's history in the loony bin—"but sometimes I think that he knows what he's talking about."

When we weren't in bed, I showed Otto some of the places on the island that I didn't think he'd find on his own, and we spent some time painting together. Mostly he painted what he saw, realistic pieces that were decent enough, though he did do a few pieces that clearly mimicked Brumfitt. When he left, he gave me a small painting showing the *Kings' Ransom* tied up to her mooring buoy in the bay, a storm rolling toward the island in the background, and something sinister and indistinct in the water by the boat's transom.

"My little ode to Brumfitt. For you. Like your father said, to show you both what has happened and what it will feel like for you when I am gone," he said. He smiled in his shy way that was so unlike the men I was used to from the island, and for a moment I thought about asking him to stay. I didn't, however, because we both knew that things had run their course. I thanked him instead, and then we stood awkwardly waiting for him to board the ferry.

We said we'd email each other, and he made sounds about maybe coming back to Loosewood Island next summer, but I knew that next year he'd go somewhere else on his vacation—Thailand or Italy or Mexico—and I didn't see myself getting to Germany anytime soon. I didn't see myself living anywhere but Loosewood Island.

Despite my fling with Otto, the summer seemed to drag forever. It felt like all I did was wait: for Carly and Stephanie to move to Loosewood Island, for the fishing season to start again. Finally, the day before the season started, in mid-August, we moved Carly and Stephanie onto the island. I'd volunteered to give them my house and move into one of Daddy's smaller rentals—it made the most sense, but it was also a peace offering—but it meant I was going to have to move in with Daddy through mid-September, when the rental house opened up. Moving me was easy, since the rental was furnished, but Stephanie and Carly were a different matter.

Daddy, Tucker, and I drove down to Portland to help them pack up and drive the rental truck, and it turned out that they had a lot more stuff than you would have expected in a one-bedroom apartment.

"I've heard of people with baggage," I muttered, "but this is ridiculous."

Carly didn't smile. "Some people have more baggage than others, Cordelia."

I didn't bother responding. My baggage didn't need to be carried down three flights of stairs.

Even with Daddy, Tucker, and I leaving Loosewood Island before dawn—which is early, in August—we weren't back to the docks on the mainland and loading up the *Queen Jane* and the *Kings' Ransom* until late afternoon. By the time we hit the island and were down to the last dozen or so boxes, I was beat. I skipped over a large box and then another one that had BOOKS written on it, and grabbed a small box marked for the bedroom. Carrying it into what used to be my bedroom, I wasn't paying a lot of attention, and I didn't see that Trudy had spread herself out across the doorway.

I didn't fall that hard—it was more of an awkward stumble—but I landed partially on the box and the side split open. I got up on my knees and started stuffing the contents back in, a few shirts, a bathrobe, a scarf, and then I saw the necklace. It had been tucked inside a delicate wooden box, and when I'd fallen, the lid of the box must have slid open. There were only a few pearls of the necklace showing. I reached out to touch it, but then I hesitated.

I stood up and carried the box into the bathroom, putting it down on the counter, and then reached in and touched my fingers to the pearls. They were cool. I pinched them and then gently, very gently, pulled them out of the wooden box that they had been wrapped inside, and held them in the light. The necklace pooled in my hands. There was no question to me: this was Momma's necklace.

I looked in the mirror while I put the strand of pearls around my neck. I could feel my fingers fumbling—I thought of how nice it would be to have Momma still alive, to have her fasten it for me—and then it was on. I touched it, trying to remember exactly how Momma's fingers looked when she touched the necklace.

"What are you doing?"

I didn't jump, despite being surprised, and I didn't turn to look at Carly. I could see her well enough in the reflection. "You've had it the whole time?"

"What are you doing in my stuff?"

For a second I thought about explaining how I'd tripped, how I hadn't been snooping, but I was too angry to bother. "I thought it was gone. You took Momma's necklace. You just took it?"

I could see Carly weighing it, trying to decide what to say. "I didn't mean to. I just, you know, clearly your place was out on the boat with Daddy, and Rena and I were home with Momma, and I wanted . . ." She couldn't look at me. "I wanted something for myself. It was on her dresser. She wasn't wearing it when she . . ."

"Fuck you, Carly. Okay? Fuck you." I started to walk past her but she grabbed my arm.

"What are you doing?"

"What does it look like, Carly? I'm taking it." I grabbed her wrist and pulled her hand off my arm.

She looked pale, like she was going to be sick. "You can't just take it." She started to reach out again, but then she let her arm fall to her side. "Please," she said. "You've already got Daddy. What more do you want? Let me have it. It's mine."

I touched it again, and the thought of giving it back to her filled me with a kind of fury. "It was never your necklace, and it was never even Momma's."

"Don't tell me you believe that story of Daddy's?" She straightened up and actually gave a rough laugh. "That *this* is the necklace Brumfitt's wife was wearing when she was delivered from the ocean? Please don't tell me you believe that. What, the necklace doesn't belong to me because it belongs to the Kings?"

I pushed the rest of the way past her. "Welcome home," I said, tossing the words over my shoulder, but I didn't have the last say.

"If you believe that, Cordelia, then you better remember that there's a price for being a Kings," Carly said.

By the time I got back to the house I'd already taken the necklace off. There was a part of me that felt terrible, and I knew that I should take it back and give it to her, but I couldn't. Not yet. The pearls were cool and smooth in my fingers, and they made me realize how much I missed Momma; there wasn't that much that she had left behind. And it wasn't as if Daddy or I knew that the necklace still existed and had decided to give it to Carly in the first place. She had just taken the necklace on her own. I thought about bringing the necklace to Daddy, but in the end I hid it in one of my drawers and then took a shower.

I cleaned up and had a bite to eat and then it was time for the co-op meeting. We always held them the night before a new season started, and we always held them at the Grumman Fish House, partly because the co-op offices weren't big enough, and partly because the Grumman Fish House had beer. Mostly the latter.

Daddy waited until we'd all had a couple of drinks and the official business was finished before he brought it up. He came right out and said it. "So you probably all know, Carly's back on the island." He said it loud and in a break in the chatter, and everybody piped down. "And you probably all know that she's brought a girlfriend."

Timmy gave me a grin and I could see the Warner brothers, who were only in their second season of running their own boat, roll their eyes the way they did anytime they thought the old men were talking like old men. They'd had the same reaction when their dad spent most of January thinking aloud about getting "one of those computers" so that he could send "electronic mail." I wasn't worried about them, or any of the younger boys. Besides, Chip and Tony owed me after what had happened with Eddie Glouster, and I figured they knew what I'd do if they raised my hackles. No, it was different when you hopped generations from ours to Daddy's: it was people like George Sweeney and Mr. Warner and those fellows that Daddy was talking to, and I waited to see how it was going to go.

"Shit, Woody," George said, "I've known Carly since she was born, and it doesn't matter if she's dating a man or a woman, long as she's happy."

"As long as it's not some bastard out of James Harbor," Mr. Warner said, and at that everybody laughed a little harder.

Daddy shook his head. He had a small smile, but that came off his face as he raised his hand and spoke. "James. Fucking. Harbor." The room came to complete quiet. "That's what we need to talk about."

"I say we just cut 'em out," somebody called.

There were a few choruses in agreement, but Daddy held his hand up again. "No. You know as well as I do how that works," he said. "We cut a few of their traps, they cut a few of ours. The James Harbor fellows who are fishing out here are running a different season than we are, and they're running big rigs, at the limit or close to it, seven, eight hundred traps. They lose five or ten traps, it's going to seem a lot less personal than if we lose five or ten. We go to war, we go to war, but let's not hasten things."

We were smaller than they were, and had many fewer traps. We didn't want to get into a trap-cutting war with the James

Harbor gangs if we didn't have to, but I wasn't sure I agreed with Daddy that it was something we could avoid this time.

Daddy finished his beer and made the rounds. By eight o'clock he was ready to take off, and I walked with him. It felt odd to be walking back home with him, to know that Carly and Stephanie were setting up house in what I still thought of as my house, but it gave me a chance to talk to Daddy without all of the other boys around.

"You seriously think we can avoid a cutting war?" I asked him as soon as we were outside the door of the Grumman Fish House.

I thought I caught him taking a glance at me, but it was hard to tell, and besides, I was sort of knocked over by what he said: "I went to see that cunt, Al Burns."

"What?" I stopped walking, and Daddy took a few more steps before he stopped, too, and turned to wait for me. "When? By yourself?"

"Yes, Cordelia. By myself. I'm not going to whack him with a hammer every time I see him. And it was in the spring, when we first started having problems. We talked civilized, and Al promised to reel his boys in, keep them out of our waters before any warps got cut. They might have a lot more traps than us, but nobody wants to get into that kind of business."

He fidgeted, and I decided that I wasn't quite ready to start walking again. "All right," I said. "I can live with you going to see Al Burns."

"I wasn't looking for your approval on that, oh daughter of mine."

"Yeah, well, I'm sensing a 'but' that you haven't said yet."

Daddy sighed. "You're too smart sometimes. Anybody ever tell you that?"

"You have."

"But," he said, "the problem is Al. He didn't look too good, and I got the impression that he wasn't going to be able to hold those younger boys together. They've got a wild crew up there, and there's been a bunch of boys who've gone into lobstering in the last couple of years, but not that many retiring. They're pushing out of their boundaries. Everybody's fishing the maximum, and they're right on top of each other. Seems like some of them might be doing more than just running lobster traps, too."

"Meth," I said.

"Yep," Daddy said.

"Good money in it. A lot more dangerous than pot, though, so I don't know why you wouldn't just stick to that. A day running a load of pot over the border can make you the same as three months of hard fishing." Daddy gave me a hard look, holding it long enough that I realized he actually thought I might be running drugs. "Oh, for god's sake, Daddy, don't be daft," I said. "If I needed money, I'd come to you."

He kept the hard look for another second and then reached out and ruffled my hair. "Sorry, kiddo. You'll never not be my daughter." He turned, and we started walking again. "Yeah, the money's good in drugs, but it's not good news for us. James Harbor's pushing their limits for fishing, and it's an easy choice for them: try to take some of our waters or go after Northport."

He had a point to that, I thought. Northport had been hit hard by meth and coke and nobody wanted to go messing there. Northport was bigger than Loosewood Island and James Harbor put together, and despite once being a good town—unlike James Harbor, which had always been run-down—Northport had fallen hard and fast. When I was a girl, it was a treat to go there. But now? There were pockets of Northport that I wouldn't go to anymore, even in the middle of the day. Lobstering was down, but gunplay was up. The one serious drug problem we'd had on Loosewood Island so far—Eddie Glouster—had been solved by a little arson, but I didn't think that it was going to be that easy to run off other drug dealers if they set up shop in our waters. Just running pot from north to south had enough money in it that people were willing to kill over it, and I figured if the Northport boys were running coke and meth, there was even more at stake than with pot. It was simple. Pot's bulkier than either meth or coke, so a boy running a boat full of cocaine or meth over the border could make a lot more money than pot. In for a penny, in for a pound, I guess.

We passed a tourist couple who were in their late sixties. They were clearly Brumfitt tourists, and Daddy nodded in greeting as we walked by. "Lubec doesn't make a lot of sense. They've got more area because they've got more boats working, ten for every one of ours. No drug scene, or at least not as bad as what Northport has, but if James Harbor tried to step in there, they'd be outnumbered." He sighed and we turned off the path toward the house. "Sadly, we're the easy choice. What would you do? Pick a fight with Northport, which is already bursting at the seams and has some serious muscle invested in moving drugs, go at Lubec and know you're outnumbered, or see what might happen with us?" He held out his hand and started ticking it off: "Limited traps, big area of water, good lobster stock, and barely thirty boats running off an island with a population of less than two thousand."

"We're vulnerable," I said.

"They think we're soft," he said.

"A soft underbelly?"

I thought that would make him stop, and I said it to see if he'd get mad, but he just shrugged, which was not what I'd expected. "What happened with me and Al Burns happened a long time ago, Cordelia. You've got to learn to let things go." We turned into our yard and Daddy opened the gate. "My guess? They think that if they push us hard enough, we'll fold."

"Will we?"

He grinned at me. "Well, tomorrow's the first day of a new season. So we're bound to find out, aren't we?"

As soon as dawn broke, men were backing their trucks up to the wharf, unloading traps and stacking them on the ground, tying their boats to the dock and loading up gear. On the first day of a season, we all pitched in, nobody worrying so much about whose traps it was that you were hauling, just as long as we kept everything moving. We'd get a boat loaded up, the captain would motor off, and by the time four or five more boats were loaded and gone, that lobsterman would have returned to help. And it wasn't just us lobstermen who were carrying traps and giving a hand. The start of the season was an event that lasted most of the day. Lobstermen and wives were the first ones down at the docks, and as the morning progressed there were usually a few tourists who decided to jump in. By noon, the teenagers had all been rousted from their beds and they formed lines to pass the traps down.

Each boat could take anywhere from fifty to one hundred traps, depending on its size, which meant that we all had to take at least two trips, and sometimes three, to get our limit of one hundred and fifty traps in the water. It was a riotous mess of yelling and cursing and laughing. The day was cloudless and sixty degrees, perfect for working, but I couldn't have cared less if it had been thirty-three and sleeting, because Kenny was back.

He was waiting for me in Daddy's yard when I came out the porch door. Kenny was sitting on one of my traps and fiddling with his knife, snapping it open and then closed. He gave a smile when Trudy started yapping and slammed herself into him. She was so excited that I thought she'd wag herself over onto the ground. She let out these little moans that sounded like she was trying to sing.

"That's my girl." He scratched at Trudy's chest. Then he looked up at me and said, "Ready to load her up?"

I sat down next to him, and with that he looked away from me. Whatever confidence he had in his voice disappeared as I stared at him. "Where the fuck have you been?" I couldn't keep my voice from cracking.

He laughed, but he still didn't look at me. "I guess we're not just going to pretend nothing happened, yeah? I sort of like the idea of ignoring the obvious and just getting back to the way things were." Trudy dug her face between his legs, and he worked his fingers behind one of her ears.

"You've been gone for months. You skipped out of here even before Sally."

"I didn't feel like being here to wave her off when she left. I figured I'd rather be the one to leave than the one to be left behind."

"You didn't say anything to me. You just disappeared."

"I'm sorry," he said. "I know I should have something more to say, but I don't. I was a coward."

"But you're back," I said. I took the knife out of his hand. It made a satisfying click when the blade locked open. "You knew about what was going on with her therapist? He had the balls to show up and help her move off the island."

"I know about it," he said. "Didn't at the time, but yeah, she told me."

We sat silently for what felt like a long time. He kept staring at the ground, and all I could do was try to break the quiet. "Would it make you feel better if I told you that the boys have been calling her Sally the Whore, like it's all one word? Like, Sallythewhore was a good teacher, but it's nice to have Carly back on the island, or Sallythewhore was never cut out for the island, or Sallythewhore seems like the kind of gal who should be living in James Harbor."

"Does that make me feel better? Honestly?" Kenny finally looked at me, a small smile creeping onto his lips. "Yeah, a little."

He had his hands on his thighs, and I reached out and covered one of his with mine. "I'm sorry, Kenny. I'm really sorry."

"Things had run their course. That happens with marriages sometimes."

I gave a squeeze but left my hand where it was. "It doesn't mean it's easy, and even if you and Sally splitting is a good thing, I'm sorry. It was probably good for you to get off the island for a while and have some time away."

"I should have called, I guess," he said.

"You guess?" I shook my head and stood up from the lobster pot and then put my hand on his shoulder. "Yeah, a call would have been nice, Kenny. I know you had a lot to deal with, but I was thinking that I was going to be going out today without a sternman."

He looked up at me with a smile and a bit of surprise. "You didn't hire somebody else on? I mean, I was hoping, but I figured you would have."

I pressed the catch on the back of the handle, folded the blade closed, and handed him the knife. "Nah. I limped along without you for the spring season. Everybody was afraid that Trudy would tear them up if they tried to replace you," I said, which was funny because the most Trudy would ever tear up would be a pillow on the couch. There'd been no shortage of boys who were interested in being my sternman. I fished on shares, which meant that the more I caught, the more my sternman made, and everybody knew that the Kings fished like we owned the ocean.

"Will you have me back on?"

"Kenny," I said, but then my voice faltered. I could feel a knot forming in my throat; I tried to speak again, but nothing came out. It didn't matter, because Kenny was on his feet and he had his arms wrapped around me, hugging me.

We have two Brumfitt Kings paintings. They are the weird, almost magical paintings that are looked down upon by Brumfitt scholars and collectors, but they would still be worth a lot of money if Daddy got it in his head to sell them. He jokes that they are his retirement fund, though if he was interested in money he would have sold the journals, which would bring enough money to buy a couple of waterfront houses on the island. The two paintings are on semi-permanent loan to the Brumfitt Kings Museum in the village, which brings the grand total of Brumfitt paintings in the museum from zero to two, though it does have quite a few sketches and studies and other odds and ends that are purported to be from Brumfitt's life. Daddy's said a couple of times that he knows where to find an even bigger trove of paintings than the one C. C. Harel unearthed, that a selkie, a mythical creature that turns from a seal into a human on land, told him where, and he'd be happy to share if only somebody would bother to ask him, but that's one of his full-of-shit stories and Rena, Carly, and I have mostly gotten into the habit of ignoring him—or, as he likes to call it, patronizing him—when he starts going off about the subject of Brumfitt's other lost paintings.

I'd be a lot more interested if I could find what I like to think of as Brumfitt's lost journals. We've got the full set if you go strictly by dates, but after the seventh journal, when Brumfitt describes how the ocean gave him his wife, the last five journals just become ledgers. He accounts for the tonnage of fish caught by the fleets that used the island, tracks his household finances, and writes down important dates, including the births—and in the case of his eldest son, the death—of his children. But none of those later journals have the visions and images that are rife in the first seven journals, the descriptions of Loosewood Island that have led some historians to claim that Brumfitt must have endured episodes of madness. And there is the paucity of them: seven journals filled in his first eight years on Loosewood Island, but only five more for the next fifty-three years? I hadn't ever thought about it when I was young and I'd slip one of the early journals out from the glass-fronted bookcase and curl up under a lamp to read. I must have just assumed that there had been something that changed him with marriage. That shows you the lack of imagination that children can sometimes have: I was willing to believe that Brumfitt's bride was borne to him across the surface of the ocean, that she materialized from the water with a dowry of bounty and doom, and yet I also believed that marriage would have transformed him into someone only interested in numbers.

Brumfitt wrote the date in the front of each journal, and occasionally dated pages or sketches within them, so that it was fairly easy to track his progress across the pages of the journals, but there was a gap between the seventh and the eighth journals. The gap is only six months, but there is no gap in dates between the early journals that lasts more than a few days. I can't help but wonder if there is another whole set of journals that keeps going, that describes what happened *after* his wife stepped from the ocean, that continues to detail the odd miracles and monstrosities that he encountered on Loosewood Island.

Kenny held me for a few seconds, and then when we heard the sound of the screen door slamming shut, he gave me a squeeze and stepped away. Daddy sauntered down the steps, a steaming cup of coffee in his hands.

"Kenny," Daddy said.

"Woody. How you been feeling?"

Daddy rolled his eyes and leaned against the wall. "I get enough of that from my daughters. Jesus. They find you passed out in the kitchen *one* time, and suddenly they act all concerned."

Kenny laughed. "Just don't go dying on us."

"I'm not planning on it. So how about you two start working?"

"Hey, Daddy?"

"I know, I know," he said. "You're going to tell me to fuck off."

I grinned. "I was going to tell you that I love you."

"Ah, save it for Kenny," he said. If I'd had any coffee of my own, I would have choked on it, but neither he nor Kenny noticed; they were already working on loading the pickup.

Daddy's pickup, which meant that his traps went on first, and then after he'd finished dropping all of his at the docks it would be my turn. I suppose I could have bought my own truck, but I never saw the point. There just weren't that many roads to speak of on Loosewood Island. Probably a third of the islanders didn't even own trucks or cars—or if they did, they kept them with relatives on the mainland—and the roads we did have were circuitous and winding. To get from one place to another, it was quicker to walk down the beaten paths of dirt and rock, or maintained paths of gravel or crushed shells, than to actually take the serpentine roads. When I needed a truck on the island, mostly just to haul my traps up from the dock when they weren't in the water, I borrowed Daddy's. He kept a second truck on the mainland, parked at a buddy's workshop near the docks in James Harbor, and the few times that wasn't available, I rented a car.

We weren't moving that quickly, and we only had a few traps on the truck when Stephanie came into the yard. She was yawning. Trudy bounced over and pushed her head into Stephanie's stomach.

"You guys sure get yourselves going early," she said. She scratched Trudy behind the ears and then rubbed at her eyes. She had an elastic around her wrist, and she slipped it off and then pulled her hair back into a ponytail. "There," she said, "my hair's done." She looked at me and then shook her head. "You know," she said, "you look put together for five-something in the darn morning. They should have a picture of you on the recruiting posters." She banged Kenny on the shoulder. "Kenny, I presume? You've got the best-looking captain on the island." I could feel myself burn hot, because of course I thought about how I looked out on the water with Kenny. Even though I had only been hoping that Kenny was going to come back, hope is a powerful thing.

Stephanie grabbed a trap and tried to hoist it into the truck. Her first try fell short, with the trap hitting the edge of the gate and bouncing back into her legs and then falling onto the dirt. I figured that wasn't the best sign for her first day as Daddy's sternman. There'd be a lot more hauling than that. Her second try went better, and by the time Daddy had finished his cup of coffee the truck was loaded high and ready for its first trip down to the docks.

Kenny and Stephanie started walking down the path, followed by Trudy and Fifth. I slid up into the cab next to Daddy. He rubbed at his hands for a second. I thought about how many times he'd hauled traps from the water, how many tens of thousands of lobsters he'd kept, and how many tens of thousands he'd thrown back when their carapaces weren't big enough for the brass measure.

He put the keys in and started the truck and then looked over at me and said, "I see Kenny's back."

"Yep."

"Guess you won't be without a sternman after all."

"Nope," I said, and that was that for the rest of the ride. The Johnny Cash tape kicked in—the same tape and the same tape deck in the truck for more than a decade—and we made it most of the way through a song by the time we negotiated the winding roads and what passed for rush hour on the island; every lobsterman was heading to the docks, same as us.

Stephanie and Kenny and the dogs cut a straight line down to the docks and were waiting for us by the time we pulled up. They started taking the traps off the truck before Daddy and I were out of the cab. Tucker came over, pulling on his work gloves, and between all of us we made quick work of it, stacking Daddy's traps near the edge of the dock so that he could tie off the *Queen Jane* and load directly up. By the time we were done, Mr. Warner was backing his truck past Daddy's, and Tucker and Kenny went over to start unloading his truck as well. Stephanie started to head after them, but I grabbed her arm.

"Aren't I supposed to help?" she said to me, yanking her arm.

"Not without gloves," I said.

"I don't need them," she said, shaking her head, making her ponytail bob back and forth. I was annoyed by her stubbornness, but I understood it. Lots of girls on the island helped their fathers when it was needed. There were enough of us who ran traps part-time as teenagers—five or six traps to make some spending money—that it's not like women never took to the water. Still, I had been the first woman on the island to try to make a full go of it as a lobsterwoman. I'd been just as stubborn as Stephanie. That was the only way to make it. The boys weren't circling me like wolves, but I wasn't set on showing any weakness, and I didn't let them treat me any differently than any of the other boys. But stubbornness and foolishness were two separate things.

"Look around you," I said. "Take a good look at everybody out here. How many people do you see wearing work gloves?"

She looked over the dock. There were already four trucks aside from Daddy's. The traps were taking shape in neat stacks along the edges of the dock. Petey Doggy turned into the lot and sat with his arm out the window, his truck running, waiting for Daddy or somebody else to pull out and give him a space to drop his traps. Stephanie shook her head. "I don't know, maybe half of them?"

"Okay, now look closer. Tell me, how many lobstermen aren't wearing gloves?"

"I don't know everybody yet, Cordelia," she said. "I can't tell who's a lobsterman and who isn't. We just moved here yesterday."

"I'll make it simple for you. Most of the lobstermen wear gloves. You start out without gloves now, this early in the season, and what will happen is that about halfway through the morning you'll start getting blisters and cuts and nicks and scrapes, and about the time you decide you're ready to throw on a pair of gloves it will be too late. And then tonight, when you're washing your hands before dinner, the hot water will sting like a motherfucker, and Carly will have to lance out whatever blisters don't pop. You don't wear gloves today, you won't even be able to unclench your hands tomorrow morning, let alone last a day at sea with Daddy."

She shook my hand off her shoulder and glared at me. "If you can do it, I can do it."

"For Christ's sake, Stephanie." I stepped over to Daddy's truck, opened the passenger door, and popped open the glove compartment. I pulled out a pair of work gloves. "I'm trying to help you. Just wear the fucking gloves."

She looked at me, raised an eyebrow, and then laughed. "You know, I've never seen anybody actually keep gloves in the glove compartment before." In that moment, with the way she smiled at me, I saw how easy it must have been for Carly to fall in love with her.

She reached out for the gloves, but I gave her a grin instead. "These ones are mine. You can get your own pair when we go back to the house. There's a pile of them on the workbench." I nodded over to the busy part of the dock and toward where Tucker and Kenny walked back to us. "We'll make another couple of runs for Daddy's traps, then when we're all done with his we'll do mine and then Tucker's." Something caught Kenny's eye, and he gave Tucker a tap on the shoulder. The two of them stopped walking and turned to look over the water, where tendrils of mist floated eagerly, Kenny pointing to something out where the boats were moored.

Kenny was wearing jeans and his boots and a T-shirt, and he looked good. He'd lost some weight while he was gone—he kept hitching up his jeans—but he still had the broad V'd-up shoulders from working on the boat, and I could see the lines of the muscles in his arms when he pointed. He brushed back his hair from his forehead, and I bit my lip and smiled. When I looked back at Stephanie I saw that she was watching me, not Tucker and Kenny.

"Huh," she said.

"What?"

"Does he know?" she said.

I felt sick for a second. I'd been careful about Kenny, trying never to let anyone—including Kenny—know how I felt about him. Stephanie was on the island less than twenty-four hours, and she already had things figured out. "Know what?" I said, and as I said it I could tell that Stephanie knew I was bluffing. Still, she seemed to understand and she nodded.

"Okay," she said. She looked down at her hands and then clapped me on the shoulder. "And thanks."

We were back and forth from the dock to the house, stacking up Daddy's traps in a solid tower of wire and rope. When there were enough, he loaded up the *Queen Jane* and he and Stephanie motored out to drop the traps. Tucker hopped off to go get a coffee. Kenny and I got into Daddy's truck to drive back to the house to start loading my traps.

The sky was aching with blue. We didn't say anything on the short drive to Daddy's house, but when I parked and Kenny reached for his door handle, I stopped him.

"Kenny," I said, "if you and Sally are done, then why'd you come back?"

"Heck, Cordelia. I fell in love." He sighed, and I could feel my head start to pound. I couldn't look over at him, and I was glad we were still sitting in the truck; if I had been standing, my legs might have given out. He kept speaking. "I fell in love with Loosewood Island and with working on the sea, first with your daddy and then with you, and I fell in love with the light and water and the rocks and the birds and the boats and the way everything comes together here when I paint." He popped open the door of the truck and slid off his seat, but then stopped and turned to look at me, his arm resting loosely on the open frame of the window. "I think you either take to living on the island or you don't," he said. "Sally's from Lubec, and she couldn't hack it. I'm not sure I helped that much. Maybe I was too wrapped up in myself, maybe I could have done more when . . ." He trailed off and shook his head. I knew he was talking about when she lost the babies. "But if you take to the island, I'm not sure it's something you can just leave. Ask Carly about it. She came back, too," he said, and then he knocked the door closed and headed over to the stack of traps.

I felt the thump and the light bounce of Kenny dropping the first trap into the back of the truck. I don't know how long I was sitting there or how long I would have sat there if Kenny hadn't appeared at the passenger-side window again, leaning into the truck.

"You planning on getting off your ass, Cordelia? I know you're the boss and all, but some help might be in order."

I got out of the truck and headed over to the stack of traps, but then I stopped and stared at him. "Why, Kenny?"

"Why what?" He had his hands on a trap, about to pick it up, but he let go and straightened up, staring at me, and I could see he didn't know what I meant.

I didn't know what I meant, either, so I said, "Why do you work as my sternman?"

"I like it," he said. "I like being out on the ocean."

"You don't need the money, do you?" I said, and it was another unexpected shift, another wave rocking the boat.

"No, Cordelia," he said, "not really." And then he grinned at me, and whatever that invisible line had been that we'd never crossed in our conversation, it was as if somebody had simply come along and wiped it away. I felt like some sort of dam had broken, but instead of water it was relief washing over me.

"I've got family money, but I like being out on the boat," he said. "I like hauling the traps, the rhythm of it, working with the lobsters, and even the smelly-as-shit bait. And I liked being out on the water with Woody, and now with you." He started moving again, making me realize we'd just been standing there in Daddy's yard, and he grabbed one of the lobster traps and threw it up into the bed of the truck. "Besides," he said, pulling at one of his work gloves, "it's not like I can spend all of my time painting. And it keeps me in shape despite my natural inclination towards sloth." He patted his stomach. "As much as chicks dig the potbelly, if I'm going to be dating again..." He raised his arms and gave a theatrical spin.

"I'm sure you can hold your own, Kenny."

He laughed, and even though we'd flirted before, had always brushed up against that edge, this was both different and familiar, with the way he looked at me and held his gaze for an extra second, and I couldn't tell how much of what he was saying was real and how much of it was a game. I think Kenny could feel it, too, because he didn't say anything else. We lapsed into the comfortable silence of work. We stacked the traps three high in the bed of the truck and then started lashing them down for the short ride to the docks.

Then we heard the bang.

The sound was elongated and softened by distance, drifting up to us from the water, but we knew exactly what it was: a gunshot.

Daddy climbed up on his chair and raised his hands. Almost all of the lobstermen and fishermen had descended on the Fish House to talk about the shooting. Even the ones who didn't drink, like Tucker, were there, nursing club sodas and Diet Cokes. I'm not sure I'd ever seen the Grumman Fish House more crowded. There were more than a handful of wives, too, and Carly and Rena and some other people who weren't lobstermen proper, but it only took a few seconds for the hush to spread out across the room, for the men to understand that we'd gotten to the point when we were going to decide what to do.

"Well," Daddy said, "what say you, George? You want to tell us how you decided to get shot in the face?" He got down from the chair and stood next to me. "Better to have you tell us the story than to go by rumors."

George's face was wrapped in gauze. Above the nose he had bandages swaddling his head, climbing up over his eyes and forehead so that there was just a tuft of hair peeking out, and below his nose there were scabs, like acne on a teenage girl. It could have been worse. Two hours in the emergency room getting worked over with a pair of tweezers, and the doctor said all George would end up with was a few scars that would fade with time. George didn't even need a single stitch. A week with the bandages and he'd be as good as new.

"Wasn't much to it, I guess," George said. "I'd already dropped my first boat of sets, and was out there with another run of fifty traps."

"Forty," his sternman, Matt Frieze, piped in. "Wasn't only forty traps that load, George."

George looked peeved to be interrupted. "Does it matter now, Matty? Does it matter if we had fifty traps or only forty traps loaded up? What difference does ten traps make?"

"You'd know if you were the one wrestling the traps instead of just spinning a wheel all day." Matty got a good laugh from us at this, and even George grinned. It looked weird to see his familiar smile below the layers of bandages, the top half of his face belonging to the Invisible Man and the bottom half—scabs aside—belonging to the man I'd known all my life. "But I'll tell you what, George, since you got shot in the face and all, if you want it to be fifty traps instead of forty, then fifty traps it is," Matt said. "Hell, let's make it sixty."

"Ah, you're a good sternman, Matt, and I'll tell you, with these bandages over my eyes, you even seem like a handsome man." Everyone laughed, and George seemed pleased. "Point is," George continued, "we was piled up with traps and steaming out to drop them. Figured I'd be out and then back in again quick enough to get the last of the traps wet before lunch. I'd even promised Matt that I'd buy him a sub at the Sandwich Shoppe."

"I'm holding you to that, George," Matt called.

"But as I come up to my grounds..." He trailed off and touched the bandages near his temple. Early season and he'd be setting his traps off near Seal Coat Cove—his boat and the bobbing buoys making a pretty view for tourists taking the Brumfitt walk—and then east of there, grounds that, like his fishing knowledge, had been passed down for generations. The law, of course, didn't officially recognize territory like that, but for the lobstermen, for all of us on Loosewood Island, our grounds might as well have been mapped to the inch. Sometimes one or another of us set traps too near somebody else's fishing ground, but it was like cutting in to dance with another man's wife: okay as long as you don't do it too often, too close, or too long, and as long as you understand there's going to be a time when the man cuts back in.

"So I come up to my grounds," he said, starting himself up again, "and I'm there, and it's one of the most pleasing sights in the world. The cliff back behind the cove, the rock beach, the Whale's Tail Rocks catching waves, the sun hitting the water all right, and the first fifty of my traps already in the water, the orange and the blue stripes just about saying my name." He scratched at his bandage again and was quiet. I could hear the way that the entire bar waited for him. I wondered if they were thinking what I was thinking, which was that George was lucky that wasn't the last time he ever saw Loosewood Island. George cleared his throat and took a sip from his beer. "And there were some other buoys out there with colors I didn't recognize. Yellow with a triple ring of sky-blue and a band of green."

"James fucking Harbor." Tony Warner, across the room.

"James fucking Harbor," George agreed. "And I figured we'd given them warning enough, so I gaffed it and cut the rope."

"You all might remember," Daddy said, "me standing here in this very spot and saying let's not get in a cutting war? That sound familiar? It should, Georgie, because I said it last night."

"Let's let bygones be bygones, Woody," George said, commanding his audience, "because the thing is, I cut the rope, and it felt good. So we moved on to the next buoy and then I cut that one off, too, and that felt so good that we moved on to the third one. And we did this for a while, but the problem is, Matty and I were so busy orphaning their traps that we didn't happen to notice the boat creeping up our ass. Seems like they'd been just around the corner, so to speak, and they'd not taken kindly to watching me cut their traps."

George took a breath and started to speak again and then

bit at his thumb. "Lucky, you know. Lucky they weren't closer. Lucky I'd just sent Matty belowdecks. I turned and barely saw anything. Didn't make out much other than that it was a boat I didn't recognize and that there was a fellow pointing a shotgun at me. He was thirty meters, forty meters. Using bird shot, too, thank god. Doctor who cleaned me out was a hunter, said it looked like six-shot. Probably his dad's old hunting shotgun, the sort of thing you take out for squirrels or rabbit. Might even have been meaning to put it over my head, but at that distance, using cheap-shit shells, the kind of open choke a gun like that would have, it's just like spraying a hose."

I saw George's wife, Mackie, reach out and take one of George's hands in hers. She looked like she couldn't decide if she wanted to be angry or to start crying. I knew how she felt.

"George," Daddy said. "Anything else?"

From across the room, Mr. Warner called out. "Who was it, Georgie?"

"I didn't see shit. Don't know if I'd even recognize him if I saw him again. All I can tell you is what I told you: buoys were yellow with a triple ring of sky-blue and a band of green, and I didn't recognize the boat." He hung his head down.

"Okay, there, George," Daddy said. "So you've heard it from him, heard it from George. Looks like we've gotten into it, then." Daddy was casual when he said it, but he was deliberate in his casualness. He wanted to make it clear that we were done just *talking* about the peckerwoods from James Harbor.

"Now, we all know what the law says about this," Daddy said. I felt Rena touch my elbow.

"Fuck the law," somebody yelled from the back, and there was a swell of support, but Daddy kept talking.

"The law says that the waters are open to those that get there first, and the law frowns upon cutting traps and letting George take a load of bird shot in the face. The law says that whomever it was that fired a gun at George ought to go to jail. The law says that you don't get to take the law into your own hands." Daddy took a few steps away from the bar, into the center of the room. He was holding a beer, the label peeled cleanly off, which was one of his habits, and the bottle hung loosely from his hand. The room was as quiet as a bar full of fishermen gets, and Daddy took a moment to look around the room, giving every man the feeling that they'd been seen. "But," Daddy said, giving that single word some space, "there's the law and then there's our laws. You all know me, and you all know that I've been fishing Loosewood Island since I could walk, and that before me it was my daddy, and my daddy's daddy, and back all the way to Brumfitt Kings. You know me, right? You know that I'll do what needs to be done to take care of Loosewood Island."

I couldn't help but think of that day nearly half my lifetime ago, when we motored into James Harbor and Daddy brought his hammer into Al Burns's office. "Daddy," I said, because as I looked around the room, it was clear to me that I was the only one who was thinking of the consequences, of what happened after Daddy smashed Al Burns's hand, of the months Daddy spent in the loony bin.

He glanced over at me and put his hand on my shoulder. "I can look behind me at the generations of my family, and I can look next to me at Cordelia and see what's coming. We do well by the island, but there isn't space enough for the James Harbor boys to come along. Does anybody doubt that?"

It was an odd pause, and for a moment nobody seemed sure if it was a question or not, and then there was a half swell of "No" and grunts before Daddy nodded and then took a sip of his beer.

In the small murmur of voices, I leaned in toward him. "Daddy? Are you sure—"

"Don't question me, Cordelia," he said. "I'm still in charge of this family." His voice was quiet enough that nobody else could have heard him, but there was no brooking it. He let go of my shoulder, banged his beer down on the bar, and raised his voice again. "There isn't much to it, then, is there? We cut them out, we run them out, we fight them out. See a trap that isn't

Loosewood Island and you cut it. See a boat that isn't Loosewood Island and you get on the horn and call us up and everybody drops what they're doing and hauls ass over so that we can run them out. Nobody confronts a boat on his own. Nobody plays a hero, because if we have to, we'll fight them out, fist or gun, and we'll do it together," Daddy said, raising his beer up. "To Loosewood Island."

And there was no hesitation there, no pause at all, just a room full of fishermen and their families, a wave of sound, a thrust of arms.

I walked back to the house with Daddy. It took a while to get clear of the Fish House. The boys wanted to talk with Daddy, were running hot on the idea of forcing James Harbor out of our waters.

It was the kind of night that is rare on Loosewood Island, with the heat staying past the setting of the sun. I was wearing a smocked peasant dress that I'd ordered just before Kenny left the island and that arrived just after he'd fled, and I thought that it was as good a night as any to wear it. It was cut lower on the top than I usually wore and fit off the shoulder, but I looked good in it, the hemline high enough that my calves were out in the open. I don't spend a lot of time in front of the mirror, less than Rena and less than Carly, but I have a good sense of what clothes flatter me. I'd even worn a pair of wedges so that my legs had a little extra shape, and I'd spent a few minutes with my hair, leaving it down instead of pulling it back in a ponytail. Rena hadn't said anything when she saw me, just shook her head. Other than my week with Otto, I hadn't put any serious effort into my looks since Kenny had disappeared, and Rena didn't ask. But Kenny said something. He put his arm around my waist and pulled me to him at the bar and said, "Glad to be back with the prettiest captain on the island."

He'd showered—which wasn't a given for the boys at the bar—and was wearing wrinkled khakis and a T-shirt with a band name on it. He was wearing some sort of cologne, or maybe it was his shampoo. It was barely enough for me to get a whiff of it when he leaned in and past me toward the bar to order a beer, and even then I couldn't concentrate on it because as he was leaning in, he said, "That's a pretty dress, Cordelia." The din of the Grumman Fish House, with all of the boys and everybody else packed in to hear George's story, was enough that he had to press his mouth up against my ear to say it, and when he spoke, I felt the words as a warm air that traveled down my body. But it was only a moment, because once the beer was in his hand, he turned back to his conversation with Petey.

Still, walking home with Daddy, I was glad I'd worn the dress. I wasn't quite as thrilled with my shoe choice, and I'd taken them off, holding them by the straps in one hand, my other arm through Daddy's arm. The air was warm. The slight dampness of the night settled on my skin. It wasn't particularly late, but the island had gone mostly dark. We kept to one of the trails, and the crushed shells held a slight glow from the moon. With my bare feet on the crushed shells and the darkness of the night, even with the familiarity of the island, we walked slowly together.

"Everything all right between you and Carly?" he asked. "You two didn't seem too warm toward each other tonight."

"Getting used to living in the same place again," I said, deciding that I didn't want to bring up Momma's necklace. I changed the subject. "Is George going to be okay, Daddy?"

"Well, I wouldn't trust it if it was just coming from George's mouth, but Mackie said so. Eyes tested fine, but the skin around them is nasty. The bandages are just for a couple of days. He's lucky. A few pellets in the eye and there isn't much you can do. It's just a ball full of jelly."

"I hope you know what you're doing with James Harbor, Daddy," I said.

"Me, too, darling." He reached across and patted my hand where it rested in the crook of his arm. I thought for a moment about telling him how reassuring it was to hold his arm like this, how solid he was beside me, how lucky I was, but I didn't want to get sidetracked.

"Are you sure it's a good idea to get the boys riled up like this instead of going to the cops? Somebody's liable to get hurt."

"Cordelia, I'm sorry I snapped at you back there when I was talking. There will be a time when you're in charge of things, but it isn't now." He sighed. "But to answer your question, yes. Somebody is probably going to get hurt, but I'm hoping that what I did will stop somebody from getting killed. You hear about one of the Warner boys getting roughed up last week?" His entire life he'd known Mr. Warner, had watched Chip and Tony growing up, and he could still never seem to remember who was who.

"Seems like the sort of thing I should have heard about, but no, Daddy, I didn't."

He nodded. "That's because I worked hard to keep it quiet. And, obviously, he wasn't hurt too bad, or it wouldn't have stayed a secret, but one of the Warner boys was in James Harbor, on a date, taking a girl to the movies, and he got jumped by a pair of James Harbor boys and took a beating."

"He's lucky all he got was a beating. Go out with a James Harbor girl and you're likely to get syphilis."

"Laugh it up, Cordelia, but want to take any guesses as to who it was who jumped him?"

"Well, if it was Chip, knowing him, he was probably taking out a girl who already had a boyfriend."

"Eddie Glouster."

The name made me stop walking. Daddy stopped, too, and then looked down at my bare feet. "I'll never understand why you girls insist on wearing shoes like that. What's wrong with a comfortable pair of boots?" He pulled his arm lightly, giving me a tug.

"Eddie Glouster?"

"And one of his friends. Ozzy or something like that."

"Oswald," I said. "Isn't Eddie supposed to be in jail?" Petey Dogger's brother had busted Eddie for trying to sell meth in James Harbor only a couple of days after we'd burned Eddie's house down. Was he out already?

"Obviously, Eddie is not in jail. But it might not be too long before he's back again. I did some asking around, and it sounds like Eddie is trying to move up from selling dime bags. Wants to be an operator."

I couldn't stop myself from snickering. "Dime bags?"

"Don't be a smart-ass, Cordelia."

"Oh, Jesus, Daddy, come on."

"But you can see why I tried to keep this quiet. Word gets out that one of the Warner boys got jumped in James Harbor, and nobody's going to be asking if maybe he had it coming." I started to speak but Daddy held up his hand. "I'm not saying Eddie is on the side of the angels, or that I think you all did the wrong thing running him out, even if I didn't like the way you went about it, but it's sort of understandable that Eddie might want to put a beating on the Warner boy. But the Warner boys are tough, and even if Eddie had a buddy, it didn't work out too bad. Just a chipped tooth and a few bruises that could be covered up. When he got back to Loosewood Island he came straight to his father instead of spreading the news. Anyway, Mr. Warner and I talked it over and brought George in. We figured, let's see if we can stop word of this spreading, try to keep things from getting out of control. But then there's today, with Georgie, so yeah, I'm trying to keep things tamped down."

"That speech of yours tonight is your idea of keeping things tamped down?" I gave him a smile to show that I was just teasing. "I'd hate to see what it was like if you were trying to start a fire."

"Truth is, Cordelia, we actually got lucky. Eddie or his buddy could have had a knife or a gun on them last week. George could have been blinded or worse." He paused for a moment and looked up at the sky. There were no clouds, and I looked up, too, taking the chance to remind myself that the sky wasn't like this everywhere, that not everybody got to see the sheer depth of stars that swam through the night. "I think there's already a fire," Daddy said. "All we can do is try to keep it under control. It's kind of like a controlled burn, you might say. You heard me talking down some of the younger fellows who wanted to head to James Harbor tonight—"

"Jessie and Matty? Don't take them too seriously, Daddy. They're sternmen. They don't even have boats of their own. What are they going to do, swim over to James Harbor?"

"If it was only them I wouldn't have been worried, honey, but I already talked about it with George and Harly and Paul." I wasn't surprised that he'd talked to George and Harly—Timmy's father—but I hadn't expected that Paul Paragopolis would be part of the conversation. Paul did a swell job with the co-op, but he wasn't a lobsterman. Wasn't a fisherman of any kind. "Thing is, there've already been a couple of other things that have spilled over. You know the Tulip boys?"

He paused and glanced at me, and I realized that he wasn't sure if I knew Frank and Dave Tulip or not. Even on an island as small as Loosewood, it was a fair enough question. There were two thousand of us, and the Tulip boys were young enough that I wasn't friends with them, but old enough that they weren't the children of people I was friends with. They didn't fish, either. Their dad was out of the picture, down in Massachusetts or New Hampshire or something working as a welder. In tourist season, they worked at the hotel, like their mother did, and they spent the off-season mostly drinking and getting into the occasional fight. They weren't long for the island, I figured. Most of the girls their age had already matched up with a boy who had better long-term prospects or had spent enough time with the Tulip boys that they knew they could do better. I didn't know either Frank or Dave that well, but I knew them enough. I actually thought they were okay, the kind of boys who could have turned out better in different circumstances.

"I know that they have too much time on their hands," I said.

"Well, this afternoon, they went over to James Harbor and jumped the first lobsterman they came across. Young kid. Twenty, twenty-one. Put him in the hospital. Broke his arm and kicked out a couple of teeth."

This actually made me stop walking again. I slipped my hand out from Daddy's arm. He took another two or three steps and then turned to look at me. He stuffed his hands in the pockets of his jeans. He shifted, and his boots crunched against the crushed shells underfoot, a sound that bothered some people but always seemed familiar to me.

"You going to keep stopping every time something comes out of my mouth?"

I sighed and started walking again. "How come I haven't heard about this, either?"

"You're hearing it now. And not everything gets run by you, Cordelia." He didn't look at me when he said it. "The boy they jumped never saw them, didn't know them, didn't even know it was somebody from outside James Harbor. Good thing, too. That's the sort of thing that escalates. The Tulip twins went looking for trouble and they found it, and you know how things are. If they go around bragging about it, word would make its way back to James Harbor soon enough that it was an island boy who'd put one of their boys in the hospital, no matter that Chip or Tony or whichever one it was got himself beat up last week."

"What about Al Burns, does he—"

"Al's old, honey. He's old, and he tried, but there's a new group of boys out of James Harbor. He's not the only one, Cordelia. I'm getting old, too." He put his hand out like he was ready to interrupt me, but I hadn't started speaking. "I'm getting to the age when things start going wrong, old enough that the beer I just finished back at the Fish House means I'm going to have to get up two, three times tonight to go to the head. How's that for making me feel like an old man, having to piss all the time? And there will come a day where I'm pissing myself. Things move on. There was a time when I just would have taken care of things, but all I can do now is try to nudge it best I can."

"Yeah, but—"

"There's no 'but,' here, Cordelia. I thought we could keep a lid on things, handle this easy, but after what happened last week with the Warner boy, after this morning, after George nearly gets blinded, after the Tulip twins' stunt this afternoon, it's clear that things are going to come to push and shove." He stuffed his hands into his pockets. "The only question is whether or not it's a couple of drunk kids doing something stupid, or if we can keep it about business, keep it about lobster traps and this being our land, our waters. We're trying to keep a lid on things best we can."

I tried to figure out how to say what I wanted to, which was that he may have talked it over with George and Harly and Paul Paragopolis, but why didn't he think to talk it over with me? I had the words ready to come out, but then he stopped walking. He was breathing heavily and he pulled his hand out of his pocket and put it on his stomach.

"Daddy?"

"I'm okay, Cordelia." He closed his eyes and took a few deep breaths. "Little out of breath."

"Your chest?"

"I'm not having a heart attack. Just a lot going on right now, and I don't care to share everything all the time. The doctor's got me on so many pills that I can't hardly keep track of them."

"You said it was just fiber pills."

He opened his eyes and looked at me. "I say a lot of things, Cordelia. I'm fine, and you and your sisters don't need to know all of my business."

"Are you taking your medicine like you're supposed to?"

"You hear me? I'm just fine, Cordelia. I've survived losing a son and a wife and raising you three girls the rest of the way. I know what I'm doing."

He turned back toward the house and waited a beat for me to catch up with him and put my hand in the crook of his arm again.

"I sure hope so," I said.

"And I hope that *you* know what you're doing, Cordelia."

"What do you mean?"

We turned the corner around the outside of the old Community Boat House, and I could see the lights up on the hill, the silhouette of Daddy's house—of my house for the next couple of weeks.

"I mean with Kenny. I hope you know what you're doing with him. You've got a good thing going with him as your sternman, and I know that he's at loose ends now that Sally's gone, but I don't want to see you get your heart broken. You might want to give him time to settle down."

"How . . ."

"You think I only worry about what's going on with you when you're out on the *Kings' Ransom*? Just because you're past thirty doesn't mean I'm not always going to be watching over you." His voice was warm, even if his words brought me to task, and he didn't say anything else.

We walked in silence the last few minutes to the house, parted quietly, and went to sleep, but I wanted to ask him if he would have loved me as much if I didn't work the water. I wanted to fall into his arms, and to tell him that I had no idea what I was doing with Kenny, but that it was too late.

By the week after Labor Day, things had settled into a pattern. Carly and I hadn't hashed out what to do about the necklace—which was still tucked away in the back of my underwear drawer—but things between us had simmered down. She no longer looked like she wanted to claw my eyes out when she saw me, and I was kind of hoping we just wouldn't talk about it. As for Stephanie, she seemed to have gotten the hang of being Daddy's sternman. She'd had a few rough days, Carly said, coming home too tired to get undressed on her own. A couple of gaffes, too, forgetting to rebait traps so that they went back into the water empty, not banding some of the lobsters' claws so that they tore each other apart in the holding tank, simple things that I take for granted after a lifetime on the water and five years of working with a sternman like Kenny. She even accidently threw one trap—baited and weighted—into the water without a buoy on it, and watched it sink beneath the water without a trace, like Scotty had done two decades ago. But despite the difficulty of her first days, she'd gotten to the point where she seemed to have a handle on things. All things considered, I was happy for her. I was honestly a bit surprised that I didn't feel jealous that she was on the *Queen Jane*, but maybe it was because it was Carly's girlfriend instead of Carly herself. And if Stephanie wasn't a natural, she was a quick learner. Daddy, who never believed in building somebody up just for the sake of building them up, said that Stephanie was ready to start earning a share, that she was contributing more than she was slowing him down. He also said that she was solid enough that I could take her on for a couple of days while he went to Saint John to see the doctor. Stephanie could be an extra crewman to help manage both my and his lines.

The day after Labor Day—or Labour Day for islanders who were feeling Canadian that week—Daddy told me that I'd be waiting *another* two weeks before I could take over the rental house as my own, since the New York City couple renting it had decided to stay on a little longer. "Didn't figure you'd mind much, Cordelia," he said. "They're a nice couple of fellows and I'll put the extra rent money into whatever new furniture you want, to make the place the way you'd like it."

Out on the *Kings' Ransom*, Kenny and I had more or less fallen into our old routines in the way we moved in rhythm, keeping the talk going, all the while pulling traps, baiting, measuring, banding, dropping, motoring, and working the waters. The difference was that with Sally out of the picture, at least to me, when we flirted there wasn't the same sense of there being a line we couldn't cross.

So it was into that second week in September that Daddy said that he was taking off with George for a couple of days. Daddy was due for a checkup with the doctor he'd seen in the spring after his fainting spell, and George had a follow-up for his face scheduled the next day. He still had some raw marks on the skin, but even with things looking good, Mackie insisted that George keep the appointment. I don't think George fought too hard. He and Daddy seemed to be taking it as an opportunity for a break. They planned, as George put it, "on drinking a lot of beer. A real bachelor's holiday."

George's sternman, Matty, was going to get put on Tucker's

boat with Colin O'Connor, and Stephanie would be going out with Kenny and me until George and Daddy got back. I knew better than to try and weasel out of it, but I made a face when he said I was inheriting Stephanie in the meantime.

"She's gotten to the point where she knows what she's doing," he said. We were eating dinner, a simple pasta that Daddy had made, and I didn't say anything, just raised an eyebrow suspiciously. He laughed and speared his fork into the pasta. It was just vegetables sautéed in garlic and olive oil, sprinkled liberally with pine nuts and sun-dried tomatoes. We'd been making him eat less meat and saturated fats, and recently he'd discovered sun-dried tomatoes. "Well, she knows what she's doing enough that she's mostly not in the way anymore," Daddy said. "Besides, I'll only be gone for two days this time. Come on. Are you telling me that you don't want me to see what the doctor has to say?"

"Like you'll give me an honest report?" I said, but he had a point.

The first day Daddy and George were gone, things out on the water with Stephanie went smoothly enough. Or, as smoothly as could be expected. She and Kenny were stepping on each other some at first, like two drunks both trying to lead on the dance floor. Even though we fished limited lines off Loosewood, running one hundred and fifty of my traps and one hundred and fifty of Daddy's together was a grind, and I was trying to keep things going double-time. I was sure it was the same on Tucker's boat, made worse by him still getting used to being a captain. At least the fellows working behind him didn't make things harder for Tucker: both Matt and Colin knew what they were doing as sternmen. On the *Kings' Ransom*, I kept sneaking looks back to see how Stephanie was faring. She wasn't as efficient as Kenny, which didn't surprise me, since he had a decade on the water against her three weeks, but she wasn't as bad as she could have been. For Kenny, pulling a lobster, slapping the gauge against the back, and banding or dropping it in the water depending on the size, seemed like a seamless action. He didn't even bother measuring some of the lobsters. He didn't need to; his eye had gotten good enough that it was obvious in many of the cases that it was a short or oversized, or, even better, that it was a keeper, a lobster we could sell. There was no wasted movement on him. Stephanie made up for all of her wasted movement with enthusiasm. The girl had a motor that didn't seem to quit. She had gotten strong, stronger than I would have expected in such a short time, and she handled the traps with no hesitation.

All morning Kenny and Stephanie kept bumping into each other. Stephanie stumbling over Kenny's feet and taking a spill on the deck. Kenny turning and accidently swinging a lobster trap into Stephanie's back. I kept Trudy with me in the cabin, afraid that she would get stepped on. Sometime after lunch, however, they settled into a rhythm, and we finished fishing my line only an hour later than we would have if it were just Kenny and me on a normal day. As Stephanie pushed the last pair of traps into the water, Kenny saw me glancing at my watch and then the sky.

"What you say, boss?"

"I say beer and burgers."

He grinned at me, and I realized that he had given me the up-and-down, and when I grinned back at him I was unable to stop the hot flush that spread across my face. For a moment the sensation of heat came so strong that I thought the sun was falling from the sky toward me. And then he looked away and clapped Stephanie on the shoulder as she straightened up.

"Calling it a day, Stephie."

"Seriously? What about Woody's traps?" She pulled off her baseball cap and pushed back some of her hair that had worked loose of her ponytail.

"Yeah, seriously, Stephanie. I'm calling it a day. It's not the way I like to do it, but I don't see us pulling Daddy's traps today. You guys have started working real well together"—she couldn't stop herself from smiling—"but I'd rather just pull Daddy's whole line tomorrow than do a portion tonight."

"Sounds good to me," Kenny said, peeling off his gloves and rubbing at his face.

"I'll give Carly the heads-up, have her meet us there," I said, thinking that it would serve as yet another peace offering. I picked up the radio. It wasn't Carly who came back at me, however, but Etsuko.

"How you feeling, Etsuko?"

"Okay, Cordelia," she said.

"Just okay, Etsuko?" I said back. She and Timmy planned to decamp for the mainland at the end of the week. She was close enough to her due date that she was going to live with Timmy's aunt in Saint John until the baby came. The boys had already divvied up taking care of his traps while Etsuko and Timmy were gone, splitting his line into chunks of twenty-five traps, so that nobody had too much extra to do. That was one of the perks of living on a small island like Loosewood. Everybody might be in your business, but when your business needed taking care of, everybody helped.

"My back's still sore," she said. Even complaining, her voice sounded sweet, like a promise of the new family she was about to have, and I wondered if, in a few weeks, when she had her baby, she'd leave me behind as a friend. The Old Maid and the Sea. "But I rang over at Carly's, and she said she'll meet you all at the Fish House."

"You and Timmy want to join us?" I asked, and as I said it, I saw Tucker's boat tied off to the dock. My brother-in-law and his two sternmen were scuttling over the decks. I decided I'd invite Tucker and Rena, too. Another peace offering, even if Rena and I weren't at war.

Brumfitt worked the fishing boats his entire life, but from the day his wife washed ashore, he never set foot on dry land anywhere except for Loosewood Island. He's buried up in the cemetery, same as his oldest son, the one who drowned as a boy, same as his other son, who lived into adulthood and from whom I can trace my line, same as Brumfitt's four daughters, same as my daddy's daddy and momma, same as my own momma, same as Scotty. But Brumfitt's wife isn't buried there.

She was given to Brumfitt by the sea, or at least that's how the story goes, and most people here think that she returned to the sea once Brumfitt died. I've heard a lot of times that she was a selkie. A selkie is a sort of shape-shifter: a seal in the water, a human on land. Some of the selkie stories are just about mischief, particularly the stories about the male selkies, who were supposed to be something fancy and cunning come to shore to seduce young women, but the stories about the female selkies are usually about romance. If a fisherman takes a selkie's sealskin while she's in human form, she's bound to marry, trapped ashore until she steals the skin back. But sometimes those trapped selkies fall in love with their fishermen husbands and regret returning to the sea, and that's where the myths become romance, because once a selkie returns to the ocean she is only allowed to return to shore for a short time, and even then only once every seven years.

Seven years. A long time to be waiting for someone you love, but at least in those stories the love is returned.

I've always been fascinated with Brumfitt's wife, selkie or not. Even though every woman in Brumfitt's painting wasn't the same, they actually *were* the same: he painted his wife in every woman he painted. In one painting, she's standing on a rock, her dress bunched about her and held by one hand in an attempt to keep it out of the spray from the ocean. The location is one that Daddy and I walk out to sometimes on our days off. It's on the back of the island. At low tide, the rock is part of a spit of land that reaches out into the ocean, but for a short while, at high tide, it is a small island peeking above the sea, no larger than a dining room table. For Brumfitt's wife to actually be standing on the rock pictured, she'd either have had to position herself there an hour early, allowing herself to be marooned by the rising water, or she would have had to get her feet wet, and risk falling, walking across the barely submerged path that connected the highest part of the rock to the Island. Unless, of course, she really was a selkie, and then she could have just swum. Either way, in the painting there's a rime of frost on the edges of the rock, and her position is precarious. The waves aren't hitting with the force of a storm—it's relatively calm for February—but there is still the thrash of water boiling below her, sending a spray that would have left her wet and should have made her miserable. She's turned in three-quarter profile, her back to the open ocean, and she has a piece of a smile, a sort of crooked, half-thought of happiness.

In other paintings, Brumfitt's wife hovers in the background. *Self-portrait, with Family*, features Brumfitt seated on a chair on the dock, his younger son and four daughters seated around him. There is an awkward space in the grouping of Brumfitt and his children, where X-rays of the painting show he covered over his oldest son, who drowned in the winter before the painting was finished. Standing directly behind him, straight and tall above the seated Brumfitt and the children, who were reclining on the dock, his wife has her hand on his shoulder, but again, she is looking away. This time, she is turned even more, looking out over the sea. When I stare at that painting I am always convinced that if we could see what happened immediately afterward, we'd see his wife finish turning, see her run toward the edge of the dock and launch herself into the water, changing into a seal while in flight.

My favorite picture of Brumfitt's wife is probably *Marriage Bed*. It's dated from the first year of their marriage. Brumfitt's wife's hair is splayed down her naked back, the sheets billowing and creased around her lower body, leaving an amorphous shape below her waist that Daddy thinks looks like a mermaid's tail. I'm not sure that I agree with Daddy, but there is something else in the picture that makes me think of the selkie myth instead: pushed partially under the table is a stool, and on the stool is what appears to be a coat made of sealskin. Maybe Brumfitt stole her skin, but loved her enough to offer it back. And maybe she loved him enough that she didn't take it up, loved him enough that she refused the gift of her skin returned, loved him enough that she let him keep her skin, let him keep her bound to Loosewood Island, bound to Brumfitt Kings.

I'd prepped Kenny and Stephanie on making an early go of it the next morning so that we could pull all of Daddy's traps and then get started on mine again before the end of the day, figuring that would work to get both lines pulled twice in three days, not a bad turn for the *Kings' Ransom*. Still, I got out of the house a few minutes later than I intended, closer to five-fifteen than five, and Kenny was already waiting in the backyard. The weather had turned, and the air hung low and wet, a thick, soupy fog. The two of us walked down to the docks together. Trudy trotted ahead of us, a ghost dog in the mist. There was something in Trudy's step that made her seem like she was inordinately happy with herself. We were three-quarters of the way down the dock when Stephanie, who was standing next to where I'd tied off the skiff, appeared out of the fog.

"Tucker and his boys just left. Making us look lazy, I guess," she said, and then stifled a yawn. "Jesus. How long is it going to take me to get used to waking up this early?" She yawned again and then waved at the fog. "Are we seriously going to work in this disaster? You can't see anything." Trudy sniffed Stephanie's crotch and then lay down on the dock. Stephanie toed at the dog. "Even Trudy thinks we should just lay low."

I hesitated for a second. I didn't actually want to go out in this kind of fog. We'd be moving slow and I'd be relying entirely on the instruments for getting us around. I could do it, but I preferred navigating by the visual landmarks that I knew. I could call it off, but the weather service was forecasting rain and waves starting the next day, which would slow us down, and I was already feeling like maybe I'd made the wrong decision yesterday to leave Daddy's traps an extra day instead of working into the darkness. He would've stayed out and pulled my line if the situations were reversed. I didn't want him coming back tomorrow in bad weather to find out that I hadn't pulled his traps either of the days. But still, the fog was thick enough that I couldn't see any of the boats moored in the bay, and even rowing the skiff out would be a bit of an adventure. I was just starting to think that his line could wait until tomorrow, that it wouldn't be that bad for his traps to spend another day in the water until the rain and wind cleared off the fog, when Stephanie said, "Shouldn't we just stay onshore today?"

I could hear a few other voices on the dock, the low hum of a diesel motor kicking on in the harbor, but it was quiet for fishing season. Clearly, most of the boys had decided to take the day off, but not all of them. Kenny glanced at me. I knew I didn't have to prove anything to him, and certainly not to Stephanie, but it felt like she was challenging me. Maybe it was because I was tired or because I liked being out on the boat with Kenny, and maybe it was because there was suddenly another woman on the water when before it had only been me, but I hardened at her question.

"Expect to be working late tonight," I said. "We'll be going long and slow."

Neither Stephanie nor Kenny said a word as I rowed us out to the *Kings' Ransom* through the thick air. Kenny tied the skiff's painter off to the mooring buoy, and then the two of them started getting set for the day as I cranked up the motor. As we left the harbor, I kept the engine low. The fog made it so that I was steering by feel.

"Fucking giant's breath," Kenny muttered.

"Giant's breath?" I repeated.

"The fog," he said, unscrewing the top of the thermos and pouring out three cups of coffee. That was one of his jobs, to stock up the cooler and the bin of snacks I liked to keep in the cabin—I turned grumpy when I was hungry, something that Kenny had learned the hard way a few times—and to make sure that we had a never-ending supply of coffee on board.

"Where'd you come up with the phrase, 'giant's breath'?"

"I've been reading," he said. "Damn, it's thick."

"You made that up."

He smiled. "A little."

I glanced over my shoulder. I could barely see Stephanie. She was all the way aft, monkeying around with some ropes. She looked ghostlike in the fog. "We could call it off," I said quietly. "Head back in and wait out the weather."

"It's up to you. It's your boat," Kenny said.

I peered ahead into the whiteness, leaning forward, as if that would somehow split the fog. The LCD screens showed a clean run in front of us, and I figured I had the first set of traps already dialed in. I knew Daddy's traps were crawling with bugs: I could feel the lobsters waiting for us, like the ocean was calling to me. We'd have a good haul. I didn't want to spend the day grounded. Or, more accurately, since Kenny was standing beside and behind me, close enough that I thought I could feel the heat of his body cutting through the chill of the water that hung in the air, I didn't want to spend the day on land by myself. "We'll keep it slow and clean and keep an ear out for anything." I palmed the wheel, grabbed the cup of coffee without looking at it, took a swig, and then immediately spit it out.

"What the fuck is this?" I peered in the cup and took a sniff. Definitely not coffee.

"It's chai, boss," Kenny said. He took a sip from his own cup with no apparent ill effects. "Indian tea with milk in it."

"And why on earth am I drinking chai?" I looked down at Trudy. She had curled up under the console—her usual place—and was taking an exploratory lick of the chai that I'd spit out onto the deck. She seemed to consider it, and then went back to sleep.

"You drink too much coffee. It's not good for you. Woody said you've been having trouble sleeping. Said he gets up to take a leak in the night and you're out there watching television or reading or whatnot." He held up his cup like he was making a toast. "This is what Woody's been drinking since you and your sisters made him give up coffee. Stephanie and I talked about it yesterday, while we were hauling traps, and we decided that what was good for the goose was good for the gander. Or, well, the gander is the male goose, I think, so I guess it would be the reverse. But whatever. Point is, I grabbed it from your dad's last night after dinner."

"I'll tell you what, Kenny, you and Stephanie and Daddy can take your chai and you can—"

"How about I go get some bait bags ready, set myself up for pulling the first set of traps?" he said, cutting me off.

"How about when Daddy gets back you can go work on the *Queen Jane*?"

Kenny laughed and turned to the bait barrel. "You firing me?" He kept laughing as he disappeared behind me toward the stern of the boat, joining Stephanie.

There wasn't much ahead of us. We were out of the harbor and the fog lay thick enough that I was mostly driving blind, letting the instruments tell me which heading to take. I glanced back over my shoulder to make sure that Kenny was occupied with the bait barrel, but he was half hidden in the fog. I couldn't tell if I could see him or if I was just imagining his form in the fog behind me. I took another sip from my cup, grimacing reflexively, but it wasn't so bad. Actually, it was kind of good. Not that I was going to tell Kenny or Stephanie that. Or Daddy.

I checked the console and then throttled down. With the motor slowed and the fog, it felt peaceful on the water. The waves were barely there. We moved forward soft and even, like we were pushing through snow. "Keep an eye out," I called back. "Should be on top of a set."

"You're going to have to hit it on the nose today," Kenny said. He'd stopped prepping bait and was standing near enough to me that he didn't have to yell. He was turned to the rail, looking over the side. Stephanie was lined up closer to stern, but she was on the same side of the boat and I told her to switch sides.

We couldn't see much, and I had half a mind to say fuck it and to head back in, but then I saw something in the whiteness ahead. I was about to say something, and then I realized that it wasn't a buoy, that whatever it was that I saw was moving. I couldn't make it out through the fog, but it matched the pace of the *Kings' Ransom*. We were throttled almost all the way back. It would have been a good walking speed on shore. The thing ahead of us stood dark in the water, and it cut a small wake. A seal, I thought, playing some sort of game with me, and I pushed the throttle up a touch. The seal sped up as well, and I had the sudden feeling that maybe it wasn't a seal at all, that it was a selkie, that maybe it was Brumfitt's wife in the water ahead of us, and that if I could only catch her she'd tell me something important. I put my hand on the throttle again, thinking I'd pick it up just a little more, when I heard Kenny call out.

I stopped us in the water and walked over to Kenny. He'd already gaffed the buoy and was holding it up for me to look at. Stephanie stood beside him looking concerned. It wasn't Daddy's buoy.

"James Harbor?" Stephanie asked. Yellow with a triple ring of sky-blue and a band of green.

I nodded. "Those are the ones, yeah? What George said he saw the day he got shot. Let's keep an eye out," I said. "Or as much of an eye as you can in this fog. You know the drill. Cut it."

Kenny pulled out his belt knife and cut the rope. He threw

the buoy back on the platform, and I watched the orphaned line wave in the water. "You see any of Daddy's?"

Kenny shook his head. "Figure they probably cut his when they dropped theirs. Must have done it last night after everybody was nicely tucked away. I went for a beer after dinner, and nobody said anything about seeing any James Harbor pots yesterday. It's been quiet."

"All right," I said. I nodded, but I felt my stomach tightening. If I would have pulled Daddy's traps yesterday I might have seen something, might have been there whenever the boat from James Harbor showed up. Might have been able to find out who it was that had dropped a load of bird shot in George's face. Now I'd have to tell Daddy that not only did I let his traps sit so that I could go get a beer and a burger, I'd have to tell him that some of them were gone. "We'll see what we can find."

If it had been clear, it would have been easy. Daddy's buoys would have shone like the sun to me, but in the heavy fog, it was hunting and pecking, and we found and cut two more James Harbor buoys in short order. I had to run slow, because of the weather, but I didn't like it. The fog was weird. There was no thunder or foulness, no sense of anything ominous. If anything, it was the opposite. There was a sort of cleanliness to the fog, and maybe that was what was so odd about it. I couldn't see much more than a half boat length in front of me, but it was light out. The sun was out there, trying to break through the dampness clouding around us. I actually had sunglasses on—it seemed like the sun was bouncing off every drop of water in the air, magnifying the light.

I was only half paying attention to the water. Mostly I was eyeing the instruments, looking for buoys. With the fog I was running blind, trusting the electronics to keep me safe, to guide my way, and when I first saw the boat in front of us, I tried blinking it away, thinking it wasn't there. And then I realized that it *was* there. The boat was solid, and I was about to run the *Kings' Ransom* right smack through its middle. I dropped the cup and spun the wheel with one hand, slamming the throttle full in reverse with the other. I heard a thump and a yell from Kenny behind me. Trudy exhaled with a coughing bark and skittered to her feet clumsily.

We had been moving slowly enough that, with the wheel cranked all the way and the engine fighting, we swung neatly sideways and pushed against the edge of the boat, the *Kings' Ransom*'s starboard gunwale touching gently against their port. It was actually kind of impressive, the sort of thing I liked to think I could do on purpose. I pushed the throttle into neutral, leaving my boat kissing the other boat.

"Holy shit, Cordelia. What are you doing?" Kenny was back on his feet, rubbing at his hip, and then he looked up and saw the other boat bobbing next to us. Trudy took a few steps over to Kenny and sniffed at where he was rubbing his hip.

"Didn't show up on the gear," I said. He stared at me and I shrugged. This wasn't a stripped-down speedboat from a television show, but an honest-to-god lobster boat, and it should have popped up on my screen.

"Whose boat is it?" Stephanie asked.

I looked closer, the fog making it hard to see even to my own rail. "Don't know. Is it one of ours?" We were quiet for a few seconds, and there was nothing but the sound of a few gulls, my engine in neutral, and the rub of our rail on theirs. We'd look an odd sight to any passersby, the two boats side by side, though with the fog, any passersby would just pass on by, not even noticing the two boats wedged together.

"What do you want to do, boss?" Kenny asked. There wasn't much to the ocean, just enough swell to remind us that it was still there, a soft bump of the boats against each other. I knew what I wanted to do, which was get the hell out of there, but then Kenny spoke again. "You know what Woody said."

"Daddy's not here," I said. "Tie us up."

Kenny looked sideways at me and then started putting out bumpers, laying line, connecting the *Kings' Ransom* to the other boat. Stephanie jumped alongside him, and I let them go about their business, turning instead to dig through the lockers in the cabin. Daddy and Kenny and news of ghost ships this spring, and James Harbor pissing in our waters, had put me enough on edge that by the time Kenny and Stephanie had us tied off, I was ready to hand Kenny a pistol.

I kept the shotgun for myself.

"I've got to be honest here," Stephanie said, looking more at the guns than at either Kenny or me. "I'm thinking that if the instinct here is to get out a rifle and a handgun, maybe we should just call in the Coast Guard or something."

"It's a shotgun," I said. Stephanie looked at me blankly. "You said 'rifle.' It's a shotgun."

Kenny popped the clip out of the pistol, took a look, and then snapped it back in. "The nuances of firearms aside, Cordelia, I think Stephanie's greater point was that she would prefer to stay on the *Kings' Ransom* and call in the cavalry. That's what Woody said to do if we came across anybody from James Harbor."

I realized that I was pushing myself into a situation I didn't want to be in so that I could show that I was the one calling the shots. I hadn't wanted to sail in this fog, and I sure as shit didn't want to be boarding a James Harbor vessel, but I'd managed to back myself into a corner. I couldn't figure out a way to change my mind without letting Stephanie get into the habit of second-guessing every decision I made, so I stepped up on the rail, balancing myself with one hand on the roof of the cabin. "There's a reason I gave Kenny the pistol, not you, Stephie. Stay here with Trudy and keep a hand on the radio. We're just going to take a look."

I didn't check back to see what Kenny was doing. I just took the short hop onto the deck of the other boat. It wasn't much of a jump, but I still managed to land awkwardly, banging myself in the shin with the shotgun. I was still rubbing at my shin when Kenny jumped down beside me.

The first thing we saw was a pair of lobster buoys. Yellow with a triple ring of sky-blue and a band of green. There were also a few lobster traps on the deck with buoys loose on top, but the traps were an odd assortment, like the crew had cobbled together their kit from cast-offs and mismatches. Kenny grabbed one and tipped it up on its edge.

"This one's shot," he said. "Head's gone, the mesh is barely connected." He fingered the bridle on another, the rope frayed and ready to be replaced. "Maybe just cleaning up some old traps? Hobby fishing?"

I shook my head. "No. Same colors as the James Harbor buoys we just cut. Nobody would poach our waters as a hobby. Camouflage?"

"What do you mean, camouflage?"

"Doesn't seem right, does it?" I said. Kenny kicked at one of the traps and then looked at me. "Maybe they aren't the old guard in James Harbor, maybe they're looking for a way to supplement their income, and they ended up here because they thought we wouldn't make a fuss."

"And the old traps?"

"Something to give cover to a casual glance? A wave and a pass to the Coasties, to other boats."

"So, are they here for drugs or lobsters?"

"Does it matter?" I poked the shotgun at one of the yellow buoys. They were actually kind of smart-looking with the triple ring of sky-blue and the band of green. It wouldn't be that hard to figure out who was fishing these colors. "Drugs or just pissbags from James Harbor, we know whomever it is working these colors isn't shy about trying to shoot somebody who is cutting their lines." The shotgun felt cool and comfortable, and I remembered what Daddy had said to me: if I ever had a gun in my hands I better be ready to pull the trigger. Even though it was silent other than the hum of the *Kings' Ransom* in neutral, Kenny and me breathing, and the water, I thumbed the safety off. Kenny looked up at the click.

"Well, that sure sounds ominous," Kenny said.

"No point having them if we aren't ready to use them," I said.

"Just so you know, Cordelia, if you accidently shoot me, I'm going to be pissed," he said, but I heard him click off the safety on the pistol. He took a few steps over to another pile of traps and kicked at them.

I shuffled toward the stern and peeked in the engine compartment. "Whoa. Whoever owns this boat is either compensating for the smallest dick in existence, or is seriously concerned with going fast. No lobsterman needs this much horsepower." I looked up at Kenny, but he was turned away from me, poking at the pile of traps, the gun in his hand hanging down at his side.

I heard Stephanie moving around on the *Kings' Ransom*, a clink of something, maybe the thermos on a cup. If anything, the fog had settled thicker in the last few minutes, and I could barely see past Kenny's back.

"What the fuck are these?" he said.

"Lobster traps."

"Don't be a smart-ass," he said. "They've got packages inside them. Drugs?"

I went over to where he was standing. These traps, unlike the ones we'd first seen, were new, but there were no bait bags. They were kitted out with bricks so they'd sink right down, but inside two of them—the rest were empty, as far as I could tell—were duffel bags. "Got to be," I said. "Doesn't seem like the best place to stash your luggage. Open it up?"

Kenny stuffed the pistol into the pocket of his jacket and then popped open the trap. The bags were puffed out and lumpy, but clearly not stuffed completely full. Kenny tugged at one, but it wasn't going anywhere. "They've got the bags rigged in there real good. Zip ties through the grommets and the handles." I looked closer and saw what he was talking about. The zip ties were black, and blended clean with the bags. "Not going to be slipping out with the waves," Kenny said. He unzipped one of the bags, and I could see that all that was inside was bubble wrap and torn plastic wrap. Kenny worked his hand through the mess and then shook his head. "Nothing in there. Just plastic. Old wrapping? What are we thinking? Pot, coke, meth?"

"James Harbor, right? So, meth."

"You even know what meth looks like?"

"Nope. You?"

"Nope, but I'm assuming we'll know it if we see it," he said, and then he spun around and pulled the pistol out of his pocket, pointing it forward, into the fog.

I moved up beside him, the shotgun up at my shoulder, and kept my voice as low as I could. "What?"

He touched his lips with his finger, and then pointed to his ear. There were only the sounds I would have expected: the low hum of the motor on the *Kings' Ransom*, the movement of the water, birds. Kenny looked over at me, but I shrugged.

He motioned with his head toward the *Kings' Ransom* and mouthed the words, *Let's get out of here*, but I shook my head. He stared at me and then shook his head, and mouthed something that I thought might have been, *Stubborn bitch.* I mouthed back, *You know you love it.*

I stepped past him, keeping the shotgun at the ready. I tried to keep my steps light as I walked forward, but even so, I heard the sound of my footstep change, turn hollow, and I looked down. Wasn't obvious, but I was standing on some sort of a panel. Kenny looked down, too, and then picked up a rotted-out lobster trap that covered a ring-pull. I stepped off while Kenny moved the trap aside. Quietly as I could, I pulled up the hatch.

What was interesting to me wasn't that there was a cargo space—every boat is fitted with nooks and crannies to stash gear, and as soon as I saw the duffel bags in the traps I figured this boat would be fitted out with something more hidden than most—but that there was nothing in the compartment space at all. Nothing. It was dead clean. There wasn't a scrap of old net or a crapped-out pair of overalls, or anything that would hint that an honest-to-god fisherman used this boat. And there weren't any suspicious packages in there, either.

"Transferring?" I whispered to Kenny. "Were they dropping off for somebody else to pick up, or were they picking up?"

Kenny took the hatch from my hand and shut it carefully. "Seems like an awfully complicated way to move drugs from one boat to the other."

"Makes sense," I said. "No Coastie would look twice at a boat hauling traps."

"But we would," Kenny said. "This a James Harbor boat. We see them dropping or hauling in our waters, and it's a different matter. Why are they carrying the same buoys that we've been cutting? This doesn't make any sense. Are they carrying drugs or are they working the water?"

"They're drug smugglers. That's for sure. Not the smartest boys on the sea," I whispered. Then I shrugged. "Maybe they're working part-time as lobstermen, part-time selling drugs. Whatever. Let's worry about that later and check the rest of the boat first."

I moved forward two more steps, and the cabin wavered in front of me, but once I was under the roof the fog seemed lighter, and it was obvious there wasn't much to see in the cabin: the key was still in the ignition, the gas tank showed they had plenty to keep moving.

I opened one of the lockers. Slickers, boots, a sweatshirt, a fire extinguisher. Next locker had fishing gear, some line, a water-stained porn magazine. I could feel Kenny's side against mine, and I glanced back at him. He still kept the pistol up, scanning around, though I didn't think he'd be able to see anything in the whiteness.

I reached out to the last locker and was about to open it when I noticed that my boot pulled sticky from the deck. I looked down and saw that the wetness I was standing in wasn't a puddle of water.

"Kenny," I whispered. I tried to keep the stress out of my voice, tried to keep from screaming, but I had the shotgun up and pointed at the locker.

In retrospect, I realize how silly it was to be pointing at the locker. The blood was clearly pooling from it, and by the amount of blood on the deck, it seemed obvious that whatever I had to worry about, it wasn't in there.

"Kenny," I whispered again. "I could use a hand over here."

I didn't want to look away from the locker to see what Kenny was doing: I kept the barrel of the shotgun pointed up and in front of me, could see the way it was trembling in my hands.

"Easy, now, Cordelia," Kenny said in a whisper. I could feel his breath on my ear, something that at any other moment would have thrilled me. "I'm going to move past you and open that locker, but I want you to back up a spell, take your finger off that trigger. Don't want you shooting me."

I backed up. My feet pulled sticky from the deck again, and I could smell the blood. I took my finger off the trigger, but kept it close. Kenny shuffled forward gingerly, each step making a ripping sound as his feet moved through the puddle. He reached out to the latch and then looked at me and gave a nod. I nodded back. And then he opened the locker.

The body in the locker hadn't spent any time in the water, but it might as well have; whoever had shot him had put a couple of bullets through the back of his head, and when the bullets exited, they ripped his face to shreds.

When Kenny opened the locker, the body fell out sideways on the deck with a heavy thud, his head almost landing against Kenny's boots, and I barely stopped myself from pulling the trigger on the shotgun. Kenny started puking right away, and I must have let out some sort of a yell, because at the same time that Kenny was bent over and vomiting, I heard Stephanie calling out to me.

Instead of answering, I stepped around the body. His hands were pinned behind him, tied together with plastic zip ties. It was the same kind that held the duffel bags in the traps, the sort that electricians used and that most of the guys I knew kept handy around their boat and in their garage for odd jobs. I could see where the band dug into his skin, and then I realized something that made me even more uneasy, though I would have thought the fact that he was zip-tied and had a couple of bullets through the back of his head would have been enough: three of his fingers had been cut off. The skin was raw and crusted with blood, and I could see the ragged tip of bone. That was enough, and I started vomiting, too.

I heard Stephanie calling out again, and this time, after wiping my mouth with my forearm, I called back and told her to stay put. There wasn't any sense in having her see this, too, and all I could think about was that whoever did this might be slinking around through the fog with their gun out, waiting to put a bullet in the back of my head or Kenny's, and that we could just as easily be lying in a puddle of our own blood as this poor son of a bitch was.

"What the fuck, Cordelia?" Kenny hissed. He pushed at the man's back with his boot, his toes coming up near the plastic-tied wrists, the missing fingers. He turned and then poked his boot in the locker the man had fallen out of. "Holy shit. Cordelia, check this out."

At first I couldn't figure out what Kenny was looking at, but it was the wedding ring that helped me figure out it was a finger. The dead man on the deck was white, but this finger was black, and big enough that it was clear that it belonged to a man. The stump end wasn't scabbed up yet. Maybe I should have been wondering how recently it had happened, but all I was thinking about was, where the hell was the black guy with a missing finger?

"We're in way over our head here," Kenny said. "I think it's time we called the cops."

The fog seemed to come in sheets, heavy and dark and then a misty trail of lightness that gave hope that everything would be normal again, that this would be just another day of hauling pots, measuring lobsters, making a living off the coast of Loosewood Island. When I'd been worried about drugs coming to the island I was being naïve. They were already here.

Kenny started to lift his hands up, but he sort of awkwardly clasped them together for an instant and then shoved them into the front of his bib. "Please, Cordelia. Let's get out of here while we still can."

I couldn't stop myself from stepping toward him, from putting my hand on his shoulder and then letting it slide down until it was resting somewhere between his shoulder and his breastbone. His hair had fallen forward, and I wanted to reach up and brush it back, but I wasn't sure that I could stand it. I wanted Kenny to reassure me, to tell me everything was going to be okay. All I could let myself do was close my hand, clenching the fabric of Kenny's shirt. He opened his mouth and started to speak at the same time that I did, and we both stopped, hesitated, and tried again, cutting each other off and falling into silence. Whatever it was he was going to say, his not saying it cleared some of the dizziness away. I shook my head, and even as I did so, I was not sure if I was trying to clean out the rest of the cobwebs or trying to send Kenny a message, but my mouth seemed to have a mind of its own. "Timmy," I said.

"What?"

"Oh, my god." I stepped away from Kenny and scooped up the finger in the locker. I expected it to be warm, but it was cool in my hand. I don't know what I expected it to feel like, but all it felt like was a finger. I held it up. "Timmy."

I held it out to him. He took it gingerly and then he looked up at me. "Oh," he said. "Timmy."

I was up and over the rail before Kenny moved. Later, when we had a chance to sit down with a beer and talk about it, he said that by the time he got his ass in gear, I had already disappeared into the fog, leaving a trail of bloody boot prints for him to follow.

When I landed on the deck of the *Kings' Ransom* I almost bowled Stephanie over, pushing her aside to get to the radio.

"Timmy? Hey, there, *Green Machine*, you out on the water this morning?"

This early in the morning I didn't expect much chatter. Anybody out early was usually busy with the start of the day, getting bait ready, hauling traps, doing something more routine than finding dead bodies stuffed into the lockers of floating ghost ships. With the fog, however, there was almost nobody on the water, and a dead silence ruled the radio. I keyed it again. "Timmy. It's Cordelia. You out there?"

The voice that came back wasn't the one I expected.

"You better be pulling my traps, honey." Daddy's voice came through easy, like he was standing next to me. "They're full up with keepers. I can feel it."

Kenny put his hand on my arm and then took the shotgun away from me. I hadn't even realized I was still holding it. I saw Stephanie staring at Kenny, and realized that what she was staring at was his free hand: he was still holding the finger. "Is that . . ." She trailed off, unsure of what she was even asking.

"Daddy?" I said, clicking the mic.

"Anybody else out on the sea have the same dulcet voice as me, Cordelia?"

I leaned against the console and then let my head drop down against my arm. I wanted to sit down, but I wasn't sure that if I backed up into the captain's chair I'd be able to stand up again. "Thought you weren't coming back until tomorrow," I said.

And then Timmy's voice came through the radio, and I didn't care why Daddy had come home early. "You looking to take Etsuko and me to dinner again, Cordelia?" he said. That was enough. That small sentence, the tone of his voice, for me to know that he was okay.

Kenny's eyes widened. "It's not his," he said, and then he straightened his arm out, holding the finger away from him like it was a rotten fish. "Whose fucking finger is this?"

"Oh, shit." Stephanie covered her mouth and jerked forward, gagging.

"Just checking in, Timmy," I said. I double-clicked the mic but didn't say anything else.

"Cordelia?" Daddy's voice was terribly clear through the radio. I wished that he really was standing beside me, instead of running somewhere out there in the fog. The whiteness had started to lift some. There was a wind, finally, and with the wetness of the fog, I realized I was chilled and goose-bumped. Later on, I expected it to be a hot day, with the sun burning off the moisture that hovered around us, but right then I would have liked to have had Kenny put his arms around me, to pull me close and warm me with his body.

"Daddy," I said, "you and George out on the water here?"

"Yep. Coming home early. George decided to skip his appointment. Long story. Well, short story, actually, but I'll tell you when I see you. No worries. We'll be docked in ten minutes. You should come on in, too, honey. No point being out here in this kind of weather. The bugs can wait another day."

"Daddy," I said, "we could use a hand out here, if you're near us."

"Like I said, Cordelia, with the fog, wasn't planning on working. Besides, I need to drop George off first."

I rested my head against the console. It felt cold and wonderful against my skin. I put the mic up against my mouth. "Daddy, I could use you out here. It's important."

There was a pause, and I wondered if he and George were having a few words, and then Daddy's voice came back. "Why don't you give me your coordinates?"

I read him the numbers from the GPS, and then almost as an afterthought I said, "Hey, Daddy? You remember that painting I like, the one we look at when we go to Halifax? It's something like that."

"Yeah," he said, and I could hear his motor revving up, knew that he understood, knew that he'd already slammed the throttle all the way forward, that Daddy was coming to me as fast as the *Queen Jane* could take him, "I remember it."

The painting was *The Ghost Ship.* I'd been to the Art Gallery of Nova Scotia, in the midst of Halifax, often enough with Daddy that he knew exactly what I was talking about. About half of Brumfitt's paintings were titled. The ones that weren't titled by Brumfitt himself have been saddled with the kind of names you might expect: *Sunrise on North Shore, Sunset on North Shore, Sunset on South Shore, Sunset by Rocks.* Imaginative stuff. Some of Brumfitt's titles are curious, however. The Art Gallery of Nova Scotia has a room devoted to five Brumfitt paintings. The one that always intrigues me, because Brumfitt named it, and because the tone of the painting seems to belie the actual title, is called *The Ghost Ship.* It belongs to Brumfitt's so-called "light" school of painting.

The painting is a shoreline scene, on the windward side of the island, in a large cove of deep water. It's a popular picnic location. Brumfitt captures the beach with a sense of smoothness that almost makes me want to believe that the rounded rocks are sand, and the color he's chosen for the sky and the light on the water would lead me in for a swim if I didn't know just how goddamned cold the water is in that cove. Nobody swims in that cove. Even in the height of summer you can often find sea ice rimming the rocks. There is a ship, of course, the titular ghost ship, broadside and hooked on the tip of the rock that is only available at low tide. The ship is rolled several degrees on its side, and every time I look at it, the hole in the boat makes me think of the gash in Christ's side in crucifixion paintings. The stern of the boat is weighted from water taken on, and it doesn't seem like it will keep floating for very much longer. The name of the ship is visible: *The Visitation*. What's creepy to me is the absence of life in the painting. Creepier still is that *The Visitation* was a real ship, a freighter headed to Boston, loaded up with the latest women's fashions, goods for market, a crew, passengers, nearly eighty men and women bound for lives as indentured servants, but when it was found, on the rocks off Loosewood Island, there was not a trace of a single soul aboard.

In the five minutes it took for Daddy and George to show up, the fog thinned out enough that we could see them coming from a couple of boat lengths away. As Daddy came along the port side, Kenny and I grabbed the *Queen Jane*'s rails to tie her off. Daddy and George both came on board packing heat.

"You can holster up, Daddy. We've already been on there, and there isn't anyone aboard," I said. "Uh, I guess I mean there isn't anyone aboard who's still breathing. We got a dead guy and an empty boat and, honestly, I'm glad you're here."

George lowered his guard, but I could see that Daddy wasn't going to put his gun away until he'd sorted things out for himself. It wasn't that he didn't trust me; he wasn't the sort of father who double-checked everything I did. But this was different. It wasn't about whether or not I'd baited a trap or tied a line or marked my bearings or any of the things that he trusted me to do, both implicitly and explicitly. This was about Daddy doing his job, which was to make sure I was safe. Didn't matter how old he was or how old I was, he was my father and I was his daughter, and he kept his gun up to his shoulder as he stepped over the other rail of my boat and onto the ghost ship. George glanced at me with a frown.

"Your dad had another one," George said, his voice low enough that I was the only one who could hear him. "Got a long lecture from the doctor about taking all of his pills as prescribed. She was just finishing up when he fainted again. He doesn't want to tell you. Figures you'll just worry. They worked him over and cleared him, but we spent the night at the hospital. He complained enough that they finally let him out near four in the morning." George rubbed at his eyes with the hand that wasn't holding a gun. "Could use a little sleep. Woody slept, but I was up the whole time. Your daddy has an uncanny ability to sleep comfortably anywhere. He was that way when we were in Vietnam, and he's that way still. Well," he said, letting out a sigh, "suppose I better get on over there with Woody, check things out." He went over the rail with an ease that belied his size, moving quickly enough that I didn't have a chance to ask him to repeat himself. Daddy fainted again?

Neither Kenny, Stephanie, nor I said anything while we waited. Kenny took the cups of chai and dumped them overboard and then refilled them hot from the thermos, while I just watched Daddy and George make their way methodically down the boat. The way they moved together looked planned, rehearsed. Daddy didn't spend much time on the body on his first pass, but once he'd made sure the ghost boat truly was devoid of life, sure that I hadn't missed anything obvious, he bent over and reached into the pocket of the dead man and pulled out an overstuffed nylon wallet. Daddy broke the Velcro seal and extracted a driver's license.

He squinted at the license, holding it farther from his face. "Got to get some reading glasses for this small type," he said. "I can read the paper well enough, but this?" He handed the license to George, who shrugged and walked it over to where the boats met.

The picture was enough for me. I didn't need to read the name to know who it was: Oswald Cornwall. I remembered the way he'd looked, lurking behind Eddie Glouster in the shadows of their campfire. I can't say that I knew him, that I'd had much more interaction with him than I'd had that night we ran Eddie Glouster off the island, but I knew enough of him that I felt a jolt when I realized that he was the faceless man lying on the deck of the ghost ship.

The sun was burning through the fog with a purpose. I couldn't see the island or the mainland yet, but it was clear between me and the ghost ship, clear between me and Daddy, and while I could see his lips moving when he said it, the words didn't sound right to me.

"You heard me," he said, and then repeated himself. "Call in the Coasties. The *Queen Jane* is clean, and you're clean, right?" He waited until I nodded, and I wondered what he thought I might have gotten into without him so that he actually had to wait until I answered. "It's one thing to handle a turf war on our own, but it's another thing entirely when we're finding dead bodies. Better to call them in and tell them what happened than to have them find the ship and maybe find something you left behind. No reason for you to be in trouble, but if we don't call it in and report it, that opens up some doors. You were all over this boat, and I don't want to have to worry that Kenny's wallet fell out of his pocket or something. You and Kenny touch anything, take anything, anything I need to know about?"

All three of us, Kenny, Stephanie, and I, turned our heads to look at the severed finger sitting on the console.

After we found the ghost ship, I had nightmares worthy of Brumfitt's scariest paintings. There were the same nightmares I'd had around Scotty's death, and then there were all sorts of new ones. I had a nightmare that I opened the locker on the ghost ship and it was Daddy's body, Daddy with the hole in his face. There was one where I accidently dropped Momma's pearls over the rail of the *Kings' Ransom*, and when Kenny saw, he leapt into the water after the necklace, but never resurfaced. Another where I dreamt that I was in the water wearing Momma's pearls, and a mermaid—the Brumfitt-style mermaid—used them to choke me and drag me beneath the surface. I woke from that one with my sheet wrapped around my neck. In another dream, Carly was the one holding me under the water, and all I could see were the pearls dangling under her chin. Probably half of the dreams included that fucking necklace, and there was a part of me that wanted to take the pearls out on the *Kings' Ransom* and gently slip them over the side, returning them to the water from whence they came. I tried keeping them in the dresser drawer, but it was like I could hear them rattling in there. I kept taking them out and wearing them around the house. They looked cold and clean around my neck, but I never wore them for long.

More days than not, we were stuck on the shore having to talk to the authorities, weeks wasting away. At least I was going to have a better Thanksgiving than the Cornwalls were: Oswald's body still hadn't been released. One of the problems with living on an island that is contested territory is that when you find a faceless body on a boat, you end up with Mounties and FBI agents duking it out over jurisdiction. And of course there were DEA agents and the RCMP Drug Enforcement Branch, plus Coast Guard, local cops from the municipalities on both sides of the border closest to Loosewood, and all sorts of people with badges. With the haggling between the Coasties and the DEA, and the paperwork of getting a tortured, drug-boat murder victim across the border, it wasn't clear when or even *if* the Cornwall family would be able to have a funeral.

Petey Dogger's brother told me that the cops were convinced it had something to do with Eddie Glouster, that there'd evidently been some sort of feud going on between Eddie and Oswald, but there wasn't anything to pin on Eddie. They'd hauled him in and searched his apartment and his boat, but they drew a blank. He was so clean, Petey's brother said, it was like he'd planned for the cops to come for him. Also disturbingly, they'd never come across the rest of that black fellow: just the finger that we found on the boat. The cops were able to identify him off the fingerprint. Not surprisingly, he was somebody who had been known to spend time with both Oswald and Eddie and who had some priors for dealing drugs, but that was the best the cops could do. Kenny's theory was that Eddie—or whomever it was that killed the guy—weighed the body down and dumped it over the side of the boat.

The night before Thanksgiving, I met Kenny down at the Fish House. He was planning to join us at Rena's for Thanksgiving proper, but we'd been spending a lot of our free time on land together, and it seemed natural to meet up for a drink. By the time I got to the Fish House, close to nine o'clock, the soft breeze had started to carry its first hint of rawness, and the people sitting outside had started edging closer to the heaters. Kenny was sitting with Chip and Tony, but they stood up to go just as I arrived.

"Taking an early night. Hitting the water tomorrow and need to be back home before the turkey's out of the oven," Chip said. Tony nodded at me, and the two Warner boys walked off into the night.

Kenny leaned forward and grabbed the empty pitcher. "Should I refill this," he said, "or do you want to walk down to the seawall?"

I looked around the patio. It was a mix of islanders and family members who'd come home for Thanksgiving. Some people only celebrated the Canadian version of Thanksgiving—which was what we were doing tomorrow at Rena's house—and some only celebrated the American, but with Loosewood Island's peculiar geography, most people ended up doing both. It made for a lot of turkey.

"This might be the last nice night of the season," I said. "Let's get out of here."

Kenny had on a heavy work jacket that I hadn't seen before, and we walked down the path toward the water. The ocean unfolded itself in front of us, endless and inviting. The wind wasn't coming hard off the water, but what wind there was had a chill that presaged the storm. I was wearing a dress and no coat, and realized that I was touching my neck the way that Momma used to touch her own neck: I'd been wearing her necklace earlier that evening, and I hadn't taken it off. There was a little gust, and I shivered. Even though Kenny just drifted along by my side, I hoped that he'd put an arm around me to keep me warm.

"How are the Warner boys?"

He grimaced. "They're trying to get me laid. Said it will help with getting over the divorce."

"It's final next week?"

"That's what the lawyer says."

I took my hand off Momma's necklace, reached out, and touched his shoulder. "I know I keep saying it, but I'm sorry, Kenny."

"You know what? It's going to be a relief." He kicked at a shell on the path. "I hate to say it, and it took me a few months to even realize it, but honestly, it was a relief when Sally left me. It was a long time coming. I think this divorce was coming at us from the day we met."

"Doesn't mean it's easy."

"I'm just ready to move on with things," he said. "And you've got to be tired of talking about it."

I looked away from the water. The old Soikie mansion, shut down for the season, loomed on the hill. Orphan clouds covered the stars here and there, and it was obvious that by the morning they would be banded together, blotting the sky. There was still enough light for us to pick our way down the stairs. Kenny lowered himself down and sat, dangling his legs off the seawall.

I sat down next to him and when my knee bumped against his, he didn't move it away. Even with the cold, the night felt intimate and close, the dark holding the two of us inside, and from our perch on the seawall we could see the entirety of the ocean spread before us.

"You're shivering," he said.

He was right, but I wasn't even sure I felt cold anymore. If anything, I felt like I was burning up, like I was in some sort of fever dream, but I didn't stop him from wrapping his coat around me. It was warm from his body heat, and I could smell the particular combination of soap and sweat and cologne that was Kenny. I leaned my head back to look at the clouds.

"It's too cold for a dress like that," he said.

"I wanted to look pretty for you, Kenny."

"You always look pretty to me, Cordelia," Kenny said. I glanced at him, but he wasn't looking at me when he said it. He was busy leaning over and pulling a rock from the ground. He cranked his arm back and then lightly swung through a throwing motion once, twice, three times before finally chucking the rock into the darkness and the water. He'd been a pitcher in high school. Not very good, by his own admission, but the throw was fluid, and I imagined that he would have been something to watch back then, young and lithe, unspoiled from the failed marriage yet to come. "You've always been easy for me to be with, Cordelia," he said. "I don't appreciate that as much as I should."

I closed my eyes for a minute, warmed by his coat, and then I shifted sideways and turned so I could look straight at him. "Do you want to talk about that, Kenny?"

He stared at me and we were both quiet. He lifted up his hand, touched the pearls around my neck, and then dropped his hands back to his lap. I could hear the shush of the water, and I wasn't sure what to do. I waited for him to move again, but when he did, it was to stand up. "Yeah, I do want to talk about that, Cordelia." He crouched down beside me and brushed the back of my neck with his hand before reaching out and tugging on the lapels of his coat, pulling it tighter around me. "But not tonight, okay?"

The next morning, Thanksgiving morning, the weather was up—a soft cold rain hovering over the island—and it had the feel of a storm coming. October leaves were burning with color, the trees starting to be stripped bare. I'd fallen asleep thinking that I'd dream about Kenny, but instead I'd had the deep, peaceful, dreamless sleep that I almost never got. I woke up feeling great, but when I went to get dressed, I saw Momma's necklace on the bedside table where I'd taken it off and put it before going to sleep. I pushed the clothes to the side and stood there looking at the pearls before finally pulling them out and stuffing them in the pocket of Kenny's jacket. Even in the rain, the coat still carried some of his scent, and I liked the way it hung large and heavy on me. It was too early to go to Rena's, so I stopped at the Coffee Catch for a while to kill some time. I kept looking for Kenny to come wandering in, but it was mostly just the old farts who were waiting for the diner to open so they could go nurse their coffees there instead. Finally, around eight, I ordered a latte for Rena and headed over to her house.

She gave me a hug, glanced at Kenny's jacket but didn't say anything, and then took the latte with a gleeful sigh. "I swear to god, the Coffee Catch is the greatest thing to happen to Loosewood Island since indoor plumbing." She leaned against the counter and held the cup in both hands. "Do you think anybody would mind if, instead of cooking a Thanksgiving dinner, I just sat down and drank my coffee? We could do frozen pizza. I'll cook turkey next month."

Like most of the families on the island, we celebrated both the American and Canadian holidays, and for somebody like Rena, who loved any excuse to decorate the house and get the family together, it was the best of both worlds: she could decorate for Canadian Thanksgiving, do Halloween, and then decorate for Thanksgiving again. She'd already hung turkey cutouts and miniature Canadian flags. "You're the one who always insists on hosting," I said.

"Please. Like you want to cook for everybody?" she said, smiling at me. "I'm just tired. Guppy had a bit of a cough last night, and it kept me up." She looked again at Kenny's jacket hanging on my shoulders. "And how late were you up?"

"Late enough," I said. "But, well, there's this." I reached into the pocket of Kenny's jacket, pulled out Momma's necklace, and told her about what had happened on the day Carly moved back to the island.

"The whole time?" Rena said. She held the necklace up by her fingertips, her arms extended, the pearls dangling down in front of her. She lowered her arm and let the necklace pool into the palm of her hand. I could tell she was having trouble not crying.

"I thought maybe Carly had told you."

"No. No, I just thought they were gone." She shook her head. "What are you going to do?"

She closed her hand around the necklace and then pulled it close to her chest, almost cradling it. I wasn't sure if she even realized she was doing it, but it gave me a few seconds to compose myself, because I was taken aback at the question. "What am I going to do? Not, what are *we* going to do?"

She was staring past me, at the wall or just into space, but when I said that, she brought her focus to my face. "Don't play that with me, Cordelia. You know as well as I do how you've set things up in this family. It's never been a democracy." She didn't sound angry, but there was an edge in her voice, and she reached out and pressed the necklace into my hand and then turned to the pantry and started pulling out flour, salt, vanilla, all of the things she thought she needed to start cooking. It reminded me of the way that I sorted gear and prepped for a day on the water, and it meant that she was done talking about the pearls. I hesitated, and then I just slipped the necklace back into the pocket of Kenny's jacket, hung it up in the hall closet, and began to carry folding chairs into the dining room.

When Tucker came home with the twins, around eleven, I took off. I had lunch at the diner and spent some more time reading at the Coffee Catch, but even though I saw all sorts of people—John O'Connor, Jessie, Matt Frieze, Petey Dogger, Principal Philips, Chip and Tony—the one person I was looking for was nowhere to be found. It wasn't until that evening, when I was turning up the walk to Rena's, that I saw Kenny.

Sometime in the afternoon the rain had turned into a heavy squall, with dark clouds and the kind of rain that hurts your face, and I ducked under the cover of Rena's porch to wait for him. He was hunched over, his hood pulled up and hustling through the weather, coming from the other direction than me. I'd planned on wearing a dress, but with the weather making a nuisance of itself, I'd ended up wearing jeans, and instead of wearing one of my own coats, I had settled on Kenny's jacket again; I had the idea that maybe Kenny would decide to walk me home after we finished dinner so that he could get his jacket back.

He popped up the steps, pushed his hood back, unzipped his coat, and then pulled a tie out of his pocket. He held it out to me. "Here," he said.

"Here?" I took the tie out of his hand. "Here . . . as in? Because, if you must know, I greatly prefer flowers. Or beer."

"Here, as in, can you tie it for me?" He gave a crooked smile and ducked his head, and I realized he was embarrassed. "She always used to tie them for me. Not that I wore a tie all that often, but, well... And I know you're the one who did it for Woody after your momma..." He sort of trailed off and then shifted side to side. "I don't know. It's Thanksgiving. Thought I should dress up."

I pulled the ends of the tie apart and reached up to drape it around his neck. He leaned over for me, lifting his collar while I slid the tie back and forth a couple of times to get the length right. While I twisted the long end over the short and then made the loop, he reached out and tugged at the zipper of my—of his—jacket.

"Nice jacket," he said. "A bit big on you." He moved his hand over and touched my chin. "No necklace?"

"Not tonight," I said.

He shook his head. "Pretty necklace, but it's not your style. You look good without it."

I cinched the knot tight and then straightened the tie. I looked up at him again, and he was staring right at me. I let my hands fall to my sides, but neither one of us moved to step back. I took a breath and put a little more weight into my toes, my body moving toward him slowly, almost imperceptibly.

"Make some room up there," Daddy called out from what felt like far away.

Kenny and I both took a step back, the space between us suddenly wide and safe. I saw Daddy walking briskly through the storm and up the steps. He stomped his feet on the porch and then unzipped his slicker. "Christ in a bucket," he said, breathing heavily. "I can't say I'm thankful for this kind of holiday weather."

"Always some kind of weather, right?" Kenny said. He tapped Daddy on the shoulder, raised his eyes at me, and then stepped through the front door. Daddy pulled his slicker off and folded it over his arm. He had a bottle of wine in his other hand. He looked at me and then shook his head.

"What are you doing, girl? You and Kenny?"

"It's none of your business."

He shook his head again. "You're my daughter, and you're a Kings, and that makes it my business. You aren't thinking, Cordelia."

"Kenny is a—"

"Kenny's a good man, and I wouldn't have a problem with you two being together, but the man's marriage just dissolved. You need to let the wreckage settle. This isn't the right time."

"There's never a good time," I said.

"Some times are better than others," he said. "All I'm saying is, give it some time. It'll be better if you do."

He stared at me, and I could see that he was waiting for me to nod, but I couldn't. "No," I said. "It's not like you have some sort of crystal ball, like you know everything's going to work out nicely in the end. You can't make me let go of this." I did my best to look defiant, but Daddy surprised me: he stepped to me and wrapped his arms around me, pulling me tight against his chest. He was warm and smelled like he'd always smelled, a mix of cologne and the sea.

"Oh, honey, I'm not trying to make you let go of this. I'm not trying to make you do anything." I resisted for a breath, and then I hugged him back. He kissed me on the top of the head and then ran his hand behind my neck and ruffled my hair. "I love you, sweetie. You can wait or you can decide not to wait, whatever you think is right, and whatever you do, I'll be behind you. You just have to trust me. Things will work out the way they're meant to. They always do."

We looked up at the sound of the front door opening. Guppy stood there, leaning halfway out into the night air. "It's raining," she said. "You should come inside."

I let go of Daddy and pointed my finger up at the roof. "We're on the porch. It keeps the rain off of us." She raised an eyebrow at me, a trick that she'd recently perfected, and we rewarded her with a laugh and followed her in.

Inside of Rena's house, all the lights were blazing, and with the heat of the oven and the crush of the whole family, plus

Kenny and George and Mackie, and with Trudy and Fifth walking around and sniffing at everything and jumping on each other and surfing for scraps, the house was cozy. Daddy was sweating and complaining about how stuffy it was. He already had his sweater off. Kenny kept fidgeting with his tie; I'd never seen Kenny wearing a tie before, but I could imagine him, in different circumstances, wearing one every day, working in some brightly lit, overwhite office, his suit jacket hung on a coat hook, shirt pressed, shoes shined. He would have been miserable.

I was glad the weather was up, because otherwise I knew that all of us—all of us except Rena, Carly, and George's wife, Mackie—would have been itching to be on the water. It wasn't as bad for Tucker. He'd actually gotten some fishing in: he'd only been having to deal with the crappy weather for the last four weeks, which still meant more days on shore than the captain of a new boat was comfortable with, but at least it was something. *We* had to deal with the weather and the law. We'd been relying on the island fishermen to help pull our traps. With the weather cutting fishing time, and with Timmy's traps already needing coverage, there was a lot of extra work to go around. The good news was that since we'd found the ghost ship, there hadn't been any more of those James Harbor buoys in the water. As sure as I was that Oswald Cornwall hadn't been spending much of his time fishing, our waters had been left alone since he'd taken the bullets through the back of his head. The other good news was that by tomorrow, Timmy and Etsuko were going to be back on the island with my new godson, and the cops of all of the various incarnations seemed to have decided they were done with us.

Daddy finished transferring the turkey to the serving platter and then slid the carving board against the back of the counter. He was sweating enough that he had to wipe his forehead with a paper towel. I watched him throw the paper towel in the trash and then lean against the counter. He looked up to see me staring and frowned at me. I knew I was driving him crazy, but I couldn't help it. I'd asked him about his fainting in the doctor's office, and after blustering, and then after being pissed off that George had told me about it at all, he'd made me promise not to tell my sisters. "They'll just worry."

Rena clapped her hands. "To the table, everybody."

Daddy picked the platter of turkey back up and set it in the middle of the table before sitting down next to Carly. Stephanie was sitting on the other side of her, and from the angle of Stephanie's arm, it looked like her hand was resting on Carly's leg. I was glad to see it. Stephanie had been quiet since we'd found the ghost boat, shaky on her feet. Daddy said she'd been fine on the *Queen Jane* the few days they'd been able to get out on the water, but it was clear, at least to me, that the whole incident had put a strain on her. At the head of the table, Tucker reached over and poked a finger in Guppy's tummy, making her laugh and squirm, and then he let her blow raspberries on his arm. Kenny sat directly across from me, with George and Mackie on his left. Rena, the last one to the table as always, stood behind her chair and then lifted up her wineglass to quiet us.

"A toast, I think, is in order. First of all, to Guppy and Fatty, thank you kindly for setting the table." Rena put her forearm on the back of her chair and leaned over. She was wearing a dress instead of her usual uniform of jeans and a T-shirt, but she hadn't taken her apron off, and it hung loosely from her neck. I noticed the silver chain she was wearing—a gift from Tucker, I guess. Almost without thinking, I touched my thigh; I'd slipped the pearl necklace from the pocket of Kenny's coat to the front pocket of my jeans.

Rena stood straight, lifting the glass up so that the straw-colored wine filtered the light from the kitchen behind her. "Perhaps it's so obvious that I don't even need to say it, but I'm going to say it anyway. I'm thankful that we are all here this year, in light of everything that has happened"—I glanced at Guppy and then Fatty, knowing that neither one of them knew about Oswald Cornwall—"and I don't want to forget how lucky we are to all be here together. Carly," she said, and my sister smiled, an openmouthed grin, careless and unguarded, like almost everything about Carly, "it makes me so happy to have my baby sister back home."

"She's not a baby," Guppy said, and we all laughed.

Rena raised her glass up and said, "To family."

I couldn't help staring over at Kenny as Rena said it, watching the way he said those words, "To family," along with us, the way he looked like he believed it. He was looking across at Carly and Stephanie and smiling, and I thought that maybe, despite everything that had happened with Sally, he recognized that there were relationships worth having.

On the island, a mermaid's kiss is what we call it when a man gets taken out of the water after floating facedown for a couple of days: the delicate bits are all eaten away. Fish get at the soft tissue of the lips, the ears, the eyes, the nose. Bone exposed, flesh torn away and left as flaps and white streaks. In the painting *The Mermaid's Kiss*, Brumfitt takes us to the rocks down right near where the wharf is now, where the fishing boats pulled up even back in Brumfitt's time. The sun glows with a creamy intensity that comes only a few days a year on Loosewood Island; you can almost feel the heat glazing off the sand and the rocks. High enough in the corner that you might not notice them at first, gulls circle greedily above the body. The boy—even if you didn't know the family history, or that this was Brumfitt's grandson, the next in the line of Kings boys to be taken by the sea, it is obviously a boy—is tangled up in nets, floating in the shallows. Two men, one old, the other in the prime of his life, stand ankle-deep in the water, hauling at the nets. There seems to be no argument that this is Brumfitt and his only living son.

The boy in the nets is turned three-quarter profile. Standing close to the painting, you see that the face shows smudges, streaks, but take a few steps back and it resolves into what it is meant to be: the victim of a mermaid's kiss. Despite the savagery of his flesh and the strain of Brumfitt and his son pulling at the nets, the boy looks peaceful. He appears to almost be reclining in the net, one hand resting languorously on his thigh, the other arm crossed up and bent high across his chest. He could be sleeping. For me, however, there are two things that turn the painting from a sad tableau into something heartbreaking and devastating. The first is that the boy is missing one of his boots. His small size, and his face, despite the ravages, are part of the reason we know he is a boy, but it is that missing boot that gives him an aura of innocence, that makes him seem so tender and vulnerable. Without having a child of my own, just looking at the painting, I can understand a mother's impulse to cradle her child, to try to protect the child from what is impossible to protect against. The second thing that just destroys me about *The Mermaid's Kiss* is that it is not complete. Brumfitt completed a triptych about the death of his eldest son, *The Drowned Boy* series, but it seems as if something about the death of his grandson broke him. He couldn't hide behind his paints and his canvas. Perhaps fishing his grandson out of the water was what made him truly understand that the bargain he had struck when he married his wife was one that could not be broken, that it would carry on through the generations of his family as long as the generations of his family carried on through. And maybe because of that, at the bottom corner of the piece, next to where there is a girl standing with a look of horror on her face, where there is a soft bundle of clothing that I think can be nothing other than a sealskin coat, there is just a blank, unmarked space where I truly believe that Brumfitt's wife should have been painted in.

By the time we finished eating and moved into the family room, the storm had gotten even worse. The rain seemed solid at times, like the ocean come to land, and lightning sheeted across the sky in an almost predictable rhythm.

"Did you know that old saw about counting between thunder and lighting is completely off?" Daddy said. He let out a small burp and tapped his hand twice against his chest before wiping at the sweat on his forehead. "Excuse me. Darn pie."

"Yes, Daddy," Rena said. She was sitting on the couch with both of the twins curled up on her lap. "You tell us that every time there's a storm."

Daddy didn't let it faze him, turning to Tucker, who had heard it as often as we had, but who was happy to listen again. "Every second is about a quarter mile, not a mile, so if you're counting one Mississippi, two Mississippi between thunder and lighting, it's hitting awfully close."

"And not much you can do about it if you're fishing in this kind of weather," Tucker said. "Just hope for the best."

Stephanie came into the living room and sat down by the sliding door, leaning against the wall and staring out into the night.

Rena had turned the lights off, so the room was lit by a pair of votive candles in the fireplace and the spillover from the kitchen. Kenny and Carly were still in there, finishing off the dishes, the music just loud enough to carry over into the living room and to mute their voices. George, as was his habit, had fallen asleep in one of the recliners almost as soon as he sat down.

"Okay, you two," Rena said, squeezing her kids, "five more minutes, and then time for bed."

I knew without having to look at the clock behind me that Rena's warning meant that it was almost eight o'clock. There was a peal of laughter from Carly in the kitchen, and then another crack of thunder. Outside, the rain came in gusts, and the harder blows made the glass of the sliding doors ripple and shake. After a momentary lull, there was a prolonged series of sheets and strikes across the sky, and the door rattled enough that Stephanie involuntarily scooted back. The wind would do anything to get inside the house, I thought, and then I decided that I was ready for another half glass of wine.

I paused in the doorway of the kitchen. At the sink, their backs to me, Kenny and Carly were framed neatly in the window. Carly had one hand on Kenny's arm, near his shoulder, and the other resting on the edge of the sink. They'd turned off the overhead lights and were washing dishes with only the fixture over the sink turned on. Past them, through the window and into the night, I could see the lighting rolling across the sky, an occasional bolt threading down to the ocean, close enough that the crackle spilled into the room and overpowered the single light fixture, casting shadows over their faces. I stood there, just watching the two of them. Their voices were low enough that I couldn't understand what they were saying over the music, but I could hear Kenny's rumble. I thought I heard my name, and then I saw Carly smile, shake her head, and then shake it again, for emphasis. She was wearing one of Momma's old aprons, her hair pulled back, and for a minute Carly reminded me so strongly of Momma that it made me want to fall on my knees. And then Carly touched her neck the way that Momma used to, and I all I could see was Momma standing at the sink, wearing her pearls even as she washed the dishes. It was a quick thought, a blink, a flash of lightning before the vision was gone, but it was enough to make me gulp at the air.

The sound I made turned Carly toward me. "Cordelia?" She took a step away from the sink. Kenny looked up. "Cordelia?" Carly said again, and this time she took another step and then another, and put her hands on my shoulders. "Why are you crying?"

I hadn't even realized I was crying, and I let her reach out and place her palms on my cheeks. She stared at me for a second and then glanced back over her shoulder. "How about you give us a couple of minutes, Kenny?" He nodded, put the towel on the counter, and went out the back of the kitchen toward the hall bathroom.

"Cordelia?" Carly said. "You okay?" I closed my eyes, and heard her give a small laugh. "Dumb question. What's wrong?" Her voice got softer and she wrapped her arms around me. I let myself fold into her, putting my head down on her shoulder.

I stepped back from her and pulled the small cloth pouch from my pocket. I could feel the pearls through the thin fabric, rubbed the seeds between my fingers and thumb, and then pressed it into Carly's hand. "I'm sorry," I said.

"Are—" she started to say, but then she closed her fingers around the pouch and felt the necklace. She looked at me and then down at her hand. "Are you sure?"

I wrapped my hand around hers and squeezed it tight. "I'm not going to be the one to tell Daddy you've had them all this time. That's a conversation that the two of you can have without me. But as far as I'm concerned they're yours. You're so much like Momma." I let go of her hand and wiped at my eyes.

Carly stuffed the pouch into her pocket and then stepped back into me, putting her arms around my shoulders and pulling me tight. "Thank you," she said.

I heard the close of a door and then Kenny's footsteps. He hesitated in the doorway of the kitchen.

"You go take a break, Carly. Sit with Stephanie," I said. "Kenny and I will finish up in here."

Kenny came to the sink and picked up a towel from the counter and slung it over his shoulder. "Do you want to talk about it?"

I pushed my sleeves up over my elbow and stood next to him, my hip brushing against his. "How about we do that thing when we both just pretend that I wasn't crying, that nothing unusual happened?" I said.

"I like that idea better," he said.

There was another crackle of lightning outside, and then, barely a full second later, thunder that rattled the windows. We both reached into the sudsy water at the same time. It was warm, like bathwater, the soap soft and slippery against my hands, a sweet smell of flowers drifting up. Our hands collided underneath the water, and he squeezed my fingers.

He was looking into my eyes, still holding my hand under the water, when the lights over the sink flickered and dimmed. They came back to full for a moment before finally disappearing, the house left in darkness aside from the candles in the family room, where Fatty and Guppy were cheering the power outage. Lightning struck again, and the room was filled with sharp whiteness, the light matched only by the sound that accompanied it: a crash and rattle that made me jump. Something banged against the glass in front of the sink. There was a scream from the other room—Rena's voice—and then others following it. Fatty and Guppy. Mackie. Stephanie.

It was Kenny who moved first, pushing past me as he ran into the living room, and I followed slowly behind him to see, in the frequent bursts and sheets of light from the storm outside, Daddy collapsed on the rug. My sisters were on their knees, over him, and I had the thought—and the thought lasted only as long as one of the strikes of lightning—that everything was going to be okay, that this was one of his fainting spells, but then I saw the way that he had his hand clutching at his chest.

Port in a Storm is held privately, and I've never seen the painting as anything other than a reproduction, which is a shame, because the size is something that everybody who sees it in real life can't help but mention. *Port in a Storm* is Brumfitt's smallest painting: it's barely the size of a magazine cover. Not that Brumfitt often worked in a grand scale, but most of his paintings were large enough to, as one pissy art critic once said, "make for good kindling." Clearly not a fan.

Size is one of those odd things about art, because it can change the way you view a painting. Monet's *Water Lilies*, which is a pace or two longer than the *Kings' Ransom*, feels, to me, intimate, despite its grand scale, while *Port in a Storm* is grand and sweeping despite its diminutive size. Maybe the compactness of *Port in a Storm* was a function of Brumfitt's age; he painted it the second-to-last year of his life, in 1780, and I imagine that the smaller canvas would have been easier for him to deal with, something he could tuck under his arm if he felt like working out-of-doors.

The lines in this painting are less clear than much of Brumfitt's earlier work, and I've often wondered if maybe his hands had started to shake. The cruel betrayal of age for an artist. That muddiness in the work is what makes it so hard to figure out if the brown daub of paint in the sea is supposed to be more than the swirling of darkened waters. I like to think that it is supposed to be something more. Brumfitt was eighty when he painted it. He must have known he was going to die soon. For me, the painting is about the voyage that Brumfitt knew he'd be taking, and the brown daub of paint in the sea is more than just a slip of the brush. I think it is supposed to be a seal, his wife, the selkie, returned to the water in order to guide him home.

Though, of course, sometimes I read too much into Brumfitt's work.

I grabbed Kenny's coat on my way out the door, but the rain soaked through my pants before I'd made it halfway down to the water; even with the choking stone in my throat, I still wished that I'd had my coveralls and boots to put on. Almost as soon as I saw Daddy lying on the floor, the lights came back on. His skin was white, like it had been treated with a thin coat of gesso; he looked dead, his hand clawed to his chest. The second Rena said that he was still breathing, I tore out of the room to get to the *Kings' Ransom*. I didn't bother waiting for Carly's call to reach whomever it was on the mainland who was going to tell her that there was too much weather for a chopper to make it out to the island.

Down at the docks, I passed by my own skiff with its oars and got into the next one over. I didn't care whose boat it was: a motor was a motor. When I primed the pump and yanked the cord, she fired up nicely. Even with a hand up over my eyes, I had to squint with the rain. I had the throttle turned all the way, and the boat skipped waves, landing like the water was concrete. The rain was already falling plenty hard, and with the speed of the boat, it felt like tiny nails of ice were being driven into my hand and face. The twenty or thirty seconds it took me to get out to where the *Kings' Ransom* was moored seemed to last forever. Once I was on board, it was a relief to have some shelter in the cabin. I was already shivering, and I tried to remember if I had a change of clothes in the lockers. I knew I had a spare pair of bib overalls, and worst-case I'd put them on over my soaked pants and take the small amount insulation that they offered. At least Kenny's coat hadn't soaked to the skin yet. I turned the motor over and Mackie's voice kicked through the radio: "—elia, soon as you can get to the dock. Please respond, over."

"I'm here, Mackie. Got her fired up."

"No dice on a chopper. Kenny and George are loading him in the truck. Your sisters will meet you down at the dock with him," Mackie said. There was the white of lightning and then, close enough that I couldn't tell if there was even a separation, the thunder that rolled with the strike. "Mainland said to meet at the docks in Blacks Harbour. They'll have an ambulance waiting to take Woody to Saint John."

"It's a forty-five minute drive from Blacks Harbour to Saint John. What about James Harbor or Northport or Calais? That would be quicker."

"Honey," Mackie said, "it's not much longer to Saint John than Northport or Calais. An extra five minutes. This isn't a thing for the clinic in James Harbor, and Saint John has a much better hospital than Northport or Calais. Doesn't matter if it's a stroke or a heart attack or whatever. We'll get him where he needs to be. Besides, if you're worried about time, why don't I hear your engine in the background?"

"Burning gas as we speak," I said, and punched the throttle. I could hear the radio start to rattle with voices, but the sound of the motor drowned them out. The goddamned radio, even on Thanksgiving, was turned on in the background. It was the background of all of our lives on the island. I knew that there were families who'd stopped eating to listen to our private drama, crowded around the radio, volume turned up. I also knew that there would already be a crowd of fellows at Rena's house, helping to get Daddy out the door, the wives inside finishing washing whatever dishes were left and getting ready to cook some more. By the time we got back from the hospital there'd be casseroles packed into the freezer in Daddy's house, tucked into the refrigerator.

The *Kings' Ransom* plowed through the waves, my knees grinding as I took each hit from the water. Even with the rain so hard that the wipers might as well not have been working, I knew where I was going. A lifetime of trips to and from the docks, a lifetime of being ready for this moment. I throttled back as I got close. I could see the headlights of Tucker's truck moving down the docks, stopping halfway, where there was a halo of clustered lights. A crowd, I realized. Two or three dozen people milling around the docks, holding flashlights and lanterns. With their heads tipped forward so their hoods kept them covered from the rain, they could have been praying. Probably were praying, a few of them. The rain gusted. Through the sheets of rain I saw Chip Warner and Paul Paragopolis reaching out to take the rail of the *Kings' Ransom*, holding her steady, while other men helped George, Tucker, and Kenny get Daddy out of the truck, helped carry him across the dock and onto my boat. Rena and Carly fussed at the edges, while Stephanie made herself useful on deck of the *Kings' Ransom*, cleaning space, chucking the empty bait barrel, an odd trap or two, onto the dock.

They'd wrapped Daddy up in a blanket like a baby. Even when I'd lip-hooked him when I was a kid, even when he'd had the flu, even in the days leading up to his trip to the loony bin when I was a teenager, he'd never looked like this—like a man who would die someday, and I was afraid that day was today. In the yellow of the dock lights and the cover of rain, his face was pale enough that until he opened his eyes and looked at me, I was sure that he already was dead. His face sagged toward starboard, his left arm slipped loose from the blanket and flopping limply at his side. It wasn't until the men tried to get him belowdecks that he showed some fire, his right arm shooting from the blanket and grabbing at a handle, the words, "No, no, no," coming out like a moan. They settled him on the deck of the cabin, near my feet. His head was resting on a life preserver, and Carly sat on the deck, her legs turned sideways and behind her, her hand grabbing the wrist of his limp arm and folding it onto his chest.

I turned to the men who were standing on the deck, looking at Daddy as if there were still something else to do. "Get the hell off my boat," I yelled. I didn't even see their faces, but they scrambled off the boat, taking the rail in stride, leaving me and my sisters with Kenny, Stephanie, and Tucker. "You all coming?" I said, and when they nodded, I called for George, standing on the dock, to let me loose.

Kenny stood by my side, his back braced against the console. He put his hand on my shoulder and squeezed it. I knew that the lights from the dock would disappear in the rain. There was only darkness behind us, darkness ahead of us. The boat caught a wave and slammed hard against the water.

"Watch it," Rena shouted.

"Fast or smooth," I said back, trying to keep my tone calm despite having to yell for her to hear me above the storm and the motor. "I can only do one in this kind of weather."

The lights of the *Kings' Ransom* came bouncing back against the rain, and I killed the spots, just leaving the running lights on, in the one-in-a-million chance that there was somebody else out on the seas with us. The rain hammered the glass of the windshield, burrowed around the edges of the cabin, misted and came after us like it was alive, like it was a cloud of mosquitoes. I glanced back and saw Tucker huddled out on the deck of the boat, unable to fit in the cabin, bent over and trying to disappear inside his slickers. Mackie was warm and dry right now, in Rena's house, getting Fatty and Guppy into bed, but I knew that Tucker wouldn't have done well staying behind. It was better to be here than to be sitting uselessly at home, waiting for some word. He was Rena's husband, he'd been Daddy's sternman, and I knew he cared for him like a father.

The wheel shook in my hands. I wasn't steering the boat, I was wrestling it. The *Kings' Ransom* beat its way across the ocean, crashing through and on the waves, bouncing and smashing. The waves were tall, the kind of sea that I would never have wanted to be out in, but it was manageable, I thought. I could feel us moving. Her engine might have been old, but the overhaul had put some extra horsepower in the *Kings' Ransom*. This, I thought, was what it must feel like for a mortal to try to control Poseidon's chariot, the hippocamps revolting at the feel of someone other than their master at the helm. And it did feel like we were galloping, like I had my own team of sea horses pulling the *Kings' Ransom*. Despite Daddy lying pale at my feet, occasionally flickering open his eyes, despite the wind and the rain and the lighting dropping from the sky, I felt a sudden surge of hope: whatever magic there was in the ocean for the Kings, it was at our backs, urging us forward and on, taking us to the land. I was sure that this wasn't how Daddy was going to die: we were going to get him to the hospital, and whatever it was that had kicked him down, a stroke, a heart attack, we'd beat it. We'd get him rested up, get him back on the water soon enough. Come the spring, Daddy would be out on the *Queen Jane*, bringing home a highliner's catch of lobster, suffering no incursions upon our waters by James Harbor boys. Come the spring, he'd be standing on the dock in the sun, browning up his skin in the first warmth that followed the winter.

Fifteen more minutes to Blacks Harbour. That's all I needed. Fifteen more minutes and we'd be hitting shore, pulling up to the docks. I couldn't wait for the sight of those cherried lights flashing in the parking lot. Fifteen minutes. Like Daddy always said, both the history and the future of the Kings family could be found in Brumfitt's paintings if I only looked in the right place. Surely if I looked hard enough I'd find those fifteen minutes hidden somewhere among the rocks and the waves, the seals and the selkies, fifteen minutes hidden among the dragons and the birds and the fish and the lobsters and the boats upon the water.

Rena was sitting next to Daddy's head. I could see her lips

moving, see Daddy opening his eyes here and there to look at her. She was stroking his hair and making sure the blanket stayed wrapped around him. Water misted on the fabric, and I hoped it wasn't soaking through. I didn't know if it mattered much if we kept him warm, but I couldn't see any upside to getting him frozen. From the floor, Carly staggered to her feet and pushed past Stephanie and then me, and barely made it out of the cabin before vomiting on the deck. Tucker pulled himself out of his shell and grabbed her by the shoulders, tried to aim her toward the rail, but the ride was too rough for him to do more than steady her. She stumbled forward, and Tucker fell over, hitting hard on his side before struggling back to his feet against the bucking of the ship. Kenny was looking like he was thinking of joining Carly in being sick out on the deck, but Stephanie was standing strong. She'd gotten her sea legs. To me, she looked like she belonged here out on the water, more than my baby sister did; there'd be some teasing coming Carly's way after all of this played out.

Even using the instruments, there was a part of me that was driving by feel. Despite wanting to do nothing more than drop to my knees and cradle Daddy's head in my hands, I tried to keep my eyes forward, at the ocean in front of me. The lightning came in strobes, the waves here and then disappearing. It seemed like the thunder never stopped rolling around us, like we were a part of the storm. Then light filled everything, burning out my eyes, and the thunder was like a gunshot. The darkness came back in spots, eating through the white of the lightning. It took me a moment to realize, through the ringing in my ears, that there was a missing sound: the motor was quiet.

The lightning strike had fried the instrument panel. The running lights had gone black. I tried firing up the motor, but there was nothing. For a few seconds the *Kings' Ransom* kept moving, and I had the fantasy that I'd been right, that I'd been driving Poseidon's chariot, that there was some magic of Brumfitt's in the ocean pushing us forward, but I was wrong. It was just our momentum, and with the motor cut out, it disappeared quickly and we started to get batted sideways. The pitch and roll sent Rena off her ass, made Daddy slide on the floor. Kenny was rooting in one of the lockers, pulling out my toolbox. In between the lightning that still carried across the sky, there was some sort of dancing orange light that spilled off the roof of the cabin. Not light, I realized. Flames.

"Fire!" I yelled, and I grabbed the fire extinguisher I kept clamped under the console, knocking hard past Carly, who was wiping her mouth with the back of her hand and coming back under the protection of the cabin.

Tucker had already seen it, and he'd grabbed a bucket and was leaning over the rail to fill it. With the motor dead, we'd turned completely broadside to the waves. His side of the boat was tilted up out of the water, the starboard side pushed down so that I had to lean at a hard angle. The fire on the roof from the lighting strike was small still, but it had a ferocity that made me think that, rain or not, it wouldn't go out on its own. I pulled the pin from the fire extinguisher and set my feet, and that's when the wave washed over us.

It happens all the time in rough weather. The best analogy I can think of is two people dancing. One partner is the boat, the other is the waves, and together they keep the beat, but sometimes the boat misses the beat, holds it too long, or the wave is dancing with too much energy and comes in high and fast. When a boat is rolled up high on one side, like the *Kings' Ransom* was, just as an outsized wave comes, the water will break over the deck, sweeping across just as the boat rolls back the other way. It's not the sort of thing that will normally sink a boat, not a wall of water thirteen stories high like they'd have you believe from the movies. You don't need a rogue wave. The amount of water that swept across the deck didn't seem like that much—it was only calf-high—but the force it brought with it, combined with having the *Kings' Ransom* rolling back to port, was like being hit with a sledgehammer.

My feet swept out from me and I smashed into the deck. I felt something hard strike me in the mouth—the fire extinguisher,

I realized, torn from my hands—and a tooth turned jagged and sliced into my lip. The water came through Kenny's jacket, soaking me, and flung me spinning across the deck. I hit knees then elbows into the side, a sharp flare of pain from my wrist, my head banging against something hard and unforgiving. As I struggled to sit up I had to stop to throw up. I don't think I lost consciousness, but when I wiped the puke from my mouth and the water out of my eyes I saw both Carly and Rena getting on their knees, straightening Daddy out, and pulling him away from the wall. Stephanie was on her ass, pulling herself to her feet on the captain's chair. Kenny seemed to have kept his balance, and was trying to get the motor to start. On top of the cabin, the flames had died, but there was still a smoldering, greasy smoke that needed to be killed completely. The wave had either caught the fire or Tucker had gotten there with his bucket.

Tucker.

Tucker was gone.

It's not a painting that people talk about. Like every famous painter, Brumfitt has a half dozen or so works that are considered iconic, pieces that people who aren't into art will still recognize. But even for people who love Brumfitt's work, it's not a painting that garners much attention. It's from the middle part of his life, and it looks, uncharacteristically for Brumfitt, as if it were rushed. I'd go so far as to say that he never bothered finishing it, and technically, it's unimpressive. Even somebody who is a hack like me could paint it. There's not much to the scene: a calm sea with an empty fishing boat floating on the water. There is nothing magical about it, and yet, I'd argue that for most fishermen it would rank as one of Brumfitt's most terrifying paintings. He doesn't need any monsters to make the painting terrifying; it's enough to have a calm sea, an empty boat, and a single word on the back of the canvas, the title of the painting: *Gone.*

I started trying to pull myself up. At first I couldn't even hold on to the rail. I was dizzy, and my left hand didn't seem to be working. Even once I got a grip, it took me three tries to get to my feet. When I finally did stand up, I wasn't sure if it was the pitch and the yaw of the boat or getting my head and my face smashed that made me stumble my way to the cabin wall. I was coughing on vomit and blood, and when I tried to wipe the water that was streaming over my left eye, it came back sticky red. My left wrist felt like it had been crushed in a vise, and I wondered if it was broken. With my good hand, I grabbed the life ring from the wall.

"Man overboard!" I yelled. The words came out of my mouth jumbled by blood, and Rena and Carly didn't look up from where they were tending to Daddy. Stephanie looked at me, but even with the ring in my hand, she didn't seem to comprehend. It was Kenny who stared at me, saw what I was holding, and started hollering.

I threw the ring over the port side, flinging it as far as I could into the darkness, praying that, if I had it anywhere near Tucker, I wouldn't have the kind of asshole luck to nail him in the head and knock him out. Kenny dropped a handful of life preservers at my feet, and ran back to the cabin. There were a couple more below, I knew. At least four of those old-fashioned squares that really just served as cushions, maybe a dozen lobster buoys that could be split into two or three groups and would serve to help keep Tucker afloat. Stephanie had my handheld spotlight and was playing it across the water, sweeping it back and forth. I picked up one of the life preservers that Kenny had dropped at my feet and was about to pitch it into the water when Rena grabbed my left wrist.

Her grip felt like a lobster claw bearing down, and I thought I could feel bones grinding together underneath my skin. I tried to scream, but with the scrum of blood and vomit and drool that half filled my mouth, I ended up coughing and gagging.

"Where is he? Do you see him?" she yelled, and then let go of my wrist to take hold of the rail. "Tucker!" she shouted. "Tucker! We're here, Tucker! Tucker!" Another wave caught us, and she banged into the rail.

Next to Rena, Stephanie slipped and fell to the deck, the spotlight torn out of her hand, its beam of light spinning around on the deck. A wave broke over the edge of the opposite rail and sent a thin wash of water across the deck, sweeping the spotlight back toward Stephanie. I chucked the life preserver out into the water. It was an act of faith to do it, but it was all I could do. If Tucker hadn't been knocked out or hadn't already swallowed too much water, and if he was swimming, I could only hope that he'd come across one of the floats. Even if he found one, unless we could get him on board, it didn't matter. He wouldn't last long, float or no float, with the cold of the water. I felt Stephanie's hand on my leg, and then she popped to her feet beside me, the spotlight in her hand again.

"Tucker!" Rena bellowed. "Tucker!" The name was a plea.

I threw another life jacket as Kenny came back with the four orange squares in his hands.

"That's it," he said.

I spit on the deck, clearing out my mouth, and then wiped the back of my sleeve against my lips. "What about the—"

"No," he said, cutting me off. "We've only got the one buoy on board. I'm going to tie it to a line. Figured it could be a sort of throw line if we . . . when we find him. Not like a buoy is going to hold much weight anyway."

I threw another life jacket in the water and then glanced at Kenny as I picked the last one up off the deck. That left me with those four orange square floating cushions, and then all we would have was a rope tied to a lobster buoy and the impossible hope of finding Tucker in the water. In a storm like this it would be a miracle, but with a dead motor, no lights other than what the lightning and the handheld spotlight offered, I thought Kenny might as well save his energy instead of getting a throw line ready.

And then there *was* a miracle: as I pulled my arm back to throw the last of the life jackets, Stephanie's light caught something in the water.

"There," I yelled. I grabbed her arm and pointed. "Out there. Maybe twenty, thirty meters. Farther." Stephanie swung the light back, but she was looking too close to the boat. "Farther," I said again.

The light moved across the water in gulping jerks, a combination of the waves rocking the boat and Stephanie being frantic.

"Farther," I yelled. "Farther. Twenty, thirty meters."

"I don't know the fucking metric system," Stephanie screamed, and despite the situation, it was actually kind of funny, and I found myself smiling when I said, "Yards, twenty, thirty yards. Same thing. Eighty or ninety feet."

Next to me, Rena grasped the rail hard enough that it had to hurt. Her knuckles bulged, and she leaned out as if that effort could make the boat move on its own. I held the life jacket at the ready and watched the dot of light travel across the surface of the ocean.

"There!" I screamed, at the same time that Rena yelled Tucker's name.

Even with the rain gusting curtains across the waves, it was clearly Tucker bobbing out on the water. He'd never been a strong swimmer, but he was trying to get to us. His arms were moving jerkily, and he already seemed like he was farther away than he'd been a few seconds earlier, when I'd first seen him. As the light hit him, he waved frantically at us, and the pause backed him away from the boat another meter or two. His head ducked below the water once, and then again. I threw the life jacket as far as I could, but it caught the wind and fluttered out barely a body length off the boat. I reached for one of the cushions, but Kenny was already there, plucking it out of my hands.

"I've got it," I said, but Kenny pushed me to the side.

"Your arm," he said.

"My wrist," I said, knowing that it didn't matter and that he was right. Even if my wrist were fine, he'd be able to get more distance than I could hope for.

He turned his body sideways and then spun the cushion. It cut through the air and carried maybe ten meters before hitting the water. "Fuck," he said, but he was already picking up another cushion. He tucked it against his body and then threw it like a Frisbee, but it had barely cleared the rail when the wind caught it under the edge and flipped it up and away from us. The boat shook and lurched, and Stephanie tried to keep Tucker in the light, but the beam stuttered on and off him. He went under the water again, leaving a dark spot on the water, but then he came to the surface, gasping. I thought that maybe he'd gotten closer to the boat, but he still seemed impossibly far. The sky seared with simultaneous lightning and thunder again. The light hurt my eyes, and there was a metallic popping sound. I could smell a funny scent wafting over us. Burning ozone, I realized. That's how close the lightning strike had been. I thought one of the antennas had taken the hit this time. Kenny threw the third cushion, and this one spun flat and true, caught a gust of wind, and landed half a boat length from Tucker, but he didn't seem to see it. I picked up the last of the cushions and handed it to Kenny. He took it, and without a hesitation tried again, but it sputtered in the wind and fell badly short.

Tucker was still swimming, but he was barely keeping his head above the waves. I couldn't see how he'd make it to us. Even if he was getting closer, it was a glacial pace. The waves or the cold would get to him soon enough. I glanced at Rena. She was still clutching the railing, still screaming Tucker's name. Her hood had blown back, and her hair was soaked from the rain, water streaming down her face.

"Fuck," I said, and then again for emphasis, louder, I said, "Fuck it," and started stripping off Kenny's jacket.

"What are you doing?" The thunder and the rain and Rena's screaming Tucker's name were all loud enough that Kenny had to yell.

"Cleat a line off. I'll tie it to my waist. I'm going in." I winced and swore as the coat snagged on my hurt wrist.

Kenny grabbed the collar of my jacket—his jacket—and started wrestling it back on. "Don't be stupid," he said. "You can't even get your coat off. You're going to be useless in the water. I'll go."

While he shrugged off his jacket, kicked off his boots and slickers, I got a line ready for him. I was more or less working one-handed, but I had it ready by the time he stood there in his slacks and button-down shirt. He hadn't taken off his tie, but with the water soaking him, beading in his hair and in the beard that he'd started trying to grow, he looked a bit like a wild man. He knotted the rope and slipped it tight around his waist. All in all, it had taken us less than a minute, and Tucker was still out there in the water, sporadically framed by Stephanie's light, not swimming, but not sinking, either.

"Wish me luck," Kenny said.

"You come back. You hear me?"

"You got it, Captain." He gave a slight smile, and then, staggering with the roll of the boat, clambered up onto the rail and dove into the water.

I looked up from where Kenny had gone in and saw the

spotlight jerking on the water. The waves were foaming, and Stephanie struggled to keep the light still, but as it circled and moved, I realized that I couldn't see Tucker anymore. Kenny was a strong swimmer. He was moving quickly, swimming hard and carried by the ocean, the line playing out behind him, but there wasn't a destination for him to swim to anymore: Tucker was gone

"Tucker!" Rena screamed his name again as I reached out to grab her arm.

"He's under," I said. "We're too late."

Stephanie was still sweeping the water with the spotlight, but Tucker wasn't there. "I can't find him," Stephanie screamed. She sounded like she was crying. "He was there and now he's gone."

"Keep looking," Rena yelled.

"No," I said. I said it quietly, but Rena heard me and spun on me. She slapped me hard across the face. I was still feeling the smash of my head from when the wave washed me out minutes before, and Rena's slap made me want to throw up again. Still, I repeated myself. "No." And then I said it a third time, louder. "No. You can stop looking, Stephanie."

"What do you mean, no?" Rena said. She held her hand up and back, like she was thinking of slapping me again. "We need to keep looking for him. We'll find him."

I turned from the water, turned from watching Kenny make distance from the *Kings' Ransom*, turned from the white line of the spotlight shining on nothing, to look at my sister. "No." I shook my head. The motion made me dizzy, and I had to close my eyes briefly. "He's gone. You know it, too."

"But—"

She didn't finish whatever she was going to say. She just leaned against me, dropping her head on my shoulder and putting her arms around me. Even though she was bigger than me and she was the one embracing me, I was holding her up.

I pulled back and put my hand on her cheek. "Daddy. We've got to worry about Daddy," I said, standing up straight. "I wouldn't be saying it if I wasn't totally sure. Tucker's drowned, and as much as I want to just collapse on the deck now and let everything go, what we need to do right now is to see about getting the engine started again."

"We've got to keep looking," she said.

"He's gone under, honey. I'm sorry. And there isn't anything we can do. We can't even call it in." I pointed up to the roof; the antenna was gone and half of the rig was missing, but at least there were no more flames. "The motor is old as shit, but I can probably get it running again. I wish it was different, but it isn't. We can't do anything for Tucker, but we can still get Daddy to a hospital."

I looked back out at Kenny, and he was treading water, out where I thought Tucker had last been. The leash was tight on Kenny's waist, the waves lifting and dropping him. He was struggling to keep his own head above water, but he was still looking around for Tucker. Stephanie tried to keep the light moving in circles around Kenny, even though there was no point: there was nothing to see but water, water, water. Just for a moment I thought I saw something, but it wasn't Tucker. It was a silken curve of darkness, but it disappeared so quickly that I couldn't tell if it was water, a seal, or my imagination. It was a moment that Brumfitt would have painted if he were there: *Man Overboard*. The boat, Kenny in the water, Stephanie with the spotlight, Rena and I on the deck, and something slick and dark moving through the water, a menace or a blessing. I stared at Rena, and finally she nodded. And maybe that nod took everything out of her, because she slumped to the deck and began to sob.

I wanted to slump over and cry, too, but instead I turned and marched to the cabin.

Carly was fussing with Daddy's blankets. His eyes were closed. He still looked pale and fragile.

"Tucker's gone," I said to Carly.

She didn't look surprised.

"I know," she said. "Daddy told me."

"What?"

"He opened his eyes a minute or two ago and said, 'Tucker's gone. The ocean has him now.' Just like that. And then he closed his eyes back up." She blinked hard, twice, and then looked down at Daddy. "Is Daddy going to die, too?"

I crouched down beside him. My knees were already stiff from the beating of the waves, and when I touched my left hand down to the deck to balance myself I let out a sharp grunt and fell over. I'd forgotten about my wrist and felt a fresh surge of pain. The burn almost felt good, taking away from the throbbing in my face, my lips, my forehead. I struggled onto my knees and then brushed my good hand against Daddy's cheek. It was cold and rough, the stubble rubbing against my skin. "No," I said, sounding more certain than I felt. "No," I said again, half to convince myself, and I stood up. "When Daddy dies, it isn't going to be like this," I said, and my voice surprised me in its strength. "I'm going to get the motor working and we're going to get him to a hospital, and we're going to get him fixed up just fine."

I looked back to make sure that Rena and Stephanie were hauling Kenny in, and then I leaned against the captain's chair and looked at the console. I could feel my wet jeans pressing against the backs of my legs where they touched the chair, and I realized I was shivering. It felt weird to be so cold and wet when my wrist was on fire. Once Kenny was here, I'd get the motor open and see what we could do. I was sure that anything with a circuit board was fried from the lightning: even if the antenna wasn't gone from the roof of the cabin, the insides of the radio were probably melted. I'd be writing a hefty check at the boatyard sooner or later. The real question was the motor. I knew enough to do basic maintenance—I could turn a lug nut like anybody else, tighten belts, gap a spark plug on Daddy's truck—but the question was how bad the damage was. I was suddenly thankful that when I'd been having problems with the engine two years ago I'd chosen to get it completely overhauled and rebuilt, rather than upgrading to something sexy. The new motors that the boys liked to run were so dependent on electronics that you needed an advanced degree just to turn them over. They were like new cars, where you needed a computer hookup to figure out that a piston was misfiring. That's why Daddy still drove the same old truck; it was old enough that he could still fix it himself, which was a nice advantage out on the island. Same went, I hoped, for the *Kings' Ransom*.

I glanced down at Daddy, hoping to see him sitting up, ready to help me with the engine. He'd be able to get it started, I knew, but he was still lying there in the blanket, looking like he was sleeping. Carly couldn't help. No point in asking her. I closed my eyes, trying to steady myself. I couldn't figure out if I wanted to throw up or just pass out, and I had to work at keeping my breathing down. When I opened my eyes, I kicked at the console. I kicked it hard enough that it hurt my toe, and it was nothing more than frustration that made me do it, but it was a tiny miracle.

The engine coughed up, sputtered twice, and then caught. The radar stayed off, and the radio didn't move, but the LCDs swam with blots of contrast, like they were trying to tell me something, and then, as the motor turned to the familiar purr, the lights blazed on fully, bathing the deck in brilliance. After all of the events of the night so far, it was the least, I thought, that the ocean could do for me, and despite myself, I mouthed the words, *Thank you, Brumfitt.*

"Jesus," Carly said. I looked down and she was shielding her eyes from the sudden brightness. And then I realized Daddy was squinting up his eyes. I nudged Carly with my foot, and she saw and then smiled. "That's something, at least, right?"

I heard Rena bark out my name and I hustled back to where she was still standing at the rail. Stephanie had put down the spotlight and was hauling at the line. Kenny was swimming toward the boat, trying to help her as best he could, but without the line tied to his waist, he wouldn't have made it back.

Stephanie saw me and yelled, "We can't find him."

I nodded. "I told you. He's gone."

"You got the motor running," Rena said. She was back on

her feet, holding on to the railing, swaying with each hit the *Kings' Ransom* took. Her voice wasn't exactly flat, but she was quiet enough that, with the storm, I had trouble hearing her and had to lean in. "Let's get Kenny on board and get Daddy to the hospital," she said.

I touched my hand to the back of her neck. "I'm sorry, Rena. You have no idea."

She let go of the railing and, without any deliberate hesitation, without making any kind of a moment out of it, slipped her wedding ring from her finger and dropped it into the water. She glanced sideways at me but didn't say anything.

I opened my arms to her and she turned fully toward me and collapsed inside them. She sobbed and shook, and I didn't know what to do other than to hold her tight, struggling to keep her upright. I didn't let her go until Stephanie and Kenny dropped to the deck beside us.

Stephanie bounced back to her feet, but Kenny stayed on the deck, shivering and curled over. The line, still attached to his waist, snaked over and under him, and the lobsterman in me made a note to talk to Stephanie about keeping rope coiled to prevent accidents, ankles snagged, bodies caught up in traps. I couldn't help but think of Scotty.

"Come on," I said. "Let's get him out of the rain, get him wrapped up in some blankets. Sooner we get to shore, sooner we get Daddy to the hospital, sooner we can get Kenny warmed up and dry."

Stephanie opened her mouth, but then she looked at Rena and then me and just let her mouth close. It was obvious, even to her, that Tucker was a lost cause. As we three women stood there, over Kenny, the rain started to bang at my face, and the sound of water falling turned to something tinny and clattering. Despite knowing better, I looked up at the sky. The stones ticked against me. "Are you fucking kidding me?" I said. "Hail?"

I reached down and took one of Kenny's hands. Stephanie took the other, and we helped him get to his feet. He leaned heavily on me, and where his arm draped around my neck, it burned with cold. It didn't help that we'd hauled Kenny directly from the water onto the open deck of the *Kings' Ransom* in the middle of a raging storm. The hail was skittering on the deck and bouncing like fish flopping out of the water. The pieces of ice were small, rock salt, and they didn't do anything more than sting, but in the twenty seconds they had been falling they had already begun to pile over the deck of the boat. Despite it being crowded with all of us packed in, it was a relief to get under the cover of the cabin. With Daddy still wrapped in blankets on the floor, Carly beside him, with Rena and Stephanie bundling Kenny up, I stood at the helm and pushed the throttle, driving one-handed. The *Kings' Ransom* started moving in the water again, leaving Tucker, leaving the emptiness of the ocean behind as we headed to shore.

The inside of the ambulance was white and loud after the darkness of the storm. Just as Mackie had promised, they were waiting for us at Blacks Harbour. The paramedics tried to take care of me first, thinking that I was the reason they were waiting—I was a bloody, broken mess—until I screamed at them to help Daddy. Once they had him on the stretcher, they made a token effort to keep my sisters and me out of the ambulance, but when they saw that Daddy seemed to be stable, they let us pile in. The last image I had of Kenny that night was of him standing on the asphalt, his arm around Stephanie; he and Stephanie were going to spend the rest of that night answering questions about Tucker for the Coast Guard.

In good weather and with a heavy foot on the gas pedal, it was a forty- or forty-five-minute drive from Blacks Harbour to Saint John, but I couldn't have told you how long it took in the ambulance that night. Rena, Carly, and I sat side by side on the vinyl bench, the paramedic strapped into the jump seat. I wouldn't let him tend to me—I wasn't doing anything until Daddy was taken care of—but I took gauze to press against my head so that I wouldn't keep dripping blood all over the ambulance. We had a keyhole view to the front of the ambulance, and I think that I spent a lot of time alternating between obsessing about Daddy's vital signs and watching the windshield wipers smear at the rain, every passing car haloing its lights on the glass. Daddy was unconscious the whole way, and Rena sat with her head in her hands, sobbing about Tucker. Carly and I took turns holding her, stroking her hair, whispering all of the stupid, useless things that you whisper when somebody has died. I wanted to tell her that there was still a chance that Tucker was out there, that maybe he'd grabbed one of the life jackets, that Kenny and Stephanie would be out there with the Coast Guards from both sides of the border scouring the water, that they could still rescue her husband, but like Rena, I could feel that none of that was true. Tucker was dead.

The paramedics banged through the doors of the hospital. We followed, coming in from the dark blow of the storm and squinting at the harshness of the fluorescent lights. The ambulance had been warm, but the hospital was chilly, like air-conditioning in August, and with my clothes still damp, I started to shiver the second the air hit me. A pair of nurses grabbed the gurney from the EMTs without breaking stride, taking a corner at a half jog. The nurse in front barked out something and a young-looking doctor—or maybe he was a resident—flattened himself against the wall. I caught him staring at me as I passed by, and I figured I probably looked a mess. Ahead of us, a young woman in a lab coat held open a door, and the nurses whisked Daddy through.

The woman startled when she looked at me, but she said, "You're going to have to wait outside."

At another time I would have stepped aside, would have gladly sunk onto one of the chairs lining the hallway, but after losing Tucker, I wasn't having any of it. "No," I said.

"Excuse me?"

I didn't bother repeating myself. I was gentle about it, but even with my injured wrist, it wasn't that hard to push her aside and walk into the room.

I could feel Rena and Carly crowding the doorway behind

me. One of the nurses threaded a drip into Daddy's arm, and the other, a heavyset Asian man, was doing something with the machine that took vitals and other signs. The four white-coats were moving deliberately as well, and despite them all looking young to me, it was clear who was calling the shots.

The doctor in charge didn't even look up before saying it: "Get out."

"No," I said to her. I felt Carly pull at my arm and I shook her off. "I'm staying."

One of the other doctors, a pair of scissors in his hand, glanced at me and then did a double-take. I realized that I'd pulled the gauze off my head, and I could feel the uncomfortable tickle of trickling blood again.

The doctor in charge still didn't look up from what she was doing. "Every time I have to tell you to get out of this room it takes my attention away from . . . is this your father?"

Rena answered. "He's our daddy."

"Your father," the doctor continued. "And if you don't leave this room I'm going to have to stop what I'm doing to make sure that you leave this room. I'm assuming you'd rather have me paying attention to your father?" She looked up at me and then frowned. "Marcus, get somebody to see to her. She's injured," she said, and then she let us away from her attention. The Asian nurse stepped away from the monitor and grabbed my arm. I let him pull me out of the room.

A before and an after.

What we had and what we didn't have.

Sixteen stitches, just below the hairline. A broken wrist set in a cast. That's what I had.

A husband lost to the ocean. An empty casket. Two children without a father. That's what Rena had.

And then, 2:46 A.M.

Woodbury Kings.

That's who we no longer had.

I kept looking back at the two coffins strapped to the deck of the *Kings' Ransom*, one empty, one not.

The wind was dead calm, the water flatlined, the late morning light white and tunneling over us. There was nothing left of the storm. The instrument panel was dead, and there was a faint smell of ash from the fire that had been on the roof of the cabin, but the *Kings' Ransom* cut through the water like a shovel through loose dirt; one night in the hospital and then another night in a hotel were enough for all of the vestigial fury from the storm to wash away.

I couldn't figure out what day of the week it was, but the ocean was deserted. Even close to shore we hadn't passed more than a handful of boats, and out here, near enough to the island that I was starting to see familiar buoys marking sets of traps, there was no activity. I hadn't expected anybody to be out today. I knew the whole island would be at the funeral. Nobody was going to be pulling traps today. We passed a line of John O'Connor's familiar white with a band of blue and a band of green, then a cluster of Petey Dogger's. I could see up to where Timmy and Harly both had a patch of buoys floating, and I knew that past that, close enough to shore that you could reach them with a set of oars and a wooden skiff, like Kings had done for generations before we moved to boats with motors, I'd be coming to one of Daddy's larger sets.

There was a part of me that wanted to stop and pull his traps. Even in my funeral clothes—we were heading straight from the docks to the cemetery—I thought there'd be something comforting in reaching a gaff out under one of Daddy's buoys, snagging the line, slapping it into the hauler, the familiar whir and then the break of the wire through the surface of the water. There'd be a fine haul in there, that I knew, and even with my broken wrist, the ache of the stitches, and the bruises on my face, I'd be more comfortable out on the wreck that was the *Kings' Ransom* than receiving mourners at Daddy's house. Given the state that they were in, I didn't think Carly or Rena would even notice if I stopped to haul a couple of traps, though I wasn't sure that I could handle it with only one good hand. Steering the boat in calm weather was one thing, but handling a trap was another. If I had Kenny out there with me, I thought, I could spend the entire day on the water instead of on land among the suits and black dresses.

I was running slow, trying to time things so that we could go right to the cemetery without having to wait, and I realized that up ahead, past the last of Timmy's buoys, the colors floating in the water were all wrong. Yellow with a triple ring of sky-blue and a band of green. James fucking Harbor. There wasn't a single one of Daddy's buoys left. Whoever it was had cut every single one loose. They'd erased any sign that Daddy had ever been here, that he'd been fishing these waters for nearly forty years, that our family had been pulling lobsters from this patch of ocean for three centuries. I turned to call for my sisters, but when I did, I saw that they hadn't even noticed.

Rena had spent the entire trip with her back to me, leaning against the washboard and looking back at where we came from, as if she wanted to wait as long as possible before seeing Loosewood Island. She looked oddly beautiful like that, in her mourning clothes, her hair fluttering in the breeze. The previous afternoon, after we'd taken care of choosing caskets for Daddy and Tucker, I'd left Rena and Carly at the hotel and gone to a department store to buy clothes for the funeral: three black dresses, three pairs of black tights, three pairs of flats, three black peacoats. Even given the circumstances, I hadn't just been able to buy clothing that we'd throw away, and the coat cut a flattering silhouette for Rena now. Carly was standing behind Rena and leaning against her, the two of them a bulkhead against the grief that we were carrying.

And as we moved past the James Harbor buoys, as angry as I was, and as much as I wanted to cut the traps loose, I didn't have it in me to stir my sisters. Instead, I kept us moving. As we rounded the point of the island and I got my first view of the harbor, whatever thoughts I had of that burst of invading colors were wiped away by the assembly of boats.

I knew that people would turn out for the funeral, but I hadn't expected this.

The entire harbor was choked with boats.

I sucked in heavy mouthfuls of air, like I'd been gut-punched. It was physically imposing, the sheer heft of it. There were three hundred, four hundred, five hundred boats. The sun glinted off antennas; the water was covered in fiberglass and wood, every inch of space marked by lobster boats, sailboats, motorboats, larger fishing vessels. There were boats anchored out past where we kept mooring buoys for the island's fleet, and I saw a stream of skiffs headed to the land. The ferry was docked, and the only open water was a path that had been left for me to bring the *Kings' Ransom* up to the wharf. I slowed down the boat and felt a hand on my waist.

"Jesus," Carly said. "They've come out in force for Daddy, haven't they?" I felt Rena's weight on my other side. "And Tucker," Carly added.

"No," Rena said. "They're here for Daddy. Some of them, the ones who knew him, are here for Tucker, too, but they're here for Daddy. The whole of them."

"It's beautiful," I said, and I realized that I was crying.

The dock was a tangle of men and women. As we came in to the space that had been left open for us, I started being able to pick people out. Some of them were obvious—George and Mackie standing with Guppy and Fatty, Stephanie in a modest black dress and blue trench coat, Kenny wearing a dark suit—and others were men and women I hadn't seen in years, people who'd moved off-island, or who lived in Boston, Montreal, and Halifax, Northport and James Harbor and Calais. The crowd stretched thick down the length of the docks, ran up the road, spilled onto lawns and in front of businesses. There wasn't enough land on the island for the greatness of all of it. Every piece of space was filled with suits and dark dresses.

As I came to the dock I realized that every single one of those people had stopped what they were doing, stopped talking, and turned to face us. I brought the *Kings' Ransom* in so softly that I couldn't even tell when we'd stopped moving entirely. Chip and Tony Warner grabbed her and tied her off to the dock and I shut off the motor.

The quiet of a couple of thousand people is something different. Off to the side, in a crowd of fishermen I thought I recognized from Lubec, a man moved to take off his hat, but otherwise the crowd was still. There were no words. There was the brush of the water against the pilings of the docks, calls from the gulls circling above. There was the hush of suit coats and leather shoes, a woman coughing, a child crying out of sight. George reached out his hand to Rena, and she stepped onto shore. She let Fatty and Guppy wrap their arms around her, putting a hand on each of her children's heads. Carly stepped her way up and over and slipped her hand into Stephanie's. I turned and looked at the coffins.

Rena had pinned my hair back that morning, and I touched it to make sure it was still up. I felt the sweet relief of the ache from where I'd gotten the stitches. Even though the seas had been calm, the coffins had been strapped down to the deck so that they wouldn't shift. I started trying to untie the knot on Tucker's coffin, fumbling with one good hand and a broken wrist. I could feel the weight of the crowd waiting for me, and it seemed like I was there forever working at the knot.

And then I felt Kenny's hand covering mine. I felt it before I saw it, before I heard him say, "I'm here." He reached out with his other hand so that he had both of them covering mine. It felt odd where his skin touched against the seam between my skin and the cast on my wrist. He bent over and his tie swung out. "Here," he said again. "I'll get it, Cordelia. Let me do it for you."

I let my left hand swing away, but he didn't push at my right hand. He left it on the knot and worked at the rope along with me. I could feel the knot loosening beneath our fingers, could feel the way that a line comes to obedience, can be melted into slackness by somebody who knows how to touch it properly. He slipped the end of the rope out of its embrace and then moved to the second line on Tucker's coffin, leaving me standing at the other end. He didn't look up as he untied that knot, moving from there to Daddy's coffin. I left the line uncoiled on the deck of the boat.

When Kenny finished, he walked over to me and took my arm. We stepped into the cabin and watched as a party of men came on board, men I'd grown up with, men I'd fished with, men who defined my idea of Loosewood Island, men now placing themselves on the edges of Daddy's coffin and Tucker's coffin. The men lifted the handles and turned the coffins, marching them to the edge of the boat and then passing them up to the men on the dock. Once they had all disembarked, they took their places as pallbearers again.

"Wait." The sound of my own voice startled me, and I called out again. "Wait," I said, and I scrambled over the edge of the *Kings' Ransom* and onto the dock. I walked over to Daddy's coffin and touched Paul Paragopolis on the shoulder. "Do you mind?" I said. Paul shook his head lightly and let me slip in among the pallbearers, taking his place from him. There were eight pallbearers, but the coffin felt almost unbearably heavy as the weight settled on my right arm. Maybe I was just tired, I thought, but I suddenly wondered if I would be able to carry Daddy's coffin as far as the cemetery. Then, behind me, I heard a few low words, and felt a shifting.

"I'm right behind you, girl," George said quietly. He said it quietly enough that, despite the quiet of the men and women lining the street, I was the only one who could hear him. "I'm here, and I'll walk with you, okay, Cordelia?"

I turned my head enough that he could see me nod, see the small smile I gave him, and I hoped he understood how reassuring it was to have him behind me. George Sweeney might have been the strongest man I've ever met. He was gentle, but he was a big man, thick with work, and I remembered a time when I was a child when I saw him haul two wooden traps from the water, one in each hand, the wood dripping from the sea, full of lobsters and weighted by bricks, and it looking like nothing to George. And then, when I turned my head forward again, I saw that Kenny had taken the place of the man in front of me, and in front of Kenny, Timmy Green had stepped in, Etsuko beside him, holding their baby. On the other side of the coffin, Chip and Tony Warner, Tucker's sternman, Colin O'Connor, and George's sternman, Matty Frieze. And though Daddy's coffin didn't feel any lighter, I knew I could carry it.

The silent mourners, packed tight along the road, made a corridor for us to pass through: Tucker's coffin, Daddy's coffin, Rena and Fatty and Guppy, Carly and Stephanie. I could feel people closing in behind us. There was no talking, and I could hear the sound of footsteps, of rustling clothing. We walked past the Grumman Fish House like that, past Swedie's General, past the Brumfitt Kings Museum, past the Five and Five, past Rena's house, past Daddy's house, past the park and the elementary school, past the bench where Brumfitt tourists liked to sketch the harbor, and into the cemetery, where there were two holes waiting in the earth.

S*tone Marker* is a self-portrait, of sorts. It's not a traditional self-portrait, but there's no question to me that the man in the painting, whom you only see from behind, is Brumfitt. The cemetery has changed a lot since 1774, but it's also stayed the same, and it's easy to find Brumfitt's grave. Mostly, the cemetery has gotten bigger, but it's still in the same place. It's bordered by houses now, and the island put a low metal fence around it sometime before the Second World War, but it still sits on the hummock, still has a clear view out over the water and the harbor. Plenty of islanders with people on the mainland, which is to say, everyone, end up making their dirt beds off the island, but the Kings have always been buried on the rock. Back when Brumfitt painted *Stone Marker*, however, there were only a few Kings in the ground.

Not all of the gravestones in the painting have survived, but enough have that, with a reproduction in hand, you can figure out that the man in the painting is working on what became Brumfitt's gravestone. Though you only see his back, you can tell by the way he's bent over, by the curve of his arm, by the thin gray hair hanging from his head, that it won't be long until the cemetery isn't a place he just comes as a guest. It's hard to see much of what he's carving into the rock. He's got a chisel pressed against the marker, a hammer in his other hand, and there's a small girl, maybe seven or eight years old, standing next to him and working as an assistant.

I suppose you could argue that the man in the painting is supposed to be somebody other than Brumfitt, but when you stand in front of Brumfitt's grave, when you rub your fingers on the carved letters in the rock, it's hard to believe it could have been anybody else.

Instead of catching the gravestone so that the painting included the water, Brumfitt focuses on the spread of the cemetery, and he positions the man, the girl, and the gravestone in the lower left of the painting, so that the majority of the canvas is grass and rock and trees, showing the empty space that would come to be inexorably filled by bodies, the empty space that would come to be marked by stone.

I'd stayed at the cemetery for what seemed like forever, standing next to Rena and Carly, shaking hands and taking hugs from men and women I'd known my whole life and from men and women I didn't recognize. Men, big men, men who worked hard for a living, who carried scars on their hands and who at one time lifted water-soaked wood traps like they were nothing, stood in front of me and cried. Women shook their heads and trembled. Through all of it, I stood there and thanked them and said yes and no and thank you, and at some point people started drifting away from the cemetery. When I looked off over the water I saw that there was a steady stream of boats leaving the harbor, people leaving the island and heading back to their lives on the mainland, able to escape as if nothing had changed. One of the boats, however, didn't seem to be steaming away from the island: it was working out among the thicket of buoys.

"I'll be back in a minute," I said, touching Carly's arm.

The day had turned warm, and at some point after Daddy's coffin was lowered into the ground, after the priest had said everything that he had to say, somebody had taken my coat. I couldn't remember who it was, but I knew that it would make its way back to me. Without it, the sun felt good on the black cotton of my dress, on my bare arms. My left hand and wrist would look odd when the doctor peeled the cast off. I'd seen the way skin came out worm-pale and soft after a few weeks or months under a cast, and I knew that it would take me a while before I was back to where I needed to be on the boat. For now, I thought, I'd need an extra sternman, somebody to help Kenny out with the things I couldn't manage with one hand. And as soon as I had the thought, I felt myself trying to choke back another round of tears, because I realized that with Daddy dead and Tucker dead, Stephanie and Colin O'Connor didn't have boats to work. There were sternmen to go around. I wasn't worried about Colin. I guessed that his father would help him buy Tucker's boat, and he'd just take over Tucker's line. It wasn't the way the O'Connors had been planning things, but Colin was an islander through and through, and he didn't need any more time as a sternman. That left Stephanie as my responsibility, and if she and Carly were still planning on staying on the island with Daddy gone, I'd be taking her on. We'd be fishing my line and Daddy's line for a while, until I had things sorted out, and certainly with my broken wrist I needed the help anyway.

I leaned against the fence and looked out over the water. The boat that I'd seen in the thicket of buoys was still there. Somebody was out working. I couldn't make out whose boat it was. I tried squinting, but that didn't seem to help. There was a time when I could have seen the boat clearly, would have known whose it was. I was barely thirty, too young to be getting old, too young to start needing glasses. Besides, I thought, Daddy was older than me, and he still didn't need glasses for distance.

It took me a beat to remember. Daddy would never need glasses.

I folded my arms on the top of the fence and leaned my head on them. The cast felt odd and cool against my face.

"You are watching the boat?"

I looked up at the sound of Etsuko's voice. After the crush of the mourners, it was good to have a few seconds alone, but seeing Etsuko made me feel like myself again. For a moment I thought she had brought me my coat, and I started to tell her no, that I was fine, that I was warm enough, when I realized that it was a bundled baby in her arms. My godson.

"Here," I said, reaching out. "Let me hold him."

"You are okay with the broken arm?"

"It's just my wrist," I said. "I'm okay."

She passed me the baby without any of the hesitation that I was so used to from new mothers. I cradled the baby in my right arm. I couldn't do much with my left hand, but I had enough movement that I could pinch the blanket and pull the fabric down so that I could see his face. "Oh, he's beautiful," I said. He really was beautiful. His skin was smooth and he was lighter than I had expected. Timmy's skin was so dense that even with Etsuko's paleness, I hadn't been able to picture the baby as anything other than a carbon of his father, but he netted out somewhere in between the two of them. "What color are his eyes?"

"Green," Etsuko said, "like his last name. Like the sea." She put her hand on the rail of the fence. In places, the metal had rusted out; it was entirely ornamental, and when there had been talk about replacing it a few years ago, the consensus was that the age of the fence was part of what made the cemetery such an idyllic place, a comfort for the bereaved.

He was sleeping, but I turned so that the baby was looking out over the ocean. "There it is," I said. "That's where your daddy works and where you'll work someday." I stopped and looked at Etsuko. "I don't even know what his name is."

"Mordecai," she said. "After Timmy's grandfather. Mordecai Ichikawa Green."

Mordecai felt so small and light in my arms that I could have been holding nothing. It was hard to believe that this was what Etsuko had been keeping inside of her for nine months. As I cradled him, I looked up over the ocean again. The sun flattened everything, and the sea seemed both endless and impossibly small.

The stream of boats leaving the harbor made a line toward the mainland, and out in the other direction, there was still that same boat moving slowly through the school of buoys. The lobster boat was closer now, close enough that when it turned away from me, I could see the name, and more importantly, the port, painted on the back: JAMES HARBOR.

Even with the steady stream of people who'd already departed the island, there were too many people for there to be a single building on the island that could handle the mourners. It would have been tough if it was raining or cold, but with the sun and the unseasonable warmth, the streets remained clogged. People spilled out of the Grumman Fish House, the diner, the Coffee Catch. They spilled out of houses and onto the streets.

I put my head down and turned and walked back to Daddy's house. Inside, it was cool and quiet. For all the people on the island, nobody had thought to come to Daddy's house yet. I closed the door behind me and then let my head rest against the door. All I wanted to do was close myself up somewhere dark. I slipped my shoes onto the boot rack and walked upstairs.

I went into Daddy's room. I didn't go in there often. The shades were open, and the light melted over the dresser and the floor. Daddy had made the bed with sharp corners, and when I sat on it, I was conscious of bringing creases into the world. I lay down for a minute, closing my eyes and taking a deep breath, but I couldn't smell anything. Nothing lingered behind in the air. I wasn't sure how long I lay there, but when I got up to pee, I went into his bathroom. I washed my hands and my face, and then I opened his medicine cabinet. There, on the glass shelf: prescription bottles. More than I had expected, but as many as I'd feared. The bottles were mostly full, and I picked one up to look at it. The date was from the spring, from when I'd found him out cold on the kitchen floor. Medicine he hadn't told me about. I touched a couple of the other bottles and found the same thing: they'd been filled months before and were still full or barely emptied. Even with my nagging, he still hadn't been taking the pills. I didn't recognize any of the names, but there was an alphabet of untaken medicine on the shelf. I wanted to be angry at the stubborn bastard, but I wasn't. I just closed the cabinet.

From his bathroom and his bedroom, I drifted down the hall to my own bedroom. It seemed small to me. I still had trophies from high school on my dresser, still had the same bedspread. There was a time when that room felt so familiar, so comforting to me, and though it felt familiar still, it wasn't a comfort. I knew I'd be coming back to this house tonight, that I wouldn't be staying in the rental house anymore. With Daddy gone, this was my house now. It wasn't a decision, really. It was just the way it was going to be. But all I could think about was that in all the days and nights I'd spent in this house, I'd never felt alone.

That's what I was thinking when I heard the knock on the door, and when I opened the front door to see Kenny standing there, that's what I said to him: "I don't want to be alone."

He stepped inside, hung his suit jacket on a hook, and then shut the door carefully behind him. He was excruciatingly gentle with the close of the door. It barely clicked as he seated it home. "I'm here, Cordelia."

"You don't have to be so careful with the door, Kenny. You're not going to wake him," I said. "It's not like he's sleeping in the back."

He tried to smile at me, but his face looked broken. He took my hand in his. "Don't," he said. "Don't try to do that. It's okay,

Cordelia. You don't have to act tough. Just, don't. Not with me. I'm here. You don't have to be alone. Okay? This isn't the kind of day when you have to be alone."

I wasn't sure if he pulled me into his arms or if I stepped into them, but either way we stood in the entrance, with him holding me.

I kissed him.

My lip was still sore from smashing it on the boat the night of the storm, and I was gentle. I had my good hand around his neck and I bent him down to me, brushed my lips against his lips, sent my tongue touching against his mouth. I pressed my body against him, and I said his name, "Kenny," so quietly that I thought maybe I'd just thought it.

"Cordelia." He breathed my name out, and I responded by pressing my lips harder against him, until the soreness of my lips turned into something good. I felt like I was drunk, my head going light. My hand was shaking on the back of his neck. His fingers were in my hair.

"Cordelia," he said again, barely pulling back, our lips still whispering against each other. "What are you doing?" I could feel him hesitate, the way he wanted to push back against me, but he closed his eyes and leaned away, into the door. "Why now, Cordelia?"

"Please," I said. "I'm asking you. I need this. I need you." I tiptoed up and pulled him down to me so that I could kiss him again, and when I did, his lips matched mine. I leaned into his body, pressing my breasts against his chest, my hips into his, and I could feel him getting hard.

"Cordelia," he said, as I moved my mouth to his neck, and let my hand slip over his collarbone, down his side, and across his stomach. My left hand felt weird and numb against his hip, like it was dead inside the cast, but the rest of my body was incredibly alive. My stomach was swimming and my legs quivered like I had a boat bucking beneath me. I pushed my good hand firmly against his stomach and then turned it so that I could slide my fingers between his shirt and his waistband.

"Cordelia," he said again. He grabbed my arm and stopped me from slipping my hand fully into his pants, but his grip wasn't that strong. "Cordelia. We shouldn't do this. You know we... You don't want to do this. You're just upset. You're not thinking."

"There's no reason not to, Kenny. I want to. I need to." I slid my hand farther down into his pants and he let the grip on my arm relax. I felt him shudder, taking a breath when I touched him. He felt hot in my hand. I wanted him inside of me more than I'd ever wanted anything. I took my hand back out and then fumbled with his belt, the cast on my hand making things more difficult than they needed to be. I fished the loop of his belt out, flicked the pin out of the hole, and then slipped the button on his suit pants.

"We shouldn't, Cordelia," he said, but he wasn't making any more moves to stop me. He closed his eyes and leaned back heavily against the solid door as I touched him again, the skin of my fingers closing around him.

"Shh," I said. At that moment, with my hand on him, I didn't care.

"I—"

I pressed my lips against his to quiet him, and then he reached back and locked the door. We moved without speaking, and it was like we'd been doing this together forever, like we were out on the water on the *Kings' Ransom*, the way we moved in concert. He put his hands against the outside of my thighs and scrunched my dress up under his fingers until he was touching my skin, and then he ran his fingers up even farther until he hooked them over the edge of my panties. I pushed his pants down past his hips and then let them fall out of my hands. I lay down on the floor of the front hall, holding his hand and taking him down with me, and he was slow and careful as he let the weight of his body press against me. I kissed him again, and we stayed with that for a few seconds, his tongue just brushing against the edge of my lip. I shifted my leg up, bending it, letting him move closer, but he hesitated.

"Are you sure, Cordelia? Are you sure this is a good idea?"

I didn't answer. I just reached down and took hold of him. He let out a thick breath and closed his eyes before pushing in all of the way. The tile was cool through the back of my dress, and I tucked my face into the hollow between his shoulder and neck. He rocked against me and in me, and the pressure of him was the only thing I could concentrate on.

There was knocking at the door, but Kenny and I stayed quiet. It was just our breathing and the rub of our bodies on each other, the slide of my back on the floor. I don't know how long it was that we were like that, but all of a sudden Kenny's breath started to catch, and then he pushed hard and stayed there, burying himself and shaking.

We lay like that for a while. His weight was warm and made me sleepy. Finally, he kissed my ear and rolled to the side.

"I hope . . ." He trailed off and then tried again. "What's it going to be like tomorrow, Cordelia?"

"Tomorrow?" I turned over and propped myself up on my elbow, resting my cast on his stomach. "I guess we'll have to check the weather report, see what the seas are going to be like. I'm hoping for another warm, sunny, calm day like this one. We've got traps to pull."

"We're going fishing?"

I leaned over and kissed him on the lips. For an instant I was terrified, because he didn't respond, but then I felt him come alive underneath me, kissing me back. I bit his lower lip softly and then pushed myself to my feet, my hand on his chest. "The lobsters won't catch themselves, Kenny."

He got to his feet and slowly pulled his pants back up, tucking in his shirttails and smoothing himself down. "You can't help yourself, can you Cordelia?" He shook his head, but he was smiling. He grabbed his jacket from the hook and then swung it on. "What do you want me to do?"

"Will you head over to Rena's with me? I don't think I can face all of them alone, all those people talking about Daddy." I frowned, and then winced. I'd forgotten about the stitches and how, when they were pulled tight, they ached.

"Of course I'll come to Rena's," he said. He reached out and pushed a loose strand of my hair back behind my ear. "Of course I'll be there."

I closed my eyes and let myself lean against him.

By eleven, the twins had long gone to bed, and the dozen or so people left in Rena's house, other than my sisters and me, collected empty cups and bottles, plates with bits of cookies, crumpled napkins. Timmy was asleep in Tucker's recliner, a half-drunk bottle of beer resting in the cup holder of Mordecai's stroller, Etsuko in the kitchen washing dishes. Chip and Tony were chatting with George—talking about how best to deal with Tucker and Daddy's lines, with my lines, I knew—when I announced I was headed to bed.

"Early start tomorrow," I said, loud enough that the other people in the room could hear me. "Stephanie, Kenny, early start." Kenny nodded, but Stephanie stared at me blankly. She looked at Carly, and after a moment's hesitation, Carly nodded.

"It's a fishing day," I said.

Stephanie looked at me, back to Carly, and then at me again. "It's the day after Woody's funeral."

"It's a fishing day," I said. Everybody in the room was quiet, and then, finally, Stephanie nodded. "Early," I said. "We'll push at five-thirty."

I started to turn and then I stopped. "There was a James

Harbor boat out in the water today." I looked at George, and he tried not to meet my eye, but then he nodded.

"I saw it," he said.

"And?"

"Looked like the same one that shot at me."

"You sure?"

"The only thing I'm sure of, Cordelia, is that things are changing."

"No," I said. "No, they aren't. These are still our waters."

I woke up a few minutes before my alarm clock was scheduled to go off. Kenny had come home with me, and I slipped out of bed, careful not to wake him. I'd forgotten to ask if I could get my cast wet, so I kept it out of the spray as best I could. I was awkwardly trying to shampoo my hair when Kenny got in the shower with me.

He picked up the soap and started rubbing my back with it. The tenderness of the gesture almost made me start crying, and I ducked my head down so that my face got wet before turning and leaning my head back so that I could rinse out the shampoo.

We weren't more than a couple of minutes late down to the docks, but Stephanie was waiting in the skiff. She'd put the oars in their locks and was sitting on the bench with her hands wrapped around the handles. She didn't smile when she saw us, but her voice was light when she said, "You ready, Skipper?"

"I guess I can't row, can I?"

Kenny laughed. "With one hand, we'd be going in circles." I stepped into the skiff and settled myself down at the bow. Trudy worked her way from dock to bench to the bottom of the boat and then waddled over to where Stephanie was sitting. She nosed at Stephanie until Stephanie scratched her neck and ears, and then she flopped down. We were halfway out to the *Kings' Ransom* when I touched Stephanie on the shoulder.

"No," I said. "Over there. The *Queen Jane*." She glanced at me and then changed course without a word. "At least until I can get the *Kings' Ransom* fixed up," I said, though she hadn't asked. "The electronics are still shot."

I ran the *Queen Jane* back to the wharf while Kenny and Stephanie started gearing up. The tank was half full, but I filled it at the co-op anyway and then we loaded up with enough bait to work through both my line and Daddy's. As I was signing my chit, I realized Kenny was looking at me like he'd accidently broken something.

"What?"

"No chai, boss. I didn't bring the thermos, and I didn't bring anything to eat, either." He looked down and then scuffed his boot on the deck. I glanced over to Stephanie, who was chatting with Paul Paragopolis near the offices.

I cut Kenny a smile. "What's the matter? Something got you distracted this morning?" I popped open the console box and rooted around. "No matter," I said. "You can run up to the Coffee Catch, get us something for the day. Daddy always keeps some cash in here. I'll get him back later." I stopped and closed my eyes, realizing what I'd said. I closed the box. "Fuck it. Just tell them I'll pay for it tonight, when we're back onshore. Grab some sandwiches—see what Stephanie wants. I'll take a coffee, too." He raised an eyebrow and I found that there was still the hint of a smile left in me. "Fine. A tea."

Kenny touched me lightly and then turned to walk up the path. He stopped and said a few words to Stephanie. She nodded and went with him. Paul looked over and gave me an unsure wave.

I waved back, but I turned to the boat. I didn't have anything left that needed to be done, but I didn't want to have to face Paul. I didn't want to face anyone. I was glad that we were headed out on the water. Even with a broken wrist, the pattern of pulling traps was something that would feel familiar. I hadn't fished with Daddy for years, since I'd had my own boat, but it was something that I'd learned from him. Everything I did on the boat, every practice, every movement, was something I'd inherited from him, and I couldn't think of a better way to be with him than to be out on the water on the *Queen Jane*. Let Rena and Carly stay at home, let them make coffee and accept condolences, let them sit on the couch and cry, I thought. I wanted to be out on the ocean, where the Kings belonged.

I ran my hand along the rail of the *Queen Jane* and let it linger on the scar that the rope had burned into the wood on the day that Scotty had gone overboard. There should be something similar for Daddy, a mark, but there wasn't, and it felt strange. It had never occurred to me that he'd die on land. I had never even really believed that he'd die at all. I'd seen him getting older, of course, seen the way his hair silvered and his skin took the sun, but I was never able to see him as anything other than the man who'd sat there calmly when I'd lip-hooked him, a lure dangling from his lip, blood dripping down his chin. Even with the fainting, the recent troubles, I'd known, but I'd never really *believed* it. Maybe it was better. He wasn't somebody who would have been suited for a recliner, for growing old gracefully.

I'd left Fifth with Rena, but Trudy had come along and didn't seem put out by taking the *Queen Jane* instead of the *Kings' Ransom*. I reboarded the *Queen Jane* and waited for Trudy to settle herself out on the deck before I went forward to the wheelhouse. I opened one of the lockers and sorted through it fitfully. It was no surprise to me that it was neatly organized. Spare slickers were on a hook, the toolbox was latched closed, lines were neatly coiled. It looked the same as the lockers on the *Kings' Ransom*; Daddy was the one who'd taught me how to stow my gear. I held on to the door and touched the stitches on my forehead. The stitches itched and I was dizzy.

I should have been happy, standing on the boat, knowing that Kenny was going to come back to me, but I felt uneasy in a way that I never was on a boat. When I closed my eyes, I wasn't sure if we were tied to the dock or if I was simply adrift at sea, and it was unsettling to not be able to tell. I opened my eyes back up, and what stood in front of me, what I stood upon, was Daddy's boat, the *Queen Jane*, but Daddy was nowhere in sight and never would be. I wasn't stupid. I wasn't dumb enough to think that because I'd slept with Kenny, because it seemed like what I wanted was within my grasp, that it would make me forget that Daddy had died, but until that moment I hadn't understood that there'd be something more than sadness.

I admired Daddy, but I knew he hadn't been perfect. There were things about him that I believed even though they weren't true. I'd mythologized him in the same way that every child mythologized—or demonized—her father. To be fair, it was probably easier to mythologize Daddy than it was most fathers. Even if I just stuck to the things that were undeniably true, he was still unlike anybody else. And I know it sounds naïve, but it hadn't occurred to me that being sad that he was gone and missing him were two separate things. I'd cried at the hospital and at the funeral, cried so hard that my lungs ached and my eyes hurt, but it was only standing there, on the deck of the *Queen Jane*, that I realized I also missed him.

Even when I was at college, I'd never gone more than a couple of days without talking to him, and when I was at home, on Loosewood Island, which is to say my entire life, he was everywhere I looked. I could trace my name all the way back to Brumfitt Kings, to the first of Loosewood Island, and for some people, that was what made the Kings the kings of Loosewood Island, but I realized that as much as I'd spent my life poring over Brumfitt's journals, looking at his paintings, painting my own versions of the landscape he'd claimed, when it came down to it, the island wasn't defined for me by Brumfitt. Loosewood Island was defined for me by Daddy, by the way he told me stories about Brumfitt and stories about his own childhood, how he'd learned to fish, by the way he'd taken me by the hand when I was a child and walked me down the crushed-shell paths, by the way he'd shown me the waters and taught me to fish myself. And it was defined by the stories that Daddy didn't tell me: the way he never talked about his older brother or his father, the way he never mentioned Billy Sweeney dying in Vietnam except for that one day on the boat, when he killed Second. He didn't talk about the time he spent in the loony bin, didn't talk about the way Scotty had looked when we'd pulled him from the water, and he didn't talk about the way Momma had walked out to the end of the wharf and then decided not to stop walking.

He'd defined Loosewood Island for me, and I realized that he'd defined Brumfitt Kings for me as well. Most people looked at Brumfitt's paintings and saw rocks and water, saw gulls and codfish and lobsters, saw the fishing boats and the contours of the island. Even when they looked at the paintings that had something else, all they saw were ghostly hands, all they saw were monsters. They never saw the things that Daddy saw, what I saw, the way that Brumfitt imagined the island as something more than a spit of rock upon which the Kings had chained their lives.

I closed the locker and then opened the one next to it. I wasn't sure what I was looking for, but I knew there was something that I wanted to find, something that I hoped would help me make sense of things. I was willing to believe that Brumfitt Kings' wife had been a gift from the sea, that she'd come with a dowry that meant the Kings would be given the bounty of the sea and a curse that meant the death of every firstborn son that bore the name Kings. But if I believed that, then I had to believe there was a way to break that curse, to stop the sea from taking back what it gave us.

My head ached, and I couldn't figure out if it was my head and my wrist and all of the bumps and bruises from the night of the storm catching up to me, or if I was just tired and dehydrated. There were several unopened bottles of water hanging from a mesh bag on the hook in the locker I'd just opened, and I fished one out. Above the hooks in the locker there was a shelf that held some papers. Maps and charts. They were organized in tabbed folders, but I doubted that Daddy had looked at them in decades. He'd built dividers lower down in the locker and he had his gun cases neatly strapped in. Two shotguns cases and a pistol, I knew. I undid the tab holding one of the shotgun cases in and laid the case on the captain's chair. The latches made a satisfying click when I opened them. I didn't pull the shotgun out. I just looked at it for a few seconds. It was oiled and I was sure that it was loaded. Daddy wanted things safe, but he'd also told me once that if he had to balance the safety of keeping a gun unloaded against the safety of having it ready to go, he'd rather err on the side of things going boom.

By the time I finished rooting through the lockers, Kenny and Stephanie hadn't come back yet, and I decided to look belowdecks. It wasn't much of a space. Enough to store gear and for some uncomfortable sleeping. The *Kings' Ransom* was newer and nicer belowdecks, but there weren't any lobster boats in the island fleet that I could recommend instead of a night at home. I couldn't think of the last time I'd been below the *Queen Jane*. Certainly not since I was a young kid, before Scotty died. There was a time when it would have been fun to play down there with Scotty and my sisters, when a small, dark space could give hours of fun, but I know that by the time I was a teenager I had no use for the dank dampness below the decks.

Daddy kept all of the sorts of things that I would have expected him to keep down there. The same sort of crap I had on the *Kings Ransom*: spools of wire for repairing traps, spare parts for the engine, life-saving gear, lobstering supplies, a rough galley that wouldn't serve for more than heating up a can of soup. The stingy bunk was made with a blanket and pillow, hospital corners making it look even less inviting than it already was. There were things that surprised me, though. He'd built a small bookshelf, cordage keeping the books in their place, and I wondered when it was that he read on the *Queen Jane*. The books themselves were nothing that I would have looked twice at—a few Shakespeare plays; two Dickens novels; Jane Austen; Hemingway; *Moby-Dick*;

a few others I'd never read. To the side, there was a heavy trunk that was lashed against the wall, and it caught my attention because it looked big enough that I wasn't sure how Daddy had gotten it down the ladder. There was something about the trunk that was familiar, and I wondered if it had been there when I was a kid and still played belowdecks.

I had trouble one-handing the latch, an old-fashioned leather tongue that fastened like a belt, but after working it a bit, it came loose and I lifted open the lid of the trunk. Inside the trunk was another trunk, but this one was designed to be waterproof, made of hard blue molded plastic. It was the kind of plastic that could spend a month floating out on the ocean with no apparent ill effects. There were a couple inches of space on top of the plastic trunk where the lid of the wooden trunk would have closed, but the sides fit so closely that it was hard to believe that Daddy hadn't built the wooden trunk around the walls of the plastic one. Then I saw the small envelope with my name written on it in Daddy's cramped writing. It was tucked under the handle of the plastic lid, wedged in so it wouldn't come loose, and I had to tug to pull it out. The envelope wasn't sealed, and when I slipped out the card I thought at first it was blank. Of course, when I flipped it over, it wasn't.

"*Cordelia,*" it said, "*these are for you for when I'm gone. You can share with your sisters if you'd like, but these are for you. If I'm not dead, get the hell out of my stuff. But if I'm dead, remember that I've always loved you and always will. You'll know what to do.*"

He didn't sign his name, but it's not like he needed to.

I heard Kenny call me and then his steps on the deck. I was wiping my eyes with my sleeve when he ducked down and saw me.

"What are you doing down there?" he said. He was holding a paper bag from the Coffee Catch, and he had a smile to greet me until he noticed my tears. "You okay?" I saw him reach out and then he put his hands on the ladder and started down. I glanced at the plastic trunk.

"No," I said. "I'm okay. I'm coming up." He stopped, looked

at me, and then went back up the ladder. I put the card back in the envelope, wedged it under the handle again, and closed the lid to the wooden trunk. I stood there for a few seconds, my hand resting on the wood. It was smooth under my fingers. I left it unlatched. I'd had enough trouble undoing the clasp. I wasn't sure I could manage closing it. As it was, with my broken wrist, I struggled going up the few rungs that made the ladder. I was glad that Kenny reached down and helped me up.

Stephanie was sitting in the captain's chair eating a bagel. I must have given her a funny look, because she blushed and then blurted out, "I know, but it looked good, and I figured a second breakfast wasn't the worst thing I could do." I didn't say anything. "Oh," she said. "The chair." She scrambled to her feet. "Sorry."

"No. It's not that. It's . . . it's nothing. Actually, really, it's nothing. I think I'm just tired," I said, but I was thinking about what it was that Daddy had left for me in the blue plastic waterproof trunk.

Kenny was already by the stern, untying us from the dock. Stephanie started to raise her hand, hesitated, and then finished her movement, touching my hand. "It's okay," she said. "We don't have to go out today."

I think she was expecting me to bristle, but her voice was so gentle that it was all I could do not to start crying again, and I turned my hand over so that I could give hers a soft squeeze. "No, I do. I do have to go out today. It's all I know how to do, Stephanie."

She held my hand and did her best to smile, but I could tell that she was holding herself back from crying, too. "Okay," she said. "Let's go fishing."

And I thought about what Daddy's card said, that I'd know what to do, and suddenly I did. "No. First we have to run an errand."

Stephanie and Kenny were quiet all the way to James Harbor. They prepped gear and bait, and then they stayed at the stern, leaning out over the water and talking. I wondered if Kenny was telling Stephanie about our new arrangement.

As we came in sight of the harbor, I reached over and opened the locker that had Daddy's guns. I was going to order Kenny and Stephanie to stay on the boat, but I didn't plan on going in to talk to the James Harbor boys alone. Even if I didn't intend to fire one, I'd be accompanied by a shotgun. I was trying to figure out which one to take when I glanced again at the harbor.

"Jesus," I said, and I throttled the boat down. The water was choked with boats that I recognized. The *Green Machine*, George's boat, John O'Connor's boat, the Warner boys', all of them. The whole fleet from Loosewood Island. I kicked the locker closed and then brought the *Queen Jane* up to the only open spot on the docks.

I felt like I was moving in a daze. I didn't remember to tell Stephanie and Kenny to stay put, and they followed behind me. As we walked up the dock, I saw a group of men rounding the corner of the building. They were laughing and smiling. It was Timmy who saw me first and called out.

"You missed the meeting, Cordelia."

I stopped and waited for them to surround me. I don't know what expression I had on my face, but Timmy started laughing. "We rounded up a bunch of their boys. Not just Al Burns, but the younger ones, too. You can turn around, Cordelia. It's fixed. They'll stay out of our waters."

George scowled, but he also nodded. "Mostly fixed. They've got one or two boys who aren't part of their co-op and who don't seem to want to listen. We'll sort them out later, but I think the message has been sent. They can't do anything about the rogues, but James Harbor as a whole is done with poaching Loosewood Island waters." He took a few steps until he was in front of me, and then he cupped his hand around the back of my neck. "I heard you last night, Cordelia. I was listening, and you're right. Nothing's changed."

I didn't say anything. Nobody else did, either, and it took me a few seconds to realize they were waiting for me, that with Daddy gone, I was the one who had the final say. It took me a few more seconds past that realization to shake my head, let a grin creep onto my face, and to say, "Well, then, I'm going fishing."

Stephanie and Kenny settled in together immediately, like we'd picked up where we'd left off before we found the ghost ship. Instead of splitting my line and Daddy's line—or what was left of Daddy's line—like I'd done in September, I fished them as if they were a single line, working the water in chunks of geography. We started on the far side of the island, where depending on what way you looked you could only see either the hills and bluffs of the backside of the island or the open sea. It was as if the mainland didn't exist.

Every trap was bursting with bugs, and despite me being limited by the cast on my wrist, I pitched in best I could. We were moving slowly, not because we weren't being efficient, but because I'd never seen a haul like this. Even Trudy seemed excited, barking every time we pulled a trap to the surface. Normally there were lobsters that were oversized or undersized. Normally there were eggers or lobsters with notched tails that told us they were eggers at other parts of the year. Not today. Every single lobster we pulled from the traps was a keeper. The good weather had carried over from the funeral, and I worked up a sweat. Even with the trip to James Harbor and back, it wasn't even nine o'clock by the time I peeled off my sweatshirt and was down to a T-shirt. My cast was itchy, and I could feel water that had trickled underneath the plaster. I was hoping the doctor had used something that didn't mind getting wet. We'd worked our way through all of the traps on this stretch of water, and I grabbed the last lobster out of the last of Daddy's traps, slapping the brass gauge against its carapace, though by that point I didn't even know why I bothered. Every single lobster had been the right size, just small enough that they were still legal, but big enough that they'd fetch a premium.

Stephanie was over at the bait barrel, but I felt Kenny next to me. I looked at him and he was grinning fit to sink a ship. "What?" I said.

"The lobsters. Nice haul today." he said. "Never seen anything like it."

I banded the lobster, securing its claws closed, and chucked it in with the others. I didn't actually know what to say to him. What he said was true for me, too. I'd never seen anything like it, even when I'd been out with Daddy. I felt like I was going crazy, but the only thing I could think of was that this haul of lobsters was, in some sort of bizarre way, a gift, like the ocean was trying to tell me that it was sorry.

Enough. To the sea, I wanted to say: *Enough*. The Kings were fragile flesh and blood, and I'd had enough of the ocean clawing away at us. It was enough for Brumfitt to lose a son, and for each son of each generation to lose a son. It was enough for Scotty to die. It was enough to have Tucker washed away on the same night that Daddy died.

I realized that Kenny was still staring at me, waiting for an answer, and because I couldn't think of what to say and couldn't think of anything else to do, I grabbed him and kissed him. We were like that for a few seconds. I think that both Kenny and I realized at the same time that Stephanie was awfully quiet.

Stephanie kept looking back and forth from me to Kenny, and then finally she crouched down next to Trudy. She scratched at Trudy's head and said, "Well, I guess that's happening. And you know what? I'm just going to pretend that I didn't see that, and I'm going to go about my business as a lobsterman. How about we drop these last two traps back in the water and head around to the other side of the island like we'd planned? Sound okay to the two of you?" There was a tremor in her lips, and then she gave up and just let herself smile.

I gave Kenny another kiss and then headed forward to the wheel and pushed the throttle. I hadn't conned the *Queen Jane* in years, but I liked the way she felt in my hands. She rolled differently than the *Kings' Ransom*, but it was a familiar movement, and I was already thinking that maybe instead of selling Daddy's boat I'd sell the *Kings' Ransom*. My boat was going to need some time in the boatyard getting worked over after having everything blown out by the lightning strike, and it made a certain kind of sense to keep Daddy's boat instead. Behind me, Kenny and Stephanie had taken seats on spare lobster traps, and Kenny was fishing a donut out of the bag from the Coffee Catch. He held it up to me, but I shook my head. He shrugged and took a bite for himself before thinking to offer it to Stephanie. I faced forward again, though there wasn't much point. The water was empty aside from lobster buoys and seagulls, and other than ramming the side of the island, there wasn't much for me to hit. As we passed the harbor it seemed as though every boat was docked. I could only see a handful of men milling about on the wharf. I wondered if maybe I was the only fisherman out on the water today—if everybody but me had come back from James Harbor and decided that it was a day to spend onshore with their families.

We came fully around to the front of the island, the mainland laughing in the distance, the harbor hiding again. I was relieved to see that there was another boat out in the field of buoys. Even with Kenny and Stephanie on board, there was something lonely about seeing the ocean without anybody else working. At first we were far enough away that I couldn't see whose boat it was. I tried matching up where it was against Seal Coat Cove, but I wasn't sure with the angle how far past my and Daddy's buoys he was working. Could have been Petey Dogger, could have been John O'Connor, but I didn't think he was far enough past to be Mr. Warner. The way the shelf rippled around this part of the island, the buoys weren't spaced as tightly as they were at other places, but the closer we got to where we could pull our traps, the more I started feeling sick to my stomach about the boat in front of me. We were still half a mile away when I knew that it wasn't Petey or John or Mr. Warner, wasn't any of the boys who had a right to be out in these waters. I let our speed creep down to a quarter of what it had been, and I felt Kenny and Stephanie come up behind me. Trudy got to her feet and pushed herself between me and Stephanie.

"That what I think it is?" Kenny said.

"What?" Stephanie stepped up until she was almost right against the glass. "The boat? What about it?" She looked at Kenny, at me, through the glass, and then back at me and Kenny again. "What?"

"It's not one of ours," I said.

"I thought—"

"You thought wrong," I said, cutting her off. "You heard what George said. Not all of them. They took care of the bulk of James Harbor, but there's always some that do what they want."

Kenny reached out and pulled the microphone from its rest on the side of the radio. I grabbed his wrist and stopped him before he keyed it. "No."

"Come on, Cordelia. You know we've got to call it in. You know what Woody said."

"I know what he said, Kenny, and we're going to take care of this ourselves. The boys went to James Harbor this morning and they took care of something that I should have taken care of. With Daddy gone, that was my job to do this morning, and while I appreciate what the boys did, I'm not calling for help every time there's something scary out in these waters." I didn't let go of Kenny's wrist. He stared at me and I stared back, and then, after what seemed like a long time, Kenny put the mic back on its clip.

I didn't say that Daddy wasn't here to take care of me anymore, and I didn't say that I was sick of things, that I'd had enough. I was tired of doing things the right way. I was tired of the ocean dictating its terms to me. And I was fucking tired of James Harbor. The ones who wouldn't listen? I planned on making them listen. These were the Kings' waters. These were my waters.

The fellows in the other boat saw us coming and were waiting. They weren't surprised when I turned the *Queen Jane* broadside, but even though I shouldn't have been, I *was* surprised to see Eddie Glouster looking back at me. I'd left a hefty gap between the two boats, almost a boat length, but suddenly it didn't seem hefty enough, and I began to regret not having Kenny call it in. I glanced over at the radio, and Kenny saw me. He lifted his eyebrow. *Let's see how things pan out*, I tried to say to him with the way I shook my head.

"Fancy seeing you here," Eddie called across. He had his arms down at his sides. I couldn't see his hands. The same went for the other man on the boat. I didn't know his name, but I recognized him as one of the men who'd been there the night we burned Eddie off the island. At the thought, the image of Oswald Cornwall, face blown through, came to me. It wasn't hard to imagine Oswald on his knees, begging, crying, saying it was only money, and Eddie standing behind him, gun to the back of his head, pulling the trigger. I kept thinking of the other body, too, the one that went with that finger.

I looked over the water. Near as I could tell, all of my buoys were still there, but Daddy's had been thinned out. I expected to see yellow buoys with a triple ring of sky-blue and a band of green, and I wasn't disappointed. "You're in the wrong waters," I called back.

He shrugged, but he still kept his hands down. I couldn't figure out if he was holding a rifle or a shotgun or something smaller. But I didn't think his hands were empty. If this was the same boat that had fired on George—and at this point, I was willing to put money on it—then there was a good chance Eddie was holding a shotgun. But maybe it was a pistol. I was hoping pistol. I wasn't sure how good a shot he was, but most people aren't as good at handling a firearm as they think they are, and pistols are a bitch to aim, particularly with the motion of a boat.

"I've heard you've got an opening, what with your daddy finally kicking the bucket. Besides, you've got plenty of lobsters," Eddie said. "You won't even notice I'm here."

"Sorry," I said across the open space between our boats. "We're full up on assholes, Eddie."

He seemed to be enjoying himself, but he was also bouncing a little, like he was full of a nervous energy, and for the first time I had the thought that he might be hopped up on something. He was thinner than when I'd last seen him, the night of the fire, and I tried to remember what I knew about meth. "You know, I pulled those traps and emptied them before I cut them." His voice faded in and out over the idle of my motor, but his words were still clear. "I don't know what the fuck your daddy was using for bait, but the lobsters sure love it." He finally showed one of his hands, lifting it up to cover his mouth in mock surprise. The other hand stayed firmly down, out of sight. "Oops. Did I say that out loud? I didn't mean to let you know that I was cutting Woody's traps. I guess he isn't using them anymore, so no harm, no foul."

"Hey, fuck you, Eddie." Kenny brushed past me and leaned on the rail. He spit the words out. Eddie flinched at Kenny's forward motion. "I get my hands on you, I'm going to kill you."

I reached out and pulled Kenny back by the sleeve. "This is on me," I said to him quietly; and then, louder, I yelled across to Eddie. "Basically, what he said, Eddie. Fuck you, fuck your piece-of-shit boat. I get near you, and I'm going to fucking kill you."

Eddie seemed to recover himself. He looked at his buddy and then he started to laugh. "Man, you should see yourself. You look so pissed off. But I don't think you're so tough without your crew of friends. And you're definitely not so tough without the old man there to take care of everything for you." He shuffled sideways until he was near the cabin. "It's hard work, you know. I thought it would be kind of fun, pulling traps, working the water, but I'd forgotten how much work it really is. Oswald and I argued about it. You remember Oswald, right? I hear you're the one who found him. And Joey's finger." He laughed. "So scared you had to call in your daddy. Shame Daddy's not here to come to the rescue?"

"Fuck you, Eddie."

He grinned. "You've already said that. Nice cast, by the way. Must be hard pulling traps with a broken arm. I guess I made your life easier by cutting some of your daddy's traps." His buddy laughed at that and Eddie tilted his head to him. "Yeah, I'm funny, aren't I? It really is hard work. That was Oswald's problem. He wasn't willing to work for it, and then he just thought he'd go off and do his own thing, and that didn't play so well with me." Eddie stared at me, trying to intimidate me. "But we're doing just fine without Oswald. Hard work, but nothing taking a few bumps can't help us get through. We've both been tweaking the last couple of days, and I know that when I come down I'm going to be sore as shit."

"You know what, Eddie? Just do yourself a favor and get out of here before somebody gets hurt. You're right. It's a lot of work, and I don't think you want to be out here any more than I want you to be out here."

He looked down at the hand that he'd kept below the rail, and when he looked up at me again his face carried an aggrieved look. "It's not your waters, you know. It's not just for you. You aren't anything special. Who gives a shit that your last name is Kings? Who gives a shit that you've been on the island for a hundred years or whatever? And you make it sound like being a lobsterman is some noble pursuit. You all are full of shit. It's just work. Hell, I don't even want to be out here. I just went along with it when the other boys in the harbor said we should make a play, because I thought it would be worth it to show you and your friends what's what. And then they all pussied out, said it wasn't worth the heat. Well, fuck them. Fuck you. Yeah, it's hard work hauling, but hell, it's worth it just to see the look on your face when I said I was cutting your daddy's traps. I make more money in a day of moving meth than I do in a week on the water, but it's been worth it. Oh, poor Cordelia, her sainted fucking father's dead. He wasn't such a good man, you know. Everybody makes him out to be such a perfect guy, Mr. Loosewood Island, but he was nothing more than a bully. Like you. "

Eddie touched his fingers to his cheek. I wasn't sure that he even realized he was doing it, and even though we were closer, we weren't close enough for me to see the small scar that I knew was still there from when Daddy had punched him. Eddie dropped his hand again. "I've been waiting and waiting and waiting for this," Eddie said. "Wish I could have seen his face." He showed his teeth. "Shame the old fucker stroked out."

The boats had drifted closer together, closing the distance to half a boat length, and I was able to drop my voice into something akin to a normal conversation. "What? You've been circling around just waiting to, what, to get back at us? Is that what this is about, Eddie? You're cutting traps because your feelings were hurt? Because you couldn't hack it? Is this some sort of temper tantrum? You want me to say I'm sorry?" I took a step closer to the rail and leaned toward him. "Sorry because you couldn't hack it as a sternman? Sorry that you started dealing meth on the island? These are my waters and you aren't welcome here."

"Your daddy ain't here anymore," Eddie said. "I don't take orders from a cunt like you."

"Fuck you," I said, lifting my left arm and pointing my finger at him.

"No," Eddie said, "fuck you." And what Eddie pointed back at me wasn't his finger. And suddenly I thought that I didn't want to take my chances, even if it was only a pistol.

The sun burned a hole in my chest. High in my chest. It was up in my shoulder, under the collarbone. No, it wasn't the sun. It was a fishhook. Somebody had slipped me onto a hook. Something banged, loud and popping. The sun was falling? Was that the sun crashing into the ocean? It fell again, and then again. I couldn't open my eyes. I opened my eyes and I was under the water and I could see scales and flesh, a mermaid turning toward me. And then she wasn't a mermaid, she was a selkie, and as she moved toward me she flickered from seal to woman to seal. I blinked, and then I couldn't open my eyes again. The back of my head hurt, and there was something wrong with everything. I could hear Trudy whining and I could hear Trudy grunting, sniffing at something. There was a coughing sound. Laughing.

I tried opening my eyes again, and I saw Trudy crumpled against the gunwale. There was something dark and shiny matting the fur near her haunches. I could see her breathing coming fitful between her whines. Her eyes were open and she was watching me, but she didn't try to get up. There was a coughing sound, coming from somewhere outside of my field of vision. I tried to turn my head to the side and had to close my eyes against the surge of light. I could feel a wet stickiness on the back of my head. I must have smashed my head on the deck when I went down. I'd need more stitches. But why had I smashed my head? I tried pushing myself up, and as soon as I moved my left arm I realized why I was lying on the deck. Eddie had shot me. The sharp hook in my chest—or shoulder, I wasn't sure where it was exactly except high and left, high enough to have missed my heart, missed my breast—was a bullet hole.

I took a few seconds to catch my breath, and then I tried again, pushing myself up with my good right hand instead. I wanted to puke. I'd gotten a concussion out on the *Kings' Ransom* a few days ago, on the night of the storm, and I was pretty sure I'd just gotten another one. Even propped up with one hand, it took me a few more seconds to be sure I wasn't going to fall over.

I heard a man laughing, and then more grunting sounds. I realized they were coming from over the rail, from somewhere other than the *Queen Jane*. I heard talking and static coming from the radio, which was smashed and half off the console. I thought I recognized Timmy's voice, even with the static.

The push against my calf scared the shit out of me, and I almost screamed. When I turned and saw that it was Kenny, I almost screamed in relief. He had his leg stretched as far as it could go, his toe against my calf. The first thing I saw was that his face was crusted in blood. His nose was bent, broken, and one of his eyes was swollen almost completely shut. Then I saw that his arms were pulled back, realized that his hands were zip-tied behind him, that he was tied to the base of the captain's chair. And then I saw that the bottom of his shirt was soaked with blood. There was a ragged hole near his belly, and the blood there was darker. He was sweating, and every time he blinked his eyes it was slow and deliberate, as if he weren't sure he could open them again. I started to move toward him, but he shook his head. The effort seemed to cost him, and then he motioned with his chin and his head toward the other boat. He mouthed her name, *Stephanie.*

I nodded, and even doing that almost sent me falling over. I knew that the water was calm, but it felt worse than any storm I'd ever been through. I tried getting on my knees, to crawl one-handed, but I couldn't keep my balance. Instead I moved my legs until I was facing away from where I wanted to go and then scrunched my feet as close to my ass as I could, planted the soles of my boots on the deck, and then slid myself backward. Each time I did it, I felt something tearing in my chest, like the bullet was shifting inside me, but it only took a couple of pushes before my back hit against the locker. I reached up to open the locker. The latch seemed loud to me, the only sounds other than Eddie or his buddy's laughter an occasional word from one of them, and the grunting that I had come to realize was from Stephanie.

The gun box with the pistol in it was the easiest to get out, but I remembered trying to fire it when I was younger, the way it kicked back at me and opened a cut on my forehead. I wanted something I was familiar with, and I worked out one of the longer shotgun cases instead. I slid it out and across my lap and then made sure my back was still braced against something solid as I worked the latches. The snap, snap of the catches made me pause, but it didn't seem to carry off the *Queen Jane* and over to the other boat. I opened the lid and found Daddy's Remington Marine Magnum. I groaned to myself as I looked at the shotgun. It was a pump-action. It held six shots, but I wasn't even sure that I'd be able to get to my feet, let alone that I could handle pumping a shotgun more than once.

Something changed in the tone of the grunts coming from Stephanie. One of the men said something, and even though I couldn't understand what he'd said, there was a sharp laugh, and then the sound of what I recognized as a fist hitting a body.

I took a deep breath and then, using the shotgun like a crutch, got to my feet, pushing myself up against the wall. I was glad to have the solidness against my back.

They'd tied their boat off to the *Queen Jane*, and Eddie's friend stood with his back to me barely an arm's length away. If I'd been able to walk, I could have taken two steps and then smashed his head in with the stock of the shotgun. He had a rifle in one hand, letting it dangle away from him. Past him, I could see Eddie on the deck, on top of Stephanie. He'd slid the pistol to the side, and was concentrating on fucking her. His pants were pushed down to his knees. Stephanie's shirt was ripped, and her pants were hanging off one of her ankles. Eddie had forced his way between her legs. He had her wrists gathered up in one of his hands and pinned to the deck; the other hand covered her mouth. A dark bruise had already started forming on her cheek, and with each thrust of Eddie's body, a burst of air was forced out of Stephanie's body, the grunt pushing through where Eddie's fingers covered her mouth. She had her eyes closed.

My head was swimming, and I could taste vomit in my mouth. The deck felt like it was bucking under my feet even though I could see that the water was barely moving. I let my eyes close in a slow blink, long enough for me to gather myself, and then I lifted the shotgun. I felt like everything I was doing was in slow motion. It was all I could do to raise the gun with my right hand and to try to steady it with my left. My wrist ached, and I noticed that there was a crack in the cast. The pain from the hole in my shoulder burned—I wasn't sure how long I could hold the shotgun up—but worst of all was the dizziness. I didn't think I could hold the gun up for long.

I thought I heard the sound of an engine. I looked to the side. I could see two boats powering toward me, and I let the shotgun waver. I was right. I'd heard Timmy's voice, heard somebody familiar on the radio. I should have known that I wasn't alone, that even with Daddy dead, as long as I was in the waters of Loosewood Island I'd never be alone. The cavalry was on their way, and it would be a few more minutes at most until they'd be here to rescue me.

I blinked long and slow again, and it was all I could do to open my eyes back up. When I did, I realized that I was looking out into the water, and that there was somebody looking back at me. It was a woman. Not a mermaid, not a seal, but a woman. She was under the surface of the water, and I could see her hair floating behind her, gathered in the current. She was upright, as if she were standing, but she was definitely below the ocean. Brumfitt's bride. She was staring at me, and she was stunningly beautiful. She shimmered. I could understand why Brumfitt thought she'd been a gift from the sea. She stared at me like she was waiting for something. I wanted to apologize to her, because I didn't know what she was waiting for. Did she want me to dive into the water to be with her? Should I head to land and wait for her to wash ashore? I stared at her, and she stared back at me, and when I blinked again, my eyes peeling back open, I realized that the woman I was staring at was Stephanie. And then she wavered back into Brumfitt's bride, staring at me, waiting. I blinked hard one more time, and when I opened my eyes I was staring at the deck of the other boat, looking at Stephanie.

She saw me focus on her and her eyes brightened. She bit down hard on Eddie's fingers. He screamed, pulled his hand back, balled it into a fist, and slammed it into her face.

And I realized what Brumfitt's wife was waiting for. She was waiting for *me*. I was Cordelia Kings, the last of the Kings. I felt something harden in me. Despite the shakiness, the ache in my body, I knew what I had to do. I was done with the blessings of the sea, done with the curses. I was done with the weight of history, done with the old stories that carried the Kings name. It was time for *me* to do something. I flicked off the safety and pulled the trigger.

Even with my back braced against the cabin, I nearly fell over from the kick of the shotgun. The sound was ferocious, and my head buzzed. The man in front of me was still standing there, but he had a fist-sized hole in his lower back. Then, slowly, and then all at once, he crumpled.

I looked back at Stephanie lying on the deck. Eddie was scrambling toward the pistol that he'd left out of reach. He snaked across the deck. I was almost detached as I watched him reach for the pistol. Eddie was flickering, changing shapes, in front of me. And then he was solid again, and I could see his weak underbelly, could see the way he looked at me with a sudden realization that I was stronger than I looked.

As he wrapped his hand around the grip of the pistol, I raised the shotgun again, hammered the pump back despite the way it made my wrist and shoulder scream, and took careful aim at the top of his chest.

And then I shot Eddie Glouster.

If I had still been on my feet I would have shot him again, but for some reason I was sitting on the deck under the wheel. It took me a few seconds to realize that the kickback had knocked me on my ass. I was leaning against Kenny. I felt something heavy on my leg. The shotgun was resting across my thigh. “Fuck,” I said, because it was the only word that seemed appropriate.

Kenny coughed, and I looked at him. He had passed out.

I didn’t hear any movement on the other ship. Stephanie was unconscious, and I hoped I’d finished Eddie off, because I couldn’t stand up again. I turned my head to look at the console and eyed the radio. It was too far for me to reach on my own. I looked down at the shotgun. I grabbed the barrel, which was warm in my hand, and then used it to knock the microphone from the clip. It swung on its twisted cord, bouncing back and forth. I missed it on the first pass, but grabbed it the second time. I keyed the mic, opened my mouth, and then closed it again. I didn’t know what to say. It didn’t matter, because I could hear the engines coming closer, could hear the boats of Loosewood Island burning furiously toward me.

Trudy whined behind me, and I tried to look at her, but I couldn’t get my head around. “Good girl, Trudy,” I said. “You’re a good girl.” And then I passed out.

Guppy flopped on top of me. "Wake up, Aunt Cordelia. It snowed."

"Snow?" I opened my eyes to see her brother standing next to the bed. Fatty looked at me and then patted my head like I was a dog and said, "Happy Christmas. It snowed."

I groaned and pulled the pillow over my eyes. "I know," I said. "Your sister told me." I was warm under the blanket, and despite Guppy pressing down on my bladder, I didn't particularly feel like hopping out of bed.

I heard Rena laughing. I moved the pillow back and squinted at my sister. She leaned in the doorway, her bathrobe cinched tight around her waist. She had carpet throughout the upstairs, and even with the woodstove, she had the furnace set to kick in early enough that on the nights I slept at her house I never woke to a cold house. "Fatty is asking for pancakes," Rena said. "I'd planned on making waffles and bacon, but Fatty wants pancakes. That okay with you?"

I rolled Guppy beside me on the bed and then sat up. "I get a say in what's for breakfast?"

Rena shrugged. "Not really. You're the last one up, which

means you get what I feed you, but I wanted you to feel like you're part of the process."

Fatty climbed into the bed and laid himself over my legs, half on me, half on his sister. "Can we open presents now?"

"Nope," I said, and then I tickled both of them until they slid off me and bumped up against the wall. I swung my legs to the floor. Trudy looked at me from the corner, where I'd stuffed her dog bed, and then she curled her head back against her side, in no hurry to get up. She still had a limp, couldn't get up on the bed or the couch by herself, and didn't have as much energy as she had before, but the fur had grown back from where the veterinarian had had to shave it for the surgery. She was doing okay. She'd be wagging herself silly once she got outside. She always loved it when it snowed, and Fifth would be waiting downstairs for her so they could go out together and play. I wiggled my toes into the carpet and then stood up. I lifted the blanket, pulling it out from under Guppy and Fatty, and then let it drop over my niece and nephew.

"You going to eat?" Rena asked.

"No."

"Didn't think so."

"It's supposed to get better in the second trimester, isn't it?"

"It's weird that you can't keep food down while you're on land, but you feel just fine when you're on a boat."

"And I still think it's weird," I said, lowering my voice to a whisper so that Guppy and Fatty couldn't hear me, "that I only sleep with him once and I end up pregnant."

"With twins," she said, giving me a squeeze. "Well, you know, Christmas miracles and all that."

I slipped past Rena and closed the door to the bathroom behind me. I kept working the shower hotter and hotter. It felt good, the steam and the water, and I stayed under until I'd used enough of the hot water that it started running cold. Doing my hair didn't take much more than running the towel over it. The doctor had to clip so much of it off to put the stitches in the back of my head that there was barely anything to save. It looked okay short, but I missed the familiar feel of it hanging down.

I wiped a circle clear on the mirror so that I could see my face. The scar on my forehead had faded nicely, and it was close enough to the hairline that it wasn't particularly noticeable. I still didn't have a complete range of motion with my arm, but the wrist didn't bother me, even when the weather was changing.

I could hear Rena calling out to one of the kids, the scrape of a chair, and then the sound of the door opening and closing, either letting Trudy and Fifth out of the house or bringing the two dogs back in. It was a nice sort of soundtrack. By this time next year I'd have two of my own babies making their own noises. It was enough to make me smile at myself, and I took my time getting dressed. We didn't wear anything special for Christmas, but once I had my jeans and my sweater on I was careful with my lipstick, touched behind my ears and the back of my wrists with a dab of perfume.

Downstairs, Fatty and Guppy were sitting at the table eating pancakes. Rena was leaning against the sink and looking out the window. I sat down at the table but then stood up again when Rena said, "Carly's here." I looked at her and mouthed, *Stephanie?* and she looked back at me and shrugged her shoulders, mouthed, *Don't know.*

The front door opened and Carly stood there. It wasn't clear to me if she had come by herself.

It seemed at first like Stephanie was going to be okay. She held everything together, but then, maybe a week after everything had happened, she just disappeared. One morning Carly woke up and Stephanie was gone. She was off the island. Gone. By the time I was home from the hospital a few days later, Carly had tracked Stephanie down at her parents' place, and had convinced her to come back to the island. But there was something broken in Stephanie. She'd gone back to her parents' for a few more trips, and even though Carly kept bringing her back, we weren't sure if Stephanie was going to be on the island for the holidays. Carly didn't talk much about what Stephanie was going through, other than to say that she was seeing a counselor, and that one of the few things Stephanie was always bright about was that I was pregnant. According to Carly, they'd even been talking about maybe the two of them trying for a baby.

Carly smiled at me and Rena, and then stepped into the house. Stephanie followed behind her. Rena let out a quick shriek and pulled Stephanie into a tight hug. "Merry Christmas!"

Stephanie had a pair of shopping bags in each hand, and after Rena let go of her she put them down on the floor. She looked embarrassed at the attention. "Just a few extra things we picked up at my parents'."

I hadn't realized that I'd been holding my breath until I let it out. I guess there was a part of me that hadn't been entirely sure that Carly was going to be able to convince Stephanie to stay on Loosewood Island for Christmas.

"There's pancakes in the kitchen," Rena said, and she and Stephanie left me standing in the entranceway with Carly.

"Hey," she said.

"Hey," I said. She shifted, and then finally let out a sigh and unzipped her jacket. "Oh," I said. And then I said it again. "Oh."

She touched at the necklace and then tried to smile at me. "Is it okay?"

I reached out and let my fingers graze the pearls. "They make you look like her," I said. "She would have wanted you to have them." The words were a surprise to me, but they were true, and because I didn't know what else to do, I hugged her. She just stood there for a second, and then she hugged me back. I saw Rena walk into the room and she leaned into our circle.

Kenny's ferry wasn't due for half an hour. We were planning to wait for the ferry before opening the presents so Kenny could be with us. That left me just enough time to go to Daddy's house.

The island looked fresh and clean with the coat of snow. There wasn't much of it; just enough to cover everything and to leave a place for me to put my footprints. It made the quiet morning even more hushed.

Almost everything was the same inside the house as it had been on the day Daddy died. It still looked as if Daddy could be living there. His coats hung on the hooks in the entrance; his reading glasses were on the table in the kitchen. The only real difference was the blue plastic trunk in the dining room.

It looked out of place in the dining room. I stood over the trunk, ran my hand along the top, and then pulled a chair out from the table. I don't know what it was that had kept me from opening it; I'd had Chip and Tony carry it up nearly two weeks ago. With everything that had happened, with Daddy dying and what went on out on the *Queen Jane* with Eddie Glouster, and with the news starting to circulate that I was pregnant with twins thanks to Kenny, and with Stephanie and Carly off and on and off the island, even Chip and Tony had started acting quiet with me. Etsuko was the only one who acted as if nothing were out of the ordinary.

I looked at my watch. Fifteen minutes until the ferry. Now or never, I thought. I flipped open the latches on the blue trunk. There was a sucking sound when I lifted the lid, the watertight seal breaking.

I don't know what I was expecting, but it was something more impressive than what was inside the crate: a thick, plastic-wrapped tube that ran the diagonal length of the blue box. I put it on the table in front of me and started worrying the tape that held the plastic wrap closed. Once I had it opened, I was almost afraid to reach in, to feel the canvas against my fingertips. I rolled the bundle open on the table. There had to be twenty-five, thirty canvases. I knew I'd be back later that day to look through all of them, but with the ferry coming in, I only had time to look at the top painting.

Despite the snow outside and the fact that it was Christmas, the spring grass of the painting seemed appropriate. Brumfitt had painted it from the promontory off to the side of the harbor. He'd captured both the ocean and the island. I'd never seen Loosewood Island look so lush before in any of Brumfitt's work. It was what the island looked like after a month of spring rain and spring sun. On the headland, he'd painted a woman having a picnic and sitting on a blanket with two children, a boy and a girl who looked to be the same age, and next to them, a pair of women standing and looking out over the water. One of the women was obviously pregnant.

I felt the drone of the ferry's horn pass through the walls of Daddy's house, pass through my body, and I knew that I had to start walking if I wanted to be there when Kenny got off the ferry, his first trip from the hospital, his first trip home since I'd killed Eddie Glouster. But before I was ready to go see him, before I was ready to leave Daddy's gifts behind, I needed to do one thing. I needed to turn the painting over.

On the back, Brumfitt had written, *Christmas, 1761*, and he had written the title of the painting: *The Queens of Loosewood Island.*

And as I read the title, I knew. I knew that I hadn't imagined seeing Brumfitt's wife the day I'd stood shot, bleeding, dazed on the deck of the *Queen Jane*.

This is what will happen.

It will be the end of April. We will have had four days of warmth and sun and we will have no traps in the water; I'll be too pregnant to work on the boat, and Kenny still won't be able to haul things the way he needs to. I'll have woken that morning craving Indian food, and in the way that boyfriends can be indulgent toward their pregnant girlfriends, Kenny will offer to take the *Queen Jane* across the water to Saint John to pick up food from Daddy's favorite Indian place on Canterbury. I'll know that it won't be the same as having it fresh in the restaurant, but it will keep fine in the cooler, and this way Kenny will be able to pick up food for as many as who want to come to dinner: me and him, Rena and the kids, Carly and Stephanie, George and Mackie, Timmy, Etsuko, and baby Mordecai, Chip Warner and his fiancé, Tony Warner and his girlfriend. They will fill the table, fill the house, and the absences—Tucker, my mother, Scotty, Daddy—won't be as noticeable.

This is what will happen. That afternoon, while we wait for Kenny to return, I'll suggest to Carly, Stephanie, and Rena that we go for a picnic. Up on the promontory, Rena will spread a blanket for the kids to sit on. She will bring an old-fashioned wicker basket loaded with glasses and a pitcher of lemonade, a batch of cookies wrapped in cloth. She'll sit down with Fatty and Guppy and laugh at something one of them says. Carly and I will stand near them until I look out over the water and see a boat coming across the distance. I will point and say something to Carly, and we will turn in profile to watch Kenny coming home. Stephanie will be standing apart from us, taking pictures with the medium-format camera that she'd brought from her studio and lugged up the hill. She won't be laughing exactly—she won't be there yet—but she'll be smiling. She will be far enough away that she can capture both the water and the stunning spring green of Loosewood Island. As Carly and I turn in profile, Stephanie will take another picture, capturing the ocean and the island, capturing Rena and the twins on the blanket, capturing Carly and me. This will be the only picture that comes out clear from the entire batch of film that Stephanie works through during the outing.

All of this will happen, and yet, I won't have told anybody about the paintings. I won't have told anybody about what Daddy left behind for me. I won't let anybody else see *The Queens of Loosewood Island*, or the other twenty-seven Brumfitt paintings. These will still all be my secret. It will be my secret that *The Queens of Loosewood Island* even exists, that there are paintings of more than just me pregnant and standing on the promontory with Carly, with Rena and the twins. There are twenty-seven other paintings: enough to make me believe in Brumfitt Kings, to believe in Daddy, to believe in Loosewood Island.

This is also what will happen.

While I am standing on the promontory with Carly, looking out over the water at Kenny in the *Queen Jane* coming home, I will feel the babies moving inside of me, and I will know that I carry both a boy and a girl, and they will be named Kings.

And this is what will happen.

I will hear Daddy's voice calling my name. Though I will look around, I will not see him, but his voice will tell me that even if he hadn't chosen me, I had earned the right to carry the Kings name upon the water.

And this is what will happen.

I will know that Rena, Carly, and I, all three of us Kings, will have sons and daughters who grow up healthy and strong, the kings and queens of Loosewood Island; they will carry the Kings name as a blessing, the bounty of the seas theirs unto each and every generation, and they will carry with them nothing else, the curse of Loosewood Island no more.

ACKNOWLEDGMENTS

I would like to thank my editor, Jill Bialosky. A good editor is an artist in her own right.

To my agent, Bill Clegg. Again, thank you.

Paul Taunton and Anne Collins.

Adria Iwasutiak.

At W. W. Norton & Company, Random House Canada, and William Morris Endeavor Entertainment, big thanks to Chris Clemans, Dave Cole, Raffaella De Angelis, Anna DeRoy, Shaun Dolan, Marion Garner, Alison Liss, Bill Rusin, Rachel Salzman, Jessica Scott, Rebecca Schultz, Matthew Sibiga, and everybody else who helped along the way.

All of the many booksellers and librarians who were advocates for *Touch*.

Téa Obreht and Jared Harel.

Matt Grice.

Jennine Capó Crucet, Shawn Goodman, Christian Howard, Etsuko Ichikawa, Jon Katz, Peter Mountford, Alison Pick, Brian Turner.

Sara, Sandy, Lynda, Mitch, Justin, Alec, Larry, Lori, Joel, Ethan, and Ari.

Ari, Kathryn, Rigby, and Teo.

Laurie, Sabine, and Zoey.

Hopper, Ditto, Tootsie, and Turtle. Good dogs, past and present.

THE LOBSTER KINGS

Alexi Zentner

READING GROUP GUIDE

DISCUSSION QUESTIONS

1. Can *The Lobster Kings* be considered a coming-of-age story for Cordelia? How does she grow into her many roles—as a daughter, a sister, a lobsterwoman, and a leader—over the course of the novel?

2. Cordelia's relationship with her father is complex. At what point does her concern for Woody start to complicate her respect for and awe of him? When does she start to see him as a man rather than a legend? Are there points in the novel where you think she should trust him more or less than she does? Do you blame her for his death?

3. What is the source of Cordelia's jealousy of her sisters and their jealousy of her? Is theirs a commonplace tension between siblings, or is it complicated and exaggerated by the mythical nature of the legacy that only one of them can inherit?

4. How do we see Cordelia's relationship with the curse of Brumfitt Kings evolve over the course of the novel, as she loses one family member after another?

5. Describe the characters of Rena and Carly. How is each sister's relationship to their father unique? How do the women's relationships with one another evolve?

6. What are some of the echoes of *King Lear* in *The Lobster Kings*? Why and how has the author made use of Shakespeare's play? In what ways has he chosen to diverge from it?

---

7. Describe Cordelia's relationship with Kenny Treat. Would you consider *The Lobster Kings* to be primarily a love story? Why or why not?

8. Each in a slightly different way, Cordelia, her sister Carly, and Carly's partner, Stephanie, subvert Loosewood Island traditions regarding a woman's proper role in a lobster fishing community. Pinpoint when and how each of these characters opens the eyes of the islanders and helps the community to evolve.

9. Discuss the relationships between some of Brumfitt's paintings and their corresponding scenes in the novel. How do the parallels between the past and the present play out?

10. Are we meant to believe, in the end, in the truth of the legend of Brumfitt Kings? Does Cordelia believe in it? Finally, does it matter whether she believes in the legend, or is it enough that she has internalized its power?

11. Do you have any family myths or potent family histories? How have they affected how you see yourself or how you live your life?

SELECTED NORTON BOOKS WITH READING GROUP GUIDES AVAILABLE

For a complete list of Norton's works with reading group guides, please go to www.wwnorton.com/books/reading-guides.

Diana Abu-Jaber	*Birds of Paradise*
Diane Ackerman	*One Hundred Names for Love*
Andrea Barrett	*Archangel*
Bonnie Jo Campbell	*Once Upon a River*
Lan Samantha Chang	*Inheritance*
Michael Cox	*The Meaning of Night*
Jared Diamond	*Guns, Germs, and Steel*
Andre Dubus III	*Townie*
Anne Enright	*The Forgotten Waltz*
Jennifer Cody Epstein	*The Painter from Shanghai*
Betty Friedan	*The Feminine Mystique*
Stephen Greenblatt	*The Swerve*
Lawrence Hill	*The Book of Negroes*
Ann Hood	*The Obituary Writer*
Dara Horn	*A Guide for the Perplexed*
Mette Jakobsen	*The Vanishing Act*
N. M. Kelby	*White Truffles in Winter*
Nicole Krauss	*The History of Love**
Don Lee	*The Collective**
Maaza Mengiste	*Beneath the Lion's Gaze*
Daniyal Mueenuddin	*In Other Rooms, Other Wonders*
Liz Moore	*Heft*
Richard Powers	*Orfeo*
Jean Rhys	*Wide Sargasso Sea*
Mary Roach	*Packing for Mars*
Akhil Sharma	*Family Life*
Johanna Skibsrud	*The Sentimentalists*
Joan Silber	*Fools*
Manil Suri	*The City of Devi*
Goli Taraghi	*The Pomegranate Lady and Her Sons*
Brady Udall	*The Lonely Polygamist*
Alexi Zentner	*The Lobster Kings*

*Available only on the Norton Web site